ABOUT THE AUTHOR

BERKELY MATHER is the pseudonym of
the youngest son of a well-known Australian
family. He rebelled against the respectable
career planned for him and set out to see the
world—sailing on tramp steamers, becoming a
soldier in 1932, and spending twenty-five years
in the Army, seventeen of them in India and
the Far and Middle East.

He is now a colonel on the active list of the
British Army reserve, and his ambition is to
write two good, taut thrillers a year.

THE PASS BEYOND KASHMIR

By BERKELY MATHER

POPULAR LIBRARY · NEW YORK .

POPULAR LIBRARY EDITION

Copyright © 1960 Berkely Mather
Library of Congress Catalog Card Number: 60-12600

Published by arrangement with Charles Scribner's Sons
Scribner's edition published in August, 1960

DEDICATION:
TO
HAROLD GILBERT
AND A SIMILAR JOURNEY

CHAPTER 1

Three of us waited there that evening. The sun was dipping
down behind the high ground towards Malabar Hill but it
hadn't taken the heat with it. You could almost see the heat.
It seeped out of the streaked, yellow-washed walls of the bazaar and it made objects in the middle distance dance and
shimmer. It was helped by the smoke of the little fires from
the alleys that ran down towards the Crawford Market where
the women were cooking the evening meal of curry and dhall
and the street traders were waking from the long siesta in
the time honored manner of the East—scratching and hawk-
ing and spitting. Ten thousand of them doing it in concert in
a square quarter-mile can drown all other sounds in the two
waking hours of dawn and sunset in Bombay.

Below the window of the room in which we sat, two policemen were trying to move a stark naked man from the side-
walk into the more decent obscurity of the deeper alleyway—
warily, because they were Mohammedans in a strongly pre-
dominant Hindu quarter and he was wearing the full Saddhu's ecclesiasticals of daubed cow-dung and ashes. The mob
was growing restive and a rotten mango sailed out of a doorway, missing the yellow pancake turban of one of them by a
finger's breadth and squelching among the baskets of an orthodox Jain sweetmeat seller. He proclaimed shrilly to the
whole pantheon of gods half-forgotten that caste was defiled
and fifty rupeesworth of trade goods were now unsaleable.
Cops being cops the world over, they left the Saddhu to carry
on contemplating his navel and Infinity and booked a Goanese taxi driver for obstruction on the corner. That shifted
the focus of things from the doorway beneath us, for which
we were grateful. The doorway was between a second-hand
cycle shop and that of a tinsmith, and from it a narrow and
indescribably filthy flight of stairs led up to a landing outside
our room and then continued upwards to the floor above
and onward to the flat roof. I could have picked a thousand
more congenial places for the meeting but the Major's son had
been insistent on this. He was telling us why for the twentieth
time in his chi-chi sing-song.

"My daddy does not want publicity, man. Those big hotels
—the High Commissioner's office—that's asking for it. Everybody watches in Bombay. Watching, watching, watching—all
the time watching. My daddy does not want—"

"Yes—you told us," said Smedley wearily, "and for God's

sake stop calling the old rip 'Daddy.' " He was shaking a little and I suspected that his next go of malaria was not far off.

The Major arrived then. I saw him come round the corner and stop at a fruitstall. He was carrying a palmetto shopping basket and he fingered some brinjals on the stall and chaffered with the woman who squatted on the cobbles beside it. He didn't buy any but passed on to another stall further down the alley. The woman looked after him and spat. He crossed over to our side then and was out of sight and we waited a full five minutes until we heard his soft tap at the door. His son crossed and unlocked it. The Major came in and said, "Sit on the stairs, Fonce, and keep your eyes skinned for any of them bastards. Go to sleep and I'll lambaste the hide off you." The son said, "Yes daddy" and went outside. The Major relocked the door and grinned at us yellowly. Everything about him was yellow—skin, teeth, nicotine-stained moustache and the rheum at the corners of his eyes. His Japanese cotton shirt had washed yellow and so had his khaki shorts and the golf hose that wrinkled round his pipe-stem legs. His battered to-pee had once been white but that too had now taken on a saffron patina.

Smedley said, "You're an hour late."

"Them bastards," the Major said in explanation.

"Suppose you tell us who 'them bastards' are?" I said. Smedley wriggled impatiently. He had already told me—but I wanted it from the old man himself.

"Baluchis mostly." The Major measured the air with outspread arms. "Not a mother-loving son of a sow of 'em less than six feet six—and built proportionate. They breed 'em special up Quetta way. They're not the moneylenders themselves—just their touts and bums. They're spread all over India and Pakistan—got a sort of brotherhood. Bloke owes them something in Bombay and he skips it for Calcutta, they're waiting for him on the platform at Howrah when he gets off the train. They never miss a point."

"I can't believe that," I told him. I could and did but I wanted all the story.

"Oh, for God's sake," wailed the Major. "Do I have to go into it all again? I've got something you fellers want. You're going to pay me for it—"

"*Maybe,*" I countered. "And only after we've seen it."

"Sure—sure—sure—but before you can see it I've got to take you to where it is. If I leave Bombay with you openly they'll be onto it like a flash—them sharks can smell money like a mongoose smells a snake. Do you *want* a reception committee the other end?"

"Not particularly," I told him. "All right—what's your proposition?"

"You got to trust me," he answered. Smedley snorted.

"To what extent?" I asked.

"Fare to Calcutta—and then from there on to the place. I've got to live for ten days. Call it fifteen hundred chips. I'll send you a letter when I get there. You can come up and I'll meet you."

There was a soft insistent rapping at the door. The Major stiffened and quivered like a bird-dog. Smedley crossed and opened it an inch.

"Bastards, daddy," said the son the other side. Smedley turned the key again and I went to the window.

The swift twilight had drawn in now and it was dark outside except for the naptha flares over the stalls down below in the alley.

I saw them immediately. You can't miss them in an Indian crowd. They were both six feet and more—and dressed alike in untidy turbans, knee-length shirts worn over baggy white cotton pantaloons, embroidered waistcoats and sandals with turned-up toes. They carried thick wooden staves almost as high as their shoulders and they walked as straight as only a Baluchi can in a crowded bazaar. Their arrogance was inbuilt not assumed. When the British ruled in India they *might* have stepped aside for a white man—but only in a well-policed cantonment. Now they just walked straight and the crowd opened up for them.

"So you've got the bums on your tail," said Smedley. "All right—all the more reason for making a deal. Pay 'em and get rid of them—or use the money to get out. Come on—who opens? You or us?"

"Fifty thousand—and no cheques," answered the Major promptly. Smedley laughed.

"You're wasting your time and ours," I said. "We'll give you the fifteen hundred you wanted for your fare, and the difference between that and five thousand in a post-dated cheque."

The Major used the same word he'd applied to the Baluchis. He used it in Hindustani, inflected and clipped insultingly. He used further words in English. He was an old man and neither of us could have hit him, but I feared for Smedley. The onset of malaria can string nerves up to an unbearable degree.

I said, "Shut up, you dirty-mouthed old varmint. Take it or leave it."

"Go up a bit." He was whining now which was a good sign. "Go up a bit. Three thousand on the nail and your chit for twenty. No cheques—just your chit."

I stuffed the wallet away firmly and walked to the door. I wanted this thing over but I knew that if I went up a rupee he would continue raising me.

"Come on, Smedley," I said. "I'm through."

Smedley heaved himself to his feet and swore weakly. The fever was gaining ground rapidly. The Major grabbed my sleeve again and almost yelped.

"All right—all right. Let's see it."

I counted out fifteen notes and let him see them in the light of a match. I could hear him gulping.

"Right, Major," I said. "Where is it—and how did it get there? Right from the beginning. I know some of it already—most of it. It's just the gaps I want filled in."

Again he seemed to be mulling—then he started; slowly at first as if he was piecing things together over a gap of fifteen years.

"You know what the column went up for?" he asked.

"Yes—I know that. Weather stations in South-west Tibet —mainly for the American fliers over the Hump from Burma to China. You reccied the sites but didn't actually establish any."

"You know what sort of a tight-lipped, dog-driving son of a bitch the column commander was? Prentice—a half-colonel?"

"I didn't know him but I'll take your word for it. Go on."

"He didn't like me. Never did, because I was an ex-Enlisted Man with a temporary wartime commission—married to a native woman. He had to rely on me though. He could tell you the Latin name of every piddling bloody flower that grew in the lower valleys but when it came to Urdu or any of the local bhats he was bitched."

Smedley groaned and said, "Come to the point, for God's sake. Where is it?" I could have hit him because it broke the flow.

"Go on as you were," I said, and kicked sideways in the darkness at Smedley's foot.

"Things blew up in the end," the Major went on, "I had it out with the whole bunch one night in the mess tent. I told 'em what I thought of the lot of them—and their bleeding parents. Then I stalked out to me own tent and left them to it. The following day he wirelesses down to Srinagar and they get through to Rawalpindi—and a week later up comes a Captain out of the Gurkhas. Their language difficulties are solved then. They leave me in charge at the base camp after that, and push on into the hills. Away a fortnight or a month at a time they are—five officers and a group of porters, forty strong. One officer stays back with me in turn—resting they called it. Maybe it was to see I didn't flog none of the supplies to the locals, the disbelieving lot of bastards. And so it goes on until the beginning of the second winter. Two of them have gone back by this time with frostbite. That leaves four besides myself—Prentice, Sloan, the second-in-command, Saunders, the Gurkha Captain, and a Lieutenant

8

called Braithwaite. They're all going out every trip now because it's nearing the end of it. Two more surveys and that's the lot. And then they get caught—bare-arsed and flat-footed —twenty thousand feet up on a ledge when a blizzard breaks. Only Sloan and Braithwaite make it back to base —with half the Sherpas. The rest of them have copped their issue in an avalanche. Braithwaite dies just as they get in and Sloan as I was bringing the remnants down the passes to Srinagar."

"All right," I said. "I'm with you up to this point. Now, what about the papers?"

"There was a drill for it," the Major said. "Each time they came in they used to spend a couple of days mucking about with maps and slide-rules and making masses of notes in the computing tent. Then they'd micro-film the lot and send it down by runner to Srinagar. What the hell happened to it then I wouldn't be knowing—Sent on to Northern Command Headquarters at 'Pindi, I expect. That's all except the last lot of notes. Sloan's still hanging on to that when he arrives at base, nigh on dead on his feet. Bloody big wedge of papers in a tin case it was. He's as mad as a coot by this time—delirious—singing, shouting and cussing. He won't leave go of the tin even when I'm trying to attend to him in the sick-bay tent. Oil, he says—all the oil in the world on top of the bloody Himalayas. Even *I* know that's nonsense. You don't get oil on top of mountains. Anyhow, as I said, he dies on the way down. I'm sitting with him in the tent and I'm dead tired—so I drop off to sleep. I wake suddenly and he's out of the blankets and crouching in the corner. He's scrabbling in the scree the tent is pitched on—and he's laughing and crying and generally carrying on. I get him back onto the stretcher and yell for a couple of Sherpas to help hold him down—but he's dead when they arrive. So next day we go on—and a hell of a trip it is. We're carrying two dead men and the Sherpas don't like it. They want to bury them there but I won't have it. We get down after five days of it and then I conk out myself. After that there's Courts of Inquiry and Summaries of Evidence and God knows what, till I'm fed up to the teeth. They ask about the papers for the last trip. I'd forgotten the damn things in the hubbub of the night that Sloan died. He had 'em when I went to sleep—he certainly didn't when I'd got him back onto the stretcher. There's only one thing for it—he must have buried them in the corner. I keep mum about that though, because I know that I'll be sent back with a search party—and I'd had a bellyful of the passes by this time. As far as I knew they were just more papers on the survey—and they'd sent in half a ton of them by this time, and anyhow, the weather station project was shelved in the spring of '43. So they assumed they'd been lost with the rest of the party higher up and the matter was dropped. Give us another cigarette."

I gave him one and lighted it for him. Smedley was twitching impatiently in the darkness. "Go on," I said.

"Well," continued the Major, "I went into hospital for a time and when I came out I was posted in command of this transit camp—and then I had my bit of bother, and six months later I found myself back in Bombay—a civilian again and on the bones of my backside—and that's how it's been ever since—job here—job there—the old woman and the kids picking up an odd rupee where they can. It was tough when the British were still here—it's tougher now—"

"When did you first realize that these papers might be—well—possibly valuable?" I asked.

"Well—that's funny now. It was back in '49. Things were a bit crummy. I'd had a job tallying cargo down on the docks but I'd lost that over—well, a bit of a misunderstanding. I'm sitting in our shanty down Worli Bunder one day when a car arrives and a copper gets out. Nasty sod he was—a detective-inspector by the name of Ram Dass. He says I'm wanted for questioning. I think it's about this cargo business so I go down looking indignant. But he doesn't take me to Headquarters. We go to a big bungalow out Juhu way. There's a European there. He's as nice as pie. Offers me a drink and smokes. He says he's interested in a project up North—airfield on the Kashmir border. They're going to start work as soon as the trouble's over between the Indians and the Pakistanis. He wants a European foreman up there —just my cup of tea. He's heard I've had some experience in those parts. Would I be interested? Would I? He starts to question me on my knowledge of the country. Pretty soon it dawns on me what he's after. He's clever but I see through it. It keeps coming back to the papers. He reckons he knew Sloan before the war. He seems to know all about those last few days. I reckon he is an Intelligence man and there's nothing in it for me so I box crafty and innocent and stick to the tale I told in the first place. Papers? I saw no papers. In the end it convinced him. Ram Dass drove me back to town and that was it. I forgot about it after that—until I saw Mr. Smedley's advertisement for much the same thing the other day—a foreman up on the Kashmir border. I answered it. You know the rest."

"All right," I said. "What you're telling us is that these papers are—or could be—buried somewhere along the route between your base camp—Kundi Hala—and Srinagar?"

"That's it."

"Could you mark the spot on the map?"

"I could—but it wouldn't help you much. I could give you the rough position from memory of where the tent was pitched too—but you'd still be looking for a needle in a haystack. You see what I mean now?"

I did, and he guessed it. He followed up quickly.

"Okay—so how about a new deal? You give me the fifteen hundred like we arranged—I find my own way to—say 'Pindi or Lahore. You meet me there and I take you on up. You'll have to fix it with the Pakistani authorities, of course."

"And on finding it we pay you a further three thousand five hundred?"

"Like hell you do," he snarled. "If you find it you pay me a further ten—that's if I take you up. If I give you a map it's three-five-hundred—but you wouldn't have a Chinaman's chance of finding it then. Use your sense, mister."

Smedley was twitching and muttering so I closed for that. And then the son was tapping softly on the door again.

CHAPTER 2

He was only tapping because he was fed up with waiting so the old man clipped his ear hard and came back.

"All right then," he said. "What's it to be?"

"We'll meet you in Lahore a week from today," I told him. "Do you know it?"

He snorted, "I know every damned town in the blasted subcontinent. Where'll you be staying?"

"Nedou's Hotel—on the Mall."

"Okay—that will be next Tuesday. I'll ring you in the morning." His hand closed over the roll of notes and he sidled to the door.

Smedley said, "Be there, Polson. Slip up on us and you'll settle for Baluchis—and gladly."

The Major said another rude word and then we heard them both going down the stairs.

My flat was in a block overlooking Back Bay. Back Bay was once the Park Lane of lower Bombay but it was now getting a bit run down. The elevator stopped running one day in four. Once lush flats built to hold a single family in palmier days now held three, and the uniformed hamal in the lobby had a tendency to forget to wear his boots and turban and he chewed betel nut. He also used to sub-let sleeping space on the stairs to a section of the city's floating population. This was one of the days the elevator wasn't working and I had to half carry Smedley up five floors, stepping over sleeping-mats and bundles. Safaraz, my big Pathan servant, took one look at him as we let ourselves in, and went off to get quinine and a bowl of some foul jallup he used to brew for me when I had the shakes. I dumped Smedley on the bed in the spare room and between us we got him out of his clothes and into a suit of my pyjamas. He was complaining bitterly that a red-head by the name of Colette had just clipped him for five thousand francs in the Pigalle by the time we got the quinine into him, and he stayed in Paris, with occasional interesting side trips to Naples and Tangiers for the next two hours before the first ague left him in a restless heat-bedevilled sleep.

It was still too hot to eat so I stretched out in a long chair with a whisky and soda. I needed it, because we'd been roasting in that damned bazaar room since mid-afternoon.

And now I suppose I'd better go back a bit. My name's Idwal Rees and I'm *not* a private detective in the accepted sense of the term. I like reading about them but the only one I've ever met was a nasty little man with no eyebrows and bad breath. My C.O. employed his agency to watch me and his wife in the latter days of the war. He wasted his money. I had lots of hobbies as a young officer, but cuckolding my comrades-in-arms wasn't one of them. The terms in which I explained this to the C.O. didn't leave me much option so I resigned my commission as soon after the war as I could and went back to Shanghai. My old man had been the Far Eastern correspondent for a London paper and he never seemed to have any money so I had spent all my life up till 1939, and much of it afterwards, in India, Burma and China. I worked for a time in an insurance office, assessing claims and smelling out skullduggery. There was a lot of skullduggery and the job proved a good apprenticeship. I stayed with them until Shanghai went finally behind the Bamboo Curtain, then I went to Hongkong just in time to get caught up in the Korean affair. I started just where I left off, as a Company Commander in an infantry battalion, but I speak languages and Intelligence apparently knew it so I was out of uniform within two months, working for our own people and the Americans. I still do when I'm asked; strictly freelance and nothing spectacular. The rest of the time I'm at liberty to run my own show, which I do from a two-by-four office off Hornby Road in Bombay. It's commercial work mostly—theft and anti-corruption. Who stole a hundred bales of silk from the Ballard Quay warehouses? Whose confidential clerk is being paid by which rival concern to sell advance market information? Mostly routine stuff and a lot of it dreary. Some of it is just plain sordid but all of it is illuminating. The man who says he really knows the Far East is talking through his hat but I *can* claim to know just enough about the undercurrents to get by and to earn my modest fees. I'm built on wiry lines and sun and fever have burned my naturally dark hide to a uniform teak colour which makes me inconspicuous in most company where the features aren't Mongolian—that's if I'm dressed the same way. I'm not a master of disguises but if you look like me and can speak Cantonese and Hindustani with a bit of kitchen Arabic and a convincing pidgin English with, when necessary, a bastard potpourri of the lot, you can get by as almost anything, from Aden to Okinawa. Somebody who didn't like me once spread it around that I was half Bengali. That wouldn't worry me if it were true, but it's not. I'm pure Welsh on both sides. I like to stay reasonably honest and I don't like treading on people's faces. Sometimes I find it hard to be the first and to avoid the second, but I do try.

These mostly negative qualities must have been known to the people who employed Smedley. He came to my office one steaming morning just before this opened. Looking back I could have wished that he'd come before he put that stupid advertisement in the Bombay Times. He was looking for an old poor white who was said to be the only European survivor of some abortive expedition into the Himalayan foothills in the early days of the war, and he mentioned oil. I'm no geologist and neither is Smedley, but the idea of there being oil up in those desolate wastes seemed absurd to both of us. The syndicate he worked for was interested, however, in the possibility of freak pockets in some of the lower valleys and had been for some time. It seemed that Prentice's wife had died recently and some old diaries of his had come into the hands of his daughter. She wondered if they might form the basis of a biography of her father's not uninteresting life and she'd shown them to somebody—and somebody had shown them to somebody else. That had been sufficient to spark things off again and the syndicate began to sit up and take notice. They had good enough contacts in Whitehall circles to be able to find out that Prentice undoubtedly had been on to something which he had referred to rather ambiguously in the last reports he had got through. He had promised fuller information in his next lot of despatches. Those were the ones which were missing. But then they found themselves up against a blank wall. The British were out of those parts now and the Indians and Pakistanis were wrangling over Kashmir. The Chinese were showing an ever increasing interest in Tibet just over the border and were, in fact, moving in on the Eastern parts of it. The Dalai Lama was in a cleft stick and the Panchen Lama had gone over to them. Things were

13

a damned sight too explosive in that part of the world for any government to give official recognition to fossickers. The syndicate was told this in very definite terms. They were also told that if they went in on their own they could expect no help if they found themselves in deep water. The governments need not have worried on the syndicate's behalf. None of its comfortable members had any intention of going in. That's what the Smedleys of this world are for.

Smedley looked like a dyspeptic missionary. He was fiftyish and built like a mid-Victorian hatstand—lean, gaunt and angular. When he wasn't working he liked whisky and women. To be quite fair he was nearly always working. His work? Well, he called himself a commercial traveller and market research expert. People from Beirut to Valparaiso who were entitled to an opinion called him many other things—reminiscently, admiringly or viciously according to which end of the deal they had been. He'd been on a fat retainer for the syndicate for a number of years and a cost-plus basis when he was actually on a job for them. He'd peddled their guns in half a score of South American revolutions, bought the right sheikhs for them up the Persian Gulf and broken a strike and lost half his right ear for them in Pittsburgh—for they were nothing if not international. They could hardly have been called public benefactors, but when wholesale importations of hashish started to make inroads on their labor force in an Iraqui oilfield they sent him to find out where it was coming from—and to do something about it. He found out in three months. It was said that he shot a Levantine gentleman in the belly in Aleppo, knifed a Greek in Istambul and drowned their chief buyer in a sewer in Mosul. Then he went back to London and put his bill in to the syndicate and retired temporarily to his semi-detached villa in Ealing where he grew prize roses and maintained in suburban dignity a large and frigid lady he invariably referred to as 'Mrs. Smedley'. He never bit the hand that fed him and he was unswervingly loyal to the syndicate. I had found out all this, and more, when it fell to me to check on him for the Americans when his masters sent him to Japan in the Korean days. He was marked on their files as "nothing known against, but WATCH"—on ours as just "WATCH" and on the Australians', who have a certain poesy in these matters, as "hard bastard—don't crowd him but don't trust him either." They ought to have known. That's where he came from originally.

I finished my drink and mixed another and sat mulling over it. I was doubtful about this job. Smedley had come to me because he had waited for three days without results after putting his ad in the paper. India happened to be one of the few places he had never worked in and he wanted experi-

14

enced help. I hadn't really earned my fee because the Major turned up at Smedley's hotel on the very day he retained me to find him. I had, however, acted as go-between in the subsequent negotiations and he had then talked me into going North with him if the Major came across with anything useful. I was committed to that now but I was beginning to wish I had turned it down; not for any particular reason—certainly not because I had any forebodings at that stage—but I'd been stewing in Bombay for over three years without a break. I wasn't short of money and I'd earned a rest. Getting into Kashmir and then onto the higher passes wasn't going to be easy. Both the Indians and the Pakistanis were touchy about the place and things were hair-triggerish on both sides of the border. At the same time I didn't like the idea of letting Smedley down after we'd more or less shaken hands on it.

I gave it up at this point and decided to shelve the decision until the morning. I finished my drink and had a shower—then I got into fresh clothes and went out to eat.

It was just striking midnight when I returned. The sleeping-mats were all occupied now and I was cursed in seven dialects as I picked my way up the stairs. Safaraz was sleeping on the floor by the door of the spare room. I went through and had a look at Smedley. The fever had broken sooner than I had expected and both he and the bed were soaked in sweat. I shook Safaraz and between us we got Smedley into a tepid bath and then into dry pyjamas. We turned the mattress and changed the sheets and got him back between them. He'd sleep the sleep of the dead now for eighteen hours or so and wake as weak as a kitten. And then the telephone rang. It was the hamal at the desk and he told me that I was wanted down below—or could the gentleman come up? I said he couldn't, and I went down—wondering.

CHAPTER 3

It was Inspector Ram Dass of the Bombay City Police.

"Hello, Inspector," I said. "Not parking again, I hope?"

"Not parking, sir," he answered, and smiled disarmingly. He had a lot of face and the smile was proportionately expansive. It was a smile that travelled upwards—first rippling each of his three tiers of chin, then twitching open his large mouth to reveal serried battlements of gold fillings, causing his button nose to vibrate like a rabbit's and then stopping just short of his eyes. It never reached his eyes. They were

15

the only part of his two-hundred-eighty pound bulk that did not radiate geniality. His paunch shook with it. His toes, visible through the open ends of his chaplis curled with it and his right hand was shaking with it even before it gripped mine. Most of the City detectives wore European clothes—shantung suits and the small flat "Bombay bowler" topee. Ram Dass, however, stuck to a dhoti or long loincloth and a turban, his only concession to Westernism being a linen jacket over his damp white shirt, and the umbrella he constantly carried in the crook of his left arm. He looked like the traditional music hall babu and knew it—and played up to it.

"What is it then?"

"Small matter, sir," he assured me. "Damn silly small matter—" he spread his hands deprecatingly "—but you know what Head Office is like. All bobbery and chufferings for sweet damn-all. We go to your room—isn't it?" He stood aside at the foot of the stairs for me to precede him.

He was the last person I wanted in my apartment at that moment. He looked like a music hall babu; he spoke like one and he oozed goodwill. It all ended there though. I had no illusions about Ram Dass—but I had no option either. I returned his bright smile and went up the stairs in front of him —thinking hard. The last time I had heard his name mentioned was by the Major. It *might* have been a coincidence, but—. I took the stairs two at a time like a man with nothing on his mind but coffee and a shower at the top of them, hoping that his bulk would slow him down enough to enable me to give Safaraz a word of warning before he caught up with me. But it was useless and he was right on my heels when I came to my door—puffing less than I. I was about to feel for my latchkey but I thought better of it and rang the bell instead. Safaraz was pretty astute and a quick wink would mean more to him than to a blind horse.

"You out for making fun, isn't it?" said Ram Dass as we waited, and he winked and grinned like the obscene fat-bellied gods they sell to tourists in Grant Road.

"I've been busy, if that's what you mean," I said coldly.

"Oh, damn busy I am betting," he chuckled. "Good—good. There's damn little fun in this city now. All prohibition and long faces. Damn funny, isn't it? Your missionaries are trying to do that to us for four hundred years and are getting nowhere. When the sahibs go we do it to ourselves."

"I mean busy in my office," I answered, and he roared and choked.

Safaraz opened then and he didn't need my warning because he flashed me one first—no more than the slightest twitch of his impassive mouth but that was enough. We went through to the sitting-room and the first thing that struck me was that the door to the spare bedroom was open and the bed showed a crisp, unwrinkled expanse of top sheet that betrayed no sign of recent occupation.

"A nice place you are having here, isn't it?" said Ram Dass. "Nice view—nice breeze. You will excuse?" He crossed to the window and looked out across the harbor and beamed appreciatively. It was the natural compliment and gesture of a guest entering one's apartment for the first time, but his passage across the room gave him a fleeting glance into my own bedroom and out onto the balcony. I shot another look at Safaraz and received a gesture of reassurance from him. Wherever Smedley was, he was safe under cover somewhere. I felt a little easier.

Ram Dass came back to the center of the room. "*Very* nice." He beamed again.

West of Suez I could now have asked him politely what the hell he wanted but I'd been East of it as long as he had, so I waited. He complimented me on my carpets and asked whether we were on main sewage or septic tank, which would be the equivalent of commending one's pictures and enquiring after the garden in Wimbledon. I told him the carpets were poor and cheap, as etiquette demanded, and informed him that we had push-pull and the full facilities of the Bombay Municipal Conservancy Board. He murmured "damn nice," and that completed the opening gambit. The next move was up to him. I anticipated that it would be another oblique reference to prohibition, because Ram Dass, though a caste Hindu, was reputed to have the capacity of a Yukon miner. I would then offer him whisky—he would accept after a show of reluctance, compliment me on the brand after sinking half a tumbler of it—I would say it was lousy and offer him some more—and once again the move would be with him. I was fretting with impatience but I knew the immutable rules. Only this time they *weren't* immutable. He just stopped smiling as if it was switched off and said, "Where is George Alfred Polson, Mr. Rees?"

It was as if a boxing opponent in the middle of the preliminary handshake had suddenly whipped a quick one in under one's ear. My counter was shaky.

"Who the hell is George Alfred Polson?" I asked.

"Convicted person of bad character—dishonorable discharge from Army but still calling himself 'Major'—semi-indigent—European birth but registered as statutory native of India by marriage and domicile. You would be calling him poor white—damn old bum, isn't it?" He was watching me closely although he didn't appear to be doing so. I had now had time partially to recover from the foul swipe.

"I hope not," I answered. "I try not to be rude—even to people I don't know."

"You were with him in bazaar room near Crawford Market this afternoon," he shot at me. He glared at me for a moment or so and then added, "Sit down, Mr. Rees."

That's an old one. The stander has the advantage over the sitter in this sort of interview, and anyhow it was an impertinence in my own home. I countered it by switching into Urdu, which was better than his English and it disconcerted him momentarily.

"I'll stand, Inspector-ji. It is impolite to sit before guests —especially when the guests are leaving." I moved towards the door pointedly.

"This man is wanted for questioning—" he began.

"Then find him and question him—not me," I snapped, and added, "Who do you think you are? One dealing with a criminal—or a poor white?"

"Perhaps the sahib would prefer this interview to be continued at Headquarters?" he said.

It was the "sahib" that did it. "Sir" or "mister" was common politeness, but the old term—and in the third person at that—meant that my flash of temper had got him a little worried. It might have been a sneer but I played it the other way.

"The sahib would," I said and reached for the hat I had thrown onto a chair on entering. "Your immediate superior is Superintendent Shanti Sarup isn't he? Good—let's go and see him."

It worked. He dropped the "sahib" but he also eased the pressure.

"I don't wish to cause annoyance but it is important that we see this man," he said. "If you can help we will be grateful."

"Why didn't you say that in the first place?" I asked. "Instead of treating me like a suspect under interrogation? I'm sorry—I don't know where he is. That's the truth."

"But you were in contact with him today."

"That was this afternoon. I have not seen him since."

"Can you tell me your business with him?"

"I cannot. It was confidential." I thought for a moment or so and took a deep breath. When you're about to tell a lie make it a thumper. "It had to do with a will made by someone in England. I have been retained by a firm of lawyers."

"Mr. Smedley is also from that firm?" This was a swift one but I managed to ride it.

"Oh, you know Mr. Smedley, do you?" I lapsed back into English.

"I know of him."

18

"Well—you're quite right. Actually he came out on behalf of this firm. He engaged me."

One can't read a face like Ram Dass's but I got the feeling that I was gaining the initiative. Straight lying he could no doubt cope with but now I was injecting a modicum of truth into it and it was getting him rattled.

"Then why did he insert advertisement into paper for foreman?" This also was a swift one and it deflated a little of my newly gained cockiness. But once more I managed to ride it.

"That was before he had retained me. He thought it might be wisest. You have said yourself that Polson is a man of bad character. Inquiries for him by name might have frightened him off."

He chewed on this for a while and I decided to make a bird of it.

"But we are wasting time," I continued. "Let us go down to Headquarters." I was taking a calculated risk. "We can collect Mr. Smedley on the way. There'll be nobody at the High Commissioner's office yet but we can phone to them later to send somebody down from the legal department."

That apparently did it. He became his old smiling self again.

"Not to worry, Mr. Rees—not to worry," he assured me. "All damn bobbery chuffering for nothing. I go to tell them at that office you are knowing nothing of this man's whereabouts."

"Like hell you will. I don't want any misunderstandings about this." I made a move to the telephone, "We'll see the Superintendent."

"No, no, no," he said hurriedly. "It is all right."

"You see," I went on earnestly, "*I'm* interested in Polson's whereabouts too. We found him all right but he was scared and nervous—he seemed to be having some trouble with moneylenders. If he's disappeared again—"

"Not to worry, Mr. Rees," he said again. "When we find him we will let you know—when we have finished with him." He moved to the door.

"What do you want him for?" I asked as I let him out.

"Damn bobbery chufferings," he growled. "I am only poor damn police officer. I am told nothing. Good evening, Mr. Rees."

"Good evening, Inspector-ji," I said and closed the door behind him. I waited a few seconds and then opened it again but he had gone down the stairs and I could hear his chaplis shuffling on the stone steps.

Safaraz came out from the kitchen. He also went to the door and peeped over the banisters. He came back and led a shaky but quite rational Smedley out of the pantry.

"What goes on?" asked Smedley peevishly.

"How are you feeling?" I inquired.

"What the hell does that matter? I've been damn near smothered in that lousy hole." He looked it.

"The policeman came earlier," Safaraz said in Urdu. "He made inquiries of the hamal then he came up here."

"What is he saying?" asked Smedley.

"Wait a minute," I told him. "Right—go on, Safaraz."

"He came to the door and made inquiries after the sahib."

"Which sahib? I or Smedley Sahib?"

"Both, sahib. I told him that you discussed business, as is your custom, in Grant Road." If he'd have flickered an eyelid I would have fined him half a month's pay. Grant Road is the brothel area.

"The policeman, being of that caste, believed me. He still wished to enter the sahib's apartment but I dissuaded him." I didn't ask him how. Not even a copper on duty will argue without reinforcements and witnesses with a Trans-frontier Pathan. They are excellent butlers but they carry foot-long knives under their shirts even in Bombay, and they have feudal ideas about their employers' property and premises.

"Shabash, Safaraz," I said approvingly. "But how did you know he had come back?"

"The hamal is a friend," he answered gravely. "He rang me on the teffeylone as the sahib went downstairs. I shall give him one rupee bakshees." He held out his hand.

I paid it gladly and then translated to Smedley.

Smedley sat hunched in a chair chewing his nails irritably.

"What does it all mean?" he asked. "Why are the police suddenly showing an interest?"

"I don't know," I told him. "But this one who was here just now is the one the Major mentioned yesterday—the one who pulled him in for questioning about his movements up North some time ago."

"Think it ties up?" asked Smedley.

"It would seem so. They must have seen that damned ad of yours and got interested. Anyhow, I should say that your immediate problem is to get in touch with the old swab again."

"What do you think happened? Those moneylender people carry him off?"

I shrugged. "Your guess is as good as mine. I told you—I'm only theorizing. Your last arrangement was that he was to ring you on Tuesday morning at Nedou's Hotel in Lahore. He *may* be on his way up there now."

"Then again he may not," said Smedley gloomily. "In which case we're going to sit on our tails up there like a pair of chumps—"

It was the opportunity I had been waiting for. I took it.

"You'll have to make your own decision about that," I told him. "I've fulfilled my part of the contract. I'm afraid you'll have to count me out as from now."

He stared at me in silence for a moment and his face went blank.

"If you're trying to jack up the price, Rees, just say what's in your mind," he said at last.

"I'm not," I answered. "You asked me to help you find Polson. I agreed to that and no more. All right, we've found Polson—and for what little I did towards it I'm not charging you."

"I hadn't counted on this," he mumbled after a time.

"I'm sorry," I said. "I admit I vacillated a bit, but I hadn't altogether accepted. I made up my mind this afternoon and I'd have told you then if you hadn't had fever."

He didn't plead and he didn't get sore—I'll say that for him. He just got up from his chair and wobbled a bit as if the room was going round, which to him it undoubtedly was, and said rather flatly, "Right—thanks for what you've done. If your servant will let me have my clothes I'll shove off back to my hotel."

"There's no need to hurry," I told him. "If you take my advice you'll rest up here for another twenty-four hours."

He nodded, grunted and staggered back to bed.

In the morning I left him in Safaraz's able hands and went to my office because I had a lot of clearing up to do and come what might I was now determined to be off to England on the first B.O.A.C. plane that had a vacant seat. My conscience was quite clear—I'd done what he asked me to and a bit more, and I'd stalled with Ram Dass in order to keep faith with him. It was England, Home and Beauty for me for the next six months; maybe for keeps if I could find a reasonable job before my money ran out. I'd been born, bred and raised out East but it was beginning to cloy.

I was still thinking along these lines when Braganza, my Goanese clerk came in and told me two police officers would like a word with me. I fumed and told him to send them in.

CHAPTER 4

These chaps were a different proposition from Ram Dass. They were thinner and younger and they wore what was currently passing in Bombay for palm-beach suits. One of them was a Sikh. I didn't know either of them. The Sikh appeared to be the senior. He came across to my desk while the other stood just inside the door, and he palmed a warrant card at me with his photo on it. I glanced at it without enthusiasm and asked him what he wanted. He signed to the other man who opened the door quickly and looked out into the other office, probably hoping to catch Braganza with his ear to the keyhole. Braganza sat at the far end out of earshot. I had caught him eavesdropping in his first month with me two years before and we had an unspoken agreement in the matter. The policeman was taking no chances though. He left the door an inch ajar and kept his eye on it. I knew the drill. Part of it was pure common sense routine—part was to impress me with their astuteness.

The Sikh leaned over my desk confidentially and said, "Superintendent Shanti Sarup is sorry to trouble you, sir."

"Good of him," I said. "What's it about this time?"

"The matter Inspector Ram Dass saw you about last night."

"I thought we'd cleared all that up."

The Sikh gave a large and impressive shrug and looked pained. "All cleared up, sir—all cleared up, then things start again. You saw one George Polson and his son yesterday, isn't it?"

"Yes, yes, yes," I agreed wearily. "I told Ram Dass all about it. I went to see him on behalf of a client—but I'm off the case now—finished—kolos—khatm hogia—samajtha?"

That was insulting. You either speak Hindustani or English to an educated Indian—not a patois of both—but I was angry. He took it well though and just looked apologetic and I felt a little cheapened. "All right—shoot," I said, "What more do you think I can tell?"

"You say you are finished with case, no?"

"Yes, Why?"

"Because the son is now dead," said the Sikh in much the same tone as he'd have informed me that it looked like rain tomorrow. I felt sick. I looked at him for a full half-minute —conscious of the fact that both of them were in turn studying my face.

"How?" I asked.

"Beaten," answered the Sikh. "You see now, sir, why we must question you more. As far as we know at this minute you are one of the last to have seen him alive. You will come with us please?"

"All right then," I said, "take me to the Superintendent."

"Yes, sir. Thank you, sir. He is out at Worli Bunder." He seemed relieved and grateful now that I was co-operating. "Mr. Smedley, sir?" he asked as we moved to the door. "You

22

know where we can pick him up? The Superintendent wishes to see him also."

I was about to tell him but I checked myself. There was no point in dragging a sick man out with us at this stage. Smedley could tell them no more than I. I shook my head. "I don't know," I said, and embroidered it because I didn't want them to waste time looking for him. "I want to see him myself. He stays at the Taj but he must have gone somewhere. Right, let us go."

They had a car waiting at the bottom of Hornby Road with another plain-clothes man at the wheel. We got in—the Sikh beside me and the other chap with the driver, and the former said in Urdu, "Worli Bunder—and quick."

We drove quickly through back streets in order, no doubt, to dodge the morning traffic on the main routes. I sat hunched in the corner not liking myself. Damn Smedley and his lousy Syndicate. I wondered sourly if this development would figure in his report and if it did whether the lunch of any of the comfortable gents who sat in well-plushed offices in London or New York would rest the less comfortably in their rounded bellies because of it.

As I reached this point in my angry and inconclusive reasoning I reached for a cigarette and then noticed for the first time that we had come at least four blocks up the Marine Drive past the turn-off for Worli Bunder and we were still travelling fast. I wondered if I had understood the Sikh properly and I turned to ask him where we were going.

"It will not be long," he assured me.

"But you said Worli Bunder," I protested. "Does the driver understand."

"He understands."

"Well I don't," I told him. "We're wasting time. I want to see Shanti Sarup—and quickly."

"We go to see him," said the Sikh, and his tone had changed and he seemed to have lost interest in things and to be almost bored. Up till now he had been polite and semi-apologetic in careful English. Now he was speaking in an Urdu one would have used to an importunate child asking stupid questions. He even yawned a little. I hadn't started at this moment to have any real doubts but I was puzzled and annoyed.

"Where the hell is he?" I demanded. "This road only goes to Juhu."

"Juhu," he repeated, and yawned again and the man beside the driver sniggered. I got really angry then and I leaned forward and rapped the driver on the shoulder—and received a smart clip across the chin from the sniggerer. I didn't return it, because he had delivered it with his left hand. His right was now resting on the back of the driver's seat and he was holding a gun in it. I looked at the gun first and then at the man. He grinned cheerfully and leaned over the seat and clipped me again—harder this time and with a greater degree of accuracy.

"He likes to hit people," said the Sikh conversationally. "Sometimes he likes to kill people. Sit down, tu."

'Tu' is a form of the second person singular that you use to somebody you don't respect, admire or even like. A decent servant will leave you because of it. It told me more than the gun and the two clips. I sat. Something obviously needed to be said but the best I could muster was a threat to report them both to the Superintendent. It sounded silly even to me. It rolled the others up. Even the driver joined in the belly-laugh. It didn't, however, disturb the steadiness of the gun which remained pointed at my midriff for the rest of the ride which lasted for another half hour and, I judged, some twenty miles.

We were well out of the city now and were headed north towards the Bassein Creek. This was an area much favored by European merchants back in the East India Company days before our dewlapped forebears got wise to the fact that malaria was carried by mosquitoes, and moved up onto Malabar Hill. There were mansions out here that might have been built along the Thames backwaters in early Victorian days, each standing in what had once been ten-acre gardens but which were now jungles of palm and peepul trees. Many of them were past habitation even by the fever-stricken squatters who lived along the banks of the creek and eked out a precarious existence fishing and raising stunted rice in the salt-choked paddies, but one or two of the less dilapidated were used by Marwaris and bunias as dried fish and rice warehouses and others as sub-divided dwelling houses for their families. The whole area, once off the main road, was lush and damp, overgrown and rotten with a fetid matted green-ness that put me in mind of the Burma jungles after the rains.

We turned off the road through a ruined archway and bumped up a long winding drive that once or twice petered out and almost lost itself in the undergrowth, until at last we stopped in front of a gabled and turreted chunk of architecture that must have looked hideous even in its palmier days. It was a mass of stained, lichen-grown brickwork and cracked stucco and one end of it had collapsed altogether and disappeared into a creeping tangle of bamboo and liana. What was left of it was still the size of a provincial town hall, and two rows of windows looked down onto the crumbling terrace

24

on which we pulled up. The windows had all been filled in with corrugated iron, giving the face of the building a cataracted blindness. The Sikh told me to get out, again in the contemptuous idiom, and when I hesitated, the driver, his hands now free and itching to join in the fun, leaned over into the back and smacked me hard across the face. I bunched my fist but a quick upward flick of the gun in his pal's hand made me unbunch it. I climbed out onto a deep carpet of rotting vegetation and, urged forward by a shove between the shoulder blades from the Sikh, went forward towards some steps that led downward to an area cellar. The whole place was as dead and deserted as a Tower of Silence but there must have been someone unseen watching and waiting for us because the cellar door creaked open as we approached it and, pushed again by the two behind me, I went through into almost pitch darkness.

I caught a glimpse of an old man in a loin-cloth and turban inside the door before it swung to and blotted out the sunlight, and then the Sikh produced an electric torch and directed its beam past me and shoved me forward again. We crossed the littered floor, our feet making squelching sounds beneath us and bringing up un-nameable stinks of damp decay, and went down a long brick-lined passage that led off from the other side of the cellar. At the end of it was a door, and the Sikh pushed me hard up against it and muttered something to the other man who screwed the muzzle of his pistol into my ribs. The Sikh's hands ran over me expertly and he frisked me of everything I had in my pockets, grunting with disgust when he came to my cigarette case, because tobacco in any shape or form is anathema to their caste. He dropped it on the floor and ground his heel on it and then kicked it into the darkness and the other man growled in protest. He pocketed everything else and then shoved me through the door ungently. It slammed behind me and there was a rattle of bolts and chains in the best tradition—and then just plain, thick, unrelieved darkness, as impenetrable and almost as tangible as an evil smelling black blanket.

I stood where they had shoved me for a long minute, and because there was nothing else to do I swore richly, lewdly and filthily. It didn't help much.

I couldn't sit down on that sponge of a floor and at the same time I couldn't continue to stand as the sheer darkness was making my head swim dizzily. I turned and groped blindly back in the direction of the door, but even in that short period I had completely lost my bearings and I knew suffocating panic as my fingers failed to encounter the wood —failed to encounter anything. I had the feeling that a black bottomless pit yawned all round my feet and that the next step would take me over the edge and I almost yelled with relief when I finally came up against the wall. I groped my way along it until I found the door and from that landmark I went on right round the place—then, because it gave me something to do, I paced it off from corner to corner, and gleaned the not particularly helpful data that it was four good paces, or twelve feet, one way and six or eighteen feet the other—and that the door was in the middle of one of the shorter sides, and that it was thick smooth wood with not a break or a projection on it, and that the walls were slimy to the touch. Greatly daring and again just for something to do, I crossed the place diagonally after that, both ways, just to prove to myself what reason told me already—that there were no pits outside my imagination.

There's a technique and a drill for this sort of thing. They used to teach it during the Korean war when the Chinese started to use pitch-black solitary confinement as a softener on our prisoners before the initial stages of brain-washing. Do something. Keep on doing something. I'd never had to put it into practice before but I remembered it now. I went over that wall brick by brick, from the floor up to as high as my fingertips would reach. I took off a shoe and tossed it above my head to gauge the height of the roof. I gained from that the knowledge that it wasn't very high and that it was a bloody silly thing to do because I had to kangaroo all over the floor to find the shoe again, but this in itself wasn't a bad thing because in the process I found that one corner of the floor on the door side wasn't as wet as the rest of it, so I took off my jacket and made a cushion of it in the angle of the wall and sat down.

I don't know how long I sat there. They had taken my luminous-faced watch from me and one loses track of time quickly in total darkness. I know I worked out the cubic capacity of that damned cellar from my estimated measurements of it—then the inside wall area of it and I remember getting up four or five times when my limbs got cramped. I must have dropped off to sleep also because, although I cannot recall anything definitely leading up to it, I suddenly found myself at the door pounding on it and shrieking and cursing and I was in a cold muck-sweat. It wasn't a pretty moment and it left me weak and shaking when I eventually got hold of myself again.

I'm going to skip the rest of that long sit. I had no means of gauging its length even in retrospect because things were too confused when I came out. I must have gone off into a deep sleep with the partial relaxing of the tension and I only woke when the door was opened. A torch shone in my face and I yelped with the sheer physical pain of it. A voice said in

English, "All right—take a good look at him, Smedley. Now am I bluffing?"

Smedley's voice said, "Sorry about all this, Rees—particularly since you don't know a damn thing. These monkeys won't get away with it. I promise you that." He sounded sick and tired.

The first voice said in Urdu this time, "Take him back upstairs but do not beat him again until I tell you."

And then there was another long wait. Whether it was longer or shorter than the preceding one I do not know. It was ended this time by the sound of the door opening, but there was no light. I took no particular notice of it at first because my ears had started playing me tricks long since. I was still a bit cagey about things even when Safaraz said softly, "Sahib—sahib—are you here?"

I had enough wits left not to yell out loud—but only just. I stood up and he struck a match and I covered my eyes against it. He dropped the match and came forward and felt for my arm. He said, "Quietly, sahib—very quietly. There are many men above. Can you walk?" I grunted an assent and he steered me to the door and down the passage and at the end of it I kicked and stumbled over something soft and nearly yelled again. Safaraz whispered his apologies and explained that it was only a Hindu, and one of low caste at that. Pathans are born snobs. He guided me across the outer cellar to the door through which we had entered and he pushed me to one side of it while he scouted outside and then he came back for me and led me up the steps.

It was night, which was fortunate for me. In strong sunlight I would have been blind for an hour or more. Even as it was the comparison between that hell-hole and the starry splendor of the Indian sky was embarrassing for a while.

Pressed flat against the wall of the house in the shadows I edged my way round after Safaraz until we got to the ruined end and then we slipped into the tangled jungle and kept going. Pathans are hill bred and prefer the open places but they can cope with jungle too. He went on at a hell of a clip and practically without noise and he could see or sense obstructions before he actually touched them and so he was able to avoid them and to lead me round them also because I was useless in that first half hour.

We came at last to the main Bassein Road and we crossed it at a crouching run and dived into the paddy the other side. There was a small stream running down the edge of it under a bund. It made a beautiful babbling sound, but that was all that was beautiful about it. It was brackish and it stank, but it served. I lay flat on my face and drank until Safaraz made disapproving noises and murmured that Hindus—*low-caste*

Hindus—probably washed and worse in it. I still drank—and then when my back teeth were nearly awash I sat up and looked at him. He seemed pleased with himself. He had reason to be—but although I love his race I also understand them. Pathans are a cocky lot. I didn't fall on his neck. I said the Urdu equivalent of, "Well? What the hell kept you?"

CHAPTER 5

Safaraz stopped preening his moustache and cleared his throat. He said, "I have a cousin—the son of my mother's broth—"

"Tell me quickly what has happened," I snapped.

"I am telling the sahib," he said with dignity, and I groaned. Pathans, dramatists to a man, have their own way of telling a story and one hears it that way or not at all. He went on, "He is a great rascal but blood is blood so, he being in this city and without funds, my friend the hamal has let him sleep on the stairs—for which I paid him rupees two per month." I knew all this but there was nothing I could do to speed things up. "Last night, the sahib not having returned, and food for Smedley Sahib being necessary, I had to go to the bazaar. Smedley Sahib was my trust and I hesitated long before leaving him but I placed that trust, with the honor of my family, on the head of my cousin, leaving him at the door of Smedley Sahib's room and giving him instructions that none but a fool could misunderstand, and I went with easy mind. The sahib will remember that we needed rice and coffee—"

It took ten minutes but I gathered at the end of it that Safaraz, a heller with the women in his off-duty hours, had gone out on the tiles leaving his cousin in charge. He had returned to find the flat empty and had sat and sweated until morning, thinking up a series of convincing lies to tell me when I showed up. His cousin had arrived back footsore and dusty about lunchtime. He also had felt the fleshpots pulling and had stepped out for a quick coffee at the local, first, Safaraz assured me earnestly, transferring the charge and the honor of the family to the hamal. Things got a little confused after this but from the welter of evasion and equivocation and calls upon the Prophet to bear witness that was Safaraz's way of telling it, I learned that the cousin returned in time to see Smedley being bundled down the back stairs by a Sikh and another man and, not caring to face Safaraz, had followed stealthily on their heels to a car at the corner of the square. He had then clung to the luggage rack and had had a long ride through the darkness to the house we had just come from. He had decided with discretion that there was nothing he could do about it on his own, so he had returned on foot to the apartment, where Safaraz had beaten him and gone to my office to try and find my whereabouts from Braganza. He had learned from Braganza that I also had gone off with a pair answering the description his cousin had given him. He put two and two together and had talked twenty rupees out of the petty cash from Braganza and had come out here by taxi, guided by his cousin. He had laid low until after darkness watching the place, and then had gained entry to the cellar through a grating at the back of the building—and had seen Smedley brought down to the room in which I had been locked—and had been surprised by the old man at the outer door, who he had knifed just before releasing me. That, at least, was the bare bones of it. Suitably emblazoned it was quite a story and reflected the greatest possible credit —on Safaraz. He hadn't done so badly at that—but I wasn't telling him so.

"And where is your worthless cousin now, slinker at the window of other men's wives?" I demanded.

"Here, sahib," he answered in no way abashed and, my nerves still stretched like violin strings, I jumped a clear foot out of the wet paddy, for the cousin was lying in the darkness within touching distance of us. Safaraz stretched out his foot and kicked him hard and poured abuse on him. "Idle one— betrayer of trusts—tomcat—besmircher of the family honor," he hissed.

I sat and pondered. The sensible thing to do now was to make our way back towards Juhu and get on the telephone to the police and leave to them the task of getting Smedley out, and I would have done just that—but for one complication. That was the Hindu Safaraz had knifed in the cellar. Self defense? Yes—perhaps. Acting in the interests of his employer? Maybe—but very doubtful. I could hear the shocked magistrate—who would certainly be a Hindu himself—telling Safaraz that he had no right to take the law into his own hands, that he should have informed the police in the first place. Safaraz was a Pathan, a man of the north and not even an Indian national. The most feared and hated of all the Moslems in the sub-continent with the possible exception of the Baluchis—to whom they were closely related by blood and tradition. If he got away with anything less than manslaughter he'd be lucky. I just couldn't risk it. All right then—what did we do? Leave Smedley there to talk his own way out? I knew I couldn't. I cursed to myself then I cursed Safaraz and his cousin. They listened in silent admiration.

"How many men are there in the house?" I demanded when I had worked some of my spleen off on them.

"Many hundreds," answered the cousin promptly and Safaraz kicked him again.

"The two who brought the sahib," said Safaraz and began to count on his fingers. "And the driver, and two more who come and go, and one who will worry nobody again—" he finished proudly, and added as the merest afterthought "—oh, and a sahib."

"A sahib?" I asked quickly.

"A sahib," said Safaraz promptly. "He is short and fat like a bunia and he speaks Urdu as well as we do, but he is undoubtedly a sahib." That accounted for the English I had heard in the cellar when they had brought in Smedley. I had taken him for an educated Indian at the time, but Safaraz was not likely to be mistaken in this. So there were six of them and all no doubt armed. The police were out—that was definite. Leaving Smedley there was out also—but what could three of us do against six armed men?

Safaraz said, "Do we return for Smedley sahib?" And I cursed him again.

"Do you know where they keep him in the house?" I asked. He shook his head. "Not in the cellar," he answered. "I searched it. He is above somewhere and they have mistreated him—and he is sick with fever." That was a clincher. On my own I might have tried to find some back door out of this predicament, but to this simple soul there was only one thing for it. He was a liar and a braggart but, like the rest of his tribe, he was not wanting in guts and loyalty. I knew the way they thought. If I had backed out now, or taken the easy way and called in the police and thereby landed him in jail, I would have rated lower in his eyes than their favorite simile —a worm in the bowels of a dog. Come what may I couldn't take that. I stood up. "How far are we from the house?" I asked, because in my confused state I had lost count of time and distance in following Safaraz through the jungle.

"About half a mile, sahib," he told me. "I brought the sahib by a roundabout way to avoid using the drive. The Sikh and the other had gone off with the driver in the car and I did not want to be surprised if they returned—"

I swore at him again then. That meant there were only three of them there at the moment and we had been wasting time.

"They have not returned," said the cousin. "I could see their lights from here."

That was a little more hopeful so I set off along the top of the bund towards the road, and we crossed it a bit further up than where the drive to the house debouched off it. My time in the hole was paying grudging dividends because I was now seeing in the dark even quicker than the sharp-eyed Pathans. We snaked through the jungle in a line parallel to the drive and came again to the terrace in front of the house. It loomed blackly before us and in the distance an owl hooted and was immediately answered by the insane laugh of a hyena nearby, and other things in that damned jungle seemed to wake and listen—and then we heard the reason for it as the noise of an approaching car came to us. It looked as if we had lost our bonus and I cursed again.

The car came slowly up the winding drive, running on its sidelights only and as it came into the open these flicked on and off three times in an obvious signal. It stopped opposite the cellar steps where I had alighted, and the driver got out. He opened the rear door of the car and we, crouched in the undergrowth a bare ten yards away, saw him haul out a heavy packing-case and set it down on the ground. I realized with relief that he was on his own and that we had lost only one third of our bonus. The driver got back and drove slowly along the terrace and round the ruined end of the house out of sight.

"They garage the car round there," whispered Safaraz. "He will return on foot and enter this way. He will expect the low-caste one to open for him."

"Come," I said, and bending double we streaked across the terrace into the shadow of the house. There was no plan. There was no time to make one because even as we got to the steps we saw the man come back into the open at the end of the terrace and I thought for one heart-stopping moment that he could not have failed to see us also—but he came on quite unsuspectingly and grunted as he hefted the packing-case and came towards us. My fingers found a rough chunk of fallen masonry and I had just an instant in which to grab Safaraz's wrist with my other hand before the fellow reached us. I had no doubt what the former intended to do, but we had one corpse too many on our hands already. I smacked the rock down on his head as he passed and he folded up at the knees and collapsed like an empty sack and fortunately the mat of rotten leaves underfoot muffled the thud of the falling packing case. Safaraz clucked disappointedly. I ran my hands over the man and could have yelled with joy when I found an automatic in a shoulder holster under his jacket. I stuck it in the waistband of my trousers. The cousin, an opportunist, was going through his pockets with practised dexterity and transferring their contents to his own.

We had nothing to tie him up with, but the bash I had given him was quite sufficient so I decided to pull him inside the door and leave him.

I hated entering the place again but the two Pathans seemed actually to be enjoying it. The Hindu was just where we had left him so we dragged him into the cell I had occupied and then, on an afterthought, sent the cousin back to bring the driver along also and we swung the door to and fumbled the chains into position. I felt sorry for the driver when he woke up—almost. We went on then guided by Safaraz who had learned the layout of the cellar. There was a flight of steps that led upward from the end of the passage and we tiptoed up them to a door at the top. I was dreading that we'd find it locked from the other side, but it yielded to our push although it creaked like the very devil.

We were in the hall of the house now, a fact that I could sense but not see because there was not a glimmer of light anywhere, but my outstretched hands came in contact with the carved balustrade of yet another staircase leading upwards over the one from the cellar. I whispered to Safaraz to hold the back of my shirt and to tell his cousin to tail onto him in the same way and we felt our way right round the hall past yawning doorways that seemed to lead only into empty rooms until we came back to the stairs. I mounted them one at a time, hugging the wall until we came onto a landing at the top and saw a blessed gleam of light under a door. I took the gun and eased the jacket back and felt it click as it cocked, then I crept across to the light, the others still tailing behind me.

I listened at the door and heard the deep breathing and the occasional creak of a turning sleeper the other side, and I knelt and peered into the keyhole, but either there was something hanging over it or it was filled with the dust of years because I could see nothing through it. I felt for the knob and twisted it gently. The door yielded so I inched it open and looked through. A hurricane lamp on a packing case lighted a large room dimly. There were three native charpoy beds in it and huddled figures slept on two of them. They slept Indian fashion, knees up under chins and heads covered in sheets against the bites of mosquitoes. I looked past them round the room and could see in the gloom at the other end another door.

Safaraz had let go of my shirt now and both he and the cousin had got their knives out and were looking at me like bird dogs waiting for a signal, but I checked them angrily. After these there was only one other—I looked round the room for something good and heavy to supplement the butt of my pistol. Two hefty simultaneous whacks on the heads

32

so invitingly demarcated by the sheets would be the answer, and I was in the act of putting my lips against the ear of Safaraz to tell him so when the nearer man grunted, yawned and sat up sleepily—and then it was too late because the cousin, who had been staring past us into the room, flew at him noiselessly and I winced as the knife took him in the side of the throat. I did save the other one, as I reached him a bare split second ahead of Safaraz and brought the butt down on his head. I turned and shook my fist at them, and the cousin looked injured in the manner of one only trying to help. Safaraz took the opportunity of kicking him again. I went on to the further door and tried it but it was locked. I turned back. Safaraz was gloating over another automatic he had found beside the man I had knocked out, and the cousin was busy frisking the other one. I took the pistol from Safaraz and slipped the magazine out before returning it to him. Henceforward he could keep it for moral effect only. He looked as disappointed as a child relieved of a toy. I swooped on the cousin who was just slipping another pistol into the folds of his voluminous pants and did likewise for him. Not being on my pay-roll he looked a little mutinous, so Safaraz kicked him again. Safaraz always came over to the side of the angels when he had no option.

And so we only had the "sahib" to deal with now—unless reinforcements arrived unexpectedly. I grabbed the lamp and went out onto the landing again. There were several doors leading off it and I tried each of them in turn. They were all unlocked and opened into empty rooms, except one. That made two locked rooms. I was in a quandary now. It was a reasonable assumption that Smedley was in one and the "sahib" was in the other—but who was in which? There was nothing for it but to take a calculated risk. I decided to try the inner one first. I slipped one round into the breech of the pistol I had taken from Safaraz and gave it back to him and told him to watch the locked door on the landing, and then I went back to the other one. I stood to one side of it out of a possible line of fire and rapped smartly on it with my own pistol. I called in English— "Police—come on—open up here."

There was silence for a moment and then I heard Smedley's voice. He said, "Sorry—I'm locked in from your side."

I said, "All right—it's me—Rees. Hang on—we've got another of these apes to deal with." And he told me querulously to make it snappy.

I went out onto the landing to the other door and repeated the bluff but got no answer so I gave Safaraz the whole magazine back and left him on guard and returned to the room. We searched the whole damned place for a key but without success. The door was solid teak and the lock was one of those massive old fashioned affairs embedded in the wood. I called to Smedley to stand clear and I fired two shots into it. The noise in that confined space was terrific and I thought they would be able to hear it in Bombay—but the two rounds might have been peas for all the impression they made on it. We searched round for something to make a battering ram out of but there was nothing heavy enough in the house until the cousin, who apparently had flashes of brightness on occasion, suggested the two beds. We tipped the two limp forms off and tore the four side pieces out and bundled them together with strips of sheeting. It was hot work and we made a hell of a row, but after five minutes we had managed to bash the lower panel out. Smedley crawled through rather slowly and when he emerged fully I saw the reason why. Both his eyes were blackened and half-closed, and the rest of his face looked as if it had been used as a chopping block. Blood stained the front of his shirt and he had a red weal round his neck. He had been worked on systematically.

He blinked at the light and said, "Where is the bastard?"

I said, "Which one? There are two there on the deck and another two down below."

"Little pursey-mouthed son-of-a-bitch, middle-aged, clean-shaven, wears glasses. Slight chi-chi accent."

"The sahib?" I said.

"Call him that if you like," said Smedley sourly. "I just want to be alone with him for a few minutes."

"We haven't seen him," I told him. "There's one still holed up in a room across the landing—"

"That'll be him," said Smedley. "That's where they did the interviewing. Lend us your gun." He held out his hand.

I didn't give it to him. "You'll have to settle that yourself —later," I told him. "At the moment all I'm concerned about is getting the hell out of here—quick."

"I'm taking that monkey along with me," said Smedley flatly.

"Don't be a bloody idiot," I said. "I know how you feel— I've been put through it too, you know. We've got two stiffs on our hands already that would take some explaining if the police arrived along—"

"I've got to see him—" began Smedley, and then keeled over. He amazed me. With the sort of fever he had had plus what he had obviously been through, he shouldn't have been standing at all. It settled all further argument though. I lifted him up with the aid of the cousin but Safaraz, officiously po-lite, took his legs from me and together they bore him from the room. I followed with the lamp and it was then that I noticed that the hitherto locked door across the landing was

34

now standing open. I yelled to the Pathans to drop Smedley and darted into the shelter of the wall and risked a quick peep round the lintel of the door. It appeared to be empty so I shoved the lamp through with my foot and then took another look. There was nobody there. There was just a rough table, a couple of chairs and a tumbled camp bed under a mosquito net. I went in and had a quick look round. There was a window in the far wall but it was securely blocked with battens and corrugated iron. The only way out was through the door. I came back and cursed Safaraz in heaps for leaving it unguarded. Now the "sahib" would probably be lying for us in the darkness ready to pick us off as we went down the stairs.

We took it very gingerly, leaving Smedley on the floor at the top of the stairs and flattening ourselves against the inner wall all the way down, but there was no sign of him in the hall or in the cellar so I sent the Pathans back for Smedley while I remained covering the bottom of the stairs—and then suddenly I thought about the car. He'd probably make for that—and we needed it. Two battered Europeans walking along the main road to Bombay were going to excite comment. I called to Safaraz to go out the way he had previously come in and to get round quickly to where the car was garaged. He was off like a shadow and then I went to the front cellar entrance.

Dawn had broken by this time and it was nearly broad daylight. As I watched I saw Safaraz come round the ruined end of the building. I waved to him and he hurried across. "All right, sahib," he grinned. "Car still there." I breathed again. I went round to it and I felt prickly round the back of the neck expecting to feel the tearing shock of a bullet in my back from out of the jungle. Naturally the ignition key wasn't in the switch so I had to go all the way back again to that damned cellar to search the driver, who was still out to the wide. He didn't have it either and then I remembered the cousin who had by this time carried Smedley to the car over his shoulder. The cousin was wearing it round his neck on a piece of string. Why? Don't ask me. Probably as a charm against rheumatism. I nearly hit him.

We got under way at last and drove back to the city. I dropped the Pathans and Smedley, who had come round again, at the back entrance to the apartments and then I went on a few blocks and left the car near Green's Hotel and sneaked back through alleys and lanes.

Safaraz was running baths and making coffee and kicking his cousin when I got back. The cousin, quite unconcerned, was squatting in a corner of the kitchen cleaning Smedley's shoes. That meant something. A Pathan cleans nobody's

35

shoes except those of his employer. It looked as if Smedley had got himself a servant. I felt almost sorry for him.

I went through to the bedroom and talked to Smedley through the bathroom door. I told him in condensed form everything that had happened since I saw him last, and he in turn told me his tale.

He came out of the bathroom eventually, wrapped in a towel. The hot water had done a lot for him and the bruises round his eyes didn't look quite so livid.

I said, "Well, that's it. Sorry I couldn't have been more helpful."

"What the hell?" he answered. "You got me out of that spot."

"That was more or less incidental to getting myself out. Anyhow, we both really owe it to those Pathans—Safaraz and his cousin. You realize, of course, that between them they've knocked off two of those people."

"Much obliged to them," he answered, unperturbed. "How much each does that run out at?"

"Not a sou if you've got any sense. If things *did* turn sour and they got pulled in, you might find yourself up on a connivance and accessory charge," I told him. "You can slip them a few rupees when you leave town, but not before."

"Hm—all right. Our immediate job, of course, is to find that old swab of a Major." He towelled his head vigorously and then looked as if he wished he hadn't. It must have felt like a bucket.

"I don't think I quite got the point over when I last saw you," I said gently. "I've quit."

That started it all over again and it was lunchtime before I had convinced him finally. We had a last drink and he was about to leave sorrowfully and a shade reproachfully when the telephone rang.

CHAPTER 6

A man's voice on the other end said without preamble, "What about a talk, Rees?" I said, "What about?" and he answered, "Things in general."

"Who's speaking, anyhow?" I asked.

"That's neither here nor there," he said shortly. "What I've got to talk about *is*."

"Such as—?" I had signed to Smedley and now he was crouching over my shoulder sharing the receiver.

"Business."

"The shutters are going up for a time," I said. "I'm off for a vacation."

"There are a couple of bundles of merchandise that might have to be explained first," he said. "I said *might;* perhaps we could come to some arrangement—and then your vacation wouldn't be delayed."

I asked him what sort of merchandise and he told me rather wearily not to be silly and that I knew damned well what he was talking about. I said I didn't and that he could go to hell.

"All right then," he said to that. "You'll be picked up and questioned—and the people who will be doing the questioning will be in possession of definite facts—and there'll be a couple of villagers who will be able to identify you as a person who was seen round that area with three other people—at the significant time—"

"I haven't the faintest idea what you're talking about," I said.

"Well think hard," he told me. "You might or might not be able to clear *yourself* as the actual disposer of the merchandise, but you're in as an accessory already—and you know it. All in all a case like this could take an awful long time to clear up *and* cost a lot of money."

Smedley was making pleading signs to me to go on. I felt I owed him that much so I said, "What do you want?"

"The answer to a simple question," came the reply. "Give that and as far as I'm concerned you're out of the matter—unless you're fool enough to come into it again. What about it, Rees?"

I said, "I'd like time to think it over."

"You've had time," he snapped. "That's why you're stalling. You can consult your partner if you like, but where is it going to get you? I've got it on him too—and don't forget that I know you both, but you don't know me."

"We do," I assured him, and quoted verbatim. "A little pursey-mouthed son-of-a-bitch, middle-aged, clean-shaven, wears glasses and speaks with a chi-chi accent." It was a shot in the dark and I could have kicked myself for it because his English was perfect. Smedley was shaking his head angrily.

"Bloody funny," said the other coldly, "but miles off the beam. You're wasting time. Well—for the last time, what about it?"

"What's the question?" I asked.

"You know that already. Polson's present whereabouts."

"What if I told you I didn't know?"

"I'd assume you were a liar and you'd find yourself down at headquarters facing some awkward questions."

Smedley clamped his hand over the mouthpiece and whispered, "Stall for God's sake."

"What about safeguards," I said. "How do I know that if I tell you, I still don't get picked up?"

"Use your sense," said the man impatiently. "Why would I want to do that? Tell me where he is and the merchandise will be disposed of and that's the last you'll hear of it—unless, as I say, you butt into things again."

Smedley was signalling frantically. He was rubbing the forefinger and thumb of his right hand together in the sign that is understood all over the world.

I said, "That's all right, but it ought to be worth something to me as well. What are you prepared to pay?"

"Not a damned cent," he said. "I've told you my terms."

"Well listen to mine," I answered. "Five thousand rupees and it's a deal—but I want the money first."

"What sort of fool do you take me for?" he asked, "If your information is on the level I'll put a couple of thousand in the post to you—*afterwards*. If it isn't—well, you know the answer to that one already. Come on, Rees, you're wasting time." He was losing his temper.

"Make it four," I said. "I haven't been paid by the other side yet, and the way things look I won't be—"

Smedley was scribbling something on a piece of paper.

The voice on the other end of the line said, "I'm giving you three seconds then I'm going to hang up and send an anonymous chit to headquarters. One—two—"

"He's with a Mr. Otto Nurlind, three-two-five Ranipeth Circle, Sholapur," I said hastily.

"Say that again."

I repeated it.

"If he is," said the voice slowly, "You'll get your two thousand through the mail the day after tomorrow. In the meantime you're being watched." There was a click as he hung up. I glared at Smedley. He sighed with relief.

"Well, that's given us breathing time," he said, and wiped his brow.

I said, "And who the hell is Mr. Otto Nurlind?"

He tore up the piece of paper on which he had scribbled the name and address before holding it under my nose, and gave the nearest approach to an apologetic grin his battered face would allow.

"Apparently the last feller Sher Ali worked for," he said.

"Cut it out," I told him angrily. "This isn't funny. Who's Sher Ali?"

"Him," answered Smedley, jerking his thumb at the kitchen door. "Your servant's pal. He has been putting the bite on me for a job and he gave me this bunch of references." He handed me a tattered sheaf of letters which had been lying on the telephone desk. I looked at them. The top one, dated the year before, stated that "—Sher Ali has been in my employ for a long time and is man of very good character and honest, willing and clean knowing all things of personal service for European gentleman and is leaving me of reasons outside control with great regret yours obedient servant Mister Otto Nurlind B.A. Oxford." It was, in fact, a forged reference. There is quite a trade in them round the Crawford Market. The others, all on embossed letterheads, were paraphrases and took in vain the names of a dozen scattered Europeans. Servants steal sheets of writing paper from employers and sell them to bazaar letter-writers who pick names from out-station directories and produce these gems at five rupees a time. They don't deceive anybody, but no characterless jobseeker would dream of approaching a prospective employer without a sheaf of them.

"That's fine," I said bitterly. "And what happens when he finds out?"

"You tell me," he said. "It was the best I could do off the cuff. Anyhow, we at least know that the Major isn't in their hands."

"Cut out the 'we,'" I snapped. "I've told you—I'm no longer interested."

"Maybe," he answered. "But it's going to be awkward for you if he does tip the cops off, and they find those two stiffs. I'm not trying to blackmail you into anything," he added hastily, "but in your own interests we ought to discuss it."

"There's nothing to discuss," I rose. "With a bit of luck it will take him twenty-four hours to get his goons up to Sholapur. With a bit more, and the little pull I've got, I may be able to get a passage out on tonight's plane—"

"Extradition as a material witness?" he murmured. I had been thinking about that myself.

"If that *does* happen," I said, "I'll just have to tell the truth and trust to luck."

"I don't blame you," he shrugged, "and I'll back you up. I'm damned sorry about this, Rees—really sorry—but that still doesn't get Safaraz off the hook, does it? Or this Sher Ali. I feel kind of responsible. What do you think they'll get if it goes against them?"

"I don't know," I said shortly—but I did. Our testimony and a good lawyer would no doubt save them from a murder charge, but the fact remained that knife-carrying Pathans were feared and hated south of the Pakistan border and I could not see them getting away with less than manslaughter.

That could mean anything from five to fifteen years. A poor return to two men who trusted me. I said, "We'll have to get them out of it—and quick."

"Sure," he said. "But where?"

"Over the Pakistan border would be their only chance."

"Do you know the drill?"

"I could do that all right."

"No fear of extradition?"

"There's no treaty between these two countries. Anyhow, they'd have to find them first."

He looked genuinely relieved and I warmed to him slightly as I realized that he did possess some human feelings. "All right," he said. "Can I leave that to you?"

"You can," I answered, "but it is going to cost you something. I can't send them by train because it's two nights and a day to the border. If things broke in that time they would be picked up this side."

"Plane?"

"No good. Two Trans-frontier Pathans with money for plane fares would arouse suspicion immediately. They'd find something wrong with their papers until the police had had time to check on them. Time's the one thing that's plentiful in this part of the world. They might hold them for anything up to a week at the airport detention center. Don't forget there's a cold war between India and Pakistan."

"What's the answer then?"

"Car," I said. "Drop them near the border and they would have to walk over at night."

"Can they drive?"

"Camels maybe. I'm damned certain Safaraz can't drive a car and I don't suppose his cousin can either. No—we'd need a driver."

"Getting a bit complicated," he said doubtfully, and then added, "How about *you* driving them? Seems to me that Pakistan might be a good bet for you also—until things blow over. Not to mention *me*." I saw then what he had been leading up to and try as I might I could not repress a rueful grin. He was as subtle as a Chinaman. He grinned back and that was the first real crack in the dyke of hostility I had been raising against him. He grinned so seldom that when he did it was a revelation. There was impish humor in it. There's no real defence against humor.

I said, "All right, you bastard—but only because it suits my book. Once over the other side and it's every man for himself."

"Good," he said. "Now what about a car? I take it that yours is no use—for obvious reasons."

"You're right," I agreed. "And I can't risk trying to hire

40

one in the city. That fellow might have been bluffing but at the same time I'd be very much surprised if this place *wasn't* being watched—front and rear."

"What do we do then?"

I'd been thinking about that even as we spoke. "There's a Parsee garage owner in Nasik—a hundred miles up the line and on our route. If we can reach there we'll be all right."

"Can you think of a way of doing that without being followed?" he asked.

"Not while you're asking stupid questions," I answered. "Shut your big mouth, Smedley. I want to think."

It made me feel a little better. He grinned again.

I was still thinking by the time I had waded through a lunch that would have put me on my back had I not had a two-day void to fill. The problem had boiled down now to the simple one of getting out of the apartment and up to Nasik without being tailed by an unknown opposition. Through chinks in the curtains I had studied the square in front and the lane behind the block for a full hour but it told me nothing except that both were full of a nameless, faceless hodge-podge of humanity that would make any shadowers' task pathetically easy.

I was going to need cash so I sent Safaraz out with a check to my bank. It was for ten thousand rupees and I knew they would boggle at it so I rang the manager and cleared it with him. I watched Safaraz from behind the parapet of the flat roof. He emerged from the lobby and took a taxi from the rank as I had told him. It may have been coincidence or it may not, but a black Morris peeled off from the parking area opposite and drove out of the square almost, but not quite, on its tail. There were still a lot more cars left there. I told Smedley, rather pointedly, what I was doing and he took the hint and wrote a manuscript draft out against his letter of credit and gave it to me. I looked at it. It was for twenty thousand.

"That covers your ten," he said. "Plus five for services rendered and five—"

"To put me in hock to you?" I supplied. "It won't make any difference. I'm still quitting once we've crossed the border. I'll let you have an itemized statement and any unexpended balance." I put it in an envelope and sent Sher Ali out to post it to my bank. I sent him the back way but it was hopeless trying to check if he too was being followed, because surrounding buildings masked all but a segment of the back lane.

I decided to put it to the test myself, telling Smedley not to answer the telephone or to open to anybody but the Pathans while I was away.

He said, "Don't worry about me. I'm my own man again, and anyhow, I've got this now." He took out one of the guns we had lifted at the house and snapped open the breech expertly.

"Don't use it, for God's sake," I begged. "We're in enough trouble already."

I went out the front way and took a taxi from the rank, and I sat where I could watch the driver's mirror. This time it wasn't a coincidence. The driver of the last cab in the rank who had had his hood lifted all the morning while he poked around in its innards, suddenly seemed to find the trouble because he closed it quickly and drew out after us—and at the corner he picked up two Hindus from the crowd. I paid my chap off while we were still travelling and then I stopped him suddenly and jumped out in mid-traffic. From the corner of my eye I saw the second taxi also stop, and even as I dived into the crowd on the pavement, its two passengers had decanted and slipped onto my tail. These people, whoever they were, weren't amateurs. Hard put to it I might have shaken them, but this was only a trial run. The problem of getting an ill-assorted quartet of Europeans and Pathans out of that damned block, through the city and up to Nasik undetected looked almost insoluble. In an Indian crowd we would stick out like crows in a snowstorm. Then the germ of an idea started to come to me.

I walked the two blocks to my office and went up and saw Braganza. I asked casually if there had been any callers in my absence. He said yes, one or two—and a few phone calls, and showed me his list, but there was nothing there that meant anything to me. I glanced through my mail then—just a few letters of no particular importance but I pretended that one —an income tax inquiry—was. I gave him some figures to get out for me in the morning and dictated a couple of letters which I told him I would sign as soon as I came in. That would give him something to say if he was quizzed by anybody. I left the office after half an hour or so and walked back to the flat, certain, although I couldn't have put my finger on anybody, that I was still being shadowed. But I had got things worked out by now.

The Pathans had returned when I got back. There had been one phone call—somebody asking for Smedley—but Safaraz had taken it and had grunted 'wrong number' and hung up. I told Smedley what I intended doing and he looked very doubtful but I snarled at him and told him to think of something better. He couldn't, so we started in on him with gusto. He is dark and saturnine so the task wasn't hard. By the time we'd shaved his head and heavy eyebrows he was well-nigh unrecognizable. A tin of brown boot polish melted over the kitchen stove and rubbed into his hands, face and neck completed it. The two Pathans howled and made lewd comments about Konkanese brothel keepers. Smedley howled too, because the polish was stinging his battered face. But it did the trick. It hardly needed the motley collection of garments Safaraz pinched after dark from the servants' clotheslines on the roof to complete the transformation. Smedley might have been anything from an Untouchable sweeper to a betel-nut seller. The Pathans, however, being Pathans, stuck to the brothel keeper. I taught him a gabbled, whining phrase—'*Huzoor-ji—Ham bahud gharib admi hain main samajtha nahin—mafi dejia.*' which, being loosely translated means 'Exalted being, I am a poor man and do not understand. Please forgive me.' It is the automatic answer of the frightened poor and usually calls for an equally automatic kick in the rump from anybody unlikely enough to address one of them. Smedley, who spoke other languages well and was no fool, got it, words and actions, surprisingly quickly. He still didn't like it, but by this time he had no option. For myself, I borrowed Safaraz's spare suit of baggy white pantaloons, long shirt worn outside them, embroidered waistcoat and loosely tied turban. I had worn these clothes on other occasions and I had, theatrical though it may sound, a false moustache that really looked genuine and, more important, stayed put when fixed. I didn't need anything else.

It was dark by the time we had finished all this. We had a meal, sitting cross-legged on the kitchen floor and eating local-style with our fingers in order to instruct Smedley. I wasn't worried about the Pathans getting out unseen. They are tomcats in other respects besides morals. I told them just as much as they needed to know—that the police were making inquiries about two dead men out Juhu way and that hanging was carried out by a casteless Hindu every second Thursday in Thana jail, and that we were heading north. That was more than sufficient. I then told them to go to the second milestone along the Nasik road after it leaves Kalyan and to stay under cover until I showed up. I gave Safaraz twenty rupees and left the rest to them—with confidence. They went joyfully like schoolboys on an orchard romp—onto the roof and over a dark jump to the next building that would have turned my stomach, and onwards, and I knew they wouldn't touch ground again for half a block.

It was going to be harder getting Smedley out. He wasn't so much frightened as horribly self-conscious in his get-up, and the more I tried to reassure him the glummer he got. We shared out the ten thousand rupees, tucked a gun apiece into our waistbands, and breathed deeply. Then I sent him on his way downstairs and told him to wander out of the tradesmen's

43

entrance and to wait for me outside Green's and to follow me when I passed. I gave him a couple of minutes and then went out openly by the front entrance.

I had no means of telling whether or not I was getting away with it. I didn't dare use any of the accepted tricks for throwing off a tail as it would have given the game away, so I just swaggered along like the off-duty servant of someone ill-advised enough to employ a Pathan, looking idly into a shop window or two, cuffing a Hindu who crossed my path and winking at anything female under sixty. I saw Smedley as I passed Green's. He was cowering like an orphan outside a ginshop in a Hogarth print, which was excellently in character. I went north up Hornby Road and past Victoria Terminus towards Byculla. It was a long walk on a damned hot night and I was worried about Smedley. He should have been in bed, but each time I glanced over my shoulder he was still there, padding doggedly along.

Our plan had been, if the coast was clear, to take a train from Byculla Station to Kalyan—but first I had to see *if* the coast was clear. I had told Smedley what I intended to do and now, as the pavements were becoming less crowded in this suburban area, I gave him the signal. I hawked loudly and spat and slipped quickly into the next alleyway I came to. I stood in the shadows and watched Smedley pass and then waited a few minutes and I thanked my stars that I had insisted on this last precaution in the face of Smedley's impatience.

Two Hindus hurried past the top of the lane. I only glimpsed them for a moment under the street light but I was almost dead certain that they were the two who had followed me in the afternoon.

Well, this would be the test. Smedley would now turn down the next alleyway. I peered round the corner and watched. Sure enough, as he disappeared, they hurried forward, waited for a moment, peeped round the corner and then went round after him.

I knew this part. Both these alleys led down to an open maidan on the other side of which was the old European Cemetery. I ran down in the darkness and stopped at the bottom. Smedley, if he did what I had told him, would now lead them back towards me. There were no lights down this end but there was a certain amount of reflected glow off the whitewashed walls of the surrounding buildings and after a moment or so I saw the blur of Smedley's figure emerge from the darker gloom of his alley. He hurried back to where he no doubt was hoping fervently I'd be, and he jumped as I touched his arm and whispered. He slid in behind me.

The other two came out and seemed to hesitate and then,

since they were faced with two alternatives, started to argue. I dropped on all fours and crept towards them in the shadow of the wall. In the manner of their race when arguing, they couldn't keep their voices down and I had learned all I needed to know long before I came up with them.

"Fool!" one of them was saying. "It was as I said—he was just a sweeper."

"But he followed the Pathan, swineface, and he came from the building—and the Pathan *was* Rees. I have seen him wear those clothes before." So I wasn't so smart. Still neither were they as it now appeared. One wanted them to split and each to go in opposite directions round the maidan until they picked up our trail again, but the other was a more timorous soul.

"Rees or Pathan or sweeper," he wailed, "they will be armed. I was engaged to follow, not to have my belly slit."

"Right—go back and tell Ram Dass that," snarled the other. "He will be pleased—"

Smedley had followed and he was now close behind me. I kicked back to caution him. The two Hindus, still arguing querulously, went off together and disappeared in the darkness and then, still on hands and knees, we went back up the alley. Halfway up we got to our feet and sprinted to the main road. There was a tramstop at the top and one was just moving off in the right direction. I grabbed Smedley's elbow and we jumped for the rear platform. Tired coolies from the night shift of the cotton mills were hanging all over it like flies but we managed to gain a foothold among them. Nobody argued with me, as a Pathan, but Smedley was elbowed and cursed. He reacted well and I heard him whining his "Ham gharib admi" plaint. We rode for three blocks and then dropped off, bilking the Bombay Transport Company of two annas each.

"I thought the general idea was to slug them," Smedley said waspishly.

"It was," I agreed. "Until I heard what they were saying." And I translated for him. " 'Ram Dass' might not mean anything," I explained. "It's common enough in India—but it *does* happen to be the name of the detective who questioned me last night. If they were referring to the same one then they were police also. Slugging a couple of toughs is one thing. Tangling with the Law is another."

"Do you think he's blown the gaff already then?" he asked anxiously.

"I don't know what the hell to think," I said. "But I'm not prepared to stack up more charges if he has. Come on." I guided him round to the third class entrance to Byculla Station. "I'll have to leave you—a Pathan wouldn't be seen dead with a jerk like you. I'll get the tickets and slip you yours outside here, then you can go on to the platform and lurk in the shadows."

"I'm fed up with bloody lurking," he growled.

"Watch me and get into the same compartment and roll up and pretend to go to sleep. It's about a forty-five minute run to Kalyan."

We had to wait nearly two hours before our train came in. It was an 'Express' which meant it was slow—fast trains are called 'Mails'—and it was made up almost entirely of long third class carriages—all of them packed to suffocation with bodies and bundles. One half of India seems constantly to be travelling and the other half to be seeing them off or meeting them, and the travelling half takes everything it owns with it including sometimes the kitchen stove.

We fought our way on through the pandemonium and to my dismay I found myself in the middle of a group of Orakzai Pathans who hailed me as a brother. I could get by in my guise with most people but I didn't fancy three quarters of an hour with the genuine article. Pathans are as inquisitive as monkeys and their first questions to a bhai-bund are about family, tribe and village. They have a sign though, which I'd learned from Safaraz. I clasped the forefinger and thumb of my left hand round the wrist of my right and pushed through them. They clucked sympathetically and opened up for me and I shoved my way up to the other end of the long open carriage. That sign meant I was on the run from the police and would rather be alone.

We rumbled through the night and it got hotter and smelt worse every minute. Poor Smedley, worn out and weakened, sat down on the floor, and a small child of unsocial habits, sleeping on a luggage rack above him, was sick. Smedley got up quickly, but not quickly enough. I felt that the bill the Syndicate were going to get after this junket was going to be a big one.

We came at last to Kalyan and we were glad to get out. This was a through train to Madras and nobody seemed to be leaving it here although, as is the custom with travelling India, everybody got out on the platform if only as a brief respite from the charnel-house carriages. We would have been conspicuous going out through the barrier, however, so I strode purposefully up the platform as if to the can, signing to Smedley to follow. Out of the dim station lights, we crossed the tracks and climbed over a fence and dropped into the road outside. He followed me through the bazaar and out onto the main road and then I waited in the darkness for him to come up with me.

"Not long now," I told him consolingly.

"*How* long?" he snarled.

"Second milestone up this road," I answered.

"It would be the bloody second." He spat and fell into step alongside me.

All in all I felt I had got even with Smedley for dragging me into this business.

CHAPTER 7

I had told Safaraz the second milestone merely to place the rendezvous well outside the dreary little railway town of Kalyan, but I had chosen luckily because here the road ran through fields of growing maize and there was not a habitation in sight. We arrived at it as the sky was beginning to pale over the hills that sweep down and bound the flat coastal plains which surround Bombay and its environs. Smedley sank down into the dust at the side of the road thankfully. I didn't know whether Safaraz and Sher Ali had made it ahead of us but I started to sing 'Zakhmi Dhil', an extremely bawdy Trans-frontier song that I had often threatened to sack the former over for howling it around the flat. I only got the first two bars out before it was taken up with gusto from the high maize, and the pair of them emerged like twin Aphrodites from the foam. I was glad to see them. They had managed to catch the train ahead of us, Safaraz told me, and I questioned him closely on the possibility of their being followed. He was boastfully positive that they hadn't been, but I took the precaution of moving a further mile up the road and then half a mile off it through the maize just to make certain. Smedley was profane about it because he had already gone to sleep and I had to shake him awake again.

I left him with Sher Ali in a mango grove right out in the blue while Safaraz and I circled back and ambushed our own track, and only after an hour was I satisfied that we had indeed shaken them. I was pretty well all in myself by this time so I set Safaraz on watch while the rest of us got our heads down. He was relieved by Sher Ali after a couple of hours, and then I took over, so it was mid-morning by the time we finally woke Smedley. The long sleep seemed to have done him good, for which I was thankful because he was going to need all the strength he could recruit.

We bathed in a nearby stream and then lay on our backs in the comparative coolness of the mango trees, smoking cigarettes and swatting flies, while the Pathans relieved each other in alternate shifts of sleeping and keeping watch over the surrounding fields, for now the villagers had come out and were working in the maize.

Smedley said, "What's the next move?"

"Wait here till dark again," I told him, "then we walk up the line and hop a train for Nasik."

He groaned and asked me how long the walk would be.

"About five miles," I said. He mulled over this for a while.

"Since we've got to do it, is there any point in wasting a whole day here?" he asked.

"I think so," I said. "Don't forget that this chap will know now that we've left Bombay. If he's carried out his threat the police will be looking for us and watching trains, the roads and the docks—and they'll know what we look like."

"In which case the train will be unsafe, won't it?"

"It would certainly be unsafe to buy tickets at a small wayside station," I agreed. "I said *hop* a train."

"Ride the rods?" The thought appalled him.

"Not quite that," I assured him. "You've seen what happens at stations; everybody gets out to stretch their legs. We just drift into the crowd in the dark—from the blind side of the tracks—singly—and mix with them."

"What about ticket checks en route?"

"We'll have to take that as it comes. Anyhow, as I remember it, Nasik is the first one after Kalyan. We'll be off the train before it need worry us. It's only a three hour run up the Ghats."

He was thoughtful for a time, then he said, "I'm damn certain he won't tell the police."

"I'm glad to hear it," I said. "But what makes you think so?"

"He no more wants the police horning in on this than I do. It's a bluff. That's why he pulled it on you instead of me. I might have called it." He looked a little superior through his mottling.

I rolled over onto belly and elbows. I was seething.

"This is a hell of a time to tell me that," I spat at him. "You sold me this pup on the assumption that *he would*—and I was sap enough to buy it."

"You can't blame me for insuring against possibilities—you do yourself, don't you? I'm only expressing my opinion."

He was right. I subsided a little, but I was still angry.

"Very well then," I said. "But before we go any further I want to know a little more about things. Who *is* this fellow?"

"I don't know," he answered.

"Then how the hell do you know whether or not he is likely to set the police on us?" I demanded quickly.

"I don't know who the feller *is*," he said, "but I can make
damn good guess who he's working *for*."

"Who?"

"A syndicate," he said vaguely.

"I've read about them," I told him. "I've got low tastes i
literature. You work for one too, don't you? I want mor
than that, Smedley."

"I'd have told you more," he said impatiently, "only I'v
been sick and you've been hollering that you wanted to g
out of it. All right, here it comes. Syndicates may sound corn
—but they exist. My bloody oath they do. The one I wor
for is big but I wouldn't be able to pick any of its membe
out in the Ritz. I get *my* instructions from a little squirt wh
runs a small agency just off the Strand. They're not crook
and I don't suppose you'd find any of them rolling into be
with Lola the Beautiful Spy. They're Business Men—capit
B, capital M—and their business is Big Money—same cap
tals. They deal in anything and everything, providing th
money *is* big. It always is, because by the time they're read
to sink a few million of other people's dough into a propos
tion they know every damn thing about it that there is t
know. I, and fellers like me, collect the info for them. Ho
we get it doesn't worry them. All they want is results—an
they don't quibble about paying for them."

I knew a lot of this, as I have already said, but I let him g
on.

"There are others besides the one I work for—London—
New York—Brussels—Hamburg—Athens—always in th
Big Money centers. *They* employ people like me too. Nic
guys some of them. We sometimes run into each othe
in pubs in Montevideo, Rangoon and Melbourne—and w
might even have a drink together—and if one tells the othe
he is travelling for combine harvesters or hula hoops it's ac
cepted. That doesn't stop one side or the other taking a dirt
swipe from time to time if interests are running counterwise
though. Some of the swipes *are* dirty. You've seen a bit of i
yourself. No holds barred—the stakes are too big to le
them be. We're business men ourselves—the field men,
mean." He lit another cigarette.

"All right," I said. "I'll take your word for it. The back
ground doesn't concern me; this particular shindig *does*.
take it that two syndicates are interested in the papers Po
son told us about?"

"You're damn right."

"And the people we've run up against are working for th
other crowd?"

"I don't even have to guess at that. Don't forget, they pu
the question to me in that dump."

"But you didn't recognize any of them?"

"I didn't. Let me put something to you. I don't know much about India—but I'm sent out here on this job. What do I do? I call in a local expert—you. You know the angles—and the language—and you've got an organization—" He pointed over his shoulder at the Pathans. "—and some of these boys working for you. Right—I leave it to you in the early stages and I keep in the background. That's the way it always is. Same with them. We've seen *his* stooges—they've seen ours—" He tried to bite it back but it was too late.

"Thanks," I said drily and he had the grace to look a little abashed.

"I didn't quite mean it that way—" he began.

"What the hell does it matter how you meant it?" I said. "That's what I've been up to now. All right—this stooge isn't squawking, but the bill's going to be a big one, Smedley."

"You're welcome. I told you, my concern's got plenty." He looked relieved. But I wasn't letting an opening like this slip.

"Pity they didn't spend a little of it in getting a good *top* man," I told him. "The other side have only let us see their stooges—but they know *you*—and they had you in the can, until the stooges pulled you out. *You* don't know your opposite number though. They've beaten you to the punch, Smedley."

He looked almost pathetic. "I was sick, goddam it—" he began, then he stopped and did a surprising thing. He fell back flat on his back and guffawed. It was the first time I ever heard him laugh. I told you—there's no defence against humor. I joined in, and although the Pathans hadn't the faintest idea what it was all about, so did they. It cleared the air, and from that moment things were easier.

We went on talking for over an hour, weighing up pros and cons. Pakistan still seemed our only bet. In spite of Smedley's opinion, the opposition might carry out its threat if only to put us out of the race. There was another aspect of it too. We knew now that they weren't holding the Major. Our last arrangement with him was for him to contact us at Nedou's Hotel in Lahore on Tuesday next—which was still two days off. Lahore wasn't far the other side of the border. We couldn't reach it by Tuesday—we'd be two or three days late at best—but if the old chap had made it at all it was a reasonable assumption that he would wait around until we arrived. Our original plan therefore stood. By the time we had settled this the shadows were beginning to lengthen.

The road and rail lay roughly parallel, running due east across the plain to the foot of the Western Ghats, so we set off just after darkness had fallen completely, padding along in single file in the ankle deep dust. Smedley was definitely on

the mend now and he kept up well, and an hour and a half
brought us to the next station up from Kalyan. It was a place
called Shevgaon and there was a huddled village of mud huts
there, and in the middle of it a chaikhana, or teahouse. It was
lighted by a glaring gas lamp and it seemed to be a
good pull-up for trucks because three or four stood outside it.
I thought for a moment of hitching a ride if any were going
up the Nasik ghat; most long distance drivers would carry
passengers for a consideration, but I dismissed that on reflection, because patrolling police often stopped trucks and poked
about in their loads on general principles. No, the train was
better. I did risk a visit to the chaikhanam though, and
wolfed some flyblown chupatties and drank a quart of tepid
tea. I bought some more and stocked up on horrible local
cigarettes and took them back to the others who were holed
up in a field outside the village. I meandered round to the station then, and because I couldn't read the Nagri timetable on
the wall outside and didn't want to be seen taking an interest
in the English one, I asked a coolie when the next train for
the North went through. He told me in an hour, but the fool
didn't add that it was the Mail and didn't stop, so we sat on
in a ditch for another two hours waiting for the 'Express'—
quotation marks mine—swatting mosquitoes and cursing.

It arrived in the end, and getting on was easy because the
platform was shorter than the train and passengers swarmed
down onto the tracks at either end of it, so all we had to do
was to mingle with them and then clamber up when the
guard's whistle sounded. There was a slight contretemps that
might have been serious though. All Indian trains have 'pur-
dah-gharries' in each class. These are carriages for women
only. First and second class present no difficulties because the
notice is there for all to read in English and Hindustani. On
the third class ones, however, it is designated only by a picture of a houri glancing coyly over the top of a harem veil.
This meant nothing to Smedley. He merely saw a carriage
slightly less crowded than the others and he made a bee-line
for it. I was busy getting into the one next to it—Pathan
style, elbows flying and feet lashing out—and the first I
knew of it was an eldritch chorus as Smedley came flying out
on his ear. Safaraz and Sher Ali were amused. Smedley was
not—neither was I when I saw two Mahratta constables
hurrying towards us, but the train was moving by now and
I managed to yank him on behind me. But it gave me an idea
for the future.

We got to Nasik in the early hours and had no difficulty in
dropping off the train and slipping over the marshalling yard
wall. I knew it was no good trying to knock the Parsee up in
darkness—people want to know who it is before taking the

chains off the front door in India—so we dossed down in a Mohammedan burial ground where I knew we would be safe from chance prowlers and Hindu police. It didn't worry Smedley or myself or, presumably, the occupants, but Safaraz and Sher Ali had a few theological doubts about the propriety of it. This notwithstanding, we slept the sleep of the exhausted until the jackals woke us at dawn. I left them there then and went off to the garage of the Parsee.

Jamsetjee R. Mechanic had been in a Field Security section with me in Burma. The 'R' didn't stand for anything, he'd just adopted it like Harry 'S.' Truman. 'Mechanic' was, however, genuine because the Parsees are like my own Welsh ancestors in that, and use trades as surnames. He was a cheery little man and, like most of his race, entirely trustworthy. I had called on his services on several occasions since the war and paid him well, so he was my man. He now owned half a dozen battered but serviceable trucks and a couplé of cars he hired out for weddings and funerals. He also leased the local cinema, so Jamsetjee was sitting pretty. I climbed over into his yard and picked my way through heaps of junk and stripped down skeletons of cars and I threw gravel up at his window. After the third handful he put his head out wrathfully and didn't like what he saw. He cursed me in three languages—a Parsee is one of the few in India who doesn't give a damn for a Pathan—and he threatened me with a twelve-gauge shotgun. I tugged off my false moustache and my turban—hastily. He goggled for a moment and then, as he recognised me, withdrew his head and came down and opened for me. He shouted up the stairs to his spouse and numerous progeny to stay where they were, after which, being a Parsee to whom one hour of the day is as good as another, he produced a bottle of 'King George Very Old Scotch Whisky (Nasik)'. I'd have settled for tea but Jamsetjee was touchy on the matter of hospitality so I drank half a tumbler of it and tried to look as if a mule hadn't just kicked me in the midriff. I told him I wanted a car and that I didn't know when he'd get it back. He said that couldn't matter less. Then I told him about the others. He insisted on settling me down with the bottle while he pulled on a pair of pants and went for them. He and Safaraz were old pals. He was back with them in ten minutes and it was typical of him that he didn't even look curious. He just set about getting us some breakfast—boiled eggs, excellent home baked bread and buffalo milk butter with lashings of hot sweet tea—a meal that couldn't offend the caste prejudices or religious susceptibilities of any of us even if we'd had any. The Pathans carried theirs out into the yard, prissily, like old maidservants who knew their place.

Smedley was looking worried at my frankness but I knew who I was dealing with. I told Jamsetjee that we were bound for Pakistan but I was worried about our clothes, as people we didn't wish to meet probably had our descriptions. He cocked an eye at us and rubbed his chin and pondered over this for a while. I could pass as practically anything, he said, while Smedley, with a bit of retouching could possibly get by in a variety of rigs—but real Pathans still look like real Pathans however you dress them, except perhaps— He smacked his knee. "Punjabi Mussalmans! That's it."

He was right. The two races are very much alike in build and general configuration and, in fact, there has been a lot of intermarriage between them. They dress differently though.

"What about clothes?" I asked doubtfully.

"A cinch," he said. "There's a lot of them guys down here from way back. There was a railway colony of them in Nasik in the British days and they've stayed on. They still dress the same and old Mir Khan runs a general store for them down the bazaar." I told you, Jamsetjee leased the local cinema and never missed a picture and his speech proclaimed it.

I said, "That's fine. Could he fix us up with a burkha, too?"

He looked startled and said, "Jesus! You got a jane with you?" A burkha is the long, all-enveloping white gown, complete with hood and eyeslits, that the orthodox Moslem woman of the North wears.

I said, "No, but my friend here doesn't speak any of the languages—as a purdah woman he wouldn't have to."

Smedley said, "Not bloody likely," with finality.

The idea appealed to Jamsetjee's risibilities. It appealed even more to those of the Pathans and gave rise to further lewdness when the Parsee came back an hour later with a gunny sack of assorted clothes. They boggled a bit over discarding their own characteristic garments but I wasn't arguing with them. Both their moustaches came off under the ungentle razor of Jamsetjee, and after a few curt words between Smedley and myself we shortly afterwards appeared as three very passable P.Ms and a downtrodden harem chattel.

Jamsetjee led me out to his garage and showed me a dated but sound Buick. The front tyres were a bit worn but he changed them for good retreads and then he started her up and waxed poetic over her noisy but sturdy beat. He filled us up and shoved a couple of jerricans of petrol in the boot as well—and he supplied us with water in canvas chagals that hung over her venerable carcass like festoons. He also fixed us up with a box of tinned provisions and stocks of cigarettes. He threw in a road map which proved invaluable and, since he never did things by half, gave me a battered portable radio so I could get the news and weather forecasts from All-India

Radio en route. And all this was just on my say-so that he would get paid in the future, because I deemed it unwise to break into our cash reserve too heavily.

We got going at mid-morning and the old Buick lived up to the reputation Jamsetjee had given her. We bowled along the Mhow road at a steady fifty, hour after hour. When the road was deserted Smedley threw off his hood and facepiece and relieved me at the wheel while the two Pathans lolled in the back like bishops on their way to Torquay, enjoying it all hugely.

I had thought up a reasonable cover story in case we were stopped and questioned at any of the village police posts we went through. I was Futrej Khan and Smedley was my wife. Safaraz and Sher Ali were my brothers. The term is 'bhai-bund' and can mean anything from real brother to members of the same tribe. We had sold our grain business in Ahmedabad and were going back to Pakistan. Safaraz was Mohammed Aziz and Sher Ali was Akbar-ud-Din—both good resounding names that pleased them mightily and made up in part for the indignity they imagined they suffered as Punjabi Mussalmans.

We knocked off ten hours that first day and put nearly four hundred miles between us and Nasik before dark. I turned off the road down a jungle track finally and we camped by a waterhole in a grove of peepul trees and had a meal and then slept like dead men.

We were off at dawn again and I refuelled in a market town and was happy to see that we excited neither interest nor curiosity, and that second night saw us level with Delhi, which I circled round by indescribably bad by-roads before once again camping in the jungle. I listened in each evening to A.I.R. in both the English and the Urdu transmissions, but although there were the usual lists of bad-hats wanted for everything from dacoity to murder, we didn't figure among them. Things seemed to be running smoothly.

And so we came on the third day to the border country.

CHAPTER 8

In the days of the British Raj, the whole pear-shaped sub-continent of India was one country, from the Northern frontier with Afghanistan to the narrow waterway which divides its Southern tip from the droplet of Ceylon. In 1947 the bottom two thirds were ruled off with an arbitrary pencil line.

That two thirds remains India but the one above it is Pakistan and now they are both independent republics. The division was bloody and bitter and the statisticians gave up counting the dead and homeless in the first months. The bleeding may have stopped now but the scars and bitterness remain. India is predominantly Hindu and Pakistan is Moslem and the enmity between those religions goes back a thousand years. Men of goodwill on both sides hope that the scars will some day be fully healed and they work wholeheartedly for that end. The question of Kashmir, however, bedevils them both. Kashmir is the most beautiful country in the world, and I make no apology for didacticism, for I have never known anyone who has been there to disagree. Geographically it lies north of the border in the corner formed by Tibet, the Chinese province of Sinkiang and Afghanistan. For that reason, and the fact that the majority of its inhabitants are Moslem, Pakistan claims it. On the other hand it has been traditionally for five hundred years a Hindu kingdom and the rulers and the people who speak for it are of that religion. My views and opinions are not important so I don't give them. I merely curse both sides for making this Himalayan paradise a squalid battlefield and for quartering their armies in its valleys, and my sympathies are with the patient, once happy inhabitants caught like unconsidered grains of wheat between two millstones.

Its climate is that of Switzerland, only more extreme—and so is its scenery, only grander—and I'd number its women, with the Italians and Chinese, as the loveliest in the world . . . and since this is neither a travel book nor a political treatise I'll leave it at that. I merely give these facts as I see them in order to explain why crossing the border from India to Pakistan is more of a business than crossing, say, from the United States to Canada.

We stopped five miles short of the border, before the patrols and check-points start in earnest, at a village called Ramabagh, which means 'Garden of God'. It was getting dark and the caravanserai on the outskirts, which had been derelict for a hundred years but which was now back in business, was filling up rapidly. Political strife notwithstanding, both sides have to eat so trade goes on as usual, but nobody moves along those roads at night if they can help it, because in addition to the patrols which stop, search and generally bulldoze travellers around as a matter of normal duty, bad-hats have taken full advantage of the tension and there is much old-fashioned brigandage on the North-west Frontier pattern. Trucks and bullock carts bound for the North therefore laager up in places like this and go forward in convoy in the morning. At the frontier itself they are stripped down and searched for contraband, and papers are checked and drivers and passengers interrogated. They snake on a couple of hundred yards after clearance, and then the process is repeated by the other side. This, at least, is the system on the main roads and also on the railway. Freethinkers and the politically irresponsible have other ways and means though, because try as they undoubtedly do, the authorities can't completely close fifteen hundred miles of otherwise undemarcated frontier.

I parked the car outside the caravanserai. It and ourselves were grimed all over with a thick coating of white dust and we fitted into that background like so many pebbles on a beach. The caravanserai was a high-walled courtyard with a well in the middle of it and it was packed tight with humanity and animals. There were dung cooking fires around the walls and their acrid smoke mixed with the haze of dust that hung over the place. There were more people outside it than there were in, and in the short time it took me to stretch my legs and light a cigarette, the car was hemmed in by new arrivals—a large open-sided passenger bus, a string of camels and some bullock carts. Safaraz and Sher Ali, with the claustrophobic intolerance of the hill man, growled in their throats and started to clear an area of lebensraum. As Pathans they might have got away with it without argument, but as comparatively easygoing P.Ms it was out of character. A Bengali spat at one of them, and things looked hair-triggerish in a matter of moments. I saw the caravanserai keeper elbowing his way through towards us. He wore a uniformly dusty loincloth, shirt and turban, but he carried a heavy staff and sported a brass armband, and that, in these parts, is the equivalent of a peak cap and jackboots in Germany. He swung the staff like a two-handed flail and it bounced off the turban of a yelling camel driver and caught Sher Ali on the shoulder. I pinned the latter against the side of the car before he could get his knife out because if he'd reached it he would have slit that earnest official from navel to chin.

I manhandled him, hissing and cursing, round the car and into a backwater between the camels and the bus. I chopped him hard under the nose with the edge of my hand and used my knee viciously. Sher Ali subsided writhing into the dust and I breathed again—but not for long because some fool, as is often the way in an Indian crowd, had started to yell that Hindus were being murdered by Moslems. The cry was taken up and it went through the mob like a flame in a dried maize field, and against it came the inevitable counter-yell of "Ulla-a-ahi' Akhbar!" and that was all that was needed. The whole place went up like a bomb.

Sher Ali, preoccupied for the moment with the nose-chop

which had all but blinded him, and what I have no doubt at all was a very uncomfortable feeling in the pit of his belly, was safe for the moment so I struggled back to the car to get Smedley out of it. I had to pull against a press of screaming, cursing bodies to get the door open and as I did I stopped what felt like half a brick with the back of my head. My turban cushioned it, of course, but there was still enough force behind it to drop me flat on my face—a posture not to be recommended in a race riot. I tried to roll under the car but there was a forest of dancing legs between me and it and things started to look really grim. Open-toed sandals are not very good for kicking, and the wearers realize it, so they put both feet together and jump on you in these parts. I don't suppose one in that crowd knew or cared whether I was Moslem, Hindu or Bush Baptist—they were in the grip of mass hysteria and I was just someone on the ground. India for Ever!—Holy Pakistan! Jump on him, brother!

I didn't know until afterwards what eased the pressure sufficiently for me to struggle to my knees and then to my feet. It sounded funny in retrospect but I'm damned if it was at the time. Smedley had seen me go down and he had tried to wrench the door open to get me inside but the press of bodies had prevented him. He had no weapon in the car that he could have used to clear them, other than his gun, and even he realized that shooting would have sent the balloon up irretrievably, but he remembered having seen a jack handle lying around somewhere. He had to strike a match to look for it among the miscellaneous junk that cluttered the floor of the rear compartment and the match burnt his fingers and gave him an idea. He balled up the road map into a rough torch and lit it, and then he rolled the window down and leaned out and started to singe the backsides of the nearer jumpers. Even mass hysteria is not proof against a burnt tail. The crowd opened up for the instant I needed to get to my feet and he yanked me inside the car—but it had drawn attention to us. There was a second of indignant, incredulous silence from those nearest to us and then they were onto the car like a pack of wolves, shrieking, howling and clawing. Smedley took over then because my eyes, nose and mouth were full of powdery dust. He wrenched open the other door which was close up to the side of the bus, and he pulled me through it and onto the ground under it. We wriggled through to the engine end and came out into the crowd again just in time to see the Buick go crashing over against the bus and stay poised at an angle of forty-five degrees. Then someone must have unscrewed the petrol cap and thrown a match in because there was a whoof of flame and a dull explosion and both vehicles were a burning mass. Blind panic now mixed

57

with the insensate fury of the mob as showering petrol had set alight the thin cotton clothes of the nearer ones, and the kneeling camels behind us had taken fright and broken free from their knee tethers and were milling round kicking and biting with wicked three-inch teeth.

Police whistles could now be heard above the din and there was a banshee-whine of sirens as two truck loads of troops came hurtling down the road from the military lines the other side of the village. A searchlight from one of them swept the seething mass and over the din I could hear a loud-speaker yelling in Urdu for stillness and silence—or else. And slowly sanity returned and with it the sheepishness and gaping wonderment of a crowd which has been yelling for blood and doesn't know the reason.

The officer in charge of that half-company knew his job. The loudspeaker crackled into life again and he told every-body to sit on the ground where they were, and the search-light flicked sideways to rest for a moment on two tin-hatted sepoys who manned a Bren on a fixed mounting. Other troops got to work on the vehicles with extinguishers but although they had the flames under control very quickly I could see that the Buick was as near a write-off as made no difference and I had the sick feeling of a man who has broken faith. Poor old Jamsetjee loved that venerable car.

The searchlight continued to sweep the crowd slowly and I strained my bunged-up eyes to try and pick out Safaraz and Sher Ali but it was hopeless. The officer and a couple of po-lice inspectors together with a fat little babu I took to be the district magistrate, were now circulating through the crowd trying to pinpoint the storm center and getting a garbled har-vest of information from a hundred expert liars. The Hindus were blaming the Moslems and the latter were calling on the Prophet to witness that they had been foully attacked by the Idolators for nothing. Things looked touchy again for a min-ute or so but the troops had got a cordon round the crowd now, and from here and there came the snick of a rifle bolt and the gleam of the searchlight on bayonet points. They sub-sided again slowly—simmering.

But the young Rajput subaltern in command obviously knew that there would be no real peace until the cause—or something that looked convincingly like it—was located and isolated. He stood in a cleared space near to where we were squatting, yelling for the truth about the trouble-makers and promising hell-and-all if it wasn't forthcoming—and then I saw the serai-keeper pushing through the crowd. He was minus his staff and turban and half his shirt, but he still had his armlet and a vestige of authority. He salaamed the sub-altern and started to howl about three P.Ms and a veiled woman in a car who molested peaceable travellers, and since that had sufficient ingredients of romance in it, the Hindu part of the crowd took it up with a will. The Moslems shouted "Liar!" and impugned his ancestors. Someone then screamed that it was no ordinary woman but one who brought fire from the skies like the Whore of Jaganath—and another that she was beautiful but damned—and another that she was as ugly as a hyena's mother-in-law. The fire theory found most favor and a half score jumped up and showed their shirttails in support, demanding compensation or blood. The officer shouted them down into semi-silence and an old hag got a word in.

"It was no woman!" she screamed. "It was a man in a burkha—I myself saw him unveil as he tried to burn innocent bystanders alive." The Moslems howled "Liar!" again, but they were outnumbered by the Hindus and I didn't like the high shrill note that was creeping back into the shouting.

"Fools!" shrieked the old woman. "Do you think I don't know my own sex? It was no woman I tell you!"

"Jahsoos ki Pakistan!" "Pakistani spies!" yelled a voice at the back of the crowd, and I shivered. I'd heard that cry before and I had seen the gutters of Calcutta running red as a result of it. It had a horrible six-beat rhythm that could grip a crowd as no other slogan I have ever heard. It started to grow in volume and the officer was yelling into his handmike but the loudspeaker was drowned in the howled chant. Troops or no troops, there would be no holding them now. There was a scurry of movement over by the serai gate and the searchlight quested and darted and then held it. A burkha clad woman had evidently got marooned in a Hindu section of the crowd and even as the light came to a halt, hands were tearing the voluminous garment off her to reveal a fat woman whose mouth showed round and black in an unheard scream. She went down under the mob and the young officer, who had his guts with him, waded through flailing his clubbed pistol to clear a way—but it was all over before he reached them. The Moslems really went berserk then and the crowd round us rose as one man and surged forward bearing us with them. I clawed at Smedley and pulled him down to the ground.

"Get this bloody burkha off!" I yelled in his ear and ripped at it with both hands. We managed to tear it off between us and then I grabbed his wrist and pulled him sideways across the tide of the forward sweep and out past the fringes of the crowd. We darted through the cordon between two troops and one of them swung at us with his butt, and then we were out of the crowd and on the edge of the open ground that surrounded the serai. We kept on running until we came up

59

against a low stone wall that bounded a field on the verge of the village and we went over it like stags and sank down into the dust the other side.

"What the hell *happened?*" Smedley gasped.

"Hindu-Moslem riot—sparked off by those stupid damn Pathans of ours," I snarled. "God knows where it will end now. You can bet your bottom dollar, though, that it will mean extra troops and police rushed from all parts—on both sides. This bit of the frontier will be crawling for days. God damn and blast them! I'm going to leave them to get out of the mess any damned way they please."

"It's put paid to the car," Smedley gloomed. "What do we do now?"

"How the hell do I know?" I snapped. "Give me time to think—or try to."

"I don't want to crowd you," he said mildly, "but if you *could* put me in the picture over that strip-tease act I'd be grateful."

I peered at him through the gloom and could not help grinning. He had an undershirt on but he had lost his shorts in the melee. I stopped grinning quickly.

"The money you were carrying—?" I began.

"That's all right," he reassured me, and raised his undershirt. He had a pouched body-belt next to his skin and I could make out the butt of his pistol against the white of his belly. I breathed again. "It's just pants I'm short of," he added rather pathetically.

"You'd have been short of more than pants if you'd got into the middle of a bunch of Hindus," I told him. "Somebody told the officer that the barney had been started by a woman singeing somebody's arse with a torch—"

"That was me all right," he agreed, "but I only did it to get *you* out of the ruckus."

"Much obliged," I said. "But did you have to lift your veil to do it? Somebody recognized you as a man—and since the burkha trick is one used by spies on both sides, that blew things skyhigh."

"Sorry," he mumbled. "I couldn't see through the damned thing when it was down." He thought for a while and then said anxiously, "I wonder if they just recognized that I *was* a man, or whether they'd know my face again?"

"Very probably," I said sourly. "One of them was comparing it to that of a hyena's mother-in-law."

"Bloody smart of him," he said after reflection. "As a matter of fact Mrs. Smedley's old woman *does* look like one. Must be a connection somewhere."

There were shots now—first a volley that was obviously aimed over the heads of the crowd because we heard the rounds singing above us like angry wasps, then three or four singles. Those would be the ones actually aimed into the crowd. The howling took on another note immediately. There was fear in it, and then came the pounding of feet as the mob broke and scattered. I yelled to Smedley to lie close to the wall and threw myself flat at the same time. Part of the mob surged over the wall and knocked loose stones down on us and then I was privileged to see one of the quickest bits of thinking on record. Smedley straightened and reached up as a straggler took the fence in a bound. He brought the man down like a sack of potatoes and he had the baggy pantaloons off him in the wink of an eye. The fellow lay still for a moment and then jumped to his feet with a yell of stark terror and bounded off into the dark without a backward look. Smedley hauled them on with a grunt of satisfaction.

But it takes more than a small arms volley to separate the East from its belongings, and I knew that the scattering mob would pull up when it ran out of breath and the bolder would start to drift back. I told Smedley this and we crawled away in the shelter of the wall and eventually found ourselves under another one which was higher than that surrounding the field. It seemed to enclose a compound, and from the other side I could hear the tantalizing trickle and murmur of running water. I had been thirsty when we stopped because we had been running through dry country all that day and we ourselves, and the radiator of the Buick had exhausted our water half-way through the afternoon. Add to that the sizable chunk of serai dust I had swallowed and you have a thirsty man. Smedley must have felt the same way because he also was cocking his ear at the sound.

"Give me a boost up," I told him.

He made a stirrup of his hands and I sprung for the top of the wall and got my fingers over the edge and scrambled up. It was high and broad. I lay flat on my belly and peered down the other side. The wall seemed to enclose a large garden and I could dimly make out a well in the middle of some shrubbery. The other side of the shrubbery a belt of thick trees blocked further view. I made certain that the garden was deserted and then I reached down a hand and helped Smedley struggle up alongside me. We dropped down the other side and crossed to the well. It was one of the sort that is topped by a cistern that is filled by a chain of buckets which run over a wheel. The cistern had been left filled to trickle down into stone gutters that irrigated the garden, and the water was cool and sweet. We drank our fill and then, since I was filthy with caked dust, sweat and the blood from innumerable cuts and scratches, I stripped off and dropped into the cistern. The water hit me with a delicious shock.

Smedley grunted his approval and climbed out of his under-shirt, belt and newly acquired pants and joined me, and we sat like a pair of water nymphs enjoying the fresh bite of it.

"I don't want to get your goat again," he said, "but have you got any ideas at all where we go from here?"

I said, "The original plan was to leave the car here with a Parsee merchant who would arrange to get it back to Jam-setjee, and then to walk on towards the border and cross to-night. You know all that."

"Sure," he said. "Well, does that stand? Apart from the car I mean?"

"More or less I suppose," I said, "but we've got to find those damned Pathans first."

"I thought you said you were going to leave them?"

"You know damn well I was only blowing off steam. I'll scrag the silly sods when I get my hands on them but I wouldn't leave them in the lurch."

"I'm glad of that," he said slowly. "All right then—how do we find them?"

"Wait until morning," I said. "We can't do anything in the dark, and anyhow those troops and police will be rounding up everybody for questioning. Start a spy scare in these parts and it takes a long time to die down."

"Where do we hole up?—Here?" he asked.

"I don't think it would be advisable. This garden is evi-dently well tended," I said. "We'd probably get a horde of coolies in here at sun-up. No—finish your toilet and let's get the hell out of it into the fields somewhere."

We climbed out reluctantly and since I didn't fancy put-ting my filthy clothes on again I soused them in the water and started to wash them native fashion by slapping them on the wet stones. Smedley followed suit with his two garments and we were crouching there like a pair of dhobies when the beam of an electric torch took us fair on our naked rumps. We wheeled and gaped in unison.

A man's voice said in Urdu, "Two twelve-gauges spread wide, my friends. Arise and turn this way but otherwise stay where you are."

I muttered to Smedley that it was a fair cop and to do what I did, and we blinked into the beam of light but could see nothing outside it and we stood like a pair of part-worn Greek athletes without the comfort of a fig leaf between us. A figure advanced into the beam of the torch, which proved that there were more than one of them, and I saw the light gleam dully on the twin barrels of a twelve-gauge. This char-acter came right up to us and then called back to the other, "They are not Moslems." I won't go into details, but there is

62

a way of telling certain religions at a glance when males are as naked and ashamed as we were then.

Somebody else said, "Shoot the idolatrous dogs then."

"The Exalted One would not approve," said the other, and my heart warmed to the Exalted One. "Put on your clothes, hubshi log," he went on, and added, "None of your jungle tricks or I'll fire."

'Hubshi log' means very low people indeed. I told Smedley out of the corner of my mouth to get dressed and the first voice barked, "Speak Urdu—or nothing."

I smiled disarmingly and told him that my brother was a poor, ignorant and benighted man who hadn't had my initial advantages, and as I spoke I tried surreptitiously to backheel my wallet and gun into the darkness, but they were too quick for me. One of them pounced at my feet and they got the lot—both guns, my wallet, cigarettes and matches and Smedley's body belt. We put on our sopping clothes and then, guided by prods from two guns, moved forlornly towards the trees at the end of the garden, through a gate in a high wall and across a paved courtyard.

There was a large bungalow at the other side of the courtyard but we could only see it dimly as we skirted round it. We stumbled on past a line of godowns and into yet another courtyard onto which a line of doors gave. They halted us here and an argument ensued between them. I could make out that there were three of them now—the man who was holding the torch and two others carrying guns. Urdu is a lingua franca that is spoken throughout India and Pakistan and it has accents and dialects that can usually place the speaker and fix his home within definite districts, but that spoken within a two hundred mile radius of Delhi is standard and uninflected, so their speech told me nothing except that they were locals. The argument went along the lines that had started at the well. One gun bearer said we were obviously goondahs (rogues and criminals) and the world would be a better place without us. The other, seemingly an older man, said that none but savages shot prisoners. I pricked up my ears at this because he actually said "prisoners" and not "khaidwalas." That could only mean one thing. He had soldiered sometime in the British Indian Army. I grabbed at this like a drowning man at a straw. I said in the third person and honorifically, "The sirda-ji is right. We of the Army do not shoot prisoners. We are not goondahs but men who have been sorely treated."

The other man grunted, "As I said—spies—jahsoos log. Let us shoot them and deliver their bodies to the Lift'nant at the barracks."

The older man said, "The Lift'nant is a Hindu—so are these. He would make difficulties."

And then a woman's voice called out from the bungalow, "What happens, Miraj Khan?"

"Goondahs, Exalted One," answered the older man. "They were armed and they carry much money."

"We are not goondahs," I shouted desperately. "We are honest men who were caught up in the trouble at the serai, and merely came into your garden to get water. Water is the gift of the Prophet, and the law of compassion is sacred."

There was silence for a moment and I could hear the thumping of my own heart.

"Lock them up, Miraj Khan," the woman called. "We will see them in the morning and decide what is to be done. They are not to be ill-treated."

My heart warmed to her too.

Miraj Khan snapped, "Forward, both of you," and we were prodded towards the buildings. I heard Smedley mutter plaintively, "if only somebody would *tell* me something—" as he was shoved through a door.

I managed to say out of the corner of my mouth, "We're not going to be knocked off—yet," as I was pushed through another door and it slammed after me.

More darkness—but this, at least, wasn't quite as Stygian as that of the last place I was locked up in. There were chinks in the door and a lantern was hung on a pole outside. I fumbled round and found a pile of corn sacks in the corner so I made myself a rough bed on the mud floor and lay down in my wet clothes and, because I was dog tired and there was nothing else to do, I went to sleep.

CHAPTER 9

I was awakened by a foot stirring me in the ribs and I sat up stiffly and gawped at the stirrer, starting at his feet and ascending. I saw a brightly polished pair of chukkah boots, immaculate white cotton jodhpurs, a knee-length, high-buttoned black coat and then a bearded face. Above the face was a neatly folded Rajput turban. If you've lived in India any length of time you read signs like this as quickly and instinctively as a printed page. Rajputs are high caste Hindus—but Hindus, other than Sikhs, don't wear beards—and Sikhs don't wear Rajput turbans. This man was therefore a Rangar—or in other words a Rajput converted to Islam. Rangars have

64

only one trade—soldiering—and they soldier exclusively in the crack regiments. I brightened a little. The face was old and the beard, speckled with grey, was trimmed and combed and the moustache above it was swept fiercely upwards in the perfection of military elegance. The eyes were bright and piercing and the whole face was distinguished and aristocratic. He was, as I have said, old, but there was a set to his shoulders and a straightness to his back that a Guardsman would have envied. He said, "Get up," and I realized that he was the older man who had been in charge of things the night before, and I was glad that I had addressed him as "sirdar-ji," which is the polite collective term for Indian officers of the old school, because that's what this man was if ever I had seen one.

I climbed to my feet and stood with toes turned out at an angle of thirty degrees, thumbs in line with the seams of my trousers and eyes fixed on a spot immediately above the center line of his turban, as without doubt *he* had drilled countless recruits to stand in the past.

I said, "Huzoor," which means Exalted One, and waited until I was spoken to. It may sound as if I'm making it all a little larger than life; I'm not. That was the way one reacted to Miraj Khan Bahadur, M.C., Indian Order of Merit, Rissaldar-major, 3rd Rangar Cavalry (retired); particularly if one was looking like an unshaven scarecrow in damp and crumpled cotton clothes and the fact that one was once an officer oneself was far back in the past.

He took me in in one long all-encompassing survey, walking round me as if he was inspecting me for guard duty and not liking what he saw. He barked suddenly at me in English, "Stannat—*ease!* Stan—deasy! Pay 'tention!" And then as I obeyed, he continued in Urdu, "And from what regiment have you deserted, worthless one?"

"None, Huzoor," I answered. "I served my time and was faithful to my salt."

"Don't bandy words with me like a bazaar lawyer," he snapped. "In what regiment have you *served?*"

It was no use trying to invent one with a man like this. I gave the one I had been in. "Second Deccan Infantry, Huzoor," I answered.

"Disbanded now," he said. "A class regiment—one company Pathans, one Sikh and two Maharatta. You are lying. You are none of these—and you wear the clothes of a Punjabi Mussalman. The truth, jackal dung, unless you wish me to defile my boot on you."

I couldn't have kept it up long. There was nothing for it. I said, "There were also British in it in my day, sirdar-ji."

"Officers only," he said.

"I commanded 'B' Company—the Pathans," I told him.

It caught him off balance for only a moment. He said, "Walk in front of me to the door."

I stepped out into the early morning light. Two other Rangars stood on either side of the threshold, dressed as this one, but younger and with not quite the same degree of sparkle. They carried twelve-gauges but they sloped them and smacked the smalls of the butts like service rifles. The old man grabbed my wrists and held up both my hands and studied the fingernails closely. He then pushed back my left sleeve and looked at my wrist. I wasn't wearing a watch but the white mark that the strap had shielded from the sun was still visible. He knew what he was about. He looked at me closely and I could see that there was doubt in his face. I glanced at the other men and said in English, "I would like to speak to you in private, sirdar-ji."

He answered, "I am not talking Angrezi well—" hesitated for an instant and added, "Sahib." Then he said, "You will wait in there please." He pointed to the room we had come from and I turned and went back. The door closed on me again and I sat down once more on the corn sacks and wondered what I had landed myself into this time.

He came back after some minutes and beckoned me out. He said, "This way please," and led me across the courtyard to the bungalow, up onto the verandah, and through a door into the hall. The hall was furnished in worn but comfortable European style and the walls were lined with mounted tiger and panther heads. He led me through it and into a small lavatory that opened off it. Soap and towels were laid out on an old-fashioned washstand and a pitcher of water stood beside a bowl. I caught sight of myself in the mirror on the wall and realized why the sirdar had not liked what he saw when he inspected me. I didn't either. Although I had bathed in the cistern the night before I had picked up another coating of dust while I slept on the corn sacks. I had lost my turban in the struggle and my hair was wild and unkempt. My left eye was sporting a beautiful shiner and I had a deep scratch from hairline to chin on which the blood had congealed, and I badly needed a shave. I said, "I had a razor in my pocket—". He nodded and went out and shortly returned with it, together with an old military shaving brush, a comb and a jug of hot water. Through the open door I could see that the other two had taken up positions in the hall. He left the things on the washstand and went out and I spent a good twenty minutes repairing the ravages. I went to the door when I had finished and found him sitting outside. He rose and led me back through the hall and along the verandah to where purple flowered bouganvillea cascaded down from the roof and made a shaded alcove. There was a table set with a yellow cloth, and a white-gowned bearer was setting a coffee pot on it, with a basket of rolls, and butter and thick honey. There was also cold sliced beef and boiled eggs in, believe it or not, individual "cosies," and finally a luscious sliced papayia, the melon-like fruit so familiar on Anglo-Indian breakfast tables. I started to slaver and I was hard put to it not to dive at the table like a Sind vulture on a carcass, but the thought occurred to me of Smedley sitting on his honkers in his cell.

I said, "My friend is—?"

"He will be joining the sahib," said the sirdar, and, my social conscience eased, I sat down and squared up.

Moslems like to feast in company much as Christians do, but caste Hindus view the assimilation of food in almost the same way as they regard the elimination of it—something to be done in decent privacy. The sirdar, being the former by religion but the latter in culture, watched me for a moment or so to see that I had everything I wanted and then dismissed himself and left me to it. I was dealing with my fourth cup of coffee when Smedley arrived. He was escorted by one of the other men and he, also, had evidently been given the opportunity to clean up. He didn't look quite as rough as when I'd last seen him but the remains of the boot polish had given him a piebald look, and the pants he had purloined had been made for a much bigger man so he had to hold them up with one hand. In short, he looked damned funny. I told him so and he swore dirtily at me and then dived onto the food.

Neither of us spoke until we were replete and rather glazed. There were English cigarettes and matches on the table so we lit up and sat back.

Smedley said, "Well? What now?"

There was a venetian-slatted french window behind us. I shot him a warning glance and went over and tried it but it was locked from the inside. I came back and sat down and said, "Parlons francais."

My French is terrible but Smedley managed to cope with it.

I said, "I can't tell you what this set-up is. The old man is obviously a British-Indian Army pensioner—but he is a Rangar."

"What is that?"

"Moslem by religion but Indian by nationality. A bit complicated."

"What is he going to do with us?"

"I haven't the faintest idea—but I have told him I am British and that I have been an officer. That has at least got us decent treatment—for the moment. I hope it will continue. The old man is a gentleman. I know the type."

"What do *I* tell him when he questions me?"

"We'll have to deal with that as it comes," I told him. "I'll probably be doing the translating anyhow—he doesn't speak much English—or says he doesn't. Don't take chances on it though—he may be bluffing."

The sirdar came back then and asked me politely if we had had sufficient, and on my assuring him, equally politely, that we had, he asked us to follow him.

He led us back through the hall and tapped at a door the far end of it. A voice told us in Urdu to enter. The sirdar went in and clicked his heels and said, "Huzoor-ji, Do Angrezi sahib-log," which means "Two English gentlemen," and told me that he knew what Smedley's nationality was even if he may have been rocky on our social status. He stood aside to let us pass and then he followed us in and closed the door.

The room was furnished like the hall, worn but comfortable, and it smelt of polished leather and good tobacco. There were kus-kus screens over the windows to keep out the glare of the morning sun and it was a moment or so before I accustomed my eyes to the dimness. When I did I saw a man sitting at a flat-topped desk at the far end. He said pleasantly, "Come in, gentlemen," and he said it in English.

He rose as we approached the desk and he indicated two chairs in front of it. He did not, however, offer to shake hands. He was tall and lean and spare and he had fair hair that would soon be all white, as his moustache was already. His seamed face was tanned a deep mahogany and he had a pair of the steadiest blue eyes I have ever seen. He was, I should have guessed, somewhere in the early sixties. We sat down and he dropped into his own chair. He was as English as the clubs in St. James's.

He said, "I hope they gave you a decent breakfast," and we assured him that we never hoped to have a better. He then apologized for our overnight accommodation and told us that a little confusion existed on our arrival. He might have been a perfectly trained maitre d'hotel explaining a mix-up in bookings to two valued guests. We begged him to think no more about it. He then asked us if we'd come far and whether we'd had a comfortable journey. I thought that this was as good a point as any to come down to brass tacks so I sidestepped the last question and whipped one back at him.

"Are you the District Commissioner, sir?" I asked.

"Good gracious no," he answered. "There are no more Europeans in those jobs. Oh—I'm sorry—I should have introduced myself. My name is Culverton. I farm a bit round here."

Things dropped straight into place then. I said, "How do you do, Brigadier. Mine is Rees—and this is Smedley."

He turned to Smedley and said, "Smedley? Dorsetshire?"

Smedley said, "No—Birmingham," and the Brigadier looked politely surprised. "Oh—and where is Birmingham, Mr. Smedley? Queensland or New South Wales?" Smedley, whose Australian accent was all but undetectable, looked startled and hipped. I was trying to help him now—by pointing to my own eyes and then to the Brigadier's. He didn't catch on for the moment, then he laughed nervously.

"You win, Brigadier," he said. "But I left there so long ago that I'm apt to forget. I live just outside London but *Mrs.* Smedley comes from Birmingham and I've more or less adopted it as my home town."

"Forgive me," said the Brigadier. "A parlor trick of mine to get you to speak. I have to place people by voices. I don't think I've ever met either of you, have I?"

"I certainly have not had that pleasure, sir," I said, "but naturally I have heard all about you."

"That clears the air then," he answered, and rose. He came round the desk towards us, "Would you mind? This is a liberty, but a necessary one in my case." His outstretched hand felt the air in front of me and then found my face. His fingers ran lightly across my features and over the top of my head and round my ears. "Um—somebody's been giving you a dusting, have they?" he said.

Behind me Miraj Khan said, "Hair black, eyes brown, Huzoor-ji."

The Brigadier moved across to Smedley and felt towards him. Smedley took his outstretched hand and guided it to his face. The Brigadier said sharply, "Don't do that, please. I prefer to do things for myself." He ran over Smedley's face in the same manner.

Miraj Khan said, "Hair brown, eyes grey. Brown patches over face—dirt, not disease, because soap has taken some away."

"That is discourteous, Rissaldar-major sahib," said the Brigadier angrily.

"That Sahib does not speak Urdu—or he is a liar," said Miraj Khan and the Brigadier told him to dismiss—in English and with a bite in it. Miraj Khan saluted and fell out, quite unabashed. They seemed to understand each other perfectly these two. The Brigadier smiled. "I'm sorry about that, Mr. Smedley. *Do* you speak Urdu, by the way?"

"Not a word," said Smedley. "What was all that about?"

"Oh, just a bit of nonsense of Old Miraj Khan's. We were sowar—that's trooper—and subaltern together when we joined the Regiment and he's been with me ever since—and he takes the most infernal damned liberties at times. Getting old, y'know." He was back in his chair now, and with the departure of Miraj Khan I sensed the subtlest change in atmosphere.

"Well now, gentlemen," said the Brigadier, "suppose we come to the point? Might I ask what you're doing in these parts—besides masquerading and stirring up communal strife? I have no official standing any longer but I happen to live here—and what is more important, so do my people—both sides of this damned artificial line—Hindu and Mohammedan."

I said, "I'm sorry if it looked like that. The strife wasn't of *our* stirring."

"Let's not quibble, shall we?" he snapped. "I went down to the bazaar last night when things blew up—and I was down there until daylight. I've talked to the police and that boy who commands the detachment, and I've *listened* round the serai and the chaikhanas. I hear more than most people. It seems to boil down to a party of four in a car that is now burnt out—bogus P.Ms and a man in a burkha—"

"There are only two of us here—" I began.

"And both bogus," he said.

Smedley broke in and I signalled angrily to him to shut up but he ignored me. "All right, Brigadier," he said. "So we're bogus. What are you going to do about it?"

"My duty as a citizen," the Brigadier told him coldly. "If you can't give me a damned good reason why I shouldn't, I'm going to hand you over to the police post for investigation."

"I'll give you a good reason," answered Smedley tautly. "We happen to be white and British."

There was a depth of contempt in the other's voice when he answered. "White and British? Then I suggest you comport yourselves as such—or as they used to. Five people were killed in that riot last night and a round dozen seriously injured—none of them white and British, of course, so it might not strike you as of much importance. It does me, though." His voice rose. "Listen, both of you. It may bore you but I've got something for your white and British ears—something you can take back to whatever jail they send you to. My great-grandfather raised a cavalry regiment in these parts—Hindus and Moslems who fought and lived and died together in peace and mutual respect. He settled here when he became too old to command any longer—and he farmed, and he taught his pensioners to farm. Then my grandfather took over and commanded the brigade that rose from the regiment—then my father—and then me." His voice dropped again and he was gazing sightlessly past us. "I lived to see

70

what those three had built over the years swept away in a deluge of fire and blood. I've seen men, women and children butchered, and the farms of my pensioners burned and their cattle slaughtered—and men who had learned to live together were at each other's throats. But the Frontier is there—the line has been drawn, and the pompous, incompetent swine who drew it have gone back to their white and British homes and collected their honors and fatter jobs, and left this festering sore that will never heal. I and one or two others like me have stayed on—and we've tried to build something out of the wreckage, and at times it looks as if we might be succeeding—then something like this happens, and we're back where we started." There was silence for a time and he sat with bowed head. When he spoke again his voice was tired. "I don't know who you are—or what. You may be some piddling politician's lackeys—you may, on the other hand, be brave men doing a job I know nothing of—in which case I'm sorry for what I've got to do. All I know is that you've brought hatred back here after two years of comparative peace." He stood up and touched a bell on the desk. "I'm going to hand you over to the non-white, non-British police, gentlemen, and when you eventually get back to whoever sent you you can tell them that it was a white and British renegade who did it."

Miraj Khan came to the door. We stood up.

I said, "All right, Brigadier. It will be uncomfortable for us for a time—but we've got a High Commissioner in Delhi to watch our interests, and we're not without friends or funds."

"I'm glad to hear it," he said without irony.

"But that only goes for the two of us here." I went on, "The other two are *not* white and British. They are Pathans, and one of them, at least, stands in much the same relationship to me as this sirdar does to you. He was my orderly in the regiment and he has been my servant since. It was they who started things last night—but they *are* Pathans—and you can as much hold them responsible as you could a monkey with a box of matches in a powder keg. They were dressed as P.Ms and the serai-keeper hit one of them with a lathi. We did what we could but it got out of hand."

"Go on," he said.

"Well—I leave it to you. It will be awkward for *us*—but that is all. It will go hard with them."

"So?"

"Hand us over if you think you're doing the right thing—but at least give me an hour to find them and send them on their way over the border. I'll give you my word of honor that I'll come back."

"If I know Pathans they'll be over already," he said.

"Not these," I retorted. "They've got old-fashioned ideas on loyalty—you and your pensioners haven't got the monopoly, you know. They will wait for me—they'll try and find me, and if they see me being taken into the police post they'll try and pull the place apart—with all that that will entail."

He was silent again for a time and I could see Smedley almost praying.

"Will you also give me your word of honor that you have no other reason for seeing them than to send them on their way?" he asked at last.

"I will," I answered. "That and to give them some money, if you will return some of that which your men took from us last night."

He opened a drawer in front of him and took out two large rolls of notes and threw them on to the desk. "Take it all," he said. "You will find that correct. Your pistols, I regret, I'll have to hand over to the police."

I rose and took one of the rolls and tossed the other to Smedley.

"Thank you, sir," I said. "Am I at liberty to go?"

He nodded. "But I am told you are wearing the rather tattered remains of a P.M's clothes," he said. "P.Ms are under suspicion. You might be picked up for questioning."

"I'll have to risk that," I said. "Perhaps if one of your people will lend me a turban—?"

He told Miraj Khan to go and get one and then turned back to me. "What about your friend? Isn't he, also, dressed in rather peculiar clothes."

"Smedley had better remain here until I return," I answered. "He wouldn't be any use to me." Smedley shot upright and gazed at me in stupefaction.

"Perhaps you're right," said the Brigadier. We waited until Miraj Khan came back with a turban and I pretended not to see Smedley's frantic signals. Miraj Khan helped me to wind it on.

"I'll be back as soon as I've found them, sir," I said.

He inclined his head and told the sirdar to see me to the outer gate. When we went out Smedley was sitting looking like a forsaken orphan.

The old man saw me to the heavy gate in the high surrounding wall and opened it a foot or so, and he saluted and said, "Acchi bhat, Major Sahib," as I went through. I wondered how he knew my late rank and then I remembered telling him I had been a company commander. I was strangely touched by the gesture.

Things were quiet in the bazaar but there was definitely an

atmosphere. Hindus and Moslems were gathered in small separate groups and there was an absence of chatter, and policemen and troops moved about in fours with bayonetted rifles slung over their shoulders. A silent group squatted in the dust outside the hospital and there was activity round the police post and much coming and going of jeeps. Two small boys were trying to hang a black flag over a shuttered Mohammedan shop, and a patrol of sepoys shouted to them angrily. The boys dropped it in the dust and scampered.

I wandered through the open square in the center of the bazaar. All shops and chaikhanas were closed but one or two itinerant tea vendors were moving through the crowd with brass, charcoal-heated urns, and where they stopped and dispensed their brew in small china mugs ad hoc clubs sprung up and men squatted and talked in low tones. There was a complete absence of women and that is always an ominous sign in an Indian bazaar.

I drew blank in the square so I turned down a side street where Mohammedan shop signs outnumbered Hindu, and I traversed its dusty length and came back up the next one and kept on until I had covered the whole area of the bazaar, but without result. I then went up towards the serai, but this area was cordoned off by troops. I could see the Buick and the bus in a charred, welded huddle. The fire must have broken out again because there was nothing left but a twisted heap of metal and near it the blackened remains of what had been a group of bullock carts—and no doubt the sole livelihood of half a score of families. Bundles of belongings lay strewn in the dust and men squatted outside the ring of the cordon and gazed silently and glumly across the littered space.

There is nothing more desolate and saddening than the scene of a riot the day after. It is worse than a battlefield—that is horrible but it is impersonal. A sacked bazaar shows its separate small tragedies.

A funeral was wending its way from the village towards the Mohammedan burial ground. The women always show their grief on ordinary occasions, and they bare their breasts and wail, but this was obviously one of the riot casualties, because there were no women, and the few men who followed the rough black-draped coffin were silent, and the short procession was tailed by an army truck with steel-helmeted watchful troops and a mounted Bren.

I saw Safaraz as the cortege passed. I thought at first that he was killing idle time, because funerals can be anybody's business or pleasure in India, but then I saw his face. He was trudging along in the dust with his eyes fixed on the coffin and his grief was not assumed. He was taking a risk because I could see armed police following on foot at a short distance. I fell in behind him.

There is no ceremony at the graveside of a Mohammedan; that is done in the mosque. The coffin was lowered into the shallow grave and dirt was shovelled over it and then we rolled stones on top of the mound to keep off the jackals that would come after sunset. I got beside Safaraz as he lifted a small boulder and I whispered, "It is Sher Ali?"

He nodded and gulped, and growled, "Some idolators will die for this. He was shot in the back."

I said, "What will it profit Sher Ali if you follow him—at the end of a rope? Come with me, Safaraz."

He shook his head. "I stay here, Sahib," he muttered.

"Then who will tell them in his village?" I asked. "Who will come this way again? Is he to lie in an unmarked grave?" That is important with these people. I saw him hesitate—but I also saw the police closing in and scanning faces. I took his arm and I remember thinking "This is it," because the police were Hindus and if one of them had touched him in that mood his knife would have been out like lightning and there would have been shooting again and more bloody murder.

And then a miracle happened. It was a very ordinary little miracle but it served. A man broke the cordon at the nearby serai and troops shouted and chased him. He was probably going to recover some of his belongings, but they were there as a precaution against looters and they were taking no chances. Other men followed him and one of the troops fired over their heads, and after a second of stunned silence, turmoil had broken out in the bazaar again. The police behind us turned and doubled back over the open maidan, unslinging their rifles as they trotted. I grabbed Safaraz and pulled him away between the rough gravestones and got him over the wall to the other side.

I harangued and pleaded for half an hour before I got him to see sense. I told him Smedley and I had to go back to Bombay for a time but that I would send for him when things had blown over. I gave him five hundred rupees and then, without feeling dramatic, I made him draw his knife and swear on it that he would cross the border after dark and make his way back to his village. He was a born liar and he would steal from anybody in the world except me or, if I'd had any, a member of my family—but I knew he would keep that oath. He snuffled a bit and I threatened to hit him —then he insisted on my taking his knife and swore he'd have another to replace it before nightfall. I tried to argue about that but he stuck it in the ground in front of me and turned

74

and went off into the maize fields where he would lie up until dark.

I stood and watched him until he disappeared, then I picked up the knife and went slowly back to the bungalow.

CHAPTER 10

The Brigadier was on the verandah when I returned. He looked enquiringly at me as I approached him. I say "looked" because I can never think of him as a blind man. The mortar bomb that had robbed him of his sight in the early days of the war had, apparently, caused a trauma of the optic nerve without injuring the eyes themselves, and they remained the mirror of his expression and emotions. That, allied with his uncanny hearing and sensitivity of touch compensated largely for his disability.

"Did you find them?" he asked.

"One of them," I replied. "My servant. His bhai-bund was one of the casualties. They've just buried him." As far as I knew, my voice was not expressing anything, but he must have sensed how I felt.

"I'm sorry," he said shortly. "Upsetting. What about your servant?"

"He'll lie up in the fields until dark and then cross. I have no worries about him after that."

"Just accepted it, did he?"

"Not quite. I had to argue—and lie a bit. Lying to a Pathan is not easy; they're such experts at it themselves."

"What did you tell him?"

"That we'd been called back to Bombay but that he'd better go on to his village and arrange for some of Sher Ali's family to come eventually to mark his grave."

"You might write to him and tell him not to make it too soon," he said drily. "In the meantime I'll arrange for the mullah at the mosque to do something about it."

"Thank you," I said. "I'd like to ask a further favor of you."

"Go ahead."

"He insisted on giving me his knife. The police will take it from me. Can I leave it with you?"

"Certainly."

I put it on the table between us. His fingers felt for it and he hefted it in his palm and then ran his thumb along the edge.

"Wicked things, aren't they?" he said. "If one could only breed the love of the knife out of them and divorce it from their explosive family honor one might eventually make something of that tribe."

"You'd have a job," I said shortly. I was getting a little tired of this small talk. He seemed to sense that too, because he shrugged and asked me if we'd both join him for a drink before lunch.

"If it's all the same to you I'd rather get this thing over without further delay," I said.

He held the knife out towards me. "You win. Give him this damned thing back yourself."

"I don't understand."

"Listen, Rees," he said. "When things blew up here in forty-seven, the Indian government offered quite generous compensation for my estate and asked me to get out. I begged to stay, and after a year of argument between myself and Delhi they agreed reluctantly—but the fact remains that I'm here on sufferance. I gave my word that I'd engage in no political activity whatsoever. Passing a couple of agents—British or otherwise—through to Pakistan is sailing too close to the wind."

I'd had enough. "Who the hell asked you to?" I flared. "What are you going to do? Send for the police or would you rather we went down to the post on our own?"

He chuckled, "You might reach there in the latter case but I think Smedley might try to cut his lucky. He made indignant signs to you when you suggested leaving him here. Flapping hands make sounds—if your ears are delicately attuned."

"I'll answer for Smedley," I said angrily. "He may not be your brand of pukkha sahib—I'm not myself, thank God—but—"

"I'm sorry," he broke in quickly. "Put it down to conceit. I'm childishly proud of my hearing. Look, Rees—will you give me your word that whatever you are doing, it is nothing subversive against either the Indian or Pakistan governments?"

"Willingly," I said.

"Good." He was genuinely relieved. "All right then, you've kept faith once—I'll risk it. I'll have you both put across the line tonight and I'll give you the address of an old friend of mine who will see you safely out of their zone *interdite* —bit of French for you; yours isn't as good as your Urdu."

"So you were behind the venetian-slatting, were you?" I said ruefully.

"Naturally," he answered. "That was how I placed your nationality. None but an Englishman could have spoken

76

French so vilely. Smedley worried me for a while; his was good enough for a Russian."

"Look here, sir," I began. "I don't know how to begin thanking you—"

"I'd rather you didn't try," he said. "Right—you might go and collect Smedley, will you?—he's in the guestroom at the end of the verandah. I'll be in my study." He turned and went through to the hall.

Smedley was lying on his back glooming at the ceiling. He grunted but did not look at me. Someone had given him a pair of khaki shorts and a shirt and he looked a little more respectable. He said, "When does the black maria arrive?"

"It doesn't," I told him. "He's putting us across the border tonight."

He shot bolt upright. "Thank God for that!" he yelled. "So the old bastard's remembered he's white, has he?"

"I don't think he ever forgot," I said coldly. "And keep your voice down, will you. He's got ears like a bird-dog."

"All right," he grinned, "don't give me the Hebe McShabbers about it. My spine was crawling listening to you two old-school-tie-ing it. *My* neck has got a vested interest in this too, you know. How did you talk him round?"

"I didn't have to. You'd better get up. He wants us to join him for drinks before lunch," I said.

He swung his feet to the floor. "By Christ—he *is* a white man. Drinks?"

"Soft peddle on them," I told him. "We've got some more walking to do tonight."

"We would have," he groaned. "Well—what about those two jays of ours? Find 'em all right?"

"I found Safaraz," I said. "Sher Ali was killed."

Smedley looked genuinely stricken. He was silent for a while, then he said simply, "I'm sorry," and left it at that.

The Brigadier was mixing drinks deftly at a side table in the study. He had gin and ice, fresh green limes and a syphon, but never once did he fumble as he made four long slings. He heard us come in and he gestured towards roorkhee chairs and asked us to sit down. We did, and then stumbled to our feet again as a woman entered the room. She was not young but she was still beautiful—perhaps some ten years younger than the Brigadier.

He said, "Ah, my dear, let me introduce Mr. Rees—" he inclined his head towards me unerringly, "—and Mr. Smedley. My wife, gentlemen."

She greeted us as naturally as if she were in her drawing-room in England and we were in normal attire.

"I saw you come in last night," she said. "I'm terribly sorry —of course I had no idea who you were, and that old rascal

77

Miraj Khan rather assumes command if my husband happens to be out."

"Quite right," grunted the Brigadier as he handed us our drinks. "Women should keep their place when there's trouble afoot."

She ignored him and went on, "I hope you weren't *too* uncomfortable."

We assured her gravely that we hadn't been and then after more small talk we had lunch—impeccably served on Kashmir lace and from fine china and glass that made bully beef and apricots straight from the tin seem a long way off. We rested during the afternoon and then, in the cool of the early evening, when all India ceases to pant and starts to breathe, he took us on a tour of the nearer reaches of the farm. It was an enormous place. He grew cotton, tobacco and the seasonal grains in irrigated plots, and round the boundaries of the vast estate were the smaller farms of his pensioners. He trained instructors on his own land and they, in turn, passed on this instruction to the tenants and their sons—and he took their produce in with his own and sold it for them at fair prices. He had rescued most of them from the stranglehold of the moneylenders and he had built model villages and a hospital, and there was a school where Hindu and Moslem children learned and played together. It was the sort of place that the professional do-gooders of U.N.O., U.N.E.S.C.O., A.I.C.E. and all the other alphabetical organizations strive to run in underfed Asia but never quite succeed—because they never could know the real love and understanding of the land and the people that this man had.

He knew every stone on the place and he could traverse its length and breadth without a guide or even a stick. When he had intended to hand us over to the police I had thought him a self-righteous, priggish old crank. Listening to him as he showed us the estate and talked quietly of his plans for the future, understanding came to me. He would have died to keep strife away from this Eden.

A young Rangar joined us as we were looking at his splendid herd of Hereford-Punjab cattle. Except for his turban and his almost too perfect features he might have been a suntanned Cambridge graduate. He spoke English without an accent and he gave the Brigadier some highly technical data about a crop experiment they were carrying out, then assuming that we too would be interested, he translated for us into Urdu.

"That's all right, Kazim," said the Brigadier. "Both these gentlemen are English—Mr. Smith and Mr. Brown. That's not their names and I'd take it kindly if you didn't mention

78

off the estate that you've met them." The boy shook hands with us and he was far too well-bred to look surprised.

"Miraj Khan's son," the Brigadier explained as the Rangar went off. "I sent him Home to get an agricultural science degree. He and his brothers will be taking this place over after me."

"You've no sons of your own, sir?" I asked.

"Two," he answered shortly. "Both killed with the Regiment. No—only a daughter left. Wanted her to be a vet but she prefers human cattle. She's running a hospital up in Kashmir."

"Doctor?" I asked.

"God no," he answered. "She's like me—expensive education—practically illiterate. No, some kind of a nurse. She and some damn silly American woman run it between 'em. Refugees—displaced persons and abandoned kids and all that sort of thing." He spoke roughly and disparagingly but I sensed pride there too.

There were baths and drinks when we got back and then an exquisitely served dinner. The wine might have come from anywhere within a twenty-five mile radius of Dijon, but the Brigadier told me his wife made it.

"Bootleg," he said. "She dances on the grapes herself, like a Dervish. Got to do it at night now we've got prohibition. Can't ask the servants to do it because most of 'em are Mohammedan." I looked at the lady with renewed respect.

After dinner and over coffee, cigars and brandy—kind friends in the Embassy at Delhi sent him over a few bottles of spirits from time to time—he told us of his plans for us.

"Things are still pretty dicy," he said. "I can tell that because there's been nothing on the radio—that means censorship has been clamped down. Best to wait until about midnight. Miraj Khan and a couple of his pals are out on a recce. I hope he doesn't make a nonsense of it. He's in his glory—but he's past it now. Getting old y'know." Indians age sooner than Europeans but I'd still have put him as younger than the Brigadier.

"About clothes," he went on. "I understand that *you'll* pass muster but that Smedley looks like a Goanese feelthy picture seller. What do you think he's most like to pass as? A burkha is no good because you've got some jungle crawling ahead of you."

"Zamindar?" I suggested.

"What the hell's that?" inquired Smedley hollowly.

"Very small farmer—usually dirty," the Brigadier told him. "Yes—that would be all right. Stick some ash and cow-dung on his face as a sign of mourning. Nobody'll expect him to speak then." I don't think he liked Smedley.

Miraj Khan came in at about eleven o'clock. He saluted and delivered his report. He gave it under the Field Manual headings and at length—eight minutes by the clock, to be precise. We gathered that the frontier itself was heavily patrolled but that young soldiers nowadays didn't know their jobs, and anyhow they were all infantry so what could you expect?—and that if the Sahib-log were ready, he, Miraj Khan, would take them straight through without trouble.

The Brigadier sent him off for clothes for the long-suffering Smedley, and when we had got him into them he returned to us our pistols and other possessions. We filed out into the darkness of the garden which Miraj Khan, who spoke Army English when he was being technical, called the "ish-tart line." Urdu speakers cannot sound an initial "S" without an "ish" before it. I started to thank our host but he brushed it aside, and as he gripped my hand in the darkness he said, "I don't know what's behind all this, Rees. I don't want to—but I do know that your job is the loneliest and most thankless in the world. Godspeed, my boy."

We went over the wall into the fields and a jackal howled in the distance, and I felt kin to it. The old man had ascribed to me, the secondhand hireling of a nameless commercial syndicate, motives of patriotism that I did not possess.

Miraj Khan might have been "getting old, y'know," but he wasn't showing signs of it now. He led us through the fields at a steady mile-eating clip that soon had Smedley gasping, and we had to pull up for him several times, and then, when he was really showing signs of wear and tear, we came out of the heavy cultivated land onto a comparatively open plain that was carpeted with thin choking dust and studded with clumps of camel-thorn. We had to slow down here because there was activity and we could hear the noise of jeeps ahead of us, and twice a searchlight fingered out of the darkness and swept the plain, catching us once full in its blinding beam. Miraj Khan and I had been trained in this and we froze in our tracks, but Smedley reacted instinctively and dropped flat on his face and a tell-tale cloud of dust rose lazily and hung in the air as he hit the ground. Miraj Khan catalogued three generations of his forebears, zoologically, in a muted growl. The light travelled on, stopped, and then quested back slowly. We prayed and sweated as it swept over us. It lingered for a moment uncertainly and then snapped out and we heard with heart-stopping relief, the jeep moving away from us. Miraj Khan was technical and instructive in English.

"For bullets drop. For lights and flares stand still and look like tree being pissed on by jackal—bloody fool man," he told the woe-begone Smedley. "When light has passed still stand—for if mans look like trees first time, then come back

80

and see no trees second time, he is knowing mans is not trees and is giving bloody hell with machine gun." They couldn't have put it clearer at the Jungle Warfare School at Ranchi.

We went on into a low forest of kika-thorn which tore at our clothes and scarified our hides, and when we had come to the other edge of it Miraj Khan pulled us down into the dust. There was a weak new moon that was helped by the blazoned glory of the stars. He pointed to a lightish patch in the distance. "That is a whitewashed house, sahib," he whispered "and it is in Pakistan, but where between us and it the line runs, not even the babus who drew the accursed thing could tell. It is four hundred yards away and all trees and bushes have been cleared, and there are trip-wires and weapon-pits that sometimes are manned. It is a soldier's passage and calls for care. Watch the civilian for he is a man of low intelligence."

I translated this to Smedley with tactful and bowdlerization, and then Miraj Khan was off on his belly ahead of us. I sent Smedley next and then I brought up the rear. We jinked and turned and scrabbled through the dust for what seemed hours, and there were times when I thought the old man had lost his way, but eventually we arrived in a clump of trees the other side of the house and we lay and panted and tried to get the dust out of our nostrils and mouths. Miraj Khan hauled a large flat flask from out of the pocket of his long jacket and passed it to each of us in turn. It was a mixture of, I should say, one part water and two parts scotch. I never needed a drink more. I had to wrest it away from Smedley. The sirdar took it back solemnly and then explained to me carefully that the Prophet, in his wisdom, had forbade wine to the Faithful, but scotch wasn't wine any more than issue rum was, and the latter had saved him from much fever over the years. When he lowered the flask it was as dry as the dust around us.

There was a further five miles of Pakistani country to be traversed, patrolled as was the Indian side, before there was further rest for us, and it was getting light when we came to a small farm. Miraj Khan went ahead of us and parleyed with someone unseen, and then came back and led us into a darkened doorway and up some stairs into a low room where there were two string charpoys. He shook hands with both of us in turn and in his execrable English gave Smedley a few more well-chosen tips on staying alive when negotiating enemy territory, and then he went. I was sorry to see him go.

Smedley felt towards his belt, "Don't we give him anything?" he asked.

"If you prefer to wear the bottom of your spine where it is and not three inches up your back, you won't," I told him, but I don't think he heard because he was already flat out on one of the charpoys—and I wasn't long in following suit.

We were awakened some hours later by another Rangar—younger than Miraj Khan and not as chockful of personality. He brought us milk in a chatthi, with a freshly baked native loaf and fruit, and when we had finished it he took us down to a stone cistern in the courtyard where we beat some of the dust out of our clothes and then bathed. He asked us where we wanted to go and I told him Lahore. He nodded but warned me that things were jittery on the roads and that police and troops were very active, stopping travellers and questioning them, and scrutinizing papers carefully. I thanked him for the tip but told him not to worry as it would be our responsibility from here on.

"*My* responsibility, sahib," he said simply. "It has been placed upon my head by the Brigadier Sahib." And I knew enough not to argue with that.

We left eventually in a bullock cart loaded with coarse maize stalks, riding buried in the dusty load, horribly hot and sticky. We were stopped by patrols on three occasions but the old zamindar who drove the bullocks, squatting on the broad shaft between them and guiding them with a tail in each hand, was known to the police sepoys and they let him pass after the most cursory of checks. We plodded on for about four hours, which, since bullocks move at about three miles an hour, meant some twelve miles, and that took us outside the border zone. We crawled out at last near a mud village and the driver told us that a motor bus ran from there to Kasur, from where we could get a train to Lahore. I gave him a few rupees and some cigarettes and he called upon Allah to increase our livestock—and as we walked on into the village scratching ourselves we realised that his prayer had been granted, because those maize stalks had been alive with something that crawled and bit like the devil.

We found that the bus didn't leave until morning so we went to the chaikhana on the outskirts of the village and I bought goat pilau and sweet tea. We squatted in the dust outside the circle of light made by the gas lamp and I instructed Smedley out of the side of my mouth how to eat with his right hand and to belch loudly at intervals as politeness demanded. He was learning fast, and with his sun-tanned face, black stubble of whiskers and semi-permanent coating of dust he was beginning to merge into his background in a way I wouldn't have thought possible a few days previously. We were getting into the North now, where grey eyes are not uncommon. He also had a quick ear for languages and an even quicker eye for mannerisms and he was picking up a useful vocabulary. He would still have been spotted in an instant as one not native to those parts had he attempted a conversation but I had told him just to grunt if anyone spoke directly to him—and if that failed, to hawk loudly, spit and scratch himself. We were both doing the last naturally.

We finished our meal and then we sauntered casually through the village and out the other side, looking for a place in the fields to sleep. It wasn't easy, because we were now well into the Punjab, and the flat plains stretched around us clear to the horizon, unbroken by wall or hedge or copse, or anything except clumps of cactus near which a wise man doesn't sleep. Further South we might have dumped down in the open, but up here the evenings were beginning to get chill and our cotton clothes were no protection against the breeze that swept down from the distant hills at sunset. There was a hint of rain in the air too, because the weak monsoon comes later as one moves north.

"No damned flop houses in these villages?" asked Smedley plaintively.

"Only the open dormitory at the serai," I told him. "Bit risky if anybody starts to talk to you."

We sat down in the dust away from the road and turned our backs to the breeze and smoked into our shielding hands.

And then it started to spit with rain. We cursed miserably and squatted on in the dust and hoped it would pass, but soon it was coming down in a light but steady downpour. I knew that a soaking in this chill night was all Smedley needed to bring on his fever again so I decided to risk the serai.

We trudged back to the village. The serai lay on the far side and was a replica of the one in Ramabagh but it was not so crowded outside. Inside there was a lean-to roof that ran round three of the walls, and under it huddled men, women, children, bullocks, goats and bundles, and the cooking fires made dense smoke that billowed out under the eaves. We paid our four annas at the gate and went through. The rain was now pelting down steadily. I looked for some corner in the mass of bodies where I could park Smedley out of the wet until I could find a bigger one where we could lie down.

At the far end of the shed a man was singing. He accompanied himself discordantly and loudly on a triangular three-stringed sitar and his voice was like that of a rabid jackal howling at the moon. The song was bawdy and the singer was extemporizing and making it even filthier, but the audience was enjoying it. There was only one man who could make "Zakhmi Dil" sound like that. Yes—you've guessed it. We had the hired help back in our hair.

He had discarded his P.M's clothes and was now as gorgeous as a bird of paradise in voluminous white pantaloons, red sash, embroidered waistcoat and a green turban to which he was not entitled, because he had not made the pilgrimage to Mecca—and was not likely to while brothels and gambling dens remained along the route. He saw me before I could duck back into the darkness and he had the gall to wink broadly at me before starting on another stanza. Yes, the audience was appreciative all right. They joined in the refrain with gusto and clapped their hands rhythmically in time to it—all of them. Or not quite all.

A Sikh sat against the wall at the back of the shed. His hands were folded on his paunch and his turban was pushed forward over his eyes and he looked half asleep, but I wasn't deceived by that. I knew he was studying Safaraz very closely indeed.

It was the man who had taken me to the house in Juhu.

CHAPTER 11

I drew back quickly into the darkness of the open square but it was too late. The Sikh had followed Safaraz's wink and although the whiskered chin remained sunk on his chest I knew he had seen me. I stood behind a bullock cart and waited until Safaraz had bellowed his way through another six stanzas. He tossed the sitar back to its owner and swaggered out into the courtyard in a storm of applause. I went forward and took his sleeve and drew him further into the darkness.

"That Sikh who sits by the wall—there— See him?" I pointed into the lighted interior, cutting short his delighted welcome.

"Too many Sikhs, sahib," he shouted. "In my father's father's day they had a way of dealing with Sikhs. How did the sahib come here?—and where is Ishmedley?—"

I had almost to club the idiot into silence. He had not noticed the man before I pointed him out, but now on studying him he remembered him.

"I am a fool, sahib," he said penitently. "I have seen the man before—yes—I remember now. He called with a beardless one at the flat—but you had left for the office. He enquired for you and for Ishmedley sahib and I told him what we did with the curious on the Frontier, and he left. Does he trouble the sahib? I shall bring him. This is not Bombay." He turned but I grabbed his arm and pulled him back.

"You've caused enough trouble this trip, damn you," I swore at him. "What are you doing here?"

"I wait for the bus tomorrow, sahib. While I waited I

bought clothes more befitting a man of the North." He preened himself. "Now we go forward again together, eh? That is good."

I let him rattle on while I puzzled over things. Sikhs come from this part of the country and are common to both sides of the border. This man's presence could mean anything or nothing. It might be the merest coincidence—even a goon like this could have a family—perhaps he was visiting it. On the other hand it might mean that we had not been as smart as I had thought—and that they had been on our tail the whole time— But this was getting me nowhere. The fact remained that the Sikh was here and that he obviously remembered Safaraz. He may or may not have recognized me in these clothes—but for safety's sake I would have to assume that he had.

I broke in on Safaraz. "Where do you sleep?" I asked.

"Here, sahib," he answered. "It is overfull of Hindus—and Sikhs—and it stinks like a Tower of Silence, but there is nowhere else." He turned again, "I will clear a space for the sahib-log. A night in the rain will not harm some of these idolators."

I grabbed him again and managed to get it through his skull in words that would have brought his knife out like a flash had they come from anybody else, what I would do to him if he started anything in this place. I knew this mood. He was laughing and he had been amusing the crowd, but underneath it all he was still seething with naked blood-lust over the unavenged killing of one of his kin, and he wanted just half an excuse to pick a fight with somebody—anybody. Buying these clothes and coxcombing it in the bazaar for half a day had probably kept his mind off things for a few hours, but seeing me had brought it all back again and he was as dangerous as a primed grenade with a half-drawn pin.

I led him out of the serai into the rain and set him down in an angle of the wall and told him to watch for two quickly invented Marwaris I had to see urgently. I described them in the greatest detail and told him that the honor of Smedley and myself and that of our families depended on my seeing them—and then, fairly secure in the knowledge that his one-track mind coped comfortably with single ideas only, I left him to cool off and I went to collect Smedley again.

The Sikh was no longer in sight when I got back to the shed, but since there was only one entrance to these serais I felt that he was somewhere in the darkness, watching—but there was nothing for it; I had to talk this over with Smedley.

He was where I had left him—sitting bolt upright but half asleep in the middle of a huddle of bodies. I waded through and nudged him and gestured to the outer darkness. He struggled to his feet reluctantly and followed me out. I told him what had happened.

"What do we do now?" he asked gloomily.

"Only one thing for it," I answered. "Give him the slip again."

"More bloody walking I suppose," he said bitterly. "Can't we set Safaraz onto him?"

"No we can't," I said firmly. "I'm going to have enough of a job to hold him in check as it is. We've just got to get out of here without being followed."

"But how? You said there's only this damned bus tomorrow."

"Exactly. He'll therefore watch it and either join it or follow it in another vehicle if we leave on it. My idea is to start walking tonight and get on a few miles up the road. If we're not on it when it leaves there's a chance that he'll think we're still hanging around here and he might wait for us to show up again."

"What if he follows us tonight?"

"We can do something about it once we get out into the blue. I don't mind that, but I'm not starting anything here."

"He might not be on his own," he said doubtfully.

"I'd be very much surprised if he was," I answered. "But with room to maneuver we can still do something about it. Well? What do you say?"

He didn't say anything. He just sighed.

We collected Safaraz and then we strolled down to the chaikhana and sat drinking tea and listening to the radio like idle men with time to kill. We stayed on until the sleepy proprietor doused the gas lamp and then we stumbled out into the darkness with the remaining handful of patrons, and started back in the direction of the serai—and we peeled off separately into alleys and waited until the place had settled down before meeting up again on the outskirts of the village.

The rain had stopped by the time we set off up the road to the north, but the dust underfoot had now turned to a liquid mud that plucked at our loose slippers and made walking difficult. We spoke little as we trudged, each of us hunched forward into the wind alone with his thoughts. Four or five times before the dawn paled the eastern sky, we halted and crouched behind clumps of cactus and waited for anything up to half an hour to see if we were being followed, but the road behind us remained silent and deserted.

We went through the next village and the next, and then when the sun had climbed high into the mid-morning sky we sat at the side of the road and waited for the bus to overtake us.

86

It came at last and we stood in line across the road and flagged it to a stop. It was the usual open-sided single decker and it was licensed to carry twenty-eight passengers. There were perhaps fifty on board and the roof was piled high with bundles and boxes and cycles. They clung all over it like flies and there was a concerted howl of protest as the driver pulled up and I began the long haggle that always precedes picking up passengers away from the regular stopping places. I struck a bargain in the end and we climbed on board gaining and keeping with difficulty the merest toehold on the back step, and we bounced and bumped for five hours through a hell of swirling dust. I tried to search the faces of those inside but it was hopeless because everybody wraps the ends of their turbans round noses and mouths on these journeys as an ineffectual barrier against stinks and dust. There were Sikhs on board—there always are—but I couldn't recognize any of them as our man—but that didn't mean a thing as any of the fifty of them could have been his deputy.

We reached Kasur and the limit of human endurance in the late afternoon and found that we had a four-hour wait for the connection to Lahore, but there was a taxi service here so we did the last forty miles expensively per jalopy, and dusk found us sitting on the steps of Kim's Gun at the end of the Mall, scratching ourselves drowsily and waiting for full nightfall.

Yev Shalom's shop was in the Anarkali Bazaar. He had a notice over it in Persian script that could be loosely translated as "We Buy or Sell Anything—Anytime"—and it meant just that. I remember once sitting for a whole afternoon in the dirty cluttered office behind his shop trying to buy something from him. It wasn't anything you could wrap up; it was, in fact, information of a highly confidential nature for a commercial house in Bombay, and a hundred thousand rupees was, to them, petty cash. The deal was murderous—because I was working on a percentage basis. He broke off twice during the negotiations—once to buy a double handful of rough-set emeralds from the absconding Prime Minister of a neighboring state, and the other time to sell a secondhand bicycle wheel to a small Punjabi boy. Both deals were as keenly contested as mine. He did all right on all three of them —but when mine was completed and he had wrung the last plugged pice from my twitching hide, he gave me an emerald which I subsequently sold for fifteen thousand rupees and, eavesdropping after he had browbeaten, threatened and cajoled the price of the wheel up to the limit, I heard him give the boy two new tyres and a lamp. The Prime Minister was subsequently arrested as he got onto the Karachi Mail, be-

87

cause there was a fifty thousand reward on his head and he had been ill-advised enough to swing five pieces of green glass onto Yev along with the pukkha article. In short, Yev was Injun honest and not without a Puckish streak of generosity, but you did business with him with one eye and both hands on your wallet and all your wits about you.

He was in his office when we arrived, a little spider of a man with greasy elf-locks and scrawny beard, dressed in the kaftan and black felt hat of the orthodox Jew.

I said, "We want clothes, Yev. European clothes."

"Anything else, Mr. Rees?" he asked. He looked directly at me but without curiosity. We might have been chaffering in Shaftesbury Avenue.

"Yes—razors—toilet things and a couple of suitcases," I added. "Oh, and baths."

"Nothing else?" He raised his eyebrows.

"Nothing," I said flatly.

He shrugged and ran an unerring eye over each of us in turn, and then he called for his son—and in an hour we would have been acceptable at any Government House garden party. We surveyed ourselves in the cracked mirror in his office and I girded my loins for the knockdown, drag-out that would follow.

"All right, Yev," I said. "Not bad. How much? Those pants my friend's got are secondhand and my shoes don't fit."

"Saville Row yet couldn't do it better," he said. "And only Pathans feel the humps of gift camels. It's on the house, Mr. Rees."

"All right," I answered. "What else are you selling?"

"What are you buying?"

"Spit it out or skip it, Yev. The job is finished and I'm leaving. It didn't pay well." I was watching him in the mirror and he knew it. He cackled drily and spread his hands. I'm sorry if I'm being enigmatic about this, but that is how it was. He had something to sell and he didn't mind spreading a bit of ground-bait to prepare things. I could sense that Smedley had guessed as much and was ready to do business here and now and was impatient with me for finessing, but I knew my Yev. One real flash of interest on my part at this stage would be costly.

Yev said, "I knew when you'd crossed. So did they. They've been watching every frontier post for days."

"Well, now you can tell them I'm here, can't you?" I answered.

"They know," he said simply. "What are you buying, Mr. Rees?"

"Experience," I told him. "Gratitude dries like the Punjab

streams in August, in the absence of a gentle rain of rupees from time to time. What do we owe you for the clothes?"

"You got my son out of Calcutta in nineteen-forty-seven when he was injured in the riots," he said. "I've repaid that three times over. To yourself alone I'd pay again—but you're only the agent of this gentleman. I'm a businessman, Mr. Rees."

"So am I," snapped Smedley. "Show us what you've got."

"A man who waits for you here. A silly old man who drinks and talks too much," said Yev softly. "I give you that with the clothes."

"The Major?" said Smedley. "Too late. We know about him. What else have you got?"

"I've got a way out of Lahore—to wherever you want to go. Mr. Rees is good—but not quite good enough. It's like poker gentlemen. You've each got two pairs—I hold the balancers that can give either side a full house. See me for a hundred thousand."

"I'll see you in hell for nothing," I said. "Deal with this gentleman when I've gone, if he's fool enough to do business with you. He's paying me for advice, among other things. Mine is that you're a busted flush, Yev—the sort that is worked by a chain." I put three hundred-rupee notes on the desk and signed to Smedley to break things off. "You've repaid nothing," I went on. "But I've paid you for everything I've had." And I added in Urdu because it would have sounded corny in English, "Your son is still my man—I give him to you. And your face and his—and his son's son's face is blackened, because you've tried to bargain on a debt which lies the wrong side."

He didn't beat his breast and he certainly didn't throw the three hundred back at me. He just grinned and shrugged and showed us to the door, but I felt that the shot had gone home. He was bargaining because bargaining was the breath of life to him and he would have been breaking faith with himself had he given us anything for nothing. As he ushered us out into the bazaar he said, "The clothes are good—worth a thousand. A present, Mr. Rees. For the three hundred I give you this—You're playing against two sides. The Pakistan government's on to it. *My* face is maybe blackened a little—but that is business. My son remains grateful. Come and see me before you go—wherever you go."

We walked back up the Anarkali and Safaraz slipped out of the darkness and took our suitcases. In the Mall we hailed a taxi and drove off to Nedou's Hotel.

Nedou's stands back from the road in a thick grove of trees. It is a long stone building of three deeply verandahed storeys and its solid Victorian comfort has not been affected by the stormy political vicissitudes of a hundred years. We checked in under our own names because there was now no point in using others. The clerk said, "Oh, yes sir. There have been two gentlemen inquiring for you—"

"Two?" I queried.

"A young one and an older one. They called a couple of times and they have rung once or twice."

"Did they leave their names?"

"No, sir."

"All right," I said. "Put them through if they get in touch again."

After dinner we sat on over coffee and brandy but we didn't talk much. The hotel was not full. There were a sprinkling of tourists, a few obvious Americans, one or two English businessmen and a number of the new generation of Europeanized Pakistani government officials. I saw Smedley running his eye over them in the wall mirror behind me.

"Recognize anybody?" I asked him.

He shook his head. Back in European clothes he had assumed his older, colder personality and I felt a restraint between us that the hurly-burly of the trip had largely dissipated.

"How much does that fellow really know?" he asked, breaking a long silence.

"You heard him," I said. "You'll have to figure it out for yourself. All I can tell you is that his shop is one of the three best sounding-boards in the whole sub-continent. Somebody has obviously been inquiring after us—somebody other than the Major, I mean."

"What about this business of being able to get us out of Lahore without being followed?"

"If he can't, nobody can," I said, and added ruefully, "and you can count me in on that too. I slipped somewhere coming out of Bombay."

"I'm damned certain you didn't," he grunted. "It must have been the Pathans." I'd been thinking that myself but I was grateful to him for putting it into words.

"What are you going to do now?" I asked.

"Wait for the Major and hope for the best," he answered. "When are you off?"

"On the Mail tomorrow night," I told him. I said it with more conviction than it really called for, and I thought I saw a slight flicker of hope in his face, but it died as he looked at me quickly. We finished our drinks and went upstairs to our rooms.

I saw the Major as we came along the darkened balcony. He was sitting on a long roorkhee chair and there was another man with him but I couldn't see his face as he had his back to us. The Major waved as we approached and even essayed a move to his feet, but he gave that up quickly and slumped down again.

"Took your bloody time about it, didn't you?" he mumbled when we reached him, "Been here five days twiddling my thumbs—"

"And lifting your blasted elbow, damn you," snarled Smedley. "You talk too much. It was all round the bazaar ahead of us."

"Not from me it didn't come—you can ask young Fonce here—" It was only then as the boy squirmed uncomfortably that I turned and recognized him. "Could have done a deal with the others before I even left Bombay," he went on. "But I didn't—and why? Because I'm a man of my word—That's me—" He was getting steamed up and his voice was rising. We grabbed him between us and yanked him into my bedroom. He belched whisky over us. Only some of it was fresh.

I turned to Fonce. "When did you come up?" I asked him.

"I just arrived on the train, sir," he answered. "My mother's people took her away to Thana—then my daddy sent me a hundi—a money order—and told me to come here."

So that was it. They, whoever they were, had probably followed the lad and this old fool's daily inquiries for us here had told them the rest. We might as well have come straight here openly and saved ourselves some discomfort. I looked at Smedley. The disgusted hunch of the shoulders told me that he was thinking along the same lines. My fee didn't seem so well-earned. It wasn't my fault, but at the same time I don't like sticking anybody. I should have given it back to him and still got out as I intended—but I stayed on and together we grilled the old devil and the boy on their every move up to Lahore. The whole thing was pitifully obvious. The other side might have lost trace of us between Bombay and the border, but that was all. I looked out over the balustrade into the night. I could see nothing but dark trees but I was never more conscious of the truth of their own proverb—"The Indian night is blind for the watched, but has a thousand eyes for the watcher."

By the time we'd finished with the Major he had sobered up a little and the idea that his value to Smedley was decreasing rapidly was starting to dawn on him. He became almost tearful.

I said, "What about this deal you were offered by the others?"

He shook his head mournfully. "Shouldn't have said that," he said. "It's not true." Smedley took him up on it, however, but after ten minutes on the grid he was still sticking to it so we had to accept it. We left him then and went through to Smedley's bedroom.

He said, "I just don't get it. They were willing to knock us both off to get this old swab's whereabouts in Bombay—but he's been on a five day bat up here and they've left him alone. It doesn't make sense."

"It rather points to the fact that they didn't know he was here until the boy led them here," I said.

"But what about that goon waiting at the border?"

"Double insurance," I said. "There's a couple of thousand miles of border, but only three points where the rail crosses it, plus about half a dozen roads. They probably had the lot covered. You're up against thinkers. It's nothing to do with me any longer, but haven't you any idea who they might be? The higher-ups, I mean?"

"There are two crowds besides our own who would be interested," he said slowly, "but who they'd have in the field for them I just wouldn't be knowing."

"Any chance of the other two teaming up?"

"Could be. My mob is the least liked."

I told him I could understand that and he grinned sourly. He said, "What are the chances of that old boy in the bazaar telling the truth when he said the Pakistan government was in on it as well?"

"That could be, too," I said. "But somehow I don't think so. They're pretty orthodox and very correct. I feel we'd have been picked up and warned off officially by now if that were so. No—it looks as if you're up against the one or two you first thought of. Sorry I can't help you any further. I *could* give you a couple of bits of advice though."

"Such as?"

I pointed over my shoulder at the other room. "Well—they know where he is now, don't they? I'd take a few precautions if you want him around when you're ready to move on."

"What the hell can I do on my own?" he snapped.

"I don't know where he's staying," I said. "Probably in some cheap hotel. You could at least move him in here—" I hesitated and was lost, but I was feeling rather a louse, "—I'll help until I leave."

He said, "Thanks. What's the other advice?"

"When Yev Shalom said he could get you out of Lahore without anybody on your tail, he wasn't shooting a line—but I've told you that already. I'd use him if I were you—but don't pay him what he's asking."

He nodded—then we went back to the Major. He was still sitting where we had left him, looking pensive and suffering

from hiccups. The boy was sitting uncomfortably on the en~~d~~
of the bed and I felt sorry for him. Smedley said, "You're g~~o~~
ing to stay here tonight—both of you—I'll fix a room f~~or~~
you."

The Major nodded and asked if he could have a sma~~ll~~
whisky for his hiccups. Smedley told him he couldn't and th~~at~~
he was drying out as from now.

The room the other side of mine was vacant so I move~~d~~
into it and put the Major and Fonce into mine and then w~~e~~
set Safaraz to sleep across the door.

Smedley and the Major were already up when I woke la~~te~~
the next morning. They were poring over maps which Smed~~-~~
ley had gone out and bought at the big booksellers on th~~e~~
Mall, and his bedroom was littered with them. The Major ha~~d~~
ringed a four mile area and now they were working out ~~a~~
route to it.

The Major was saying, "Get out of this place without th~~e~~
cops and half the damn Pakistani army on our tail an~~d~~
there's no problem."

I said, "That's going to be easy—maybe. Which way ar~~e~~
you going?"

"Up to 'Pindi by train—car from there to Srinagar," th~~e~~
Major answered cocksurely.

"The way the tourists used to go in the old days, in othe~~r~~
words?"

"Sure—Where else?"

"Try it," I said. "You can get to 'Pindi all right—but you'~~ll~~
need papers from there on."

"Not the way *we're* going," he smirked. And then Safara~~z~~
came in from the balcony and said that there were two polic~~e~~
sahibs asking for us outside. I didn't understand the "sahibs"
and I asked him what the hell he was talking about. Ther~~e~~
are no British left in the Pakistani police.

He said, "They are police because my scalp prickles, an~~d~~
sahibs because they are Europeans, though not gentleme~~n~~.
Doubtless they have heard that we are rich men and war~~e~~
bribing." Safaraz was a cynic as far as the Law was con~~-~~
cerned.

"What does all that mean?" Smedley asked.

"Trouble, I should say," I told him, and translated.

"Your servant's right," grunted the Major, and spat. "Pa~~y~~
the bastards and get rid of them."

"It'll come high," said a voice at the door. I spun round.

"Hello, Rees," said the taller of the two men who stoo~~d~~
there. "I heard you were in on this. Silly fellow. Now who d~~o~~
we do business with?"

CHAPTER 12

They weren't policemen, but Safaraz could have been excused for thinking they were. They hadn't got particularly big feet nor did they wear their hats on the backs of their heads, but they brought into that room the same sort of indefinable something that makes some men finish their drinks quickly and leave bars unobtrusively. I knew the one who had spoken. The last time I had seen him he was bailing out three Liverpool firemen from the Harbour Court in Karachi and escorting them back to their ship. They hadn't particularly wanted to go but he was coping quite adequately. He wasn't on the staff of either the High Commissioner or the Consul, but both retained him on an as-required basis to deal with undesirable Britons, firmly but discreetly. The other was an Eurasian and at a guess I'd have said ex-sub-inspector—pensioned off when we handed over, but still retaining all the earmarks. I didn't like either of them.

I said, "Hello, Sutcliffe. I hope we didn't keep you waiting. We didn't hear you knock."

"Think nothing of it," he said. "I'm here to help—if I can."

"You can't," I told him.

He raised his eyebrows and pursed his lips. "You'd better hear what I've got to say," he said. He turned to the other man and jerked his head at the Major. "Take him into the other room," he ordered.

I moved across quickly, cutting off the Eurasian's advance. He shouldered past me and I brought my elbow up sharply into his chest. Smedley's hand disappeared into his pocket and he shifted his position round towards the door. Safaraz said to Fonce, "Out of the way, boy, while my master shows how we deal with goralog and others of low caste." The Major started to wail that he didn't want trouble. Only Sutcliffe didn't move—except to shake his head sadly.

"Now isn't this silly?" he said mildly. "I come here to try and save everybody from some trouble and you start making difficulties. Mr. Smedley, if that's a gun you're going for, take my tip and forget it unless you've got a current licence. Under the present emergency possession is worth seven years—using, fifteen."

I said, "Show us some paper, Sutcliffe."

"Paper?" He looked hurt. "Don't be bloody stupid, Rees. You know damn well that if I was here officially I'd have the local law with me to see me serve it. Paper's the *last* thing you want at the present moment. This could be serious."

"All right then," I said. "Suppose you come to the point?"

"What am I trying to do?" he enquired reasonably. "I've got something for you and Mr. Smedley as British subjects, but I'm damned if I'm going to tell it to you in front of witnesses. I've got a job to think of."

I said, "The others can go next door, but my servant goes with them. Tell your man to stay here with us—and also tell him that if he tries to strong-arm past me again I'll really hurt him."

"Fair enough," agreed Sutcliffe.

We waited while Safaraz shepherded the Major and the boy out. Smedley said, "Suppose you introduce us, Rees?"

"Mr. Sutcliffe," I said. "He works sometimes for the High Commissioner—and I think he's implying that we're undesirable aliens."

"You're damn right I am," Sutcliffe said earnestly. "If we can sit down and behave like adults I'll tell you the form." He sat on the end of the bed and mopped his brow. I took a chair facing him but Smedley remained leaning against the wall by the door. The Eurasian was rubbing his midriff and looking murderous.

"Go on," I said.

"Undesirable?" he said and whistled softly. "At the present moment you're two pork chops in Jerusalem. My boss wants you out, Rees—both of you—and bloody sharpish. How you go, and where, doesn't matter, just so long as you go before the Pakistani police pick you up."

I said, "He must be confusing us with somebody else. There's nothing they could pick us up for."

He snorted. "Now we're playing silly muggers, aren't we? You had no entry permits. We don't know how you came in —we don't want to know. We *do* know, however, that you didn't come through any of the authorized channels—and you didn't get your passports stamped. All we're interested in is getting you out again—and quick."

"I'm not admitting you're right," I said, "but assuming you were—how could we get out without questions being asked about how we got *in?*"

"Just give us your passports and get yourselves on the Karachi Mail tonight. Our people will put you on the Bombay boat—or the Timbuktu one if you like—without any snags whatsoever."

"We'd want to know a bit more about things than that. Why the interest of the High Commissioner? If we're just un-authorized visitors all he's got to do is to disown us if we're picked up."

"Talk sense, Rees," begged Sutcliffe. "If you'd busted a bank in Bombay and were on the run with the boodle, he'd do just that. Politics are another matter though."

"Politics?"

"Listen." He sighed like one dealing with a rather dim child. "I know, you know, we all know that that old nit out there—" he jerked his head towards the next room, "—has been skulldugging for the Pakistanis in India for a long time. Now it looks like he's doubling his take by skulldugging for the Indians in Pakistan. Okay—that's his business. He's no longer a British subject and he carries an Indian passport. If he's picked up it's no skin off our asses—*but*, if two of the pukka article from Blighty get hauled in with him you can imagine the squawk that will go up—'Imperialism Raises its Head Again in Pakistan'—'Two Britons Arrested for Espionage'—et cetera—et cetera. Work it out for yourself, Rees, for God's sake. You know local politics as well as I do."

"I do," I said, "but thanks for telling me again. Tell your boss not to worry. We don't know a thing about the Major's politics and we're not interested."

"I believe you—maybe—but that doesn't alter the fact that he's going to be pulled in by the Special Branch here—"

"How do you know that?" asked Smedley quickly—and we both watched for the slightest hesitation on Sutcliffe's part. It wasn't forthcoming.

"We know—that's all," he flashed back. "The ins and outs of it are neither here nor there, but if it will make any difference I'll tell you. It was a tip-off from the High Commissioner's branch office in Bombay to our people in Delhi. It was repeated to Karachi—" he paused and looked at us both closely in turn, "—and it names you two as contacts of Polson's. That is our only interest. We want you out of Pakistan when Polson is arrested."

"Is it certain he will be?" I asked.

"Not that you'd notice. The Indians themselves will put the finger on him. They're bloody angry at being made monkeys of."

"Why haven't they done so already?" Smedley asked him.

"Because they didn't know where he was. They still don't—but they damn soon will. He disappeared out of Bombay after having some dealings with you. They put tails on you two then—but you gave them the slip. *We* picked you up as soon as you arrived here. We put two and two together—" he shrugged, "—it looks like we were right."

"You're not actually," I told him. "We've had certain business dealings with Polson but that's all. All this other is news to us."

He rose and stretched. "I said I believe you—maybe. But I

won't be sitting on the bench when you go up. There won't be a damn thing we can do for you then."

"All right," I said. "Suppose we take you up on your invitation and you get us out quietly—how do we know we're not going to be picked up by the Indian authorities in Bombay? They could frame us just as readily as the people this side."

"That's your lookout," he answered. "All *we* want to do is to get you off *our* doorstep before the balloon goes up. Anyhow, I told you, you don't have to go back there if you don't want to. Name any place you like. If it's ticket money you're short of, that will be forthcoming. What do you say?"

I said, "I'd like to talk it over with Smedley."

"Go ahead," he said. "Only for Pete's sake make it quick." He went to the door followed by the Eurasian.

"Just one thing," I said. He turned impatiently.

"No more questions, Rees. I've already told you more than I should."

"Only one," I answered. "I've told you—we've had certain business dealings with Polson. We're under no obligation to him but I don't think either of us would care to walk straight out on him without warning. How much can we tell him?"

"Tell him what you like," he said. "Only in your own interests I wouldn't make it too much. When he has the screws put on him he'll squawk. The more he knows the more he'll involve you. Still, that's your affair—once you're out of our parish."

They went out onto the balcony and halted at the railings a few yards away. I stood and watched them. Sutcliffe took the hint and they moved further down and round the corner.

"Now what?" asked Smedley.

"We accept," I said.

"But God damn it—" he began.

"Shut up!" I said. "I know what I'm talking about. We'll get him back in a few minutes and dicker—and then accept reluctantly. Keep your eye on the door."

All these bedrooms had their own bathrooms which opened from the rear walls and in turn gave out onto a narrow service corridor. I went through quickly and along to the room where the Major and the boy were waiting nervously. Safaraz squatted on the floor by the balcony door, ostentatiously cleaning his nails with the point of his knife. The Major started to wail but I cut him short.

"Safaraz," I said, "take these two to the shop of the Jew in the Anarkali. Go quietly by the servants' entrance and out through the back. If you are followed I shall blacken your name wherever men gather to talk."

"Look here, Mr. Rees—" began the Major.

"Go, damn you," I told him urgently. "And do as the Pathan tells you. Tell Yev we'll be along later—and then do as *he* tells you."

"Come, you," said Safaraz as he darted through to the bathroom. "You heard what the Sahib said."

I watched them along the corridor and down the steps at the end and then I went back to Smedley.

"They're off," I said. "Now keep your fingers crossed and play up to my leads." I went out and walked along to the corner of the balcony. The main staircase lead from here down to the lobby. Sutcliffe leaned against the bannisters smoking a cigarette. The Eurasian waited on the landing lower down.

"All right," I said. "But there are a couple of points we'd like cleared up."

"Such as?"

"Better come back to the room," I told him.

"Wait here, Snaith," he said to the other and followed me.

"Both of us know a brick wall when we see one," I said, "but we'll have to have help on a couple of personal problems."

"I told you—if it's passage money—" he began.

"We can take care of that," I said. "Passports are the thing. Smedley's is with his kit in Bombay. I lost mine when our car was burnt out on the way up."

"Routine," he said. "You sign a Statutory declaration in the H.C's office that you've had your papers pinched and they'll issue temporary ones. Anything else?"

"Yes— Neither of us fancy Bombay for obvious reasons, but I've got an office, and my bank balance is there, and I've got things to wind up—"

"Listen," he said impatiently. "Time's running short. Snaith will be going down to Karachi with you on the train. Give him a letter to your bank manager—give him a list of anything else you want taken care of—"

"There's the lease of my flat—"

"Shove it down."

"I'll want my stuff forwarded—" I ticked off the points on my fingers worriedly. "There's my clerk to pay off—and the office rent— It's all very well for you to say 'shove it down' just like that—"

"Rees, for Christ's sake—" he started, then took a deep breath and went on with heavy patience. "Look—if you get knocked off and shoved in Lahore jail nobody's going to worry about your personal affairs for a very long time. As it is, I'm giving you my word—the H.C's word if you like—that all you've got to do is to give Snaith a list of what you want

98

attended to and a note of authority to the Bombay office and that will be it."

"If I could be assured of that—" I began anxiously.

"I've told you, haven't I?" he shouted. "What the hell else do you want?—a blueprint?"

I sighed resignedly.

"I think it's a dirty trick on that poor old bum in there," Smedley said heatedly. "I don't know what his politics are— I'm not interested—I know we haven't been mixed up in anything—"

"That's fine," sneered Sutcliffe. "So you've got nothing to worry about—much. Listen—both of you— With things as they are between these two countries you've only got to raise the whisper 'Spies—Imperialists'—'Indian subversion' or 'Pakistani sabotage' to start screaming, blue-bloody murder. God Almighty, Rees, I don't have to tell you that, do I? You've been around long enough."

I nodded glumly. "He's right, Smedley," I said. "I'm sorry and all that—" I suddenly lost my temper. "Good God! Who have I got to be sorry for except myself? If the old soak wants to get himself mixed up in local politics that's his affair. I'm being chased out of Bombay and I'm losing my business—I'm losing everything—"

"Whose fault is that?" snarled Smedley. "You took the job on—and you'll be paid what you asked. What the hell have you done for it anyway?—except drag me all over hell's half-acre for sweet damn-all—"

I turned on him. "Look, Smedley," I said, and I found my voice was shaking with real rage. "I don't want to begin muck-raking at this stage, but if you want me to start telling Sutcliffe one or two things about this business—things that I haven't been altogether happy about from the very first—"

"Tell him what you like!" shouted Smedley. "All right, Sutcliffe—ticket to London for me—by air—quicker the better. I don't know where my friend is going—all I ask is make mine a separate reservation. Contact men? Local fixers? My God!" He stalked out.

"Sorry about that," grinned Sutcliffe sympathetically. "Ask me, I think you're well out of it. Nothing to do with me, of course—but how the hell did you get mixed up with him? Our info is that he's a tout for an oil company. Bit out of your line that, isn't it?"

"That's what I haven't been too happy about," I said darkly. "I think it's a load of bull myself. He doesn't tell me a damn thing. I tried to get something out of Polson but Smedley has him frightened. He just shuts up like a clam. I'll tell you this much, though—" I went on confidentially, "—there's

99

others interested in whatever it is—" I stopped suddenly and went to the door and looked out. I came back to him. "Here —I'd like a bit of advice. I'm completely up the pole in this business—and I've got to live out here when it's all over— Both sides of the border."

"Hm—" He rubbed his chin and cocked an eye at me. "Anything I can do—willing to help, of course. Off the record I think the H.C. would appreciate a spot of frankness. It might do you quite a lot of good. Couldn't promise anything, of course."

I mulled over this for a moment or so. He lit another cigarette and then looked at his watch and cleared his throat.

I said, "I can't tell you here—this is his room. Wait for me down in the lounge—the small one behind the bar—better not be seen going down together."

He winked and went to the door. "All right, Rees," he said loudly. "We'll send a car round for you both just before six. You might be packed and checked out by that time, will you? The train leaves at half-past. Be seeing you." He walked along to the main staircase. I gave him a couple of minutes and then went through to Smedley's room.

"Come on—quick," I said and led him through the bathroom and down the back stairs.

I knew Nedou's. The trees and shrubbery in the front continue up one side of it to the hotel dhobi ghat and they shield it from the lounge and the verandahs. Behind the dhobi ghat stand the servants' quarters, and a gateway in the back wall leads into a lane which runs parallel to the Mall onto which the hotel itself fronts. A couple of taxis usually stood there as the management wouldn't allow a rank on the main drive. I was praying that there would be at least one there now. There was. We hopped in and I told the driver to take us to the station. It is only a three minute drive. I paid him off there and watched him slide away into the evening traffic and then I hailed another one and we drove to Museum Square—and then it was only a short walk to Yev's shop.

The old man was sitting in his office when we went through. He nodded in response to my look of inquiry and grunted something to his son who was writing in a large ledger at a desk just outside. The son jerked his head and led the way through a door in the dark and dusty nether regions of the shop. We followed him out into a small closed yard and through another door and up some steps into a large storeroom that stunk to high heaven of old camel saddlery. He pulled an enormous yakdan—the leather box that swings on each side of the pack saddle—out from a wall, and lifted a trap—and that is all I can recall with any exactitude of the next ten minutes or so, because we went down more steps,

100

into other cluttered rooms, hefted further extraneous junk to one side, went up more steps, down others, traversed pitch dark passages, sending up the dust of ages that made us choke and sneeze, until finally we came to a small room, windowless and lighted only by a guttering oil lamp in the middle of the floor. The son turned to me and held out his hand.

"Wotcher, Mr. Rees," he said in the rich accents of White-chapel. "Rahnd the bleedin' 'ouses, eh? Sorry I couldn't tip you the old how-de-do back there. The old man is very partic-ular abaht pleasantries with the customers in business hours. Some of 'em don't like it—not 'arf. Sit dahn and I'll get you a drink."

He got a bottle of Johnnie Walker from a recess in the wall and three brass Moslem drinking vessels. The scotch didn't taste any the worse out of them.

"Okay," he said, wiping his mouth with the back of his hand. "Just sit tight, will you? The old man will be along in 'arf a tick. Help yourself to another tiddly when you feel like it. Be seein' you."

He started to bustle out of the door.

I said, "Did my servant arrive with two others, Solomon?"

He said, "Be seein' you, Mr. Rees," and went. I should have known better.

Smedley reached for the bottle and poured himself another.

"Knock twice and ask for Alice," he said drily. "What the hell does all that add up to?"

I grinned. "Old Yev always felt that his own English was a bit academic for purely business purposes so he sent Sol-omon home to a fourth cousin in the East End of London. He was there five years."

"He didn't waste his money," said Smedley. "I wasn't re-ferring to that though. Would you mind putting me in the picture as to what has been occurring since we ditched our pal Sutcliffe?"

"Sorry," I said. "All right—here goes. I got Safaraz away with the other two when I left the room—"

"I gathered that."

"Well—you know the rest—except that after you stalked out I hinted to Sutcliffe that I was ready to make a deal. I told him to wait down in the lounge for me. I should imagine he's just about feeling the hot seat now and getting ready to go back to the room to look for me."

"That's fine," he said. "But I still don't understand. We had the police—and somebody—up against us when we arrived. Now I take it that we've got the High Commissioner as well? I'm not bitching about it—" he added hastily, "but you must forgive a slight bewilderment on my part."

"Sutcliffe was no more from the High Commissioner than the man in the moon."

"I thought you said he was?"

"I did—and I really thought so at first—but the damned fool overplayed his hand. He does do some devilling for the consular branch but he'd never be sent on this sort of job. We'd have had a very smooth operator by the name of Bentley call on us and we'd have been invited to accompany him to the H.C's office in Karachi. We'd have been warned off and invited to leave under our own steam. If we didn't accept the invitation we'd have had to take the consequences from the Pakistani police. Good God! They'd never connive at a felony —forge entries and exits on a passport and cough up our fares to wherever we wanted to go. The whole thing stunk."

"It struck me as a bit funny at the time," Smedley mused. "Well now—who's *he* working for, I wonder?—and what did he hope to gain?"

"That's your side of the house," I said. "You know who you're up against—or you don't. My guess is that whoever they are they wanted to get us out of it so they could grab the Major. He was probably telling the truth when he said the old varmint had given them the slip out of Bombay. The boy led them back to him but then we arrived on the scene and gummed things up again."

He pondered on this for a while. "Hm—maybe you're right," he said after a time. "I still don't see quite how they'd have played it, though?"

"Pretty obvious, isn't it? If we'd worn it we'd have left on the train. That Eurasian—Snaith—would no doubt have left here with us to lend weight to it. He'd possibly have jumped the train sometime during the night when we were asleep, and we'd have gone onto Karachi like a pair of chumps. By the time we got back here they'd have had the gallant Major and they'd be making him sing."

He was silent for a long time, then he said slowly. "Yes— yes—it fits. But I'm still puzzled—I'm *badly* puzzled now."

"About what?"

"About who the hell they *are,* Rees."

"As I said before—that's your side of the house. Didn't you tell me that there were two or three other syndicates who could be interested?"

"I did—but I hadn't cabled then."

"Cabled?"

He felt in his pocket and handed me a buff envelope. I took the form out.

"Smedley care Cable and Wireless Lahore," I read. "Buy any good quality cotton available at current market prices.

102

Urgently needed Manchester market. Particularly interested in long staples. Ventnor."

"Sorry," he apologized as I looked at him blankly. "Things have been happening so damn quickly that I haven't been able to explain. I was too sick to get a cable off in Bombay before we left and I haven't had a chance since, until this morning when I went out to buy those maps. I inquired in code what the form was—who was in the field against us. That answer came up as you were talking to Sutcliffe after I left the room. It is telling me not to worry—we're up against nobody, as my principals have made a nice comfortable deal with the opposition. That sometimes happens. It also tells me to get a bloody move on and to stop idling out here on the fat of the land."

"Splendid," I said. "So we're being chased all over India and Pakistan by figments of our own imagination?"

"Looks like it, doesn't it?"

"I'd send them another cable if I were you."

"What's the good?" He laughed bitterly. "I could tell you the answer now—they'd instruct me to buy more cotton and authorize me to go three points above current market prices —and so on and so on."

"Meaning?"

"Loosely decoded—'Get on with it you bum. What are we paying you for?' I tell you, my mob deal only with results. How we get them is our own affair."

"Ever strike wild jokers in the pack before?" I asked.

"Once or twice—but an inquiry home has always placed them for me before. This is the first time I've been left right out on a limb—and certainly the first time they've been quite as rude as that." He sighed. "I must be getting old," he added. "I should have taken Mrs. Smedley's advice and quit a year ago."

I stared at him in silence for a full minute. He reached for the bottle again.

"Listen," I said at last. "Isn't it time we tried to tidy things up a bit?"

"Go ahead," he said glumly. "At the moment I'm too tired to think any more."

"All right." I started to check points on my fingers. "The Major has certain papers your people want—or rather he *says* he knows where those papers are. You make a deal with him. Simultaneously some other crowd start to show an interest. Let's call them the 'X mob'. For reasons of his own— the Baluchi moneylenders—the Major has to leave Bombay quickly. The X mob obviously assume that we know where he is, so they get hold of us and put us through it—"

"Oh, for Pete's sake," he began wearily. "We *know* all this so why—?"

"Do we?" I retorted. "We don't know a thing. We've just been assuming all along the line—running like headless chickens, without really knowing who we've been running *from*. We've got to go back to the beginning and do some re-thinking. Right—we give the X mob the slip, but they counter by threatening to involve us in a murder charge. Once again we manage to duck them and we reach this place—where they pick us up again. We assume that they managed that by keeping tabs on the boy and following him here."

"What about that Sikh at the frontier?"

"Normal precautions. They knew we would be making north so it would be a fair bet that they would have had every crossing covered. With me so far?"

He gave something between a nod and a resigned shrug.

I went on. "Now, as far as I can see, their only real interest in us has been to get us to lead them to the Major. If they could get us off the scene and put their hands on him they would make him cooperate. It would appear that that is just what Sutcliffe has been trying to do—so I think we are justified in putting him down firmly as an agent of the X mob. All right, let's sum up so far and see what they are fielding against us." I counted on my fingers. "Sutcliffe and the stooge with him, Snaith. A European who you described as a pursy-mouthed type with a chi-chi accent. The Sikh and the Hindu who shanghai-ed us—the former of whom we've seen again at the frontier. Four assorted Indians at the house—two of whom are no longer with us—"

"The feller who put the frighteners on us over the phone?" Smedley suggested.

I nodded. "That makes ten—"

"You're forgetting the cop—what's his name? Ram Dass?"

"I'm not. I was coming to that. I think we've got to put the police in as another factor. My guess is that their interest is purely incidental—so far, at least. They've always had their eye on the Major and that advertisement of yours would have sparked things off again. Unfortunately we've put ourselves on the wrong side of the law though—and the X mob hold that as a trump card against us, ready to play it or with-hold it as it suits them. Right—if we accept that we can regard ourselves as one corner of a triangle—the X mob and the police form the other two. The other two *could* combine against us, but at the moment that is unlikely because—"

"Well that's something," Smedley broke in with heavy irony. "So we can rule out the police and it leaves us only with the X mob—who my bosses say don't exist anyway—"

And then Yev arrived. He stood in the doorway and clucked disapprovingly.

"I try to run a respectable business, Mr. Rees," he said. "A little bit of smuggling maybe—and sometimes we oblige a gentleman who has got himself disliked locally. But murder yet—that's not good."

"Who's murdered who?" I asked.

"Warrants for you. Two Indians in Bombay."

"So the bastards weren't bluffing," said Smedley thoughtfully.

"Where did you hear this?" I asked hollowly.

"A small bird," said Yev primly. "Gentlemen, this is going to be expensive."

"Don't come that one, you old swab," I said savagely. "We didn't do it—and even if we had, there's no extradition between here and India."

"No," he agreed. "But there is *deportation* from here to England—and there is extradition from there."

I stood up. "Come on," I said. "I've had enough of this. I'm going to take a chance. Lead us back through this rabbit warren."

"You'd be taking a big one, my friend," he said drily. "The Lahore police look for you also—on other matters."

Smedley grinned mirthlessly. "So your triangle is now a square, Rees. We're up against the X mob, the Indian police *and* the local force. Can't anyone drag in the fire brigade, just to make it really interesting?"

CHAPTER 13

I said to Yev, "I am prepared to believe you about the Bombay matter. There are circumstances that could link us with it—but we still have an answer to it. You're lying about the Lahore police though. If they had wanted to they could have picked us up any time they liked—right up to half an hour ago. Now listen to me—my friend wants to go somewhere and he wants to take someone with him. He is willing to pay anything in reason, so there's no need to try and jack the price up."

"I'm not," he said. "I don't want anything for myself."

"You're a business man, Yev," I said. "You've always driven a hard bargain—I don't blame you for that—but now you're shaming me. Why lie like a bazaar tout to a tourist? You just said it was going to be expensive—now you say you don't want anything for yourself."

"Name your price," growled Smedley. "If it's too high I'll tell you—and we'll walk right out of here."

"And you may call me a liar again and spit in my beard as you go," said the old man softly. "But hear me first. Sit down, Mr. Rees." He lowered himself onto the carpeted floor and the light from the lamp in the middle which was only knee-high, was now on his face. I followed suit. There was silence for a full minute and Smedley wriggled impatiently. I nudged him to keep quiet because in an Eastern bargain he who speaks first is at a disadvantage.

Yev was combing his straggly beard with clawed fingers and he gazed past us into the shadows. "The Polish Refugee Camp in Delhi," he said at last. "How many did it hold between nineteen-thirty-nine and nineteen-forty-eight?"

"I don't know," I answered. "What has that got to do with it?"

"Come to the point," snapped Smedley. "What's your price?"

"Twenty-seven thousand, four hundred and thirty-three." The old man was talking more to himself than to us. "The line ran from Warsaw—through Rumania and down to Istambul—on through Syria and Persia to Afghanistan and then over the Frontier and finally to Delhi. It was *my* line—and it is strewn with the skeletons of Jews and Christians and men without a God at all. I refused nobody passage over it—nobody who was running from death—and I charged nobody a toll. It cost money, my friends, and I mortgaged everything I had to keep it open. I am still paying on my bonded word. The line remains, but whoever uses it today pays for a life of yesterday."

"How much?" persisted Smedley. Yev ignored him.

"You, Idwal Rees, have a life in credit. My son's. You use it free," he said.

"I'm not going," I told him.

"Then you'll rot in Lahore jail. Bargain for your friend then. What does he run from? Death? Injustice? Tell me that and the line is open—but if it is for profit, his or another's, the price is high. What is it, Idwal Rees?"

"The hell with that," said Smedley. "I'll do my own dickering. Okay—I could say I was running from death—and I'd be telling the truth. Rees can bear me out on that. They've had a crack at us both."

Yev looked at me for confirmation. I didn't like making it tougher for Smedley but the old man had me in a cleft stick. "That's true," I said. "But we're both being paid for our risks
106

—and the people Smedley works for don't do anything unless there's a percentage in it. Call it both—*from* death and *for* a profit—but we're both free agents."

"You *were*," he said, "but now you're leaves before the wind. All right, Idwal Rees, the line is open. If your friend comes back he pays me a fair man's price. Where do *you* want to go? Show your face in the bazaar and you'll be arrested for espionage—go to India and you'll stand trial for murder."

"How do you know all this?" I asked.

"Sutcliffe?" He looked at me inquiringly.

"A small man. He sometimes works for the High Commissioner," I said.

"Don't under-rate him," he answered. "And he hasn't worked for the High Commissioner for over a year. Ram Dass?"

"If we're talking about the same man, he's a detective-inspector in Bombay."

"We are talking about the same man—but he's in Lahore now, with Sutcliffe. Sayed Din?"

"Another policeman—this side of the border. He used to be on the Karachi force."

"Also in Lahore—with Sutcliffe. Snaith?"

"Never met him before today. Eurasian. He was with Sutcliffe too," I said.

"Late of the Punjab police. Discharged by the British for corruption. You ask me how I know all this. *That* is how I know. Where vultures gather there is a carcass."

"What is the carcass?"

"Is it for me to tell you that? Aren't you also vultures?"

"Skip the riddles," said Smedley. "Tell me who they're working for—and you can add it to the fair man's price."

"Is it information or confirmation you are asking for?"

"Bit of both."

"Who does Kavronski work for? You must ask in Moscow and Peking for that." He was watching us closely under his heavy brows.

I shot bolt upright. "Kavronski?" I said. *"That* bastard?"

"In spades—doubled," said Smedley feelingly. "You know him too, do you?"

"A bit," I said drily. "So all these others are working for Kavronski are they, Yev?"

He spread his hands wide and hunched his shoulders right up to his ears. "So it was *in*formation yet? That comes dearer than *con*firmation. Tell your friend that, Idwal Rees, when he reckons up the fair man's price. Tell him also that if Kavronski never crosses this or any other frontier again, *I* pay a fair man's price in gratitude. A bastard, you call him? Use another term. I fathered a few bastards in my youth—but they are all honorable men." He spat.

"Where is he now?" I asked.

"I don't know. He came here some weeks ago—but I didn't know until it was too late by one short hour—or he wouldn't have left again. He went through to Kabul. Egyptian passport. My son Solomon beat three of my agents, and I turned my face to the wall and wept."

"He was in Beirut last I heard of him," mused Smedley. " 'Fifty-three."

"In Hongkong in 'fifty-four," I supplied.

Yev rose creakingly to his feet and smoothed down the creases in his kaftan. "So now you know as much as I, gentlemen. Remember—a fair man's price if there is a profit— I'll sell your executors a tombstone—cheap—if there isn't. The score is settled if Kavronski should die—and if it's slow there'll be a bonus. God forgive me, because I'm a merciful man. Where do you want to go?"

"Up through Kashmir," I said. "Four of us. I've changed my mind."

"Who are the four?"

"Me, my friend here, the old man who came earlier and my servant."

"What about the boy?"

"Oh hell—I'd forgotten him. Could you get him back to Bombay?"

"As you wish," he said. "All right. Rest here five or six hours. I send some food up." He went out.

"How far can we trust him?" asked Smedley.

"You can please yourself," I answered. "For me?—one hundred per cent. He'd skin a flea for its hide and tallow, just for the sheer love of bargaining—but when he gives his word he keeps it. All the East knows that."

"That bit about the escape line—?"

"Perfectly true. They say it cost him five million of his own money. Seven governments, including our own, promised him medals and recoupment. The medals came through but they ratted on the recoupment. He never squawked, but he prefers to deal with *individuals* now."

"Don't blame him." He poured himself another drink. "What do you know about Kavronski?" he asked.

I said, "I could tell you the lot in six well-chosen words— but if you want it in detail it's a long story."

"Time's the one thing we're not short of," he said. He pushed the bottle across to me. "Let's have it in detail."

"Hearsay, the first part of it—but I've no reason to doubt it," I told him. "He came to Shanghai as a child, after the

Russian revolution in nineteen-seventeen. The whole of North China was full of emigrés at that time. His parents died and he was brought up in an orphanage in the International Concession. I remember him as a young man who used to come to our house to play chess with my father—I was just a kid myself. I always knew him as 'Mr. Stewart'. Kids are not interested in adults' backgrounds but harking back I remember vaguely that he had a good job with an engineering company, and that we always thought of him as an Englishman. I think he was keen on my elder sister at one time, but she married somebody else and we didn't see so much of him thereafter. He was a magnificent linguist—that I know with certainty, because my father was an Oriental scholar of some repute but Stewart could lose him. He used to amuse us kids by taking off Cantonese tradesmen arguing with Shanghai mandarins and things like that. You'd have to know as much about the Chinese dialects to do that as you'd have to know English if you were doing a skit on a Cockney talking to an Oxford don.

"There are gaps now. I don't remember seeing much of him when I was a youth, but I met him in Burma in nineteen-forty-three. He was a major in the Indian Army Intelligence Corps—I was then a subaltern with my battalion. I had dinner with him one night in the Headquarter mess. He told me he had got out of Shanghai with one of the last parties of refugees when the Japs had finally moved in after Pearl Harbor. They had come right across China into Burma and then down into India. It was quite a story—and a true one, because I subsequently met others who were with the same party.

"Well—that was that; just a chance meeting with an old family friend. The next time I saw him he was in close arrest at Fourteenth Army H.Q. I and everybody else who had known him in the old days were sent down there for interrogation—"

"In other words, that was when he was first rumbled as a spy?" said Smedley.

"It was certainly the first time it came into the open. Intelligence said they had the finger on him since before the war but that they gave him rope purely to uncover his lines and contacts—and then they pulled him in in their own time, but that may have been a face-saver."

"Who was he actually working for at that time?"

"The Japs. You see Japs, or any other Oriental race, are up against a severe handicap when they went to spy on Europeans. They can't pass as Westerners themselves so they had to borrow trained personnel from the Germans, or recruit stateless Europeans. Stewart was a natural for it. He passed as an Englishman and had an almost perfect background.

109

Dammit, I was prepared to swear to him myself—hadn't he almost become my brother-in-law? Hadn't he played chess with my father and cricket with the English Club? Didn't he used to bring me toys when I was knee-high to a bean-pole? Stewart a spy for the *Nips?* Bloody nonsense. Most of us reacted the same way at first—right up to the time he escaped."

"How did he escape?"

"Damned cleverly. There were no facilities for keeping him in close arrest in his own quarters during the inquiry—like an officer and a gent—so he was put in the guardroom of an Indian regiment each night. The regiments changed over. He marched out in command of the rear platoon of the old one. You couldn't blame the sepoys—it was pitch dark and all they knew was that a sahib was marching behind them checking them for getting out of step and talking. Sick and wounded officers were always being replaced by reinforcements. By the time he was missed by the new crowd, the old one had entrained for Manipur—but he wasn't with them. God knows how he did it, but we heard afterwards that he'd slipped away and walked nearly a hundred miles slap through the jungle to the Jap lines. Clever bloke."

"Can you fill in from there?" Smedley asked.

"Only hearsay again," I said. "I've never seen him since—but he has worked for the Chinese in Korea and we once almost got our hands on him in Hongkong. He did a liaison job for the Communists in Malaya and some anti-Dutch stuff in Indonesia. He gets around—always where there's trouble, or where there's going to *be* trouble. I'd like to meet him again. He's the only man I know who I'd shoot while he slept."

"Anything personal in it?—or just on general principles?"

"Both. I don't particularly like professional spies who work for the highest bidders, but I'm not a prig about it. Yes there *is* something more to it. Just one little detail I missed out. When he escaped from the guardroom he was wearing the kit and equipment of his officer escort—a subaltern of the regiment. They found the kid under Stewart's mosquito net next morning with his throat cut. He must have drowsed off and Stewart just jumped him. They had been playing chess together apparently. Somehow or other that made it *very* personal."

"If it's personal enough to make you want to stay on with me, I'm grateful," he said quietly.

"Let's get it quite straight, shall we?" I answered. "I've just said I'm not a prig in these matters—or I try not to be—but the fact remains that I work better if there's something at the end of it besides a check. Up to now I've thought it a case of

110

one commercial concern against another—and damn little to choose between the two of you. If Stewart—or Kavronski—is on the other side that puts me with the angels. Incidentally, does the knowledge that he is in it help to place any of your wild jokers?"

"Not altogether," he said slowly. "But it does knock a few possibles out. The big boys pay for results and to hell with how you get 'em—but I don't know of a single one who would risk retaining Kavronski. He'd take their money all right and he'd give them something that *looked* like results—but at the final reckoning he's only got one set of bosses—and they wear fur hats, whiskers and snowy boots. Whatever the cynics may say, big money and politics do *not* go together. No—if *he's* in it someone the other side of the Curtain—Iron or Bamboo—is interested."

"In which case someone this side will be interested too—damned interested. I want to make a deal, Smedley," I said.

"Shoot."

"Whatever we uncover in this affair, I reserve the right to make a full report to—well, to somebody I know."

"I can't make side deals," he said. *"I've* only got one set of bosses too, thank God. At the same time, I don't see how I can stop you. Shall we leave it at that?"

"Suits me," I said "—just as long as we understand. All right then—I've told you what I know about Kavronski. What do *you* know?"

"Less than you. He's only a name to me—a name that stinks. I've never actually met him. He's a sort of bogeyman—a shaggy dog. Every job I've done out East for my people since the war, somebody has always said at the briefing—'Watch Kavronski'. To still be around with so many people wanting him dead, he must be quite a guy. I wonder if old Yev is shaggy-dogging too?"

"Write me down amongst the naive," I said. "But if Yev says he's in, he's in. I'm worried about the police angle though."

"In what way?"

"Sutcliffe I can understand. He'd work for whoever paid him. That goes for the other stooges we've met also—but Ram Dass and Sayed Din are different. They are accredited, and as far as I know, fairly honest cops—for India and Pakistan respectively."

"He buys cops," Smedley yawned.

"Maybe—but I'm damned certain he wouldn't buy them just like that—straight off the force. A government job with a pension at the end of it is the height of that type of Oriental's ambition. I'm wondering if he's bought some of their *bosses*—and just how high it might go. There are factions in these governments, you know. This could mean something really big—and very nasty."

"Too big for me," said Smedley. "My people want a set of papers somebody has buried up there. Fine—if I can get them for them I eat and pay the rent for another year or so. Who's bought who among the opposition doesn't concern me but if, as an incidental, Kavronski gets rubbed out in the process I'll save the office some overhead, get a bogeyman out of my hair and apparently make you happy also. Wake me up when chow arrives." He stretched out on the carpet and went to sleep. He was an amazing man.

I gave it up after an hour's puzzling and went to sleep myself.

Solomon woke us some hours later and we sat each side of a big brass dish and ate pilau and kebabs. He told me that the Major and Safaraz had left already and that we'd meet them at his uncle's house in Srinagar, which is up at the top of the Kashmir valley.

"Which way did you send them?" I asked.

"'ave some more kebabs," invited Solomon. "Cooked by me old woman 'erself." I didn't pursue it but Smedley asked how much walking we had ahead of us.

"To Srinagar?" asked Solomon. "Not a bleedin' step. You're going up by car as a couple of Hoos."

"Whores?" yelped Smedley. "What! In those damned burkha things again?"

"Nah—doctors—W.H.Os—World Health Organization. The old man don't like doing it but things are getting tight on that road."

"Thank Pete for that," said Smedley feelingly. "If it means riding."

"You'll have to be careful," went on Solomon. "You're supposed to be Swiss—one German-Swiss, one French-Swiss. Broken English and as much Urdu as you'd have picked up on the train from Bombay. You're not likely to meet any Europeans on the road but some of the officers at the control posts might have a word or two of French. Educated bastards some of 'em nowadays. Any preferences who's Kraut and who's Frog?"

"I speak German," grunted Smedley. "What about you, Rees?"

"Bit of French and not so hot," I said.

"Right—finish your supper, gentlemen," said Solomon. "I'll be back in a few moments."

He returned with a Leica and flashlight attachment and pinned a white sheet up on the wall—then he worked on the long-suffering stubble on Smedley's head with some dope that turned it a dirty blonde even as he applied it. When his eyebrows were done also and he had a pair of horn-rimmed glasses the effect had to be seen to be believed. Then he cropped my hair down to crew-cut length, took our photos and left.

There has been much nonsense talked about the extent and efficiency of Yev's organization. I had always discounted a lot of it myself. I wasn't quite so sure when I looked at the two Swiss passports and the set of, as far as I could see, perfect W.H.O. papers Solomon handed us some hours later. The supporting props were so good too—just the sort of things a couple of doctors travelling in advance of their heavy kit would carry—an oil-immersion microscope that Dr. Gantzmeier didn't want knocked about, a couple of tropical medicine textbooks in German, stethoscope and a leather case of drug phials. Dr. Laporte had a complete medical pannier with him—both had snaps of their wives and families with affectionate messages in German and French respectively written on the backs. We each had properly franked letters addressed to us care of W.H.O. Bombay, and receipted bills from hotels along the way were clipped to an expense-diary. Put it this way; if I'd been turning over a couple of kits I'd have been absolutely convinced of the bona fides of the owners on this showing—and I'm supposed to be trained.

"You should be all right with that lot," Solomon said with some understandable satisfaction. "Nobody is likely to be giving you the works—they're used to Hoos going up and down the road and they got a sort of diplomatic immunity, but if any cocky young bugger does get officious you should be able to blind him." He handed me a type-written sheet. "There's a few pointers down there—where you came from, when you landed, where you're going and what you're doing. Let's have it back when you've got it pat. But understand, gentlemen, this takes you to Srinagar only. You hand over all this stuff to my uncle there and you're on your own from then on."

He gave us half an hour to study it and then he came back and led us from the room again, and once more we traversed passages and stairways and crossed flat roofs and went down into courtyards and through houses and shops where the occupants, if they saw us at all, were not interested in our passing. Never once did we come out into a street until at last we arrived in a quiet walled garden where a big black saloon waited. Solomon gave us a thumbs-up sign and vanished without a word.

The driver was a little black man in a neat khaki uniform and an over-large topee on the front of which was the globe-and-laurel badge with serpent-entwined staff of the W.H.O. He took our kit and loaded it into the boot and then held the

113

rear door open for us and said, "Ha-ji doctor sahibs, am first class senior motorman driving very dam' fast, okay."

We rolled out of the double gates of the garden and turned left and then right and I was amazed to find that we were under the walls of the Old Fort near the Secretariat offices, a good half mile from the Anarkali. We crossed the Ravi Bridge as the sun was rising and dispelling the low-hanging mist over the irrigated fields to the north of the city. Progress was slow at first because we got into a stream of crawling trucks which we couldn't pull out of as the road was choked with an opposite moving stream of panniered donkeys and camels and almost as heavily burdened women head-loading vegetables and baskets of grain into the morning markets. There was a crowded bus on our tail, and behind that a black car similar to our own—and both worried me not a little until, after an hour or so, the traffic thinned out and we were able to drive "very dam' fast, okay" and lose them in the dust.

We covered the hundred and eighty miles to Rawalpindi by midday. I had expected we would stop somewhere to eat, but the driver had obviously had his orders because he skirted the old cantonments and turned onto the Murree Road and swept along towards the hills without checking until, just before the road starts to ascend sharply to Tret, he stopped under some trees and topped up his petrol tank from jerricans he carried in the trunk. He produced sandwiches and bottled beer for us after that, and retired a short distance to eat chuppatties and cold rice himself in decent seclusion. Then we pushed on—up to Sunny Bank, with its memories of Kipling, red-coated soldiery and Victorian nannies, on to Murree, a tree-embowered jewel in the peerless air of an eight-thousand foot altitude—and then down the sickening five thousand foot drop to Kahala on the Jhelum River.

There was a check-post here, and just across the river was the actual Kashmir border but they hardly bothered us at all. A police sepoy sauntered over and glanced into the car and saluted us perfunctorily. The driver chattered in Punjabi and the sepoy waved us on. It was as simple as that—until, twenty miles on we came to Domei, where the road from Abbottabad joined the one we were on, and there was a knife-edge barrier barring our way, and troops sat in a sandbagged emplacement behind a mounted Bren gun.

Smedley swore nervously and the driver started to chatter again. But it was only routine. The road was closing for the night and traffic both ways was being halted and diverted into a transit camp. Inspection of papers seemed to be more thorough here though, and it was being done by an officer. I watched him dealing with a couple of cars and a bus which

114

had come up the Abbottabad road and had reached the barrier ahead of us. He was taking plenty of time over it, and in the gloom I could see that the passengers had dismounted and he was shining a torch into their faces as he scrutinized their papers. The cars themselves were getting attention too; a rummaging squad under an N.C.O. dragging cases and bundles out of trunks and off roofs and going through them minutely.

The officer reached us at last and told us curtly in Urdu to get out. I said "Excuse please—you speak English, no?" He saw the badge on the driver's topee then and he was civil and apologetic—too damned civil by far. "Ah—doctors, eh?" he said in English, and returned our papers after the briefest glance. "You see the first car there—ahead by the barrier? Okay—you just pull out and follow it. We'll put you up in the mess. The dak bungalow is full." He cut short our protestations and roared at his squad to leave our kit alone. We thanked him as he directed our driver and sat back glumly as we bumped up a side road that skirted the crowded transit camp.

"Any way of ducking this?" asked Smedley.

"Not without giving offense or rousing suspicion," I said. "Don't worry though. We'll struggle with our English, take a drink and something to eat off them and then plead tiredness and ask if we can go to bed."

The car ahead of us pulled up in front of a group of tents in the shade of a slump of neem trees and we rolled to a stop behind it. It was a battered open tourer and the occupants had evidently suffered from dust on the way up because we could see them, a tall man and a shorter one in khaki bush jackets, shaking and brushing themselves off in the middle of a group of orderlies who came from the lighted mess and pounced on their luggage. I tried to see who or what they were, but the next minute we ourselves were coping with orderlies, and by the time we had supervised the unloading of our kit they had gone into the mess tent. We followed them in. They were standing with their backs towards us being greeted by a fat little Bengali captain.

"Ah—nice to see you again," he was saying as he shook hands with them in turn. "You are tired, is it? Damn hot dusty run. Some drinks will fix that—" He saw us then and came past them with outstretched hand. "More visitors—more the merrier in this place. I am Captain Bannerjee— Asgaon Rifles—gentlemen—"

Smedley was clicking his heels and bowing and saying, "Doktor Gantzmeier. You are so kind."—but I was looking at the other two.

The shorter was a girl and, in spite of the dust on her face and in her dark hair, a very pretty one. And she was undoubtedly English.

CHAPTER 14

The girl returned my look with a friendly grin. She really *was* pretty—but it wasn't that that was making me stare; it was the red cross brassard she wore on her arm. I followed Smedley's example and bowed and murmured "Laporte," and sounded to myself like a fifth rate impersonation of Maurice Chevalier. Bannerjee took over then and effected further introductions. I missed her name in the babble but the man with her was one Railton, a middle-aged American engineer on a hydro-electric project further up the valley and, thank God, a talker. He monopolized things for the next few minutes and I slipped out on the pretext of seeing to the unloading of our kit. Smedley was coping splendidly getting in a word here and there in a mixture of German and guttural English, shaking hands and thanking Bannerjee and the other officer who just then arrived from the checkpoint.

This was a facer. I was prepared to keep up the masquerade in front of a couple of Indian officers, but if this girl was a doctor and happened to speak French we were sunk. The cover story was worrying me too. Ours was all right as far as it went, but there wasn't many hospitals in Kashmir and if she was in the business she would know them all and she would naturally be interested in our tour—where we were going, and what we were doing—and would ask questions. There was only one thing for it. I had to go sick quickly with a dose of fever and Smedley would have to attend to me, and that would be sufficient reason for keeping us out of the mess tent.

I went back to the door of the tent and tried to catch his eye but he had his back to me, and Bannerjee was being hospitable with a bottle of whisky and glasses all round. The girl refused a drink, however, on the score of wanting to bathe and change first, and the checkpoint officer led her out through the rear entrance of the tent. I went in again and accepted a drink myself and slid round quickly alongside Smedley who had sunk his first in one gulp and was holding cut his glass for another. The American greeted me in French which was, if that were possible, worse than my own and then apologized for it and switched back to English.

116

"Sharma tells me you're from W.H.O.," he said. "Fine—fine. We can't have too many of you people up here. Claire's going to be interested in talking to you—"

"Comment? Claire?" I asked. "Oh—the young lady? She is a doctor also?"

"Nurse," he answered. "She helps a countrywoman of mine run a camp for displaced kids up in Bhavnagar. Neither of them are doctors but they do a mighty fine job all the same. You must have heard of them—Ethel Platting and Claire Culverton?" I had guessed it by this time, of course. "Expensive education," the Brigadier had said. That would no doubt include French. I wouldn't last two minutes. I caught Smedley's eye and put my hand to my head wearily.

"I fear I have the fever," I said.

"Hell, that's bad," said Railton sympathetically. "You must have picked it up down-country. There's none up here this time of the year. I got some stuff in my baggage—very good—"

"Thank you," I said. "I think perhaps I leave it to my colleague—"

"Oh, sure," he said hastily. "I didn't mean to horn in. You got plenty of blankets? First-timers often don't realize they're needed up here—"

Bannerjee looked genuinely stricken. He had the earmarks of a man planning a party. He said, "Let me telephone for our own M.O. He is knowing the local fevers and will fix you damn quick. Man, one dose of his horse jallup and you are dancing like a devidass."

I told him hurriedly that we couldn't dream of putting him to the trouble. "No trouble," he assured me. "It will take him only one hour to get here—half an hour if he thinks there is a party—and it will save your friend from bus-driver's holiday." He put his drink down and made for the door. "I telephone," he said firmly—and it took ten minutes solid arguing, invoking medical etiquette and insisting that it was probably only a headache anyhow, to talk him out of it. Through it all Smedley, the swab, grinned like a Cheshire cat and kept up a sustained attack on the bottle. I was really worried but at last I managed to get away and an orderly took me to the tent they had allotted us. There were two mosquito-netted camp beds in it and I got into one of them quickly.

Smedley came in some minutes later and I swore at him. "You bloody fool," I growled. "Why the hell couldn't you have backed me up instead of standing there belting that bottle? Don't you realize that that could have been serious?" But he just grinned and made a very vulgar gesture. I could have hit him. He said, "Relax, cobber. We're doing all right. You sounded just like a Marseilles jig-a-jig pimp, and my German is blinding them. What did you want to turn chicken for?

Nice bit of stuff that—and I think the Yank's a high-principled type—and me?—I'd never do anything Mrs. Smedley wouldn't approve of. You'd have been sitting pretty."

I hung on to the tattered remnants of my temper with difficulty. "You realize who she is, I suppose?" I asked.

"Sure. The old Brig's daughter. So what?"

"So this," I ground. "We're supposed to be going up to Srinagar in the first instance. After that we're supposed to be doing a tour of hospitals and camps like hers. Do you think she's not going to be interested? Ask questions? Isn't she likely to discuss us with other medicos and missionaries that she meets? Aren't people going to wonder when we don't turn up? And finally, isn't word likely to filter back to W.H.O.? Use your savvy for Christ's sake."

"We're far more likely to rouse suspicion if we rabbit out of it," he said. "These two officers want to throw a party."

"That's just what I'm afraid of," I answered. "I know what you're like when you've got a load aboard. Now listen to me —I'm sick and you're staying here to look after me."

"If you're as sick as that, Bannerjee is going to send for their own quack, who he assures me is the best fever-physicker east of Suez. I'm having a hell of a job to talk him out of it as it is. No reflection on my professional ability, of course—they only want to be helpful. Better leave it to me, Rees—and don't worry about my getting a load on board, either." He was sore now. He turned to the door of the tent.

"If we're uncovered," I told him, "we're going to drop old Yev in the cart. If that happens I quit on the spot."

"Forget it," he snapped and went out.

I was really anxious now. Sober, he might have carried it off—but if there was whisky around Smedley would drink it, and booze reacted on him quickly. I lay and sweated it out for half an hour or so and then an orderly brought me a light meal on a tray—and that didn't improve my temper because I could have coped with a heavy one. Smedley came and saw me sometime later and the two officers stood in the tent doorway and made sympathetic noises. They were all a bit owlish by this time, but I must say that Smedley did it well. He took my wrist and studied his watch solemnly and then got a thermometer from the pannier and stuck it in my mouth. It was the wrong way round but nobody seemed to notice it but me. He looked at it and then shook it down professionally. "Iss good—will live," he grunted and this seemed to strike all of them as damned funny because they roared and rolled off back to the mess and shortly afterwards I heard Smedley howling a German song at the top of his voice. I couldn't understand a word of it but it had a sort of beery "Ein, zwei, drei" refrain to it that the company, now swelled by the arrival of a carload of other officers, took up with gusto. This cheered me a little—not the singing, but the fact that no woman would be likely to stay in the mess with that crowd—certainly not a nicely brought up one. I went off to sleep eventually and only wakened when Smedley came in some-time during the small hours and thrashed round the tent cursing and belching, finally flopping onto his camp-bed and collapsing it. I went back to sleep a little happier.

I woke him again as dawn was breaking. He was a sick man and a sheepish one. I went out into the chilly morning and found our driver who was sleeping on the back seat of the car, curled up in that incomprehensibly small compass that only Indians can manage. I got some coffee and bread from the duty cook and we loaded the car and drove down to the barrier and got a place at the head of the queue, then I found Sharma's tent. He was in as bad shape as Smedley but like the rest of that hospitable crew, his manners were good. He wrapped a blanket round himself and came muzzily down to the control office, stamped our transit voucher and yelled to the sentry to lift the barrier for us. I thanked him nicely in French, assured him that my fever had now abated and gave him an old Provençal remedy for hangovers which I trust he no more understood than I, and we drove through.

We now had a further hundred and thirty miles to cover to Srinagar and I hoped that with this early start we could make it well ahead of the car that Railton and the Culverton girl were sharing, and for the first couple of hours it looked as if this would be so, because the driver took the ascending slopes and sickening hairpin bends with a verve that soon had Smed-ley green round the gills. Twice on the section above Garhi, where the road is cut into the sheer wall of the cliffs, we hung miserably out into space. Smedley sat back in his corner shivering and retching and snarled, "All right, you son-of-a-bitch, so I got a load on—but so did they, and I'm damned certain we got by better because of it. If we hadn't made it a buck party the girl would have stayed on and asked ques-tions, and the others would have been sober and they might have got interested."

"Sure," I agreed. "That's just what I was thinking—when you were bellowing bush songs in pure Australian."

"You're a liar," he said. "I knew what I was doing—every minute of it."

"Maybe," I told him. "But get drunk once more before this is over and you go on alone." He went back into sullen silence after this, breaking it only to curse the driver peevishly on the stiffer turns, and eventually he went to sleep.

We were getting into the mountains now, before the road descends into the valley of Kashmir itself, and it was striking

119

cold and a thin mist of rain was sweeping down from the higher peaks. Through rents in the cloud I could see in the distance the soaring, ragged edges of the Karakoram range, and already there was snow on the upper slopes. Our way lay up through there and it looked damned unpromising.

Despite the cold the radiator was boiling before we got to the highest point of the road and we had to stop to let it cool off before we refilled from a wayside torrent. I went back to a bend and surveyed the way we had come. The rain had stopped for a moment and under the canopy of cloud the air was crystal clear and I could see miles down the valley behind us to where the road snaked round the surrounding hills, twisting, winding and often bending right back on itself. Away in the distance microcosms were moving up towards us and when the sun shone fitfully through gaps I could see flashes of light off windscreens. This was the first upward moving convoy of the day—cars and lorries geared to the speed of the slowest of them, and on whom we had stolen a lead of at least an hour. I cheered up considerably, and when I went back to the car I was almost civil to Smedley, but he was now wrapped in gloomy dignity and would have none of it.

We got going again, downward now, and both of us sat hunched and tense, gripping the edge of the seat on the bends as the driver took them two-wheeled—a blackened butt of a cigarette dangling in the corner of his mouth except when he took one hand off the wheel to flick the ash delicately out of the window. That usually occurred on the extreme tip of the hairpin, before, with a shuddering last-second bash on the brake, he pulled the hurtling car screaming round on itself to take the next descent. Hill drivers are a race apart with a technique all their own. Petrol costs good rupees and no man in his senses wastes it, so they coast down the slopes in neutral with the engine switched off and rely on their brakes and Allah. This was a private car and one in good condition. In the hired ones there is usually a notice on the back of the driving seat; "Please not to be interfering with driver. He is knowing best. Penalty fifty rupees." I had had previous experience so I just sat and sweated while Smedley ground out agonized curses through clenched teeth, and at times even prayed a little with his bloodshot eyes tight closed. He said, "Can't you do something with this ape?"

"It's his way or not at all. I know these—" I began, but that was as far as I got, because the moving finger had written, and this particular pitcher had had its tally of trips to the well. We came screaming round a blind bend to meet an upward straggle of loaded donkeys, fat-tailed sheep, sundry lean cattle and many goats. Behind them a Kashmiri family of father, mother, all four grandparents and hordes of yelling

120

children drove them in a solid phalanx towards us. By a miracle of split-second co-ordination the driver got foot and hand brakes hard on and his wheel wrenched over to the inner side of the road, and we did the last twenty yards broadside, all four wheels locked hard. The livestock escaped; animals that use the hill roads are either quick or dead—and the farmer's family seemed to get away with it also, leaping for the upper slope or bounding over the lower one like chamois. Only the car suffered—or so we thought in those first stupified moments after we had slid to rest in the ditch.

We crawled out and gazed at the debacle. The radiator had met an outgrowing stump and was pushed back over the engine block, and the near-side front wheel was twisted round crazily on its stub-axle. That much we saw at a glance and we needed to look no further. The car had had it.

The driver was shrieking abuse at the Kashmiris who were hurling it back while still slithering round the hillside rounding up their scattered animals, and Smedley was adding to the din, threatening mayhem all round, so it was some minutes before we noticed the old man half hidden between the car and the cliffside. He had been caught by that wild slide and pinned against the rocks, and what we saw when we looked closer silenced even Smedley. The family, once the animals had been collected again, came drifting back and sent up a concerted wail but offered nothing constructive until I had cuffed some of the elder males quiet, then we heaved and sweated and lifted the car out a foot or so and pulled the old man clear. Smedley said, "The poor old devil's a write-off. I *told* you to do something about this crazy bastard."

He looked a write-off, but as we laid him down on the edge of the road he whimpered faintly and that set the family off again. I bent over him and examined him closely and my heart sank. I can cope with field dressings and rough-and-ready first aid, but this was patently beyond me. I said, "Get the pannier out." Smedley got it and between us we made shift to stanch the bleeding from the more obvious wounds and I straightened and splinted an arm and a leg with pieces of wood torn from one of their packsaddles. We got blankets out of our kit and wrapped him in some, and made a shelter against the rain with others. The family were by this time sitting in a circle round us, patiently waiting for the miracle that the blasted driver was promising them—for were we not doctor sahibs from beyond the sea, of a wisdom greater than that of the nine Gurus themselves? To get those eyes off me while I worked impotently on the old man, I set them all collecting wood from the hillside and then they made a fire in a way known only to a people who live half their lives in mist and rain. The driver had completed his inspection of the car and

121

he was walking round in circles repeating dolorously "Khatm hogia—kholos—no good—finish," and calling down curses on all Kashmiris. Smedley, with his unerring nose, had found a bottle of brandy in the pannier and had taken a two-fingered belt at it before I wrested it away from him. I followed suit myself and then forced a little between the toothless gums of the patient before sending the bottle over the edge of the cliff. Smedley moaned hollowly.

There was nothing more I could do now. I sat back on my heels and lit a cigarette and tried to think. By my reckoning the convoy behind us should be up within the hour. They could take the old man the hundred miles or so on to hospital in Srinagar if he lasted that long—and us too. But that would mean police inquiries, statements from ourselves and witnesses and perhaps even an inquest. Alternatively we could now leave him here with a reasonably clear conscience and get under cover—hitching a ride into Srinagar on a later vehicle which we could leave before we actually got to the city. That seemed the more sensible course. There would be a hue and cry for us, naturally, but with luck we could be under cover and on our way before it got really serious. I was on the point of telling Smedley this when a car came round the bend behind us.

Like ourselves it had been running free in neutral and our first knowledge of it was when it skidded to a stop alongside us. Railton and the girl got out and came across.

Railton said, "Hell—what's happened?" I mumbled, "The accident," and beckoned frantically behind my back for Smedley to come and take over. He climbed out of the car where he had been sheltering from the rain and gave a quick thumbnail sketch in broken English and German. The girl stooped under the blanket shelter and looked at the patient and then came out again quickly.

"He is bleeding badly," she said in perfect French.

"Ja—ja," said Smedley. "It iss bad. We must get him to hospital. You take?"

"Our car would be no use. He must travel flat. Surely you can see that?" she answered, still in French.

We both nodded, profoundly and she looked at us curiously for a moment and then turned back to the old man. She examined his bandages closely and evidently didn't like what she saw because she made certain quick, deft changes and then, catching sight of the pannier, she started to go through it. She pulled out a couple of bottles and looked at the labels. "Plasma," she said. "Don't you think it might be advisable to give him some?"

Smedley and I exchanged quick glances. The girl turned back to the pannier and continued to go through the contents.

122

Smedley said, "Fraulein—mam'selle—my colleague and I —we—we are hit in the head. We do what we can but—" he rolled his head from side to side and essayed, successfully, to look a very sick man. "We shall be grateful for your help," he finished, and smiled wanly.

She nodded abstractedly and went on with her rummaging, and then she bent over the patient again. She sniffed closely. "With that headwound I should suspect concussion, shouldn't you?" She flung the question over her shoulder at us both.

"Ja—jawohl, gnadige fraulein," agreed Smedley. "Concussion—oh, yes."

She straightened and wheeled on us. "Then who has been giving him brandy?" she demanded.

Smedley played it straight back. "The driver," he said, and added confidentially, "A great fool."

"All right then," said the girl, "if you agree about the plasma, shall we get on with it?"

We both nodded. She stood looking at us for a further full moment and I didn't know what to do with my hands. Our sham was hanging about us like tattered rags. She shrugged and turned back to the pannier and thereafter addressed all her remarks to Railton. In a matter of minutes they had rubber bandages and transfusion needles ready and she chased the two drivers round in circles getting seats out of both cars and making a bed, heating water and preparing the plasma bottles. Smedley and I she ignored completely.

The head of the truck convoy arrived as she finished, and we halted it and Railton got a space cleared for the patient in the back of one of the leading vehicles. The family now set up another howl but the girl dealt with them calmly and gently and had reassured them before climbing into the truck herself. Smedley and I, by common consent started to slink away down the column. She stood up and looked over the tailboard at us. "I think *one* of you might come up here and ride with the patient also," she said accusingly. She pointed at me. "You," she added. There was nothing for it. I went forward like a man onto the scaffold. Fair play to Smedley, he moved with me. "One of you, I said," she repeated. "There's no room for you both. Bring the pannier with you."

"You sure you'll be all right up there?" asked Railton anxiously.

"Perfectly," answered the girl. "You take the other—doctor—with you in the car. Take it slowly and don't let this driver pass you." There was the faintest stress on the word Doctor.

I climbed up beside her, and passengers and drivers from the other vehicles got back amid a storm of chatter, and we lurched forward. She sat on the floorboards and watched

123

the patient closely, bolstering him against the roll of the truck as we took the bends. I sat down the other side of him and did the same and we rode for a long time in silence. I dreaded the inevitable breaking of it. When it came it was another question in French, and one I hardly understood, but it had something to do with where I had qualified. I had had enough.

I said in English, "You know perfectly well I'm not a doctor—or a Frenchman, either."

"I rather guessed it," she said drily.

"Your mother and father are very well," I said irrelevantly. "We stayed with them a few days ago."

"If that's meant to reassure me, it doesn't," she said coldly. "I've got rather strong views on masqueraders who usurp medical privilege."

"I'm sorry," I told her. "It was forced on us. We were being pressed rather hardly."

"I don't know who or what you are," she blazed, "and I'm certainly not interested in your private intrigues, but a few —a *very* few of us, are trying to do what we can for these people up here. The W.H.O. are trusted by both sides. If you thugs start sheltering behind their badge for your own rotten little ends they're going to be barred—"

"I'm not a thug and I'm not sheltering behind anything," I said. "The accident was not our fault—and we did what we could."

"So I noticed," she said contemptuously.

"What the hell else could we have done?" I demanded. I was getting angry myself now.

"Keep out of Kashmir altogether—you and all your kind," she spat. "There's enough trouble here without carpet-baggers bringing more in."

"All right then—we're carpet-baggers. What are you going to do about it?" I asked.

"*I* don't need to do a thing. The Srinagar police will do it. I hope you've got some strong backing. You'll need it," she said with vicious satisfaction, and bent over the patient.

I said, "I suppose it's no use trying to explain—"

"Not a bit."

I swallowed hard. "All right, Florence Nightingale," I said. "Suppose you stop waving your lamp in my eyes. We've got a long journey ahead of us in a confined space—too confined. Just leave it at that until the police take over."

"I'd be glad to," she said, and there was silence thereafter. The convoy stopped at the dak bungalow at Rampur as dusk was drawing in. It was raining heavily as we climbed out stiffly and I put up my hand to help her down but she ignored it and jumped to the ground unaided. Tea and a meal of sorts was available here and I joined Smedley in the queue well behind the girl and Railton.

"How're you making out?" he asked perkily. "I'm doing all right so far."

"That's fine," I said grimly. "I've blown the gaff."

His jaw dropped. "Oh my God," he groaned. "And I've been telling that Yank what to do about his duodenal. What did she say."

"That she'll be damned glad to see the Srinagar police gather us in."

"She kidding?"

"She's not. I've met these do-gooders before. If you really want something savage I'd commend you to a mish or a near-mish who thinks you're horning in on his or her vineyard. The hers are the worst."

"Hell," he gloomed. "You really think she'd turn us in?"

"How do I know?" I snarled. "You can judge for yourself. *I'm* not riding another yard with the prissy little bitch."

"It's no good climbing up *my* frame," he said. "What are we going to do about it?"

"Nothing—until we get to Srinagar," I told him. "We'll just have to try and slip off in the dark then and hope for the best."

I finished my mug of tea and went out to find the local bus contractor to arrange for the car to be towed in, because the wretched driver was still camped alongside it up in the hills behind us. The contractor was a Sikh and an opportunist, and I had a blasphemous twenty minute session with him before we came to an agreement. When I got back to the dak bunga-low the head of the convoy had already started to move off. I searched for Smedley but could not find him, and then some-one told me that the swab had continued on in the car with Railton, so I started to look for a place on one of the remain-ing trucks but when I eventually found one I saw the girl in the light of the dak bungalow verandah humping out a mat-tress to put under the patient, and she looked wet and tired, and although I would gladly have cut her throat I felt like a heel, so I got down again and went across to help her. We got the old man settled more comfortably and then, as I held a lamp over him, she rearranged his dressings and finally gave him another shot of morphia. By the time she had finished, the rest of the convoy had moved off and we were the last vehicle. I hung the lamp on a hood strake and yelled to the driver to get going.

All this had been done in silence, but there was nothing strained about it while we had something to occupy us, but now, as the truck jolted slowly through the night and we sat with our backs braced against the shifting load I think we both

125

felt uncomfortable. I fumbled for two damp cigarettes and handed her one but she refused it with a curt shake of her head, so I shrugged and lit my own. I smoked it through with averted eyes and then flicked the butt over the tailboard into the wet night—and it *was* wet, because the rain was now coming down in a solid sheet and there was a hole in the canopy through which water was trickling down over the bags of grain behind me and I was sitting in a puddle. I pulled myself to my feet and tried to find a drier spot, but it was impossible in that confined space, so I strap-hung miserably and pulled my wet shorts away from my chilly rump with my free hand, and in doing so our eyes met. She did her best to keep a straight face but it was no good. A quirk started at the corner of her mouth, developed into a twitch and finished as a grin.

She moved her feet and said, "You'd better come over this side of the mattress."

CHAPTER 15

But the thaw didn't last. If anything things grew a little chillier after she had hunched up her knees and made room for me because, having refused one of my cigarettes, she now lit one of her own and silence clamped down again until about an hour later when we came to a checkpoint and she asked me to move to let her pass. She jumped down over the tailboard and moved off through the darkness towards the lighted police post—and this, I thought, was it. Her moment of off-guard amusement at my wet tail was not going to stop her turning us in.

I gave her a minute or so and then jumped down myself and ran through the rain to the head of the column to get hold of Smedley. Our only chance now would be to make a run for it in the darkness and then set off on foot for what I judged to be the last thirty miles or so. I splashed through puddles and sideslipped once into the brimming ditch at the side of the road and when I climbed out, soaked to the skin, the wind cut through my sodden cotton clothes. Damn the self-righteous little prig, I thought savagely.

There were some twelve trucks between ours and the barrier and they had not closed up when we halted, and since police sepoys were routing sleepy passengers out of the vehicles to check their papers by the light of guttering hurricane lamps, and I had to push through them, it took me some minutes to cover the couple of hundred yards—and by the time I got there they had raised the barrier and the first vehicle, which was the car Railton and Smedley were riding in, was actually driving through. I stopped short, cursing blindly. That meant she hadn't been quite quick enough and he had got through but I was left holding the bag. I stood irresolutely wondering just what the hell I should do now. Smedley could be written off, as the police would undoubtedly ring through from here and he would be picked up at the barrier outside Srinagar—in which case what was the use of my leaving the column and hoofing it over the last thirty miles in the rain and cold? I might as well sling it in here and now and spend the rest of the night in the comparative comfort of a cell. On the other hand the thought of this wretched girl having the satisfaction of scuppering us a few miles short of our goal brought gall and aloes to my mouth. If only I could reach Srinagar on my own and find Yev's brother, at least I would still have a slim chance of getting out of Kashmir undetected.

Horns were sounding and passengers were milling round and getting aboard again as the sepoys cleared them, and the next vehicle was already rolling through the barrier. Either she was having some difficulty in making them understand, or they were passing the buck to Srinagar, because nobody in authority came out of the post, and very soon the whole column was lumbering forward and the sepoys were hurrying back to shelter. I thought of making a jump for one of the other vehicles but while I was still weighing it up I saw her come out of the post, pause in the light for a moment and then, as the door closed behind her, run back towards our truck. So *nobody* was being stopped here. Worried and puzzled I went back myself and climbed up over the tailboard.

She was bending over the old man again and because she was kneeling in the place where I had been sitting I started to move back to my wet patch, but she finished her examination and moved her feet and made room for me again. I sat down and asked her how the patient was faring.

"He should be dead," she said shortly, "but if we can get him into bed before morning he'll have a fighting chance."

"Where are you taking him?" I asked.

"To our own place at Bhavnagar," she answered. "They're sleeping in the corridors of the Srinagar hospitals."

"Where is Bhavnagar?"

"Fifteen miles this side of Srinagar," she said. "There's a turn off from this road. Mr. Railton has gone ahead to arrange for an ambulance to pick us up."

This sounded more hopeful and I would have liked to have followed it up, but she broke things off at this stage by leaning back against the load and closing her eyes. So she hadn't squawked? Perhaps she never intended to. I sat with my elbows on my up-drawn knees, chin in hand, looking at her. I had noticed on my first meeting with her that she was pretty, and that was all, but now, with my anger abating and curiosity mounting I was able to study her closely. She was about middle height and nicely built—very nicely. Mid-twenties, I put her —but this type of genuine raven-wing brunette who has managed to keep a flawless complexion in spite of the ravages of hill wind and sun can be deceiving. Half sleeping and relaxed and with some of her earlier spleen gone, she could have ranged five years either way. If I hadn't seen her wipe her rain-wet face vigorously on the sleeve of her damp bush-jacket I would have said that her perfectly arched eyebrows had been carefully made up with black cosmetic. Her nose was straight, with delicately chiselled nostrils like those of the carved women outside the cave temples of Ellora, and her mouth was generous in repose but relieved from fullness by something of the firmness of that of her father's—a firmness that extended to the chin and saved it from soft ovality without making a snowplough out of it. I was trying to remember the color of her eyes when she opened them and they met mine, staring straight at her. She was the less confused. In fact she wasn't confused at all. She returned my look coolly and then her eyelids drooped again and I felt a complete fool until I noticed a faint flush, perceptible even in the dancing light of the lamp above us, creeping up from the line of her jaw, and I was maliciously pleased. Her eyes were blue-black, like pools of ink, and I liked them better when they weren't flashing cold sparks at me. She must have been uncomfortable because she opened them again a little while later, but this time I was prepared and I was pretending a deep interest in my nails. I caught her glance, however, and grinned at her and she looked angry. To cover it she bent over the patient again, feeling his pulse and rearranging the blankets round him, and thereafter she stayed awake until the truck ground to another stop an hour later.

The driver came round from his cab and stood blinking up at us. "We are at the road to Bhavnagar, miss-sahib," he said. "But nobody waits here and there is no light in the dak bungalow."

"Drive up towards Bhavnagar then," she told him and he started to wring his hands.

"But there is nowhere to turn round if we meet the ambulance—and I can't reverse in the dark," he wailed.

"Then we remain here until the ambulance comes," she said coolly.

"But, miss-sahib—" He was hopping with anxiety. "I have

been running at half-speed as you ordered me, and now the convoy is miles ahead. If I lose more time the barrier will be shut against me at Srinagar and I will have no time to unload before the down trip tomorrow and I am a poor man supporting many children and all my wife's family and—"

I cut him short and told him to pull into the side of the road but she snapped at me that it was no use being high-handed and told us to get the patient down and moved onto the verandah of the dak bungalow. I hate capable women and I'd have liked to have told her to go to hell—but I found myself meekly letting the tailboard down and doing as I was told. With the help of the driver and the two cab passengers we got the old man out on the mattress and carried him across the squelching compound to the bungalow, she lighting us with the hurricane lamp and cursing us like a Peshawari camel wife when we stumbled. When we had laid him down in a relatively dry spot, the others scuttled back to the truck and we watched its tail light bumping down the track and out of sight.

The dak bungalow was a wretched affair—just one room and a dilapidated verandah with a leaky roof. I took the lamp and examined the door. It was secured by a rusty chain and a huge bazaar padlock, but the wood round the staple through which the chain ran looked rotten. I went out into the rain and found a big stone and bashed at it until it gave, and the door creaked open. The room was ankle deep with dust and litter but at least it was drier than the verandah, and it was sheltered from the wind, so we dragged the mattress inside and I held the lamp while she made the old man comfortable again. She looked up at me when she had finished and I saw that she was desperately tired. I asked her how long Railton was likely to be.

She said, "It's seven miles up the track from here. That will take them over half an hour—and the same back—but Mr. Railton was going to push ahead from the last checkpoint, while we have been running at half speed so he should almost have made up the time." She sat down wearily on the end of the mattress and I perched on the medical pannier. I risked another snub and offered her a cigarette and this time she took it.

"It's good of you to wait," she said after I had lit it for her.

"What else did you expect me to do?" I asked.

"You could have gone on with the truck."

"Hardly, under the circumstances. Anyhow, I have to wait for my—er—colleague."

"Mr. Railton will take you both on to Srinagar," she said.

"Good of him," I said drily, and added, "but I'd hate to get him involved with the police."

"There's no reason why he should be," she said, blowing smoke straight ahead of her. "He can drop you both on the outskirts before you reach the last checkpoint."

"Wouldn't that make you both accessories or something?"

She shrugged. "I don't know—and quite frankly, at the moment I couldn't care less. All I want to do is to get this old man into a ward and then go to bed myself." She ground out her cigarette on the floor beside her, leaned back against the wall and closed her eyes, and this time it wasn't just to end the conversation. She was all in and she went out like a light.

I started to nod myself and once I dropped off altogether, waking up just in time to save myself rolling off my precarious perch. I looked at my watch and was startled to find that we had been here over an hour. It was getting really cold and even in her sleep the girl was shivering. There was a rough stone fireplace in the corner and leaves had blown down through the open chimney and were littering the floor. There was also the broken frame of a native bed and the remains of a roorkhee chair there, and that gave me an idea, so I carted them outside and smashed them up with the stone I had used on the door, and in a matter of minutes I had a blaze going. The girl woke up and together we dragged the patient into the warmth—then she looked at her watch and I could see that she was worried.

"They must have been delayed up there," I said.

"They shouldn't be," she answered. "We've got an ambulance from the government, and a jeep fitted for stretchers that we've done ourselves. One or other of them is always on call."

"Washaway on the track perhaps," I suggested. "This rain has been pelting down for hours now."

"Could be," she agreed dubiously. "But the road is pretty solid. Cut out of the rock mostly. Snow's the only thing that worries us and it's too early for that." She stretched out her hands to the fire gratefully. "Oh well, this helps a lot—even if we have to wait until daylight," she said.

But the dry wood was burning down rapidly, and having chalked up a few marks on the credit side I found myself as absurdly eager as a schoolboy to keep things that way, so I went out into the night to forage for more fuel. There was a lean-to shed built onto the back of the bungalow and the supports were of wood that was rotten in places. I got busy with the stone again and bashed a few of them down, ripping a chunk out of my left hand in the process. I carted the wood back and made up the fire. She saw the blood in the light of the flames and reached out and took hold of my wrist and inspected the cut, which wasn't as bad as it perhaps looked, and, brushing aside my protests, she got stuff from the pannier and cleaned and dressed it. I sat on the floor by the fire as she bent over her task, studying the top of her head and the way the lustrous hair fell away from each side of the parting and curled round the delicate column of her neck. She kept her hair short but there was nothing she could do about its thickness or the wave in it. It was almost Indian in its texture and color and I found myself looking at her nails as she worked, to see if a tell-tale darkened half-moon betrayed a trace of mixed blood in her, but they were wholly pink and her skin had that magnolia transparency that is purely Occidental. She looked up and once more caught my eye. She gave the bandage a last pat and said, "That will hold it, but you really ought to have an antitetanus jab. That lean-to has probably been used for stabling goats. Get one at the hospital when you get to Srinagar. And now if you'd stop staring at me I'd be obliged."

"I'm sorry," I said, and to cover my confusion, added, "I was just thinking how like your father you were—apart from your coloring."

"I'm not actually," she answered. "But since we're on the subject, when did you see him?"

"Two or three days ago. We stayed there overnight."

"Did he know you were coming up here?—under false colors?"

"No."

"I'm damned certain he didn't—or he'd have had you both locked up."

"As a matter of fact he did just that. We passed the night in the forage barns—with Miraj Khan and some of his boys on guard with shot guns."

"Why did he let you go?"

"Because he took my word that nothing I was doing, or was likely to do, was in any way detrimental to either Indians or the Pakistanis. I'm sorry I can't convince you of that also."

"Were you in the war?" she asked.

"I was."

"Didn't anybody ever mention a little thing called the Geneva Convention to you?"

"If you mean by that did I ever use the Red Cross as a cover for military operations, the answer is no. It wouldn't have been any use, anyhow. The Japs didn't respect it."

"Well the people up here do—both sides—but they won't much longer if you—er—"

"Carpet-baggers?" I supplied.

"Well—whatever you are—start abusing it."

"We've already gone into all that," I said, nettled. "I told

you—we had no option, other than probably getting ourselves bumped off. I've also told you I'm sorry. We'll drop the
whole wretched business when we get to Srinagar. Now can't
we forget it for the moment?"

"Who brought it up?"

"Certainly not I."

"You did. You said my father had you locked up."

"I merely said you were like your father—"

"Which is nonsense anyhow."

"—and you then asked me when I'd seen him—"

"And you said you'd been locked in the forage barn. There's
no need to shout."

"God damn and blast it—who's shouting?" I roared.

"You are—*and* swearing," she said, primly. "Please stop. I'm
not the slightest bit interested in your affairs—just so long as
you stop mountebanking as a doctor."

"I told you—we're going to. If it comes to that, we have already."

"I hope you have."

"Oh, for Christ's sake," I said wearily. "Dry up, will you."
And then I saw that she was laughing at me and I could have
wrung her neck.

"Who's been trying to bump you off?" she asked.

"Never mind," I snapped. "Anyhow, you just said you
weren't interested in my affairs."

"Only that bit. You sounded like something out of a horror
comic."

"All right. Forget it." I got up and stumped to the door and
stood for a time searching the darkness in the hope of headlights coming down the track, but there was nothing but rain
and wind and it was damned cold so I went back. I sat down
the other side of the fire and tried to go to sleep again.

I succeeded and I woke some time later stiff and cold because the fire had burnt down to a handful of embers. The
hurricane lamp was guttering too, and it looked as if it would
soon go out altogether.

I peered at my watch and saw that it was nearly two
o'clock. The girl wasn't there but I could hear her moving
about on the verandah and she came in shortly with a few
pieces of wood I had overlooked. I took them from her without a word and shoved them among the embers and blew a
little life into them and it was while I was on my hands and
knees that I heard the sound of the approaching car and I
was never gladder to hear anything in my life. She had returned to the verandah by the time I straightened. I followed
her out and we stood together watching the approaching
lights.

The car came on right to the edge of the compound and pulled up with a squeak of wet brakes. We went forward and she ripped out a stream of impolite Urdu at the driver that I couldn't have bettered myself, and then she stopped short as a man got out of the vehicle and stood between us and the lights, bulking blackly against the glare. He was only a sil-houette and completely unrecognizable—but his voice wasn't nor was the gun he held in his fist.

"Stand right where you are, Rees!" he said. "*And* you young lady!"

It was Sutcliffe.

CHAPTER 16

There were others there too because I could see figures mov-ing round the back of the car and coming up behind us. The girl reacted first. "Who are you?—and how dare you point a gun at me?"

Sutcliffe chuckled throatily. "At you? Never let it be said. It's pointed at *him*. I didn't want you getting in between us, that's all. All right—let's all get out of the rain, shall we?" The girl didn't move—so I stood my ground also. "Who are you?" she demanded again. One of the men behind us got me by the arm and spun me round. The other must have done the same to her because as I turned, her arm swung in a full arc and she caught him a magnificent open-handed slap straight across the kisser. It sounded like a pistol shot and it must have hurt. He yelped like a pi-dog and staggered back.

Sutcliffe said sharply, "Hold it, Rees, or you'll get it. Don't do that again, Miss—"

She wasn't listening though. She was pouring out blistering invective at the man who had touched her. I saw that it was a big Punjabi and his eyes were literally blazing red like those of a rabid animal. It may have been a trick of the headlights but the effect was blood-chilling. Women to him would rate be-low his cattle and possibly only just above his dogs, and he'd been struck in the face by one in front of witnesses, and was now being scientifically insulted in three languages—and he had a gun in his fist. Things were poised on the finest of razor edges and Sutcliffe realized it. He lumbered past me like a charging elephant and struck downwards at the Punjabi's

133

wrist with the chopping edge of his free hand. The other dropped his gun and Sutcliffe planted his foot on it, and the situation was under precarious control again. I tried for a split second to profit from the diversion but the man behind me jammed something hard into my ribs and the moment was lost. Sutcliffe was roaring at the Punjabi who was shrieking with rage and trying to get his hands on the girl. I said sideways to her, "Take it easy," and she told me to mind my own bloody business. Sutcliffe wheeled on her and snarled, "You do as you're told, you silly young trollop, or I'll let him at you, just to knock some sense into you. Now get going—both of you."

I thought she was going to swing on *him* then so I got my arms round her and clamped hers down to her sides and urged her forward to the bungalow. She just about came up to my shoulder but it was like handling a bag of wire snakes, and she back-heeled me in the shins. For a moment I was almost on the side of the Punjabi.

We got inside in a struggling mass and I was pushed against the wall by the fireplace. I hung on to her wrist and managed to keep her beside me. Sutcliffe said to the third man who I now saw was Snaith, "Get this ape back into the car and tell him to stay there." The Punjabi was standing in the doorway still gibbering, and Snaith had to coax him to get him out of it. Sutcliffe turned and glowered at us.

"All right," he said. "I was prepared to talk sweet reason to you, but you know the score now. Sweetness is out. Where is he?"

"Who the hell are you talking about?" I asked.

"You know who I'm talking about," he roared. "Don't give us any chalaki, Rees. Polson. Come on—spill it, or have it the hard way—like your pals."

"What pals?"

He nearly blew a valve. His lips were working soundlessly and small muscles between jawline and temples twitched. He took a deep breath and got a grip on himself. "Look here," he said in a strained, unnaturally soft voice, "Lahore is Lahore, but Kashmir's Kashmir—"

"And there's still a long term jail in the Andamans," said the girl. "Who are these louts?" She looked at me with raised eyebrows.

Sutcliffe ignored her and continued talking to me, emphasizing his words with the muzzle of his gun which he kept jabbing towards me like a pointer. "You were bloody smart down there, but not smart enough. He's up here and you're meeting him here. We know that because he was seen at the barrier this afternoon. Okay, where's he holing up? Tell us that, and give us time to check and I'll see you on your way back to 'Pindi—and that goes for Smedley and the Yank too—"

The girl turned towards me again. "For the last time—will you *please* tell me who this man is, and what on earth he's talking about?" she asked coldly.

"I'll get that Punjabi to explain, outside in the dark, if you don't shut your blasted mouth," Sutcliffe said. "Come on, Rees, what's the use of finagling? You know the ways of making a man talk as well as I do. Are you going to make us use them?"

"They don't always work apparently," I said. "You must have found that out from our pals." I was fishing now.

"Don't talk bloody silly," he snorted. "They told us within three minutes flat that they were meeting you here but they couldn't tell us where Polson was, simply because they didn't know. *You're* the guide, they said, and man, they were speaking the truth—just like you're going to, sooner or later—"

The old man on the mattress had started to stir uneasily and he was moaning faintly. The girl went forward and dropped on her knees beside him. "Get back against the wall," snapped Sutcliffe. She took not the slightest notice but went on taking the patient's pulse. He stepped towards her and stood looking down at her. "Did you hear what I said?" he barked. He might not have been there. She replaced the old man's skinny arm under the blankets, tucked them in and lifted one of his eyelids and studied the pupil carefully. Sutcliffe stood for a moment or so uncertain what to do, then he backed to the door and whistled into the night. The girl got to her feet and crossed to the medical pannier and got out some dressings. Once on the Burma border I saw a rogue elephant defied and finally brought to bay by a small terrier. This reminded me of it.

Sutcliffe had the gun on her but he couldn't keep it there because I was across the room at an angle from her. He started to swivel it back and forward between us—and now the lamp was almost going out. If only I could have relied on her to drop flat I could have done something, because in the hurly-burly they had neglected the elementary precaution of frisking me, and my own gun was still under my left arm between my shirt and my skin. But in a moment it was too late. Snaith came to the door.

"Put that bitch back against the wall," Sutcliffe told him.

Snaith hesitated. He looked at the girl and then at me and then back at Sutcliffe. "Get on with it," Sutcliffe roared.

Snaith advanced on her uncertainly. She remained on her knees rummaging into the pannier. "Come on, miss," he begged. "We don't want trouble. Do as this gentleman says." The girl carried on as if she had not heard him.

135

"Move her, damn you," roared Sutcliffe. "The bloody lamp's going out."

Snaith put out a wavering hand and touched her on the shoulder, and then screamed like a wounded hare. I've never seen anything quicker, with the possible exception of a she-cobra. She must have had the long surgical scissors in her hand all the time. She wheeled on her heels and jabbed upwards and he got them right in the pit of the belly. Sutcliffe fired but it must have been sheer reflex because an aimed shot shouldn't have missed either of us at that range. The blast of the heavy gun and the resultant eddy in that confined space put paid to the last guttering glim of the lamp. I dived for the floor tugging out my gun at the same time, just as Sutcliffe blinded off his second shot. I fired at the flash, and the two reports and his bellow were blended into one. I rolled sideways to get out of line of his next, but there wasn't one. Yelling to the girl to lie flat I crawled round the wall towards Snaith who I could see in the faint light of the fire writhing and blubbering on the floor. I got right up alongside him and shoved the muzzle in his ear which added to his grief because he evidently thought I was going to blow his brains out. But I only wanted his gun and when I had it I put my knee under his up-turned rump and hefted him into the middle of the room where I could see him without taking my eyes off the still bulk of Sutcliffe. He *was* still but I didn't know whether or not he was foxing. I said to the girl, "Can you handle an automatic?"

"Tell me the knobs and switches," she answered, as if we were discussing an electric toaster, "and I'll manage."

I wasn't risking it though. I pretended to do things to it and then passed it to her. "It's cocked now so for God's sake keep your finger off the trigger until I tell you to let one of these clients have it," I told her, and then I crept up on Sutcliffe. He was lying prone with both his hands outstretched and empty so I felt around until I found his gun on the floor in front of him. There was only the Punjabi to worry about now, and he was making things easy by calling nervously from the direction of the car, "Sahib, sahib—kya taklif hai?"

I said to Snaith, "Can that fellow drive?" but he only moaned, so I crossed to him and shook him by the shoulder.

"Don't do that, you fool," said the girl sharply. "He's probably got a punctured peritoneum." And preoccupied as I was the coolness of it nearly took my breath away. Snaith whimpered, "Oh man, I am bloody dying."

"You probably will if the Punjabi hops it in the car," I said. "If we can get you to hospital you might have a chance." It worked.

136

"He can't drive," he said, and relieved of that immediate worry I went over to Sutcliffe again and had a closer look at him. He wasn't dead, but from the pool of blood he was lying in it would only be a matter of time unless something was done for him quickly. I turned him over. The bullet had taken him on the right side and had ploughed upwards through his ribs and come out in the region of his shoulder blade. He was quite unconscious and was breathing stertorously. I passed this information to the girl and then went and had a look at Snaith. Dawn was breaking now and grey light was creeping through the half-opened door. I had to tear his hands away from his belly and almost cuff him into keeping still. *His* main trouble was he was just plain yellow. She'd certainly ploughed a ragged furrow upward across his guts, but as far as I could see it was only a fleshwound. I told her that also and then went to the door and peered round the lintel. That Punjabi was no doubt possessed of a full measure of explosive masculine pride but he was short of elementary savvy because he was standing outlined against the dark bulk of the car in full view. I called to him to put his hands up but he slid round the other side out of sight. I studied the position for some time in that tricky half light and after a full minute or so I thought I saw his turban move past the rear window and I took a shot at it. He broke cover then and ran across the compound towards the road. I was taking aim at him again when that damned woman came up behind me and grabbed my elbow.

"That's quite enough," she said.

"Sure," I agreed bitterly. "We've got to get out of here—and presumably take these people with us—and there's a Punjabi with a gun laying for us in amongst the rocks."

"If you're referring to the patients, two of them can't be moved without an ambulance. You'll have to take the car and go up to the hospital," she said.

"And leave you here?"

"Naturally."

"Don't be stupid, woman," I nearly spat.

"Very well then," she said. "I shall go and you can remain."

"That's out too," I said firmly. "We'll both go."

"And leave the patients unattended?"

"They won't hurt for an hour."

"Possibly not—but I'd prefer somebody remained with them."

I counted ten and took a deep breath and had another try. "Listen," I began, patiently—reasonably. "The position is as follows— One—" I started to enumerate on my fingers.

"I'm neither a child nor an imbecile, Mr.—er—Rees, isn't it?" She was being patient and reasonable too. You could

137

have cut it with a knife. "Either you go up for the ambulance and I stay here—or *I* go and *you* stay here. We surely don't need a blackboard demonstration."

"No," I said. "You're neither a child nor an imbecile. I could make my point with either of those. You're just an insufferably smug, self-satisfied young woman, and you're striking attitudes. Who the hell are you trying to impress? Me?—or yourself? If I go, that Punjabi would be in here before I'd got half a mile up the road—"

"I can protect myself," she blazed.

"Yeah? What with? That gun? You don't even know how to hold the damn thing, let alone fire it—and it would take more than a pair of scissors to hold *that* goondah off. On the other hand if you attempt to go up the road on your own he could pick you off from under cover and we're right back where we started—on our flat feet. Be sensible for Pete's sake. We go together. You drive and leave me free to cover you. Now come on. We're wasting time." I went to the door and looked out again. The light was improving rapidly and there was an open space of some fifty yards between us and the car. I grabbed her arm and shot out of the door and raced for it. She dragged back at first but then gave up and ran with me. I think she saw the sense of my plan but she just hated agreeing with me. We tumbled into the front seat and she slid behind the wheel, switched on and searched for the starter button—and when she found it there was a dull, reluctant churning under the hood and then nothing. The battery was flat. Cursing a blue streak I scrabbled round on the floor for a starting handle—but there wasn't one, so I wrenched the keys out of the ignition switch and climbed out and went round to the trunk to see if the wretched thing was there—and it was then that the first shot came. The bullet shattered the glass of the rear window right above my head as I bent over the lock. I hit the wet ground before the echoing reverberation had died away and shot round the car on all fours like a jack-rabbit, putting its bulk between me and the firer. I yelled to the girl to lie flat and I peered round the front wheel hoping to place the flash of the next one. From the bungalow I could hear Snaith's voice raised in bleating plaint. The girl called, "Have you got the handle?"

"No I haven't," I snarled. "But I damn nearly got a bullet in the backside."

"How far away is he?" she asked.

"How the devil do I know? Lie flat on the floor and shut up," I told her.

"That's not going to get us anywhere," she said coolly. "We're on a slight slope here. I suggest you nip back inside and I'll release the handbrake, and roll."

There was something in that though I hated admitting it. I didn't answer for a moment or so then reluctantly agreed. "All right," I said, "only you stay where you are and let me do the driving." I darted out of cover and dived for the door and another shot rung out, but it was wider than the first. She was already in the driving seat and I swore at her again but she just held out her hand for the key, switched on, shoved the car into gear and let go the handbrake. We crawled forward a few inches and then almost came to a stop. I bounced frantically up and down on the seat to try and gain some momentum, but the slope was too gentle. "I'm going to give her a shove," I said and wrenched the door open again. I got my shoulder against the front door post and heaved and we made another foot or so and then the slope increased and we started to roll. She could drive—I'll say that for her. She didn't make the mistake of slipping her clutch in too soon but held on until we had gathered speed and then, when we were almost in the ditch at the side of the road, she let her left foot come up and banged her right hard down. Cars don't start easily in damp hill air and if she'd missed the first time our front wheels would have been bogged hard in the ditch, but it came off and after one agonizing hesitation the engine took up and coughed and sputtered. The girl slipped her clutch again and revved up hard before engaging and then we bumped up onto the road and shot off towards the junction. I hadn't heard any more shots in the flurry of that last couple of minutes, but now a bullet smacked through the coachwork above our heads—and then we were round the corner of the junction and speeding up the track. It was only one car's width and the surface was rough and uneven and she was taking it too fast. I said, "All right—you can ease up. We're out of range now." She didn't answer. She took the next three turns almost flat out and I was clinging to the edge of the seat in a cold sweat.

"Ease up, for God's sake," I shouted at her.

"Suppose you leave it to me," she shot out of the side of her mouth. "You haven't been too brilliant so far." It was nothing but temper, of course, but I was damned if I was going to let her break my neck because of it, so I reached forward and switched off.

"Get out of that seat," I said, "before I pull you out."

Her eyes blazed hate at me for a moment then, because I think she realized that I meant just that, she opened the door on her side and got out. "All right, Mr. Rees," she said coldly. "You do better. There's something wrong with this car. If you don't keep your foot hard down she'll stall. Don't forget I rode up from 'Pindi in it." It was only then that I realized that this mud-caked veteran was the car that Smedley and

139

Railton had been riding in and the one from which she had changed into the truck. I slid behind the wheel and she walked round and got into the seat I had vacated. I switched on again and pressed the starter—and got the same dull thump from the almost dead battery. I didn't dare look at her but I could sense her satisfaction and from the corner of my eye I could see her hands folded primly in her lap.

We were on a sharp upward slope so I slipped into reverse and ran back but the slope ended in a bend and all I did was to jam our back wheels into the ditch without starting the engine. Nearly choking with rage I got out and went round again to the trunk and unlocked it. It was a large trunk, which was fortunate—because Smedley, trussed like a chicken and gagged with an oily cleaning rag, was in it.

The girl heard my startled yelp and looked round and, seeing me standing there staring goggle-eyed, her curiosity got the upper hand and she climbed out and came back to us. I was already pulling off the coils of sticky insulating tape that were keeping the gag in place and it must have been painful because he was telling me so when the rag came out of his mouth—richly and expressively. I clamped it back again quickly and said, "Cut it out. We've got company."

He was bound with the thin strong cord hill drivers tie loads onto the roof with, and they had done an expertly cruel job on him because his wrists and legs were swollen and purple. We didn't have a knife between us so it was a hell of a job getting the knots undone and it took some time. The girl pushed me aside when we finally got him free. She started to chafe some circulation back into his limbs and he squirmed in agony. She wouldn't let him talk as we got his cramped limbs straightened and eased him gently out of the trunk—not that he wanted to after that first outburst of obscenity. He moaned as his feet touched the ground, and his legs buckled under him. We got him into the back seat and I left the girl with him and went round to look for the starting handle again. I found it this time and after several abortive swings I got the engine running. Smedley was a little recovered by the time we got under way. I wanted to ride with him to get his story but she had gone all Florence Nightingale again now that she had another patient on the slab, and she insisted on staying in the back and continued to chafe his wrists.

She was right about the car. Her way was the only one with that cranky rattletrap, and I had the very devil of a job over the few miles to the top of the rise and although I roared questions at Smedley over my shoulder his answers were drowned in the tortured scream of the engine, so I gave it up.

We got to the hospital at last. It was quite a big place, com-

140

pletely isolated on the end of a spur that jutted out into the valley. It was built of stone and surrounded by a high wall and it was only as we drove in under the crumbling archway that I recognized it for what it once had been. It was one of the old Sikh forts that dot those hills and date back to the days of Ranjit Singh. It had started to rain again and the courtyard was deserted but there was activity inside the main building and smoke rose from most of the godowns that lined the inner walls. I pulled up inside and looked round at her inquiringly and she pointed to a small bungalow that stood on its own to the right of the archway. I drove across and a woman came out onto the verandah as we stopped. She was middle-aged, matronly, garrulous and American. She ran down the steps towards us with her arms flapping like semaphores.

"Claire! What on *earth* has happened to you? Where have you *been?* Henry Railton I've a good mind to scalp you. *You* told me on the phone—"

"Henry's not with us," the girl cut her short. "We've got a patient here and another three down at the dak bungalow. We'll want the ambulance."

"But we're full! Lands' sakes girl, you know that," shrieked the other, but we were already pulling Smedley out of the car so she shrugged hopelessly and shot back into the bungalow ahead of us and as we came slowly up the steps we could hear her yelling, "Bhimabai— Bhimabai—three beds—no four beds. Where? I don't know, but get 'em—"

Smedley grunted painfully. "I don't want a bed. I'll settle for a drink." We lowered him into a chair and the girl left us.

I said, "I've got to go down the hill again with that virago. Can you tell me what happened in about six words?"

"Just like I said in the car," he said wearily. "We're driving along in the dark last night—Railton reckoned we had about another six miles to go before we turned off to this place— when there's a light in the middle of the road. The driver pulls up and I heard somebody yaking in the language. The driver says it's another police check and would we get out. We did, and I could just make out four Indians in the dark. One of them spoke a bit of pidgin English and he asks us our names. Railton gives his and puts his hand in his inside pocket to get his papers, and that was it. He just got beaned on the spot by someone standing behind him. I tried to duck round the car and get my gun out but I hadn't a chance. Something weighing half a ton hit me right on top of the head and I went out like a light. I came to in a little low-roofed dump that stunk to high heaven of goats. I'm lying on the floor and Railton is sitting up being sick. There's a couple of Indians there with guns. They're eating curry and—"

"Never mind the details," I said. "That girl will be back soon and I want the outline first. Go on."

"Well, later on those two yegs we saw in Lahore arrived by car— You know—the European and the half-chat—"

"Sutcliffe and Snaith?—get *on* with it man."

"Aren't I doing it? Well, they look at *me* and seem quite happy, but the big one—Sutcliffe—raises hell with the Indians when he sees Railton. I couldn't understand what they were saying, of course, but it was pretty obvious that he's ticking them off for bringing the wrong bloke. They're all shouting the odds together when Railton gets up and joins in. He's sore —and can you blame him? He still thinks they're police and he'd demanding to be taken to headquarters in Srinagar and he also wants them to send up to the hospital to get an ambulance down to the road junction to meet Miss Culverton who's following up in a truck. In other words he throws the whole thing. Not his fault of course. He even enlarges on it. He says 'This gentleman,' meaning me, 'is an official on highly confidential business—and so's the other one with Miss Culverton' —which is what I told him when he found out I wasn't a doctor or a German—'and some cops in this division are going to lose their jobs.' Well—that was it. They had all they wanted. Sutcliffe apologizes to him and tells him there are wheels within wheels and that it will all be sorted out in the end blah, blah, blah—but that he's afraid Railton will have to remain here for a time while he takes me off for questioning. Railton says the hell with that, he's going to see the top policeman *and* his consul, and starts to stalk out to the car— or so he thought. They just bean the poor devil again before he'd taken two steps. That's the last I saw of him because then they bring in some rope and adhesive tape and truss me up and carry me out and stick me in that damn trunk and we drive off. It seemed like three weeks. I heard all the shooting and I'm waiting for one to come through the trunk—and then you open up."

The older woman came back then followed by a couple of white-saried ayahs and despite Smedley's roars of protest they started to get his clothes off. I left them to it and went out onto the verandah just in time to meet the girl hurrying up the steps. She said, "I've got the ambulance ready. You're under no obligation to come with me, but the couple of Indian servants we've got here wouldn't be much use if that wretched Punjabi is still on the rampage."

"I'll come," I said shortly, and followed her down the steps.

Smedley, deserted, was raising Cain and trying, apparently without success, to hold on to his pants and his dignity.

CHAPTER 17

There was no argument about who was driving this time. *She* was; foot hard down and two-wheeling on those sickening bends, with me squirming and cursing on the seat beside her, and two scared Kashmiri ward-boys bouncing like peas in the back of an ex-army ambulance that I'll swear had no brakes. We slithered to a stop in front of the dak bungalow compound after fifteen minutes of absolute hell, and she whipped into reverse and backed across the uneven ground to the verandah, halting a bare foot clear of the steps. She jumped down and hustled the boys into the bungalow with stretchers before I had time to get my paralyzed legs working again, which, since the Punjabi might quite well have been inside waiting for us, was stupid of her. However, he wasn't, and as I got down and started to scan the hillside above us, they brought the patients out—first the old man and then Sutcliffe and finally, whimpering but on his own feet, Snaith. The old man had come round and he was swearing weakly and querulously, but Sutcliffe looked as poor an insurance risk as I've ever seen. His face was ghastly—bloodless and yellow under his tan and his almost white lips were drawn back in a fixed grin of pain. He seemed to be coming round a little because I saw his eyes open and roll from side to side as they brought him into the light.

We slid the two stretchers into their clips then I motioned one of the ward-boys up into the passenger's seat and climbed myself into the back with the other. The ambulance started forward with a jerk and swung round in an arc, and we were off on our return trip within a matter of minutes. This time, thank God, she took it slowly and I was able to breathe again. I sat on watch with my pistol in my hand peering out over the tailboard until we turned up the track again and started our ascent. I asked the ward-boy if he spoke English and he shook his head, so I shifted my seat and sat down beside Snaith.

I said, "You're in a lot of trouble, Snaith." He snuffled and swivelled his oystery eyes sideways at me but didn't answer.

"Armed hold-up, abduction and attempted murder," I went on. "That should hold you quite a time. This young lady is the daughter of an influential man and she stands ace-high with Government. Martial law up here—and now the Americans will be interested too. You don't stand a chance."

143

"Can't you leave a man alone?" he whined. "That damn woman nearly disembowelled me. The law works both ways you know, Mr. Rees."

"Don't talk like a sap. She was entitled to. You were attacking her. Attacking her while she was in the act of succouring an injured Indian. Can you imagine what a military court is going to do to *you?*"

He wriggled like an eel on a hook and it hurt him, because he turned green and groaned. "You know I wasn't, Mr. Rees. You know I was only asking her to move to the wall while Sutcliffe was getting things sorted out," he wailed.

I shook my head. "You and your gang of thugs had already attacked and carried off two law-abiding citizens—one of them an American—then you stuck us up and attempted to manhandle the lady. You were impersonating police officers. Work it out for yourself. If she gets through to headquarters you're sunk."

"What are you trying to do, Mr. Rees?" he moaned. "Aren't I in enough trouble without you trying to frame me further? Give me a chance, for God's sake."

"Nothing to do with me," I told him. "She's the one who'll be laying the charges. I don't *want* to be called as a witness but if I am I'm not going to pull any punches—neither are Smedley and Railton. How about a deal?"

He looked at me sideways. "What deal?" he asked suspiciously.

"I can't promise anything," I said, "but come clean and I'll do what I can for you."

"I don't know anything, Mr. Rees," he said earnestly. "Nothing that signifies anyhow. Sutcliffe's the man you've got to talk to— *He* dragged me into it."

"Pity," I said, and lit a cigarette. I blew out a lungful of smoke and flicked the match over the tailboard and then leaned back and closed my eyes. I could feel him wriggling beside me.

"I don't *know* anything, I tell you," he squeaked at last.

"That's fine," I said wearily. "You just came along for the ride. All right—stick to that. They might believe you. It won't stop you swinging a pick on the Indus dam for the next ten years or so. You know these people as well as I do. Better."

He took one hand away from his belly just long enough to wipe the sweat from his face and I could hear him almost sobbing. I still kept my eyes closed. Then I felt him clawing at my sleeve.

"Listen, Mr. Rees," he said. "Listen—this is the God's truth —as true as I'm sitting here. I'm trying to pick up a few rupees round Lahore station doing commission work for Mohammed Aziz, the bus and taxi contractor. Sutcliffe gets off the Karachi mail a couple of mornings ago and he sees me and takes me for a drink. He asks me if I want to earn five hundred chips. What was I to say? As far as I knew he was still working for the H.C.'s office. I said okay. He said all I had to do was to look official while he was talking to a couple of Europeans. We go along to Nedou's and we see you—and as God's my judge I knew nothing more than that. We went down to the lounge like you said and we waited for you for half an hour, then Sutcliffe gets a bit uneasy so we go back to your room and you've all gone. He nearly goes mad. He tells me to get the hell out of it, and doesn't pay me what he's promised—only a hundred chips. I got sore but there was nothing I could do about it. I go back to Mohammed Aziz's office and when I get there there's a car just leaving with Polson and that Pathan of yours in it. I make some inquiries and find out that it's a special booking for Abbottabad, and that the driver's got to go like hell to connect with the Kashmir mail truck in the morning. I go back to Sutcliffe and ask him what the information's worth—and when he coughs up the four hundred he owes me I tell him. What happened after that I can't say, but he does a lot of telephoning, then he promises me another five hundred if I'll stay with him, and we go out to the airfield and get the plane to 'Pindi. We get a car from there and come up the road, and Sutcliffe is scattering baksheesh like confetti to pick up news about the lot of you. Nobody knows about you two, but we find out that Polson and the Pathan are on the convoy ahead of us—going by the Abbottabad road—so we come the quick way and try and cut them off here. Sutcliffe has brought some toughs of his up from 'Pindi and we lay up at the side of the road and stop all cars coming up on their own—and leave the toughs five miles further down to deal with any that come up the by-pass. We stop three but draw blank—and then the others send word up that they've got hold of two Europeans who answer to the description of you and Smedley. They've taken them to a goatherd's shanty just off the road. We go down and we find Smedley all right, but the other fellow is an American and he's raising hell. We have to knock him out."

"What have you done with him?" I asked.

"We left him tied up there."

"Anybody with him?"

"Yes—all the goondahs—less the Punjabi—"

"Where is it exactly?"

"Just this side of the Abbottabad turn-off. It's a hundred yards or so off the road on the right as you come up—"

"All right—go on."

"Well, we know now that you and this bloody murdering woman are coming up with the convoy and that you've got

145

an accident case with you, and that an ambulance is supposed to meet you at the dak bungalow—and, well, that's it. You know the rest, Mr. Rees. As far as I'm concerned it's government work Sutcliffe is on—I didn't ask questions—and you can't prove anything to the contrary. I know the law—I've been a police officer. It's all legitimate as far as I'm concerned—I was only trying to help and all I got was an assault with an offensive weapon and suffered grievous bodily harm —she can get into trouble herself for that—under Section 17 Indian Penal Code— It hasn't been changed—I know the law—" He was blubbering and howling.

I let him be until he had run down like tired clockwork and when there was silence except for an occasional shuddering sniffle I whipped a quick one in. "Who's Sutcliffe working for?" I asked.

"I tell you I don't know!" he screamed. "You bloody bastard—I've told you all I know." He was beside himself with stark fear. He had rolled off the seat and was pounding on the floor with both fists, and the ward-boy was sitting bolt upright in the corner, bewildered and scared. If Snaith had anything more to tell, now was the time to get it out of him. I doubted it, but it was worth another half-twist of the screw.

I said, "You're a liar—and I'll see you go down for ten years—" Then I realised that the ambulance had stopped in the courtyard and that the girl was looking at us over the tailboard.

"You filthy, bullying, beast," she said to me—slowly, distinctly and with a pause between each word. Snaith stopped in midpounding and looked at her, mouth open and drooling spit—and it dawned on him slowly that here was somebody who disliked me and was therefore a potential ally.

"Miss—miss, please—I'm a sick man and I've been cheated and lied to by that damned Sutcliffe—and now this man is threatening me with more lies—" he quavered.

"That's enough," she said sharply, and dropped the tailboard. "Come on—down with you, and up those steps." Snaith shot me a vicious look and scuttled down from the ambulance quickly, and then remembered his wound and crawled painfully up the steps into the bungalow. The girl watched him go, then turned back to me.

"Mr. Rees," she began coldly. "While you're here you will please remember—"

"Skip it," I cut in. "I'm going. You might tell Smedley that, will you? If he feels up to travelling he is at liberty to come with me; if not, he can make his own arrangements."

"*I* shall decide when Mr. Smedley is fit to travel," she said.

"Tell him that too," I snarled, and started to walk to the other car. The American woman came out then, shrieking

146

questions and waving her arms. "Oh, for God's sake, Ethel— later," I heard the girl say. "Shift these patients into bed and try and get Dr. Mitra down from Srinagar. I think the European is going to die."

I wrenched the car door open and started to pull the luggage out of the back and dump it on the ground. I had no intention of leaving Smedley there but I felt that if I stayed within arm's length of this female for another minute there would be a regrettable incident. I also had to do something about Railton. With four or five armed goondahs guarding him, what that something was to be I hadn't the faintest idea, but the first thing was obviously to locate the hut Snaith had mentioned. I got the last bag out and then took the starting handle round to the front of the car and I saw her walking across towards me. I turned my back on her and started to fit the handle into the hole.

She said, "Oh no you don't, my friend. There are several things to be cleared up before you go."

"They'll just have to wait," I told her. "I've got more urgent things to attend to at the moment. Suppose you give Smedley my message?" I gave the engine a hefty swing and for once it started first time but before I could get the handle out she had walked back to the driving seat and switched off and removed the key. We stood looking at each other in silence for a full minute, I trying to get a grip on myself before risking speech, she hefting the key in her palm.

"Give it to me," I said at last, and my voice was shaking.

"You heard what I said," she answered.

"And you heard what *I* said." I stepped towards her, but before I could grab her wrist she had dropped the key down the neck of her shirt. I stopped short and for a moment I was tempted to stand her on her head and shake the damned thing out of her. She seemed to guess it because she said, "I wouldn't try it if I were you. Now you listen to me. The sooner you and your friend are clear of this place the better I shall like it—but I've got to get a doctor down to that man. Even if he doesn't die, a bullet wound has to be explained. There'll be questions asked—and I don't know any of the answers. You'll wait."

You don't *have* to have the key to get an engine mobile; you can always short the wires through the ignition switch— but I knew that all she would need to do would be to stand by and jerk them free each time I went round to the front of the car. The bitch had me cold, and, to add to my impotent rage, a ring of small children now stood round us regarding us with stolid curiosity, and the other woman was back on the verandah yelling, "Claire! Claire! The doctor's on his way down— but will you come in here, girl, and *tell* me something?"

"All right," called the girl. "Now get through to the police post and tell them I want the inspector down as well."

That settled it. I said, "You win—but in the meantime your friend Railton is in trouble—"

"That's the first point I want cleared up," she answered. "Where is he?"

"A few miles down the road. Whether you believe it or not that's where I was going."

"I think you're playing it off the cuff," she said.

I shrugged. "All right. Have it your own way—but you can ask that little rat you stuck all about it. I had it from him on the way up."

She stood pondering for a moment, and in the meantime the other woman had shot back into the bungalow. I went on, "Get the police down if you want to, but it will take time for them to get here—and from what I gather, Railton is in a bit of a spot. He's tied up like Smedley was—in a hut, with a bunch of goondahs."

"What could *you* do?—on your own?"

"That remains to be seen. All I wanted to do in the first instance was to find the place. They *may* have pushed off now that they know that Sutcliffe and Snaith have had it. Even if they haven't, they'll be a bit demoralized."

"I still think we ought to have the police down," she said, but there was a shade of doubt in her voice.

"Please yourself," I said, and I tried to sound casual, but through the open door of the bungalow I could see the other woman twisting the handle of the telephone and jiggling the hook up and down. The girl hesitated a few more seconds, then she turned and walked quickly across and went up the steps. I followed her, sweating.

"All right, Ethel—hold it for a moment," she said, and I halted in the doorway and breathed again.

The woman jammed the receiver down on the hook and turned round exasperatedly. "Claire—just what *is* going on? You know the police are the *last* people we want here until—"

The girl cut her short with a look and gestured to an inner door and they went through and closed it behind them.

The bungalow appeared to be their private quarters and the large central room in which I stood was furnished spartanly as a sitting-room. Doors led off it to a couple of bedrooms and a short passage ran down to a kitchen in the rear. The rooms the other side seemed to be given over to patients, however, because I could see the ends of white-sheeted hospital beds, and nursing ayahs were hurrying in and out with trays. Through an open door I saw Smedley sitting disconsolately on the end of a bed wrapped in a blanket dressing-gown. I went through to him and he jumped up as I approached.

"For Christ's sake get my clothes back and let's get the hell

148

out of here," he said plaintively. "That damn woman's mad. She got four of those bints in to undress me and give me a bath, and I was too stiff to do anything about it."

"How do you feel now?" I asked him.

"All right. There was nothing wrong with me except cramp and a headache—but try telling them. Well—what goes on?"

"The young one was all for phoning the police at first, but I think we're safe for the moment," I told him. "We'll have to go down to where they took you and see what's happened to Railton."

"That's going to hold us up some more," he grumbled.

"Maybe," I said. "But we can't leave the bloody man there. The only alternative would be to let them call the police and that would snooker things completely."

"Um—I suppose you're right," he agreed reluctantly.

I heard the women come back into the big room and I went back with Smedley cowering behind me. The girl said, "All right, Mr. Rees. If you're ready we'll go off."

"We?" I said, startled.

"Naturally. You wouldn't be much use on your own if those people are still there. Besides, you can't handle that car properly." She turned towards the door.

"I'd rather you stayed here," I said. "Smedley is all right now. He'll come with me."

The older woman noticed him for the first time. "Back into bed," she said firmly. "You've got a temperature." Smedley sidled away from her like a startled mare. I hurried after the girl.

"I know it's no use arguing with you—" I began.

"Splendid," she answered drily, leading the way towards the car.

"At the same time," I went on, "I think Smedley ought to come with us. There will quite likely be trouble."

She hesitated for a moment then nodded and went back and I heard her voice in argument with the other woman, and after a while she came back and got behind the wheel and fished for the key. I swung the engine again and as it roared, Smedley came galloping across to us tucking his shirt into his shorts and looking back over his shoulder. I got in beside the girl and he climbed into the back. As we drove out under the archway I handed him Sutcliffe's gun which I was still carrying as well as my own.

It all ended in anti-climax, because Railton was coming towards us, trudging along in the middle of the road with his hands in his pockets and his shoulders hunched against the rain which was just starting again. We squealed to a stop and I jumped out and ran towards him.

He looked a mess. Blood had trickled from under his tousled hair and had congealed in a streak down one side of his face. One eye was blackened and closed and his lips were swollen and cut. I led him back to the car and helped him in beside Smedley. He was dazed and confused and the girl didn't want him to talk, but as we sped back up the road I could hear him carrying on a muttered conversation with Smedley.

We drove into the courtyard again and helped Railton out. The American woman's bewilderment seemed to have given way to resignation because she stopped flapping and took charge of him and he went off to the ward stumbling blindly and almost out on his feet. The girl said to us, "Wait here for a moment," and disappeared down the passage. I lowered myself into a chair and realized for the first time that I myself wasn't feeling too chipper either, and neither was Smedley. He sat down heavily in the one beside me and said, "What a bloody do."

"Did Railton tell you what happened?" I asked wearily.

"He doesn't know much about it," he answered. "He came to some time ago and found his ropes had been cut so he just got up and started walking. The poor bastard hardly knows what hit him yet."

He yawned, and so did I—and then I must have dozed off. I woke up some time later as somebody shook my shoulder gently and for a moment or so I didn't know where I was. A white-coated bearer was standing over me and past him I saw that a table had been laid and from somewhere came the divine smell of coffee. I hauled myself to my feet, my mouth salivating.

"Breakfast, sahib," said the bearer, and turned to wake Smedley.

There was coffee, bacon and eggs—a huge platter of them —mounds of toast, butter and marmalade. I turned and looked at Smedley.

"And I called 'em bitches," he murmured. "God forgive me."

Neither of us spoke for the next half hour, and the platter went out for refilling twice, and then, when we had finished I fished out my last two cigarettes and we sat back and stretched our feet towards a blazing wood fire somebody had lit while we slept.

I looked at my watch for the first time and was amazed to find that it was nearly four o'clock. We had got back before midday.

"If we get away now," I said, "we can make Srinagar barrier before dark. We'll leave the car a mile or so short of it and go on by foot."

I turned to ask the bearer where the miss-sahibs were, but at that moment the girl came in.

"The police are just arriving," she told me.

I stared at her.

"Bitches stand," said Smedley and stopped just short of spitting. "In spades and doubled."

CHAPTER 18

My first feeling was, illogically enough, one of sickening disappointment. She owed us nothing, but somehow I just didn't think she would do it. Smedley was glowering at her and cursing in a long unbroken rumble. I looked at her, then crossed slowly to the window. Two black police cars stood inside the archway, and armed sepoys and a couple of turbanned plain clothes men were tumbling out. The girl said, "Don't stand there, you fool—they'll see you. Help me shift some of this stuff." She was gathering up our plates and cups. It didn't penetrate until she hissed at me, "Get a move on for God's sake. They'll probably come in here, and they'll know damn well that Ethel and I don't eat breakfast at four in the afternoon." She shot across the room with a pile of dirty crockery and disappeared down the passage towards the kitchen. Smedley stopped in mid-flow and said, "So! We're still in business. Come on—you heard her." He picked up some more things and followed her, and I gathered up the four corners of the tablecloth with the rest.

She was waiting for us in the kitchen. We dumped the stuff on the table and she opened a door which led out into a small yard in which firewood was stacked round the walls.

"Over the wall and get under cover," she said. "I'm going to say you left these people here and went on your way. If they catch you outside you'll have to do your own lying. I'd keep off the roads if I were you."

"This is damned good of you," I mumbled. "But I don't like leaving you to face the music."

"Good nothing," she said contemptuously. "You don't think I'm worried about you two, do you? We've got thirty-seven Tibetans here that we're trying to run into India and we just can't afford complications, that's all. Now go."

So that was it. Things dropped straight into focus as far as this weird girl was concerned. It certainly explained her nerviness and tension, and in that moment I saw her in a different light. Smedley had already taken a run at the wall and was scrambling up over the firewood but I still hesitated. I started to put my hand forward but she shook her head impatiently and turned back to the door. I said, "Thanks all the same—" but she had gone and the door closed behind her.

I climbed over the wall after Smedley and dropped down the other side. The rain was coming up the valley in sheets, and clouds were closing in on the heights behind us, and the short twilight was drawing in. Smedley was crouching in the dripping lee of a clump of holly-oak and he was swearing glumly and monotonously. He said, "What now?"

"Get moving," I said. "If they start questioning the servants or patients we might find them on our tails immediately."

"Can't we find shelter somewhere and go back after they've gone?" he asked hopefully.

"Not a chance," I said. "Firstly, there's no shelter on a hillside like this—secondly, we don't know how long they're likely to stay—and thirdly, we've involved those women enough already."

"But what about the car?" he asked.

"We've had that," I answered. "It'll have to be by foot again—and across country at that."

"Oh, my God," he moaned. "How far this time?"

"From what I can remember of these parts, we're about fifteen miles south-east of Srinagar—by road. What it will work out at over the hills I'm damned if I know." I slithered down into a watercourse at our feet and, crouching in the shelter of its shoulder-high banks, started to climb towards the low summit behind us. By clinging to outgrowing roots and jumping from rock to rock I managed to keep out of the miniature torrent that rushed past us, but Smedley was clumsy at this sort of thing and he slipped in several times before we got to the top, floundering about waist deep, gasping curses and howling to me to help him.

The crag overlooked the hospital and from it I could see right down into the courtyard. I lay on my belly and craned over the edge and peered into the gathering gloom. The cars were still there but there was no activity outside except for a tiny black figure climbing up the broken masonry onto the top of the archway, and then I saw that others had climbed to the roof of the building and they seemed to be studying the ground all round. I called to the still struggling Smedley to keep still, because this last bit was in full view of the courtyard, and the police in these parts are hillmen, with eyes like kitehawks even in tricky half-light. He flattened himself against the muddy bank, up to his knees in icy water while I wriggled round and studied the lie of the land in the other direction.

This crag was only a false crest and the hills further back ran steeply upwards to a line of ragged peaks. To my left and far below I could just make out the blurred line of the main road clinging to the side of the cliffs until it disappeared in the gloom round a shoulder of the main massif. It confirmed what I had already been fearing—that from this point right down to the lake on which Srinagar lay it was a case of road or nothing because on one side the wall rose perpendicularly to the crestline, while on the other it dropped sheer into the valley which was now a swirling sea of cloud that hid the bottom. There was no chance whatsoever of following a course parallel to the road, and one would either have to walk on it and accept the risk of running into patrols in the dark, or strike out across the hills. Compassless and with cloud masking the stars it would be well-nigh impossible to maintain direction once darkness fell completely—but it was out of the question to stay here until morning because the rain was turning to sleet and the wind was cutting through our soaked clothes like a knife. I looked over the edge again at Smedley and almost grinned. He had looked miserable throughout most of the journey, but this was his nadir. He was wet through and covered in mud from head to foot, still clinging to the spot where I had told him to stay. But it was getting darker momentarily so I called to him to crawl up to me slowly.

He pulled himself up to my side squelchily and lay flat on his belly, shivering like a wet poodle, and I started to point out the two alternatives to him, but he just wasn't interested. I had half decided to take the imperceptibly lesser of the two evils and descend to the road when away in the distance the faintest twinkle of a light caught my eye, and then, as I strained my eyes towards it, there was another to the side of it—and then another—and another—and soon there was a whole minute carpet of them close together and I realised that I was looking at Srinagar. Providing that the weather didn't worsen I now had a beacon to home on, though I dared not think what lay between us and it. I hauled Smedley to his feet and we started off to climb to the next ridge.

Darkness had now fallen completely, as suddenly and dramatically as the drop of a curtain, as it always does in those hills, and we floundered through a villainous knee-high scrub that had long sharp thorns which tore through our trousers to our skins, and we kept falling into deep fissures in the slope which had now turned into rushing torrents, and all the time that cursed rain came down solidly and inexorably.

Three or four times I completely lost the patch of lights when we either got round the blind side of one of the higher spurs or cloud came down between us, and when that happened I knew panic; but each time they came up again after a few minutes and we struggled on until eventually we reached the top, and the patch got bigger and spread out round both horns of the dark void I knew to be the lake—far below us and a long way off still.

If climbing to the top had been difficult, going down the other side to the long plateau that overlooks the last few miles of the road was absolute hell. We slipped, slithered and rolled and kept losing each other, but at last we fetched up on fairly flat ground and, our eyes being now more accustomed to the darkness, we were able to make better time. Smedley was past even swearing by this time. He trudged along in my tracks in a semi-trance, and every time I stopped to negotiate some obstacle he ran into my back. I'm probably sounding a bit superior about all this. He was a considerably older man than I and he was not long over a nasty bout of fever, and those two things considered, he did extraordinarily well—but I was in neither an appreciative or a compassionate mood that night and I didn't ease up even when he stumbled once or twice and stayed down for some time. He got up each time, however, and broke into a shambling run until he was back on my heels. We had lost the lights now because they had dropped below the edge of the escarpment we were crossing, but I could see the glow they made in the sky quite plainly and I kept course on the center of it. When we eventually reached the edge they were appreciably nearer and I could pick out the streets and canals by the brighter pinpoints of the electric standards that lined them, and even see their reflections wriggling in the water below them.

The first mile of the road out of the city is lighted also, and at the end of this stretch is the last checkpoint before you enter. This, thank God, was now right at our feet beneath us. I couldn't believe it for a moment, but then it occurred to me that though the road distance from the hospital to the city was about fifteen miles, our route, more by luck than judgment, had been nearly a crow-flight and it must have halved it at least.

I sat down on a boulder at the edge of the slope and Smedley just subsided in his tracks. I said, "Good show, old boy," which, in certain circumstances can be the smuggest and most priggish phrase which ever cheapened the English language. Smedley evidently thought this was one of them because he merely cleared his throat and spat noisily and invited me to do something anatomically impossible. We rested for some minutes and then, when I felt myself getting stiff and cold, I got to my feet and he wearily followed suit. We skirted the edge of the crest for about half a mile and then started to climb down towards a point near the Jhelum Bridge from where we could move parallel with the road, but out of the light, into the outskirts of the city.

The descent itself was easy because here the slope was gentle, but at the bottom the irrigation canals started and they run at right angles to the road, where they join a main one. They are normally only a couple of feet deep and about four wide, but now they were swollen to the size of small rivers and their banks were quagmires, and in one of them I lost a

154

shoe and had to spend ten minutes diving and groping in liquid mud to find it again.

The Jhelum runs through the center of the city like a spine and it is joined at frequent intervals by canals that criss-cross through the bazaars and the main cantonments and make of the whole place a hotch-potch of islands. On the islands are carved wooden houses, some of them several stories high, which overhang the canals and in places almost touch, turning the waterways below into tunnels. There are narrow tortuous lanes winding through the buildings that sometimes open out to a width of twelve feet or so, but along most of which it is possible to walk with outstretched arms touching the walls either side. River and canals are lined with covered boats that house the city's floating population, and they are crossed by dozens of carved wooden bridges. From the hills the city had appeared to be brightly lighted, but his had been due mostly to the arc lights on the main roads that led out of it. Once in the maze, we had to find our way by touch alone. There were a few lights in some of the houses but these were mostly in the upper stories and they didn't pierce through the gloom to ground level. Sometimes the lanes ran along the banks, but never for long, and following the line of the river we often had to jink back inland between the houses, tracing and retracing our paths and often finding ourselves back where we started. I had spent leaves in Srinagar and I knew the old European quarter and the lake which stretches away from it to the north-east fairly well, but this wasn't helping me now.

The house of Yev's brother in Srinagar was near the Sher Garhi palace, where the main canal joined the river with the lake. Solomon had pointed it out to me on a map of the city, but finding it from memory was like trying to traverse the Hampton Court maze blindfold and I was on the point of giving it up and waiting until daylight when I recognized the post office, and next to it the Bank of India, and then what had once been the European Club—all stone buildings in Victorian gothic which fronted onto the river and backed onto the polo ground—and I realized that we had come right through the old city, overshooting the Sher Garhi by a mile. It was easier after that because here I was on fairly familiar ground and the lanes were wider and there was even an occasional dim oil lamp on some of the bigger bridges. We followed the bank of the river back until we came to the junction of the main canal and then crossed to the other side and found ourselves under the ruined walls of the palace.

The house was one of a row of high wooden buildings that faced the palace across a small open square. All of them were in pitch darkness and their windows were teak-shuttered and barred. We found the lane that Solomon had described to me.

It ran down to the canal between the end house and the high wall of a mosque, and it opened onto a cluttered terrace built out over the water. There were houseboats moored to the terrace and from one of them a dog started to bark, and it was taken up by others until that whole section of canal sounded like a hunting kennel at feeding time. Angry voices rose from the boats and a child started to cry and someone at the far end crawled out with a hurricane lamp and looked around sleepily. Across the canal a torch flashed and a man's voice called sharply, "Kya hai, tum log?"—which is the universal challenge of the Indian police. In the dim light of a lamp at the other end of the bridge we had just crossed, we saw movement and the dull glint of metal. The bearer of the hurricane lamp called out something about accursed dogs and thrice-accursed rats and started to lay about him with a stick. There were yelps and then whines and then silence. The man went back to the bosom of his family and the patrol the other side passed on.

We waited for five full minutes and then I felt along the wall and counted doors. The third from the corner of the lane, Solomon had said. There was a niche beside it—and within the niche a tablet with Hebrew characters on it—and above that a rusty chain which disappeared into a pipe in the wall. You pulled the chain and counted ten slowly, then pulled it again twice, then counted another ten and pulled it once more. The niche was there but I had to take the characters on trust, and then I couldn't find the chain because the whole front of the house was covered in bas-relief Kashmiri carving and it was hidden in the crevices—but finally my questing fingers found it and I pulled as directed.

More minutes passed and then we heard bolts being withdrawn the other side, and the door was opened a bare inch or so. I said, "Peace be on this house—and on the one below." The door opened further and we went in. We couldn't see who had admitted us but we heard him rebolting the door and then he shone a torch ahead of us and grunted to us to follow him. The air was warm and somewhat musty and there was a compound of smells in which that of dried apricots, old leather and turmeric predominated. The man led us across the large room between piles of bales, teak-wood boxes and pyramids of drying fruit laid out on squares of matting. We went up some stairs the other side and emerged into another storeroom, and then up a further flight into a workshop where the torch played across carved walnut tables, boxes and screens and there was a stink of glue and turpentine—and on up two more flights until we came to the attic. He left us here in total darkness and went off between piles of junk and we heard the sound of heavy articles being humped across the floor as if he was shifting furniture. He came back for us after a time and led us through a low doorway set amid the rafters and then put his torch down on the floor and lit a brass lamp which stood on a box in the middle of a tiny room. It was evidently formed by a gable because we could only stand upright in the center of it and we could hear the rain beating on the roof. There was a pile of Pachmina rugs in one corner, which are woven from the coarser type of Kashmir wool but are still as soft as thistledown. He pointed to them and we needed no second invitation. We dived on them and made up beds on the floor and then he left us to it, and as we stripped off our sodden muddy clothes we heard him shifting stuff back against the door the other side.

Neither of us had spoken a word to each other for the last hour and we didn't break the silence now. We just crawled under our respective heaps of rugs and, speaking for myself, went out like lights.

I awoke hours later. There was a small window in the sloping roof and through it I could see grey murky daylight, and rain was lashing against it. I was warm and relaxed in my rugs and at that moment I wanted nothing more than to stay there. I turned my head and looked across at Smedley. He lay flat on his back, mouth wide open, snoring like the Bull of Bashan. He hadn't shaved for the last three or four days and the stubble on his chin was as long as that on his head. I ran my hand over my own chin and realized for the first time that I was sporting a promising beard also. We hadn't a vestige of kit between us by this time other than clothes in which we had left Lahore and which now lay in two sodden heaps on the floor between us—except, of course our guns. I felt for mine under the rugs and pulled it out and examined it. It was already rusting and it was choked with mud, and because things like that worry me I sat up and took it to pieces and started to rub the parts clean with the corner of a rug.

I was engrossed in this when I heard the junk the other side of the door being shifted and then it opened and a man stooped and came through. He was younger than Yev but, even apart from the orthodox Jewish clothes he wore, there was no mistaking the family resemblance. He stood just inside the door and bowed gravely.

"Good morning, Mr. Rees," he said courteously. "I must apologize for putting you up here but it is safer. I have many Kashmiris working down below and they talk too much."

"It's dry and warm," I said. "We are grateful."

He said, "Do you intend staying in Srinagar long?" and although he made it sound like a polite inquiry I detected a note of anxiety under the question.

"That depends on a few things," I answered. "Certainly no longer than we can help."

"I had a letter from my brother yesterday morning," he

157

went on. "He tells me you wish to go further up into the hills. It won't be easy. Things are getting very difficult."

"That's normal in Kashmir since partition, surely?" I said. "Anyhow, we're not going towards the India/Pakistan military area."

"Where to, then?"

"North-east—towards Tibet."

"You won't do it," he said positively.

"That remains to be seen," I answered. "We've got another month before the snows close the passes."

"I'm not referring to the snows," he said.

"The army and the frontier guards shouldn't worry us. Neither side patrols up there from what I've heard. They're too busy watching each other down here in the valleys."

He shook his head. "Not any more," he said. "You'll find Indian and Pakistani troops patrolling together on the lower slopes. There's a common enemy that binds them together now."

"The Chinese?" I laughed. "That's a bogeyman the army people use in both Delhi and Karachi to scare money out of their Finance ministers. Lower down perhaps—and maybe along the Sikkim and Eastern Nepal frontiers. The Karakorams are for Tibetans and yaks only."

"You are neither."

"Are you telling me?" I answered. "We're only going up a *little* way. Higher than the patrols go, no doubt—but well below the actual frontier."

"Can you tell me where exactly?"

"I can't."

His expression didn't change but his voice was colder when he spoke again. "My brother has told me to offer you every assistance, Mr. Rees. If I'm to do that, you'll have to trust me."

"I trust you implicitly," I assured him quickly. "I wouldn't have told you as much as I have if I didn't. I can't be more specific because I don't know myself yet. We have to rely on a guide from here on."

"Have you any idea what you will require in the way of equipment?" he asked.

"I understand it's a three day march for fit men," I said. "But we'll have an old man with us—"

"Polson?"

I nodded. "Yes. We'll have to add another day on each way for him and a couple of days rest at the far end. Say ten days altogether."

"How many of you all told?"

"Four." I pointed to the still sleeping Smedley. "Him, myself, Polson and my Pathan servant."

158

He made a rapid mental calculation. "Forty days rations," he said. "Even with tsampa and buttered tea that would total eighty pounds for Europeans. Two tents—spirit lamps—sleeping bags—blankets—ropes—cooking utensils and extra clothing. You'll never do it under two hundred pounds at the barest minimum. That's a fifty pound load each."

"The food load gets progressively lighter," I pointed out.

"And all of you, except perhaps the Pathan, will get progressively weaker unless you're used to the mountains."

"Others have done it," I said.

"Fit men—your own words," he answered. He pointed at Smedley. "Is he fit? And the man Polson?—he's old, and a drunkard. He'll never be able to carry a load."

He was beginning to convince me so I changed the subject.

"Where are Polson and the Pathan now?" I asked.

"In the attic of the house next door," he said. "I thought you might wish to eat and dress in dry clothes before I sent for them."

"We would," I agreed gratefully. "Did they have any difficulty in getting here?"

"None. Their papers were in order—as were yours." He seemed to inject a note of reproof into the last words.

"We had bad luck," I explained ruefully. "We had an accident on the road and then we fell in with a young woman who runs a children's hospital. She guessed we weren't doctors and was very angry."

"Miss Culverton?" he said, and smiled. "I heard about it."

"How?" I asked, startled.

"Word travels fast in these parts," he answered. "In this case you happened to be riding in one of my trucks and the driver told me."

"I wonder who else he told—and what?"

"This particular man, nobody—and nothing. He is one we can trust." He looked past me and bowed and said, "Good morning," and turning on my elbow I saw that Smedley was awake. He blinked at us both and worked his mouth gummily. No, he certainly didn't look fit.

The man said, "I'll send up some food and a few articles you may need." He bowed again and went out.

Then the Major came in. "Well, you took your bloody time, didn't you?" he said. "What the hell kept you?"

I couldn't just at that minute find an answer.

CHAPTER 19

We left at midnight, after a feverish day trying on the mass of clothes Yev's brother brought up for our inspection, weighing and packing loads, testing and rejecting, unpacking and ruthlessly discarding and then repacking again, until we got down finally to what I considered the irreducible minimum— and even then I was doubtful, and I had to lighten the packs of the Major and Smedley considerably—thereby increasing those of Safaraz and myself. We wore heavy Kashmir underclothes and socks, and over them quilted trousers that tied round the ankles, then we pulled on felt Gilgit boots and woollen smocks. Over all we had sheepskin coats with the wool inside, which had hoods like parkas that could be brought up over our fur Tibetan caps. The clothes were old but serviceable and they smelt of the rancid butter people higher up the hills anoint their bodies with each year when the snows begin. Yev's brother advised us to do the same, but with the exception of Safaraz we all jibbed. Later on we were sorry because he was the only one the lice didn't worry.

We left the house singly and slipped across the terrace into a small lake boat and we lay down in the bottom while they piled firewood, sacks of parched barley and tins of kerosene on top of us. This was a regular supply boat that made trading trips twice a week up to the top of the lake, and it was owned, as most of them were, by the Shalom brothers. It got under way when the load was finally adjusted, and we lay in the dark listening to the rhythmic clunk-clunk of the poles and the scuffle of the boatmen's feet as they ran forward to the bows, shoved the poles against the mud at the bottom and walked down to the stern again. Two or three times in the first half-hour we were hailed from the banks of the canal, and once we were halted and heavy boots sounded on the deck above us and we saw the flashing of torches through the interstices of the firewood, but the check was only a perfunctory one and we were not stopped again.

After about half an hour the easier motion of the boat, and the fact that the men had changed their poles for paddles, told me that we had reached the open lake.

One of the boatmen came along the deck and pulled back part of the load and let us come out into the air. We were glad to because in spite of our clothes we were beginning to get chilled and cramped.

The rain had passed now and the night was clear and cold and a late moon was rising. It made a silver path across the lake to the black pines that ringed the distant shore and cut a sharp dividing line between the dark water and the snow-topped hills behind them. The boatmen had hoisted a patched and ragged square sail and the breeze, dead behind us, was moving us at fair speed and making the water sing past the low gunwales. There was no other sound save the musical honk of a skein of night flying geese, heading for the south high above us. It was the sort of night one used to get in the winter in North China, and I found my thoughts going back to the days before the war when I sometimes went out with my father overnight to catch the early flights of Siberian geese as they came in to water at dawn. We used to go out in a sampan under a sail something like this one, and then, just before the sky started to pale in the east, we would lower it and drift into the bank and cut reeds to camouflage the boat and ourselves, and we'd wait with our villainous punt-gun that had a bore like a drainpipe, for them to alight along the mud-flats—and then, as they came in with their outstretched wings pink in the first rays of the sun, the old man would always find that the range was wrong, or he'd lose the lanyard or forget the priming or something, and he'd curse both me and the boatmen in Chinese and Welsh, and we'd grin at each other behind his back because we knew, as he did, that the damned old gun wouldn't fire anyhow. Mr. Stewart and some of his friends from the bank came out with us once. My father, who knew the river like the palm of his hand, put them under the opposite bank where the sun would catch them and they'd stand out stark against the reeds, while we went on to our accustomed place. Mr. Stewart wasn't so dim though. He moved during the night and took up a new position on our side. There was nothing wrong with their gun. It scattered far and wide and they collected half a boat load of birds with one withering blast. The old man never went out again.

Smedley and the Major were arguing in low voices not far from me. It was nothing that mattered—about the distance to the further shore or something equally footling, but it spoilt for me the spell of this wonderful night, so I moved away from them towards the bow of the boat. Smedley broke off the argument and sidled along the gunwale towards me.

"Do you think there'll be a police patrol where we land?" he asked.

I shook my head. "Not very likely. It's just a landing in the wilds—and I've still got the feeling that the police up here haven't got wind of us yet."

"Then what about the posse who came to the hospital?" he asked in surprise. "Who were *they* after if it wasn't us?"

161

"There's an answer to that. You'd gone over the wall when she told me. Those two women are running Tibetan refugees into India and Pakistan."

He looked at me for a moment with his mouth agape, and then he chuckled. "The hell they are? No wonder they didn't want us around drawing attention to things. There's big money in that. I know a feller who's making two thousand dollars a head running them into Hongkong. Smart gal. At the same time I don't quite understand—"

"No, you wouldn't," I said. "You wouldn't understand anything unless there was a fast buck attached to it. I find it a bit difficult myself at times—I've been dealing with people like you and your bosses for too long. There are some left though, who can't take the look in the eyes of poor driven devils marching in front of armies. Yev Shalom is one—she, apparently, is another."

"Hey—wait a minute—" he began defensively.

"Jump in the lake," I told him, and moved round to the other side of the boat. And for the life of me I couldn't understand why I was so angry.

The flat bottom of the boat ground into the mud at the top of the lake in the small hours of the morning. It narrows here to a long winding creek, from the banks of which the hills run up steeply, making a funnel down which the wind comes clear from the snow slopes above, giving, at this time of the year, a difference of anything up to twenty degrees lower than the temperature of Srinagar. Thin ice crackled under our feet as we stepped over the bows into the reeds and waded to the shore. I confirmed the pick-up time with the boatmen again and then, as they poled silently off, I spread the map on the ground and put the prismatic compass Yev's brother had given me on top of it, and checked our position in the light of my torch.

"No need for any of that bull," said the Major. "I remember the bloody place. This is the way we always came. Only one track out of it—straight up the valley."

I insisted on pinpointing our spot, however, and then, when I had finished, we shouldered our packs and set off; myself leading, then the Major followed by Smedley, and Safaraz bringing up the rear.

The track was narrow at first, but well-trodden and although ascending all the way, the slope was easy and we made good time to the top. The defile up which we had come now opened out into the upper valley and there was cultivated land each side of us—small stone-surrounded fields from which the harvest had long been lifted, and which now lay white under the sharp frost, and groves of walnut and apricot trees. There were tiny hamlets of wooden, turf-roofed houses at fairly frequent intervals, and when we approached these

I led off the track into the fields and detoured round them. The Major was petulant.

"You don't want to worry about them bastards," he grumbled. "They hole up from dark to dawn—doors and windows tight shut. They wouldn't open up if you hammered."

But I was having none of it. I just kept up a steady clip which I felt would not tax him too much before the real climbing commenced, and continued to skirt the villages.

We had only put some five miles behind us before the tops of the hills to our right started to lighten, as I constantly had to slow up towards the end to allow the ever increasing gaps between myself and the old man to close. But even allowing for a fifteen year diet of curry and bootleg gin, he didn't do so badly that first night. I led off the track across the fields and climbed up through dense spruce to a ledge in the lower slopes and we hollowed out shallow trenches in the fallen pine needles for our sleeping bags and got down to it.

We woke when the sun was well overhead. The wind had dropped and the cold of the night before was a thing of the past. Besides a few tins of bully beef and some packets of issue biscuits of vintage '45, we carried only Tibetan tea and tsampa. The tea is strong black stuff, made up into blocks with an admixture of butter and then compressed under weights and dried, until two pounds of it becomes only a cube of a few inches. You hack chunks of it off and drop them into boiling water. It tastes like hell to an unaccustomed palate, and looks worse, because the resultant brew is the colour of treacle and has yellow globules floating in it, but once down, it is heart-warming and even in the absence of solid food it possesses a sustenance of its own. Tsampa is parched barley ground fine. You can eat it straight, mix it with butter or stir it into your tea. *It* doesn't taste nice either, but it possesses everything that is necessary to enable a Tibetan porter, or a Sherpa, to carry a ninety pound load on the upper slopes, day after day for eight hours. I told the others all about the virtues of both as I prepared a meal of it over the spirit lamp. They gulped it down glumly but were not impressed, and, since it was originally made by Tibetans, who are Buddhists and therefore, in Safaraz's simple lexicon, idolators, the latter rumbled under his breath about offence to his religion. But I'd seen him eat pork and beans in Korea when all else failed, so I wasn't worried.

We lay in that place all day and through a pair of good binoculars watched the track, up and down which people came and went without ceasing; villagers, traders from the lake boats, and once a party of Tibetans—six men and a couple of women in clothes like ours, trudging wearily behind a yak which bore blanket-wrapped bundles in panniers, and on whose back, half hidden by its flowing black hair, perched

163

a brace of small children. They looked as if they had come far and they did not seem to be chattering, singing and laughing as Tibetans normally do among themselves. Even the yak seemed distressed at this relatively low altitude, because, as we watched, it stopped and sank to its knees and stayed in that position, head touching the ground and haunch up like a foundering ship, until it quivered and collapsed and finally rolled onto its side. The women shambled forward and plucked the children clear, and then they all squatted in a circle and watched the exhausted animal dully and with the lack of interest of the hopeless. Villagers passed with averted eyes, which struck me as strange at first, because Kashmiris are kindly folk and will usually help a traveller in trouble. And then we saw, or rather guessed, the reason.

From the direction of the lake marched a party of police; four sepoys and an N.C.O. bringing up the rear, with Stens over their shoulders. Smedley, who hadn't been talking much since I told him to jump in the lake, heard my muffled exclamation from where he had been lying on his sleeping bag, and looked at me in inquiry. I handed him the glasses and pointed. He watched for a while, swearing under his breath.

"So that's *it*," he said at last. "The bastards were on our tail—and now they're ahead of us, and we've had it. We should have pushed on while we had the chance." And that's what I had been thinking too, but then, as I took the glasses back and looked again, I saw them halt at the party of Tibetans. We couldn't hear what they were saying at that distance, but I could see a lot of gesticulation from the police, and finally, after some quarter of an hour's parleying, the Tibettans got up and turned back in the direction from which they had come—and now they were carrying the children and the bundles. They didn't look back—they just walked. And the foundered yak lay where it had fallen—a black hairy mass at the side of the road. The policemen stood round it for a few minutes, and through the glasses I could see that their attitudes were those of men who did not like what they had done. They, too, turned then and went slowly back towards the lake. I handed the glasses to Smedley and heard his sigh of relief.

"Going back," he grunted. "Thank Pete for that. Now what the hell was all that in aid of?"

"Tibetan refugees," I said. "The Indians and Pakistanis have every sympathy with them—but they don't like encouraging them over the border, in case it offends the Chinese."

"What will happen to the poor devils now?" he asked.

"You tell me. Perhaps they'll hole up somewhere and try again. Perhaps they'll give it up and go back to whatever they were running from. Perhaps they might just give up, and do

164

what the yak did. They tell me there's a lot of money in running them through to India."

He was silent for a time, and then he said quietly, "You made your point last night, Rees. There's no need to rub it in."

I spent the remaining hours of daylight redistributing the contents of the packs, stripping that of the Major down till he was carrying only his sleeping bag and blanket, then I made them take their boots and socks off while I examined their feet. It was as well that I did, because one of Smedley's socks had a rough cobbled darn in it and it had started to rub a raw patch on his heel even in the short distance we had covered the night before. I made him change to his spare pair and then we had another meal of tea, tsampa and, since they all looked so miserable, I opened a tin of beef. We rested a further hour, then, when darkness had finally fallen, we shouldered our packs and set off once more.

The cultivation ended after another mile or so and there was only one more village before the real ascent began. It was gentle at first and followed the contours of the slope, but as we got higher it showed a tendency to cut corners and shoot upwards in sharp little jinks that soon had the Major, then Smedley and finally me, gasping and sweating under our thicknesses of clothes in spite of the cold which was now increasing in intensity as we climbed. We had to stop more frequently for the Major and I started to worry about the time because there was a police post at the top of the pass and we had to be well beyond it before daylight came. Only Safaraz seemed to be enjoying it. These were not his hills; he came from Waziristan which is much further west—but they *were* hills, and he had stewed too long in the turkish bath of Bombay. I could actually hear him singing his eternal "Zakhmi Dil" in the rear, extemporizing lewdly and comparing Smedley's struggles up the slope to those of a pregnant camel, and worse, and I had to shut him up, not because I wanted to spoil his fun, but because voices carry on that still, clear air.

We stumbled over the Tibetans after two hours stiff climbing. They were sitting huddled in the middle of the track, shapeless bundles of sheepskin, and the first I knew of them was when a child cried out suddenly and startled the very devil out of me. They thought we were police again and they started to gather up their bundles in silence. I don't speak Tibetan, but most of these border people have some Urdu, and these understood me. They told me they were nomads and although Chinese troops had been in their province for some time they hadn't bothered them much at first because they were able to keep moving, but now the numbers were increasing. The Chinese were everywhere and they were rounding up the nomads, men, women and children, and they were

165

marching them to the north-west, but nobody knew where exactly although there were wise men who said that it had all been written by the Fourth Buddha in ages long ago. The Tiger of the North would mate with the Dragon of the East and their offspring would bring the fires of hate and murder and rapine to the plateau of Tibet, and the God-King would be forced to flee from Holy Lhasa and his children would perish unless they could find shelter—but there would be no shelter.

If an Indian had been telling it there would have been drama and histrionics, complaint and accusation. These people told it in the flat dull tones of acceptance. It had been written. It had come.

There was little we could do for them except to deplete our stores by a block of butter-tea and some tsampa. They had nothing left but a small amount of rancid butter which they offered us in exchange. We stayed with them for as long as it took Safaraz to boil some water on the spirit stove—which was not long at that altitude—and I told them to have another go at it in the dark and to get to the lake and bribe some boatman to take them to Srinagar—and then to walk fifteen miles down the road the other side and turn up a track to a hospital. I translated most of this to Smedley.

He said, "The best of luck to them, but those bum-boat wallahs won't carry them for honor and glory." And I heard him fumbling under layers of clothes to his money belt.

They didn't thank us. Thanks for simple kindness are neither expected nor given in those high places, but they stood up as we left and bowed gravely and poked their tongues out, which is the polite Tibetan greeting and farewell, and one of the women followed us a few steps and gave Safaraz a crumpled white scarf which she said had once hung on the bronze Buddha at the monastery of Gatkon and which was therefore a sure specific against impotence in a man or barrenness in a woman. Safaraz did thank her for that and whipped in an improper suggestion, and because Tibetans are as joyously bawdy as Pathans there was laughter among them as we went on our way.

We paid for the delay in that we didn't make the top of the pass by a good two miles before dawn was upon us, but I had had time to re-think our journey. The Major wouldn't make it at the pace I had planned, nor perhaps would Smedley. Safaraz, however, was in his element. We would press on at the best speed we could make without foundering the weaker members of the party and if we found the ten day limit creeping up on us I would send Safaraz on ahead on the return journey to make fresh arrangements with the boatmen.

Once more we got off the track and stumbled round the

166

contour of the hill until we were out of sight of anybody coming up or down it, and I found a hollow in among some rocks that gave us cover, but from where we could see right down the pass up which we had come. We were on the edge of the snowline now, which solved our water problem. I made another tea and tsampa meal which was this time eaten a little more gratefully, and then we crawled into our blankets and sleeping bags. The cold was really killing but the bags were good. After an hour in them one became aware of their grateful warmth.

I studied my map before going to sleep and was able to fix our position fairly accurately by two peaks which lay above us. We had only made fourteen miles from the top of the lake but we had climbed some sixteen thousand feet. We had another two thousand to go before we came to the first plateau and after that it would be fairly level going for a couple of days before we started to climb again.

We slept and smoked through the day. Nobody came up or down the track in that time and as night fell we set out again rested and fitter than we had been the day before. We came up to a spot over which I judged the police post to be after an hour's climbing and I left the party in the lee of a big boulder and went forward to recce.

I saw it sooner than I expected. I had imagined it to be a stonebuilt "sangar" type of place, made to accommodate perhaps an N.C.O. and a couple of sepoys. Probably that is what it had been originally, but it had obviously been enlarged recently because now there was a large Nissen hut there also and the whole area was sealed off by barbed wire. It probably held fifty men which would make it an officer's command. Against the moonlit sky I could see a radio aerial and I could hear the coughing of a motor-driven generator. Clearly this was a place to be avoided, if only for the tracks we would leave in the snow.

I went back to the party and led them off in a wide detour that must have put at least five miles onto the march and involved some climbing which had us in a muck-sweat before we had once more got back onto line, with the lights of the post behind us and on the correct compass bearing. Fortunately there was a stiff breeze blowing now and that both prevented the snow from getting too deep on the track and at the same time obliterated our tracks on that which did manage to lay.

The night was crystal clear and when the moon came up it was almost as light as day. It did something for all of us. The going was level and smooth and the air was like champagne. Three of us were soldiers and we knew something of that mystic rhythm of the march that pulses with the blood and blends muscles into coordination when once its swing has

167

gripped you. We fairly bounded along at one-hundred-and-twenty to the minute and when Safaraz's invention had temporarily run dry on "Zakhmi Dil", that of the Major went back over the years and he came up with a quavering but equally filthy variation of "Colonel Bogey." We carried Smedley, the despised civilian, along with us, and when dawn came we had put, detour notwithstanding, a good honest twenty miles behind us.

We were in a different world now. The plateau was ending and ahead of us the main range rose in a solid wall with the tops of the higher peaks shrouded in grey snow clouds. The track was becoming increasingly difficult to follow because a heavy fall of snow swept down from the hills just as the sun rose, and spread a flat white blanket over everything, and in the last minutes before we halted we lost it completely, until, in casting around for it, I stumbled over a prayer cairn. These are heaps of stones which dot the sides of roads and tracks in Tibet, and it is an act of merit for Buddhists to add to them in passing. Some of them are surmounted by poles on which flutter tiny white prayer flags which help a lot against a dark background but become lost when the snow falls. Having found it, and sent Safaraz ahead to find the next and stand on top of it, I took a compass bearing on it for future reference and once more led off the track a few hundred yards and we made camp in the middle of a tumbled pile of high boulders. We pitched our tents for the first time. They were small affairs, three feet high at the center ridge and just wide enough to take two sleeping bags side by side. One of them was made of white windproof cotton and it merged into the background perfectly, but unfortunately the other was of a brilliant yellow nylon and I had some doubts about using it until I saw that the heavily falling snow was soon likely to cover it.

We brewed tea and I made a stew of corned beef, tsampa and melted snow, and then we crawled into our bags and slept like dead men for some hours.

I woke at mid-afternoon. Smedley, invisibly cocooned in his bag beside me, was still snoring like a grampus. I unlaced the flaps and looked out. It had stopped snowing but it had obviously been falling heavily while we slept because I had to dig through a two foot drift. It was fuggily warm inside, but the cold struck me like a knife as I put my head out. I took the glasses and scanned the slopes above us. The clouds had cleared from the summit now and I was able to make out the pass we were heading for. It was just the merest dip in the razorlike crestline that stood out white against the threatening grey sky, and what lay between us and it appalled me. By my early optimistic reckoning we should have been up there by this time, and the Major's camp should have been only half a day's fairly easy march ahead of us, but now I had to

168

recast things. That climb, even under light snow conditions, was going to take us a good twelve hours at least. If any more came down, and the sky certainly looked as if more was on its way, it might easily double it. Food was starting to worry me now also. I had allowed for a ten day round march plus a four day reserve, but our freakish generosity with the Tibetans had all but washed the latter out. Things were going to be tight at best. I decided to take the rest of the daylight as a bonus and start the assault on the slope as soon as we had had some tea. I shook Smedley awake with difficulty and left him yawning and mumbling peevishly while I crossed to the other tent to call Safaraz and the Major.

Safaraz answered immediately and stuck his head through the flaps, grinning from ear to ear, and as I filled the tin kettle with snow and crawled back into our own tent I heard him roaring, "Awake, ancient one! Awake from dreams of houris and whisky-soda! Reveille is upon us!" And the Major cleared his throat noisily and snarled, "Aw, pipe down, you black bastard," in English.

We finished our tea and then struck the tents with difficulty, because our breath had condensed on the inside of them and they were frozen to the stiffness of boards. We got them rolled and packed at last and then we adjusted our loads and stamped some life into our freezing feet before filing back to the track.

It was Safaraz who saw them first. One minute the frozen white wastes had been empty of all life except ourselves, and then they had appeared—a row of tiny black dots emerging from the foot of the slope at the spot I had judged the track to enter the bottom of the pass. He grabbed my arm and pointed. I told the others to get back under cover and I went behind a rock and unslung the glasses.

They were still too far away to make out what they were with any certainty. There were twelve of them walking in single file and I judged it would take them a good half hour to get abreast of our position, and another for them to pass out of sight behind us, and I cursed as I realized that our bonus would be reduced. I called Safaraz up beside me and handed him the glasses, but, as is usually the case with hillmen, although his natural sight was magnificent he was no good with binoculars and couldn't tell me any more than I knew already.

Smedley had come up behind us and his breath was steaming past my ear. "What the hell are they?" he asked.

"Could be anything," I said. "Indian troops. Tibetans or even Chinese—but I hardly think the last. We're still a good twenty miles inside the Indian border. We can't take any risks though. We'll just have to wait until they're past us—and that will be an hour at least."

The Major snorted. "We could have had a longer nap," he said petulantly. "There should have been somebody watching."

"You're right," I agreed. "We'll go on a sentry roster in future. *All* of us."

We watched them as they crawled nearer, stamping our feet and blowing into our mittens as the cold crept in remorselessly. I was able to make them out as Tibetans after a time, from their high-pointed, ear-flapped caps, and I had almost made up my mind not to wait any longer but to lead out onto the track and pass them. I turned to tell the others this when Safaraz pointed again.

A second party was emerging from the pass.

CHAPTER 20

This party was larger than the first. I counted seventeen of them, and they were travelling faster. We could see, even in those early stages, the gap close rapidly between them, and there was something about the very way they were moving that was different from those in front.

Smedley, his breath forming a frozen rime round the sheepskin of his hood, said, "Christ! How many more of them? What's the use of waiting? Let's get on—we're freezing solid." But I shook my head and continued studying them through the glasses.

The front party was now close enough for me to pick out details. They carried small bundles on their backs and, in two cases, equally small children, and they appeared to be as worn out as the previous party we had seen. They did not seem to be aware of their pursuers. They were marching in a straggling file, their hoods pulled down over their heads, hunched against the wind and sleet that was beating into their faces. The rearmost figure in the front party paused once as we watched, and turned and scanned the track behind him, but although we could plainly see both parties from our position on the flank, there must have been a rise between them that cut off the watcher's line of sight, because, after a moment or so, he turned again and slogged along behind the men in front of him.

And then the rear party was hidden by a dip in the ground from our view also, and we waited for a repetition of yesterday's pitiful little tragedy, heartsick but helpless to do anything about it. Less than four hundred yards separated them now.

The others came into view again. They had deployed while they were out of our sight, and they were now strung out in line abreast, moving forward at a shambling double. They had gained ground too, and the gap had narrowed to something less than three hundred yards—and then, with a horror that struck chiller than the wind itself, we saw the middle section of the line drop prone and the two flanks of it start to swing inwards to each other in a pincer movement.

The volley reached the Tibetans before the sound of it came to us. We saw the rearmost man pitch forward onto his face and lie still; and another figure, halfway up the file, spun, dropped and thrashed about in the snow. The others halted and turned, and through the glasses I could see them staring stupidly at the two fallen men, and it was only then that the thin ragged tearing of a sub-machine gun burst came downwind to us. One of the figures at the front of the halted column started to run back towards the rear. It was one of those that had been carrying a child on its back and I could see now that it was a woman. She ploughed through the snow at the side of the track until she had reached the still figure, and then she dropped on her knees beside him and tried to turn him over. The others had gathered round the wounded man and seemed to be trying to do something for him.

The pursuers had now come up to the Tibetans. A couple of them hauled the kneeling woman away from the fallen man and bent over him, and then I saw them pull his sheepskin coat and high felt boots off him. The woman was struggling to get back to him, and one of the others clubbed her. She knelt in the snow, both arms clasping her head and slowly rocked to and fro. They rounded up the Tibetans then and started to hustle them back the way they had come, hauling the woman to her feet and pushing her along with the rest.

There was a pounding in my ears and my mouth was dry and my tongue felt too big for it. I couldn't hold the glasses steady any more so I passed them to Smedley and leant against the rock in front of me, weak at the knees and sick in the stomach. Death doesn't worry me unduly; I've seen it in many ugly forms—but this coldblooded shooting down of exhausted men—in the back and without warning— Then I heard Smedley swearing. "The dirty bastards—they're taking the coat and boots off the wounded man— Oh, my God—and now they've shot him and they're leaving them both lying in the track."

We remained behind the rocks watching the receding dots get smaller as they filed back and eventually disappeared into the pass. None of us spoke for a long time, then Smedley said shakily, "Who were they?—the bastards with the guns, I mean?

"Chinese," I told him. "They could only be Chinese. The Indians and Pakistanis might stop them and turn them back, but they'd never murder them."

The Major said, "The hell with this. I never bargained for none of this. I'm going back. The hell with it—" and he kept repeating it complainingly until Smedley turned on him and blasted him. I sat down in the lee of the rock and fumbled for a cigarette with numbed fingers and tried to think. Smedley watched me for a time and then said impatiently, "Well, come on for God's sake. What do we do now? We'll freeze solid if we stay here much longer."

"It's up to you," I said. "According to my reckoning we're about fifteen map miles from the spot the Major pointed out —most of it climbing. I'm willing to go forward with you if you still want to go—but I'm not forcing anyone who doesn't."

Smedley turned to the Major. "Okay, you heard that. I'm not being gypped this close to it. What are you going to do? Stay here on your own?"

"No he's not," I said. "If he won't come I'll send him back with Safaraz."

Smedley said flatly, "Right—you've broken your contract, Polson, so I don't have to pay you a sou—"

"It wasn't in my contract to get murdered by a bunch of Pongs," the Major wailed. "I'd settle for Indians—Baluchis even—I understand them—but not these yellow bastards. I didn't know we'd run into any. How was I to? For Gawd's sake, we're inside the Indian border, aren't we?"

"Shut up," I said wearily. "All right, Smedley. That seems to be it."

"It isn't," he snapped. "Listen, Polson, come forward with us and show us the place and you get paid. Even if we don't find it, I'll still pay you what I agreed—but rat out of it and I don't even cough up your fare back from Srinagar."

"I'm an old man," shrieked the Major. "Mr. Rees—you're not going to let him do that—"

"I'm not going to try and persuade you to go forward," I said, "and I certainly wouldn't leave you here on your own. You heard what I said. Anything beyond that is between you and Smedley. I have got a suggestion though."

"Let's have it," said Smedley.

"If he won't come forward, he gives us a map of the spot —and the closest directions he can from memory. If we find it you pay him. If we don't—well, that's up to you."

"He comes forward—or not a goddamned cent. Okay— what about it, Polson?" He turned to the Major.

"It's there, I tell you," the old man screamed. "But what the hell good is a map going to be to you? I told you, it'll be like looking for a needle in a haystack. I've got to see the spot again—see it in daylight."

172

"Then come on up and show us," Smedley snapped.

"And get murdered? What good would that do any of us? I've done me best but it's no go. Pay us what I'm out of pocket —a few thousand miserable chips—and call it a day. Gorstrewth! It'd only be a fleabite to a man like you." He finished on a whine.

"You heard my terms," said Smedley relentlessly. "Come and get paid. Go back—and you go on the bones of your ass."

They wrangled for over an hour while Safaraz and I prepared tea and tsampa in the lee of the rocks. It was, I think, a mixture of cupidity and the dread of seeing the party split that eventually won the Major over. As night fell we moved out again onto the trail.

We stopped in the moonlight and looked at the two dead men in the snow. There was nothing we could do for them— not even bury them in that frozen ground—so we dragged them to the side of the track and left them in the shadow of a snow-covered prayer cairn. Safaraz said, "Some Japanis will die for this, my brothers." To him all the yellow races were Japanese. And that was their epitaph.

This march was easier than I had been fearing. The moon was up and the night was still and cold and we were able to follow the track in the trodden snow of the party which had gone ahead of us. Once in the pass the ascent was steep, but not nearly as bad as it had appeared through the glasses. My main fear was that we might stumble on the Chinese and their prisoners camping somewhere along the track, but I knew that that was hardly likely in the pass itself. The top would be where we would have to be careful, and we would not reach that before daylight.

We kept at it all night, plodding upwards at a steady snails pace—and as the first streaks of dawn lightened the sky I saw the crest just above us. Once again I lead them off the track and got them under the cover of an overhanging ledge —then I moved further out to a flank and climbed the rest of the way to the top.

The view from up here was magnificent. Behind us the range ran down steeply to the plateau we had crossed, and in the distance to the west rose the lower range that was the barrier between us and the Kashmir valley. In front of me was the second plateau, and overshadowing everything was the sheer rearing wall of the Himalayas themselves. The sun was just appearing through a gap and where it struck the snow it turned it pink, while in the valleys below me, where it wouldn't penetrate until high noon, the shadows were still deep purple.

I scanned the ground ahead of me for some minutes but there was no movement of any sort, so I got out my map and checked my position by bearings onto some of the higher peaks, and I was relieved to find that they confirmed my

173

estimate of where we should be. And then, as I was about to scramble down to rejoin the others, I saw the Chinese.

They had camped for the night about a mile from the top of the pass, and they were now emerging from a hollow at the side of the track. I watched them through the glasses as they set out—soldiers in front, then their prisoners, then more soldiers bringing up the rear. When they had become dots in the distance I turned and slid down the hill again, and for once I hadn't much appetite for breakfast.

We stayed under the ledge for the rest of the day, Safaraz and myself relieving each other at the post at the top of the hill at hourly intervals, watching the track behind us and in front—and I had a final huddle with the Major. He had got over his blind panic of yesterday and was now more specific about the place. There was a stupa there, he told me—a sort of stone Buddhist totem pole. There were many such along these tracks in the proportion of about one stupa to ten prayer cairns, but he'd know this one when he saw it. It was just beyond where the track left the upper plateau and started to climb again—about half a mile up the pass itself. The path was narrow each side of it. In the old days if a yak was too widely loaded it couldn't make it. The wall ran up perpendicular on one side and dropped as sheerly on the other a couple of hundred feet to the gorge below. He might have been describing a dozen similar places that we had seen on the way up, but he said he'd know this place as soon as he saw it, because it had been used as a staging post by the mail runners when he was here before—in fact, he himself had chosen it because the wall bent back and made a hollow that was sheltered from the wind, and even in the depth of winter it remained free from snow. There was just enough space to pitch one tent there although further down it opened out again, and that, in fact, was where the Sherpas had camped on that wild night years before.

As he was telling it now it might have appeared easy for us to have gone on ourselves and found the spot, but I knew it wasn't. He was describing it graphically enough but I realized it was as he said—he would actually have to see it again.

"Of course," I mused. "It's still pretty dicy. If the spot is just as you have said, it would be frequently used as a camping site. People scrabbling about in the scree could have unearthed it."

"What people?" he demanded. "I told you, there's a stupa there. Tibetans wouldn't defile the place by camping under it. They didn't like us doing it either. This track is not used much anyhow. The main trade route is south of here—through Ladakh. Rees—those bloody papers are *there*, I tell you."

I had intended to make this a day march, but the happen-

174

ings of yesterday had now ruled that out as unwise—at the same time he said he would want to see the place in the light. I decided, therefore, to camp where we were until the early hours of next morning and then to go on and reach the foot of the pass as day broke.

We continued watching from the top of the hill for as long as we could see, and as it was getting colder, we pitched our tents again, had a meal and turned in.

That last march was the easiest yet. It was flat going the whole way and we had reached the pass long before dawn. Smedley wanted to go straight on up for what we judged half a mile and save some time but the Major jibbed, and I saw his point. He was looking back over fifteen years and, however clear the picture of the place might be etched on his memory, he didn't want to take the slightest risk of missing it in the half light. That ten thousand rupees was really needling him now.

So we huddled in the shelter of some rocks for nearly two hours and when the snow behind us was once more pink, we started up the pass—the Major this time leading.

He was absolutely right in his description of the track. The pass itself was wide—perhaps nearly a mile from side to side where it opened into the plateau, and never narrowing to less than four or five hundred yards, but the path clung to the side of the sheer northern wall and I soon appreciated his insistence on daylight, because, as we mounted higher, bending and twisting round its contours, it petered out to a precarious five feet in width, with bits of it, as it went round the shoulders of the cliff, even narrower. Below us, the floor of the pass was of snow-covered ice, but we could hear the murmur of water underneath it. When the snow melted higher up, the Major told us, it was a raging torrent.

We came to the Sherpas' camping ground just when I reckoned we should have done, and now the fever of it had got into us all—even Safaraz, who didn't know what the hell we were looking for and probably cared less. Behind me Smedley was chattering and cursing in an unbroken undertone, and, in spite of the cold, I could feel my palms sweating inside my mittens.

And then we came round a bend and it was there.

It was just as if a giant spoon had scooped a chunk out of the face of the rock. You couldn't call it a cave because it was too shallow. The track just widened out at this point to some twenty feet or more, and the cliff overhung the broad shelf thus formed for some yards, and then it narrowed again and disappeared round the next bend. The stupa was set on a ledge above it. It was a truncated, conical pillar with a rough representation of the Lotus carved on its side. Between the inner edge of the track and the rockface was a short expanse

175

of pulverized shaly rock—not scree, as the Major had described it.

The Major halted and I could hear him breathing like a foundered horse. He pushed back his hood and wiped his face with the back of his mitten then he turned and looked past me at Smedley. "There you are," he said hoarsely in a strained cracked whisper. "Look at it, damn and blast you. Now tell me if I dreamed this one up. Think I didn't hear you whispering together back on that boat? I'm a liar, am I? Mr. Rees, I'm calling on you to witness that I've brought this man to where I said I'd bring him—that there's a bargain been made and accepted—that there's—"

Smedley said, "All right, Polson—save it until we've looked for it. If it's here you'll get your money."

"I get half even if it isn't—" began the Major.

"Oh, for Christ's sake stop it—both of you," I said, and swung my pack off my shoulders. There was a small tool in the tent roll that was half spade, half pick. I got it out. "All right—now show me. Where were you pitched?"

He walked to the edge of the loose shale and measured in the air with his outstretched hands. "Here," he said. "Just as I'm standing now. 'Tents, twenty-five pound, Indian pattern. L.P.' Remember your Ordnance Store vocab? Twelve by six them sort were. Narrow side this way—right smack under the stupa. See what I mean?"

I did. It was the only way it could have been pitched, because the shale fell away sharply each side.

"We put it as far back as we could to get it out of the wind," he went on. "Six foot high at the ridge, so it couldn't go back too far because of the overhang. I'm five foot eight—" he walked forward until his head touched the rock above. "—all right, the rear pole must have been a bit in front of where I'm standing now—say about here." He reached out with his foot.

I paced off the small rectangle and marked it with the edge of my spade. "Right," he said. "Imagine the stretcher lying here—with him on it. I'm sleeping across the other side—here. When I wake up he's crouching in this corner—right here."

I turned and offered the spade to Smedley. He licked his lips and then shook his head. "You're doing all right," he muttered.

I started to dig.

I was still digging an hour later. Why, I don't know, because I'd long given the whole thing up. The Major had stopped shrieking and scrabbling in the shale with his bare hands by this time. Smedley had smacked him open-handed across the mouth and I got in between them and pushed them apart

176

and he had nearly gone over the edge. Now he was sitting hunched against the cold looking savagely miserable. The Major had unrolled his sleeping bag and had crawled into it pulling the flap over his head. From time to time a convulsive heave came from the sausage shaped bundle and he kept repeating monotonously, "The bloody thing is here I tell you. The bastard had it when we carried him in. He didn't have it when we carried him out. It's *here.*" He went to sleep after a time.

I found it fifteen feet from where it should have been. The shale must have shifted in the weathering of the years. I knew what it was when the edge of the spade struck it but I had to stop scratching the dirt and get my breath back before I could bring myself to uncover it fully. I felt round the edges of it with my fingers and drew it out. It was a flat steel mapcase about eighteen inches by a foot, and some four inches deep. It was black japanned and rather battered but it had stood the test of time well and was undamaged except for the hasp, which had rusted through. I looked at Smedley. He was staring at the case. He didn't move for a full minute, then he got up and crossed to me. I handed it to him. He squatted on his heels beside me and opened it and the hinge on the back snapped off clean as he did so. Inside was a large oil-silk envelope, nearly the area of the box. He took it out and untied the tapes that secured it. There were three large-scale Ordnance Survey maps of the area and clipped to them a mass of notes and meteorological data on squared paper. There was also a small field service notebook in a faded red cover. We carried the papers out from under the overhang because it had now clouded over and the light was dim.

We didn't speak. We just spread the maps over our knees and tried to peel the notes apart with our gloved fingers. It wasn't easy because the damp had got into them and they were stuck together, and the ink had run badly. The wind had risen now and, mutton-fingered with the cold, I let one of the sheets go and it whirled away down the pass like a leaf in a gale. Smedley yelped and I thought he was going to hit me for a moment.

I said, "All right. So you've got them. Put the damned things away before we lose the lot, and let's get the hell out of here." He stuffed them back into the envelope and I got to my feet and walked up the track to where I had posted Safaraz on lookout for anybody who might come down from the top of the pass. "It is finished," I said. "We go back. Take the rear again and watch behind you. We don't want to be caught like the Tibetans were yesterday." He nodded and fell in behind me.

Smedley was stirring the Major with his foot when we returned. The old man stuck his head out of the sleeping bag like an angry tortoise and spat at him.

"Okay, Polson," Smedley said. "You get your money. I'm sorry. Now suppose we forget it." He held up the steel case.

He couldn't believe it at first—then he started to chatter like a monkey. I couldn't understand what he was saying, then I realized that he'd lost his false teeth inside the bag. He realized it too and he squirmed down inside it and came up with them, wiping them on the canvas and cramming them into his mouth. Safaraz started to guffaw, and that broke the tension. Smedley's face cracked and his belly started to heave, and then we were all laughing like fools—including the Major.

We were still laughing when we came to the foot of the pass, and the rocks above us were throwing the echoes back.

We stopped as the squad of Chinese troops rose from the snow in front of us and covered us with sub-machine guns.

There were six of them. Northerners they looked like; squat and broad and deceptively slow moving. They were the sort they used for really tough jobs in the winter in Korea. They must have heard us long before we came into sight because they had had time to deploy properly in inverted arrowhead formation, point away from our line of march and flanks enclosing us, so that any or all of them could have mowed us down without hitting each other. They looked at us stolidly, blankly, and when they closed in on us they did so like perfectly drilled automatons. We stood one behind the other, just as we had been marching. One of them—the man forming the point of the arrow—reached up slowly with both hands and clasped them at the back of his neck and then sunk to his knees. He rose again and pointed to us. We followed suit. Behind me the silence was broken only by a shuddering noise, almost a sob, from the Major. The man walked towards us. He was dressed, as were the others, in heavy grey quilted trousers and parka, felt boots and a sheepskin hat that came down over his ears in flaps. Over his parka he wore light field service order of belt, cross-straps, ammunition pouches and a small haversack. They were all armed with light sub-machine guns rather like our Stens.

He came right up to us and stopped in front of me, and I got the old familiar smell of sour rice, cooking oil, wood smoke and unwashed body. He grunted something and one of the others handed his weapon over to the man next to him and circled round behind us. His hands came over my shoulders feeling for the fastenings of my sheepskin coat. He undid them and then tugged at it and I stretched out my arms while he removed it. He threw it to one side and then grabbed my gun which I was carrying in the waistband of my trousers. Then

178

he pulled my woollen smock over my head, and then my vest. He put his hands on my shoulders and jerked me flat onto my back and the snow seared my naked skin like hot metal. He pulled my boots off then, and my trousers, socks and underpants, leaving me finally stark naked, numb and petrified in the cutting wind. They let me get to my feet while the first man made a rapid search of my clothes. He put my gun, binoculars, map and compass to one side and kicked my clothes back to me and signed to me to get dressed again. I took the first real breath since they had come up to me, because up till that moment I had thought they were removing my clothes merely to save them from the damaging effects of a short burst at close range from one of their guns. Smedley, immediately behind me, spoke for the first time. "What happens, Rees? What happens? Say something for Christ's sake," he mumbled. The man who had undressed me was now starting on him. He stopped and moved round in front of him, and sitting on my coat pulling my socks on, I saw him drive his fist straight into Smedley's mouth. The man in front of us raised his forefinger and tapped himself on the lips. We all understood perfectly.

The soldier went slowly and deliberately about his task until all of us had been stripped to the pelt and searched. He had some difficulty with the Major at first because the old man's knees wouldn't hold him any longer and he sagged uncooperatively. The soldier corrected that by moving to one side of him and taking a swinging kick at his ribs. I was frightened stiff about Safaraz's reactions when it came to his turn, but I managed to shoot him a warning look which, thank God, held him.

They went through our packs then, sharing the contents of mine between themselves and packing the guns, compass, maps and oil-silk envelope and Smedley's bodybelt with the money in their place. This the first man slung over his own shoulder and then he barked an order and the others fell in in file, prodding us into position with their butts—first a soldier, then me, then another soldier, then Smedley and so on —alternating us so we couldn't talk to each other. The whole thing had taken no more than ten minutes, and not a word had been spoken—but it was as well-drilled and mounted an ambush and frisking as I'd ever seen. It was frightening.

The leader gave another order and the first man led off to the north, skirting the foot of the slope right-handed. He went at a cracking pace which I, the fittest member of our party with the possible exception of Safaraz, found killing within the first hour. I tried to turn my head to see how Smedley and the Major were making out but the man behind me unslung his burp-gun and drove the butt into my back.

179

The Major was the first to crack. I could hear him wheezing and gasping and then there was a sudden check behind me and one of the soldiers in the rear called out sharply. The man in front of me halted and turned round. I started to do the same but I got another thump from the fellow behind me so I eyes-fronted quickly. There was a colloquy between the leader and the others then—the first time any of them had spoken other than to bark orders—and although it was in a Northern dialect with which I wasn't very familiar, I found I could follow the drift of what they were saying—and it told me quite a lot. Briefly, one of them said the old man would never do it so why not shoot him now? The leader told him not to be a fool and that all four of us were wanted, and to fall the two fittest in each side of him. They hauled me out of column and shoved me along to where the Major was lying face down in the snow and I saw Safaraz being chivvied forward at the same time. The leader made signs to us to pick him up and then once again tapped himself warningly on the lips. We hauled the old man to his feet. He was as skinny as a crow but his clothes made up for his lack of weight and we had our work cut out to keep him upright let alone to make him walk. Somehow or other we managed to do it, however, and we went on at that same merciless pace for at least an hour before we had our first halt. They let us rest for about ten minutes and then we were off again—and we kept it up until late in the afternoon and then, when I knew we couldn't go another half mile, they turned off from the cliff-bottom path up a narrow defile. I thought this meant a climb right to the top and I was just about to throw the towel in when we emerged into a small round valley, surrounded on all sides by the hills.

It was about two hundred yards across, and round its circumference were rough, stone-built huts. In the center of it was a loop-holed machine gun emplacement that commanded the defile by which we had entered. We halted alongside it and a sentry looked out of one of the slits and nodded. We went across the open space to one of the huts the other side. They shoved Smedley through a door and clanged it to after him, then we moved on to the next and they signed to us to drop the Major, then finally Safaraz was peeled off and we continued on to the next, rather bigger hut and they let me sink down onto the ground. They stood around me in an untidy silent bunch while the leader went inside and I sat with my head down between my knees only half aware of what was going on. Then the leader came out again and grunted something to them and they filed off, leaving me there alone.

Then somebody in the hut behind me said, "Come in, Idwal."

CHAPTER 21

He hadn't changed much since I saw him last. There was a little grey at his temples but it did nothing to age him. He was sitting by a charcoal stove as I entered, and he got up and put his hand out. I had taken it before I realized what I was doing. It was still the same warm grip. There was the same laughing sparkle in his blue eyes and the same wide friendly grin.

He said, "Well, you made it."

"Yes," I said wearily. "I made it."

"I did try and stop you, you know?"

"I didn't even know you were in it," I answered.

"Surely Yev told you?"

I shook my head. He laughed. "I'd be willing to take you up on that. I'm an obsession with the silly old devil. Well—it doesn't matter. The point is that you're here. Now what are we going to do with you?"

"Play chess with me and then cut my throat, I suppose," I said.

He looked puzzled for a moment and then slightly hurt.

"There's no need for that sort of thing," he said. "If there had been any other way out I'd have taken it. I was with the opposition remember, and I was about to face a court-martial and possibly a firing squad. War's war, Idwal. Anyhow, that's over and done with." He sat down and pushed a chair towards me with his foot. "Sit down and tell me all about yourself. How's Maire?" Maire was my sister.

"She's living in Wolverhampton," I told him. "Three kids."

"Give her my love when you write."

He caught me flat out. I tried to check my look of surprise but it was too late.

He roared. "Good God! What did you think I was going to do to you?"

"What the hell could I think?" I mumbled.

"Well, if *that's* what you're thinking you can forget it. What damn silly melodramatic nonsense. The only killing that's been done in this business has been done by that bunch of plug-uglies of *yours*. Don't forget *that*, young Idwal." He got up and crossed to the door and clapped his hands. "Now go on, hop it. Have a bath and a change and come back here to dinner in a better frame of mind."

A soldier came to the door.

I said, "What about the others?"

"They're being looked after," he said shortly. "I said hop it."

I followed the soldier to the next hut. He opened the door and stood aside to let me pass. It was small and delightfully warm. A charcoal fire glowed in the corner and in front of it was a steaming canvas bath. There was a camp bed made up with brightly coloured Tibetan rugs, and on it a set of under-clothes and a woollen shirt similar to the ones I was wearing, only these were clean. The soldier grunted and left me. I wallowed in the hot water until the greasy rime I made on the surface of it started to congeal, then I got out and towelled myself until I was raw. As I finished dressing again, the soldier came back and knocked at the door. I followed him back to the first hut. It was dark now and starting to snow heavily.

The table was set for two with a coarse white cloth and enamel plates, but there was a shaded lamp in the middle of it and it looked as cosy and inviting as a corner in Raffles. He always was a dainty feeder, even when we went out shooting. He was stirring the contents of a big stone casserole on the charcoal stove and the smell from it made me slaver. He turned and grinned at me.

"Only stew I'm afraid," he said. "But at least I know what's in it. I do my own cooking up here. These Manchurians are so bloody dirty. Help yourself to whisky and pour me one." He jerked his head at a bottle of Johnny Walker on a trunk by the wall and I poured two drinks. "Cheers," he said, and we drank. I said, "I don't want to harp on it, but those blokes of mine *are* being fed, I take it?"

"They haven't left off since they arrived," he answered. "Now, for the Lord's sake stop worrying about them." He filled a plate and put it down in front of me. "Get on with that," he ordered. "No talking until we're finished. *I've* been out in that damned cold all day too."

I think I beat him by a plateful, but as the Duke of Wellington put it, it was a damned close-run thing. He produced a box of long Burma cheroots when we finished and we stretched out in two rough-made but comfortable chairs each side of the stove, with glasses close to our elbows. I don't know when I've ever felt a greater sense of sheer physical well-being—nor, simultaneously, one of such cataleptic un-reality. I seemed to be two persons; one relaxed, warm, com-fortable—the other tensed and uncertain.

"Well?" he said at last. "Any questions?"

"I wouldn't know where to start," I answered.

"Nothing mysterious about it," he said. "I'm in oil."

"I noticed the wells as we came along."

"I'm not pulling your leg. It's a fact."

"I've heard rumors—" I began sceptically.

182

"Of course you have. That's what brought you up here. That crowd Smedley works for are a naive lot. All oil concerns are. Start a rumor about oil being found in the most unlikely spot and they'll bite at it, whatever their geologists may say. They *must* poke into it—just in case. They've wasted their time and money here though. There isn't any. Not yet anyhow."

"Put it down to the march, the stew and this whisky," I said. "I'm just not following."

He didn't answer for a time. He sat with his feet stretched out to the glowing stove, chin sunk on his chest, slowly swirling the whisky in his glass. "Those papers?" he said at last. "Did you have time to go through them?"

"We only unearthed them a matter of minutes before we ran into the patrol."

"They wouldn't have told you much—unless you already had the full background—and nobody has that, except us. Want to hear it from the beginning?"

I nodded.

There was another long silence. He leaned forward and put a scoop of charcoal into the stove and then settled himself back into his chair again. "What beat the Japs?" he said at last.

"Us—and the Bomb."

He shook his head. "They were beaten long before the Bomb fell. It was oil, my boy. Their whole war machine was grinding to a stop early in 'forty-four. They were running on synthetics and the piddling amounts they were able to get from the ruined wells in lower Burma—and that wasn't much use to them because the Allies had sea and air control and they had no proper lines of communication to get it back to Japan. The Chinese have known this for years. They're not going to be caught the same way. They've got everything else they want growing in their own front garden. Coal, iron, tungsten, copper and, when they've taken over Malaya, tin and rubber. They've got the biggest manpower reservoir in the world—indoctrinated—disciplined. Food isn't going to worry them, because the whole of the far East is going to be their rice bowl without firing a shot. Lord, man, you can see that for yourself—it's happening already."

"Rockets, the nuclears, the know-how," I put it. "They haven't got those yet—and I can't see anybody making a rod for their own back by giving them to them."

"Some of you people who should know better, make me sick," he said. "You were saying the same thing about the Russians as late as nineteen-fifty. You stopped feeling cosy one morning when somebody's seismograph picked up a nuclear explosion in the middle of Siberia though. Not even

183

Korea has altered the picture for some of you, of the Chinese being a race of docile peasants digging their paddy fields with wooden spades. Who the hell invented gunpowder? Who had mastered the mathematics of astronomy and navigation while the Greeks were still living in caves? Haven't got the nuclears? You'll learn one day—maybe. No, my boy—oil is the one thing that limits their potential at the moment; and it will continue to do so until somebody stumbles on the knack of making it cheaply from seawater—or they've got it flowing through their back door. When they've got that, the world will have a chance of survival—because China will be at least the equal of the other two power blocs in so-called conventional forces and will hold the balance—and the nuclears will have cancelled themselves out."

"So all we've got to wait for is oil from seawater or a tap at their back door and we'll all be dancing round the maypole again waving olive branches?" I said. "Give us another drink."

"Sneer if you like," he answered as he passed me the bottle. "But it's as simple as that. I don't know about the seawater—that's a bit too philosopher's stonish for me. I'm an engineer."

"So you pipe it in through the back door?"

"Just that. Go easy on that bottle. It's all we've got."

"Can't you get some more—through the same pipe?"

"Do you want to hear the rest of this?" he snapped.

"I do. Forgive the iconoclasm. Carry on, Uncle Stewart."

"Where is the world's greatest natural oil reserve?—or didn't the Christian Brothers tell you in our Shanghai alma mater?"

"The Persian Gulf, isn't it?"

"Exactly. And how far is that from the nearest point of the Chinese frontier—as it now stands?"

"How the hell do I know?" I burped slightly and lay back in my chair. The warmth and the food and the whisky was taking the tension out of me, and the relaxed me was getting the upper hand.

"Well don't go to sleep while I'm talking to you, for God's sake," he said in mild reproof. "Actually it's just a little over two thousand miles—I'm counting Tibet as Chinese territory, of course, and when we've made a deal with India about this disputed bit we're in now, it will be considerably less. Here, I'll show you."

He crossed to the trunk on which the whisky had been standing and lifted the lid, and when he turned back I recognised the oil-silk envelope in his hand. He put it on the table and then gathered up the plates we had been using and dumped them on the floor. He shook the contents of the envelope out onto the white cloth. He disregarded the maps and took up the notebook, leafing through it quickly. "Here

184

we are," he said, and laid the open book down under the lamp. "That chap Prentice did some pretty wild guessing but he wasn't far off the mark in this particular aspect of it."

I bent over and followed his pointing finger. It was a section of the top of the Indian sub-continent, freely but quite expertly drawn, with the mountain ranges beautifully hachured in fine pen-strokes. "See what I mean?" He traced a line obliquely down from the top righthand corner of the sketch towards the outer edge. "The Tibetan plateau running down south-east on this side—got it? Right—now follow this dotted line running straight west from it—across to Gilgit— on, north of the Indus outside Pakistan territory—just nipping through this southern bit of Afghanistan and so onto the Persian plateau and then going straight across the deserts to the head of the Gulf. That's as Prentice saw it. Actually he was wrong about Gilgit. He was assuming that we'd follow the valleys. The line will be more direct than that. He couldn't conceive of our tunnelling through the ranges a hundred miles at a stretch."

"I'm right with him," I said. "Neither could I."

"Neither could the stupid bastards who sent him out here in the first place. He'd been preaching the gospel of pipes across Kashmir for two years but they were still thinking in terms of Kipling's Kim and the Great Game. Russia was the bogeyman to be watched. Russia with her eye on Afghanistan and then British India. South to the north—yes. Pipes from the Gulf up to the shores of the Caspian they could understand. But this crazy idea of west to the east? Good God, what would John Chinaman want with pipelines?"

"Who and what was Prentice?" I asked.

"Their Man in Kashmir. The finest dumb linguist in the British Secret Service—but they didn't know how to use him."

"Dumb linguist?"

"He knew every dialect in this part of the world—but he never spoke anything but English. He just puttered round collecting rock specimens, butterflies and eidelweiss, and wrote books on them—but he was the best Private Ear the British ever had. He *told* them—he kept on telling them—about the survey parties up in the higher Himalayas. Russian reconnaissance, they said. The Chinese would take care of them when the time came. You wait until we've settled with the Germans and Japanese, and China is our strong, gallant and grateful Ally in the East again—in the meantime you just get on with siting those weather stations. Then he stumbled on something that he thought would convince them—"

"What?"

"A Chinese engineer lost in an avalanche and then uncovered by the winds months later—survey notes on him. Prentice told them about it in his second last report—and said he'd let them have the lot when he'd translated them." He flicked the pile of notes with his finger. "That's them. The stuff that never reached base."

I picked them up. They had dried now and were no longer stuck together—sheets of foolscap covered with smudged figures and words in technical English, alternating with rice paper that bore Chinese ideographs. I looked at them for a moment and then put them down. He was watching me closely.

"That's all it was, my boy. Old stuff now, and never very important—but it *might* have let a ray of light into their thick skulls if they'd seen them in those days. It might still—*if* they saw them. I doubt it though. They're too preoccupied with the sideshows—Korea first—then Malaya—Indo-China—Burmese border—scuffles between Chinese and Indian frontier guards—whether the Chinese will be offended if the Indians give the Dalai Lama a house in Mussouri—what's going to happen in Hongkong?—is there going to be a major flare-up in the Straits of Formosa? Brother Mao allee time makee monkey dance with left hand but keepee right hand behind him—still digging. And it will keep on digging—ten years— twenty years—just keeping pace with the new boundaries. As they get wider, the line gets longer. No fightee—just makee monkey dance. Nehru, or whoever comes after him, will make a noble gesture and buy him off with this useless bit of upper Kashmir that nobody wants to go to war over. Afghanistan will give no trouble. They're frightened of the Russians— they'll be only too glad to make a treaty with a strong China. Pipeline through our hills? Sure. And so into Persia—and by that time a perfected technique of tunnelling five hundred feet or so underground—a million Chinese burrowing like moles—just as thousands of Tibetans are doing at this moment right underneath us—and finally a take-over bid for a piece of the Persian oil country and an atom-proof pipeline smack into their back door. Have another drink."

I held out my glass. "All too big for me," I said.

He poured me another drink. The bottle was getting low now.

"Of course it's too big," he said. "But that's the way it's going to be. I've over-simplified it—but that's it."

"Where do *you* fit into it all?"

"Me? Oh, I'm only a small man—relatively. Call me a trouble-shooter for this section. Nothing technical. I just watch points. Keep the Tibetans from breaking out in large numbers—watch who comes up and down these passes—listening posts in India. The last's the most difficult. *You* know that already."

186

"Me?"

"Yes you. Good God, I knew Smedley had contacted this silly old chump Polson. I knew you were working for him. All I sent word down to do was to nobble Polson. I'd talked to him myself years ago and was convinced that he knew nothing. At the same time I didn't want a couple of professionals working on him—just in case. Well, what sort of a shambles did they make of it? First of all they lost Polson—then they picked you two up to find out where he was—then *you* gave them the slip—then they picked you up again in Lahore and same thing happens, and I lose sight of you completely until you pop up again north of 'Pindi. I managed to move Sutcliffe up ahead of you to cut you off on the road—then you bump him off."

"I didn't. He was alive when I saw him last," I said.

"Well he isn't now. You can take my word for that. I sent a posse of my boneheads down to turn that mission hospital place over as soon as I heard what had happened—but you'd flown the coop and he had just breathed his last—blast him."

"So they weren't police?" I said.

He shook his head. "No. I've got a few venal cops on my payroll in India itself, but none up here in Kashmir. Too risky. The force is riddled with Section B counter espionage men. That's the whole trouble. I'm tied up here and things are getting badly unbuttoned down there. I had five Europeans —four now—half a dozen Eurasians and a hundred or so allegedly intelligent locals—and they couldn't get their hands on an alcoholic poor white or stop you getting up here. And I *did* want to stop you. Believe that, Idwal." He shook his head sorrowfully and finished the whisky in his glass. "You kids were the nearest I ever had to a family—and I owe a lot to your old man. It was he who started me in the business."

"What business?"

"Uh?" He looked up at me absently. "Oh—sorry. What was it we were saying?"

"I said what business did my old man start you in?"

"Oh well—you know—he pushed a bit of work my way from time to time. Have another drink."

I shook my head. "Let's come back to this business. What was it?"

"What the hell does it matter?" he said impatiently. "The thing that's worrying me now is that you're up here—and what we're going to do with you."

"You told me you were going to let us go back."

"I'd like to—but use your sense laddie. You know the lot now, don't you?"

"Why have you told me?"

"Why? I don't know. Probably because I haven't talked to one of my own kind for a long time. A man gets lonely."

"I see," I said slowly. "So I don't go back?"

"Now don't go jumping to conclusions. I didn't say that at all. But even you can see that it's not going to be easy without —well, proper safeguards."

"Such as?"

"We'll come to those in a minute. In the meantime have you considered your own position in the matter."

"That's what we're discussing, isn't it?"

"I don't mean here. Down below—back in India?"

"In what connection?"

"Good God boy! There are two dead men in a house near Bassein Creek—"

"I didn't kill them."

"Don't quibble. It was your party—and you know the law of accessories. You *did* shoot Sutcliffe though."

"Self defense."

"Fine—you prove it. Listen—Sutcliffe worked for me—but he and that half-chat he had with him also worked for the Indian government—Tibetan refugee control. Those women at the mission are up to their ears in refugee running. Can't you see what it *could* look like?—particularly if Snaith were to testify? You could quite easily be in the racket too—they were on your tail—you and the girl made murderous assaults on them. Indian military court, don't forget—bit rough and ready—touchy position up here. Fair trial and twenty years— *if* you were lucky. Maybe the same for the girl—but that doesn't concern us; it's *your* position we're trying to sort out?"

"From what you're saying, that's pretty clear, isn't it? If I go back and start saying the wrong things to the wrong people, you can make it tough for me. As long as I keep my mouth shut you're not going to wake up any sleeping dogs. Isn't that it?"

"You make it sound pretty squalid—but that's it, more or less."

"And that goes for the others too?"

"We'll come to them in a minute. Let's stick to you. You're right. I not only don't wake sleeping dogs—I bury them— finish."

I shrugged. "There's no problem then. What sort of bloody idiot would I be to make trouble for myself?"

He grinned. "I think we're getting somewhere. All right then. That's hurdle number one over—but it's not a hundred per cent in itself. The safeguards must be steel-hard and binding."

"What else is there?"

"How about a job?"

"What sort of job?"

"A retainer of five thousand pounds sterling a year and a good expense account—and you can still run your own business on the side. In fact I'd insist on that. First class ready made cover."

"What would my duties be?"

"Allee same number one boy in Bombay—and that means all India. Just my contact man down there—keep your ear to the ground—keep me informed—kick that idle bastard Ram Dass up the arse when it's needed. Remote control adjutant if you like. What do you say?"

"It sounds wonderful—except for one thing."

"What's that?"

"I happen to be British. You're asking me to work against my own country."

He looked at me for a moment open-mouthed, then he said, "Say that again."

I said, "You heard me."

There was a depth of contempt in his voice. "Yes, I heard you. You're British. My God! How melodramatic can we get? British? *British?* What the hell are the British nowadays? Fifty million or so of them living in a welfare state in an island-and-a-bit off the north-west coast of Europe. Doing all right too—on a strictly 'damn you Jack, I'm all right basis'. The Empire on which the sun never sets? Dirty word now. That's all been handed back to the locals—pro tem. They did it because they loved the locals. Like hell. They did it because they no longer had the strength to hang onto things. Yes—it's all handed back and they've withdrawn to their free-milk-fair-shares-for-all burrows. You go back and try and horn in on it—you people who were born in the far places—and see where it will get you. Where's your union card? Where's your National Insurance Stamps? Are you *sure* you're *quite* British? Go and ask the poor bastards that Nasser threw out of Egypt after Suez. They were British too—they had British passports didn't they? Most of them are living in hostels in the Midlands on the same footing as any other refugees. British be damned. You're no more British than I am—than your father was. He stopped being British when he finished a five year stretch for forgery in Cardiff—and came out to Shanghai and changed his name—"

I hauled myself to my feet. "You dirty bloody liar!" I choked. He pushed me back into my chair.

"Okay," he said. "Take a swing at me later if you like. I'm telling you just what he told me himself—when I boggled at the job he offered me. 'I'm not British,' I lisped, 'but the British have been very good to me. They let my parents live in their Concession in Shanghai—and gave papa a good job spying on other Russian emigres. Who's Red?—Who's Pink?—Who's White as the driven snow? And the Christian Brothers educated me at cut rates for eleven dollars a month.' That's what I said. And do you know what *he* said? I'll tell you. 'There's no British, my boy,' he said, 'There's no Russians—no Chinese—no Hottentots—when it comes down to the simple mechanics of living. There's the man who pays you. For him you'd go to the stake—*while* he's still paying you.' That's what he said. All right—I'm offering you his philosophy. Take it and live, as he did. He worked for Chiang Kai Shek—and served him well. When Chiang double-crossed him he went over to the Japs. I went with him. When the Japs folded up I went back to the Chinese. Did they look at me reproachfully? Not a bit of it. I was a professional. They knew the code of the professionals. They're realists. They hired me and gladly—and I'm their man. Think it over. If you want proof of what I'm telling you I'll give it to you—later. I'm leaving here in the morning at first light. When I go, you either come with me, and I'll brief you on your job—and then you go back to India—or you stay here, and the troops will do what's necessary. It's as simple as that, Idwal. I'm sorry. I didn't want you to come—but you're here. That's your choice."

I sat hunched with my hands covering my face. "The others?" I mumbled. "What about the others?"

"The Pathan can go back with you. He's your man—and their philosophy is as simple as ours. The old soak? Think nothing of it. He wouldn't make the journey anyway."

"Smedley?"

"Smedley? Ah, yes—there's still Smedley, isn't there? When you come over, you come over for good, Idwal."

I looked up at him. He was measuring the last of the bottle against the light.

"What do you mean?" I asked.

"You shoot Smedley through the back of the head before we leave. *That's* the ultimate safeguard. Have another drink—there's just two half pegs left."

CHAPTER 22

There was the pattern. It must always run to the pattern. That is the weakness of it. There's no flexibility. First the physical stress—forced marches—lack of food and rest—exposure. We had done that for him already. After that came the easing of the tension—warmth, food, friendliness—swiftly, so that it hit one with a traumatic shock. 'Stage one schizophre-nia', in the book. You are two people—one relaxed, one taut-ened to screaming point, and you're pulling against each other and there's a hiatus in between. Then into the gap the casually dropped reference to one's family—photos if one's carrying them—"This your wife? How old's the boy?—Um, I've got two myself—eleven and seven."—"How's Maire? Give her my love." Common ground. A hand reaching to one through the darkness. Then pure, cold logic. Then back to the personal. Your problems and his—common ground again. A hint of something shameful in the past—a trump card if they've got it. The tiny creeping doubt—and you're whirling in the dark. The hand again—guiding, counselling, What have you got to lose? What have you got to gain? This? or this? The means justifying the end—oil for the lamps of China and the nuclears cancel each other out and there's hope for the world's survival. Then the Shock. The pit's at your feet—one step—you're in it, or you're over. Lean on me and you're over—one step—one step—

I said, "No." But I didn't look at him.

"Four men die your way, Idwal. For what? A blazoned in-scription—'he kept faith'? Faith with what?—and what do you blazon it on? That's the rub. Nobody will ever know—except me. Four heaps in the snow—and no trumpets. That's your way. My way there's only two—and still nobody knows—except me."

"And me."

"And you. The next line is 'I've got to live with myself after-wards.' Forget it. We're all living with ourselves. Do you think this has never been done before? Good God—I could give you the names of three high-ranking officers in Korea alone. You'll live with yourself all right. That's the operative word—'live'."

"Let the troops do it," I said.

"The ultimate safeguard, Idwal. *You* do it."

"I can't." My fists were bunched and I was pressing them into my eyes and I was swaying backwards and forwards like a peasant woman mourning.

" 'The mechanics of living,' " he said softly. "Your old man's words."

I whispered, "How?—When?" I still wasn't looking at him.

"Into the hut. One round in the gun. The troops will come in when they've heard it. Now."

"I've got to have a drink," I said.

"Afterwards. There's only two half pegs left."

"No—now. All of it." The bottle was on the floor between us. I reached for it. The neck rattled on the rim of the glass as I poured. He sat looking at me. There was understanding and even sympathy in his face. 'Stage four—human relationship as the patient breaks.' Both were blotted out as the bottom of the bottle took him in the mouth. I reversed my grip and tried to brain him before he yelled but he jerked his head sideways and the blow missed. My forward rush took him backwards as he was struggling to his feet, and our combined weight tipped his chair over with a crash. We fell over it and as we hit the ground I got my right hand on his throat. My left was fumbling frantically for his right because he was trying to get at his belt under his smock. He had to stop that, however, and use both hands to try and break my grip on his throat. But now my thumbs were each side of his windpipe and I had the mad strength of blind fury. His fingers were clawing at my face—ripping—tearing—and in a convulsive heave he managed to get his knees up under my belly and twist me sideways, but he had no power to break that grip. I couldn't have done so myself because my fingers were locked. We thrashed about like two landed fish—and then he stiffened and went still—but I still pressed with both thumbs. I was pressing a full five minutes later, when the madness receded, leaving me weak and sick.

I got to my feet and waited until the room stopped spinning. I wondered dully why the troops hadn't come in. Surely there must have been a sentry somewhere. I remember looking down at him and saying aloud, "*Five* heaps under the snow, Uncle Stewart," and giggling foolishly.

I leaned against the wall sucking air in great gasping sobs and waiting for something to happen. But nothing did—and gradually my wits returned to me. I crossed to the door and opened it the barest chink. The wind was howling outside and the snow was being blown horizontally against the hut. I closed it again quickly. That explained the absence of a sentry on that side at least. I began to wonder if there was one outside at all. Surely if there had been he would have heard the noise.

I crossed to Stewart again and stood looking down at him. His head was twisted at an unnatural angle on his neck and his eyes stared sightlessly back at me. His smock had worked up, exposing the pistol he had been trying to reach. I stooped and took it from his belt.

I weighed it in the palm of my hand—and I wondered—slowly, because the fogs had still not cleared. My eyes went round the room—past the overturned chairs and the now dying charcoal fire, and finally came to rest on the opened trunk from which he had taken the envelope. I went over to it. Lying in the bottom of it were the things the troops had taken from us, ranged out neatly in order—two pistols, binoculars, compass, maps, body-belts, Safaraz's knife. Mechanically I started to gather them up and stow them away in the pockets of my smock. I went to the table and crammed the other maps and the notes back into the envelope feverishly. I knew what I was going to do now. Without equipment and provisions we wouldn't have a chance in this blizzard—even if we could succeed in getting out—which was absurd anyhow. There was only one way into this tiny valley—the narrow defile through which we had entered, and that was covered by the machine-gun emplacement. That was bound to be guarded even if there were no sentries on the individual buildings inside. There *was* one faint chance though. Safaraz might have a hope in a million of making it if he could creep past under the loopholes. Whether he could cover the twenty or thirty miles back through loose snow to the last Indian post we had passed was another matter. I was damned certain he couldn't. Having dealt with us when the alarm went up, the troops would catch him as soon as there was light enough to follow his tracks. Still—there was that millionth chance—and Smedley and I, if I could get them out of their huts, with three pistols between us might be able to hold things up for a time before we were overwhelmed. Anyhow, it was better than waiting tamely for the inevitable end—and maybe there would be more than five heaps under the snow at the final count.

I was about to slip through the door again when my eye fell on Stewart's sheepskin coat hanging behind it. I had left mine in the hut in which I had bathed. I slipped it on and pulled the hood up over my head. I looked at the lamp. It would be better to put that out before I opened the door again. If anybody looked in they might conceivably think that he had gone to bed—and that gave me another idea. I went over to him and got him by the shoulders and dragged him across to the bed and struggled to get him up onto it—then I covered him with the blankets, leaving only the top of his head showing. I straightened the room up after that, and finally doused the lamp.

The cold hit me like a solid wall as I went out. I closed and latched the door behind me and stood for a second trying to get my bearings. Unless they had moved the prisoners, Safaraz was in the next hut. I wondered if there would be anybody in with him—or a sentry outside. If there was, that would be the end of the venture—but at least there would be six heaps. I took out one of the guns, eased back the jacket and cocked it—then I sidled along the wall towards the next hut. It was one of a row of about six if I remembered aright—small isolated affairs that looked like storehouses for explosives or ammunition. I wasn't noticing much when I arrived, but the impression remained that there were two bigger ones that were probably barrack huts one each side of the defile—then there was the one I had just come from, and finally the one I had bathed in. I hoped fervently I was right.

I peered round the corner. There was a deep drift here and no black bulk broke its whiteness. I ploughed through the snow to the next hut. Like all the others, it was windowless. I felt along to the door. There was a huge baulk of timber securing it and I had to discard my gun while I fumbled it out of the slots each side with frozen fingers. I pushed the door back creakily and stepped inside, gun in one hand and torch in the other. I pushed the door shut with my back and shone the torch. There was only one figure there, huddled in a sheepskin coat in the corner. I breathed freely again. I crossed to it and stirred it with my foot and Safaraz sat up and blinked into the light.

I said, "Silence, Safaraz. Follow me."

He bit back the delighted yell that was forming and got stiffly to his feet. "Shabash, sahib!" he said. "And now some Japanis die."

"Not yet," I said. "Listen carefully. Do you remember from whence we came—and how?"

"From the south, sahib, skirting the foot of the hills the whole way."

"How then, would the track run back to where we passed the Indian fort, at the head of the first pass?"

"East across the plateau, sahib. As we stand at this place to our front and our right."

"Could you find your way back?—in the dark and in heavy snow?"

"Sahib," he said reproachfully. "You, my sahib, ask me that? I, Safaraz, son of Wazir, son of—"

"All right—all right—" I shut him up. "Here—take this packet—" I handed it to him and waited while he stowed it away inside his sheepskin. "Now—you make for the fort. You tell them, without lying, of me and Smedley sahib and the old man. Where we came from—how we came. You tell them that Kavronski—repeat that—" He had three or four tries before he mastered it. "Right—Kavronski was here with the Japanis—but he is now dead. You give the officer these papers and you say one other name—Prentice. *Prentice.* Say that."

"Prentish."

"Good—now all of it from the beginning."

"We came from India and there was much fighting, and the idolators shot Sher Ali in the back and—"

It took me five minutes to strip the message down to its bare essentials and to get it into his skull, conscious as I was doing it that it was a waste of time because he would never

194

make it, but at last I got the names over to him at least, and I hoped that *if* he reached the fort, the officer in charge would have the savvy not to waste too much time trying to sort the wheat from the chaff of Safaraz's boastful mendacity, and would push him on down the line to somewhere where a trained Intelligence interrogator could get to work on him before the details became too blurred.

"And where do the sahibs go while I am away?" he demanded as I gave him his knife and a gun.

"The sahibs have other work here," I told him.

"Then we stay and do it together," he said flatly.

"You will do as I tell you. It is an order."

"The sahib would not give an order that would blacken my face."

I knew that this would arise and I was prepared for it.

"My honor, and the honor of my father is in those papers. If they do not arrive *my* face is blackened," I told him.

"Why don't we go together to deliver them?" he grumbled.

"Because the old man could not march—and then we would all be caught on the plateau—then we all die and the papers are not delivered, and my face remains blackened— and I have no son to clear my name!" Excellent argument, theoretically unanswerable by a Pathan—that is a Pathan with an ounce of intelligence—but Safaraz had no intelligence —only an animal cunning and a blind loyalty. He said flatly, "I don't go."

"It is an order," I told him.

"I am no longer a soldier—and the sahib is not an officer. He is a box-wallah from Bombay and I am a servant and I have not had my wages for this month or last, therefore I am not in the sahib's service any longer and the sahib cannot give me any orders."

"I could give you a thrashing."

"And I would take it—but I remain true to my salt. Am I less than a man? The sahib should not ask this of me."

"Owl! Ox! Frontier camel spawn! Do you go or do I spit in your face as one who is afraid of the snow and the dark?" I raged.

"Spit in my face. We go together or I stay here."

We were wasting time. It was like trying to move a mountain. I said, "Come with me then—and quietly. If we fail it is on your head, and that of your family."

"Yes, sahib," he said happily, and followed me.

We crept through the snow to the next hut. Safaraz opened up and remained at the door while I went inside. The Major was snoring loudly. I sank on one knee and put my hand over his mouth. He woke and started to struggle and it took me some time to make him understand who I was. I helped him

195

to his feet. He was shaking like a leaf and his legs were buckling under him. I knew he wouldn't make more than a few yards but there was nothing for it. I helped him outside and then we went on to the next hut. Smedley was awake, sitting hunched against the rear wall. He blinked into the beam of the torch.

I said, "We're going to try and get out. We haven't an earthly but they're going to butcher us in the morning anyhow. What do you feel about it?"

"Up to you," he said.

"Come on then. We'll crawl to that guard post by the entance and try and sneak past. I'll send Safaraz in front but you'll have to help me with the Major— He's about had it."

We snaked through the snow, Safaraz a length in front and Smedley and I dragging the old man by his hood. The machine-gun post was now a shapeless hump half buried in a drift. We circled round it as widely as we dared without getting too close to the bigger huts that flanked it. A door in one of the latter opened just as we were abreast of it, and a man came out. He stood framed against the glow of a stove inside and we were near enough to hear the muffled sounds of sleeping men and to feel the draught of warm fetid air that came out. I thought this was the end of it—but as we lay flat in the freezing snow he hawked, spat and then urinated— then shivered and went in again. We crawled on.

It was an anti-climax. If there was anybody in the emplacement they were snugged down for the night. We couldn't even see the slits, and after covering another five yards on our bellies we couldn't see the emplacement either. We had no difficulty in finding the defile because the wind was howling right up it into our faces. We got to our feet and leaned into it. The Major seemed to have rallied a little, because he shook off the supporting hands of us both and battled along on his own. I thought of trip wires, but if there were any there the snow had covered them to a depth that made them useless.

We came out into the plain, and the wind, no longer funnelled in the defile, seemed to abate a little. The snow had had no chance to drift here and the path was clear. We turned left, the way we had come, and set off. I came up alongside Smedley.

"Pretty hopeless," I told him. "They'll find out before long and they'll be on our tail as soon as it's light." I passed him a gun.

"Where are we making for?" he asked.

"I hadn't even thought. I tried to persuade Safaraz to make a run for it on his own to that fort but the bastard won't leave us."

196

"Hat's off to the bastard," said Smedley. "What's been happening?"

"Quite a lot. I saw our friend Kavronski—"

"How's he keeping?"

"He's not. He gave me three months brainwashing in two hours. Then I choked the son of a bitch."

"Hat's off to you too. So the trip's on Yev."

"One way only. We've got no equipment and no food and a two day march ahead of us in breaking weather. Those Chinese will just come out and fan over the plateau till they pick us up."

"Do we have to keep on the plateau?"

"What the hell else? The alternative is to start climbing— but then we're going away from any chance we've got of safety. Anyhow, the Major couldn't climb. No—that's our way—to the right—and they'll know it."

"Why did we come out at all then?"

"I told you," I said. "There might have been a faint chance of Safaraz getting through—but that's out now. He won't go. I'm too tired to argue any more."

"You're tired all right. I can tell that. Are you open to a suggestion?"

"Smedley," I said. "I can't even think any more. I'm sorry."

"Okay then—for what it's worth. This way we're going to get picked up. Turn to the left and it *may* fox them. You say we're going to die anyhow. All right then, let's turn left if it's going to inconvenience them. Let's sit up there among the rocks and watch them looking for us. Let's climb—if it's only for the laughs. What do you say?"

I didn't say anything because at that moment a curious thing happened. It was the normal reaction but I didn't know that then. I didn't know anything. I stopped walking. I stopped doing anything. I didn't keel over and I was still fully conscious. I just stood—rock-still and rigid. Smedley ploughed on—head bent into the wind—still talking, and the Major and Safaraz walked into my back. Sarafaz said, "What now, sahib?" and waited expectantly. I didn't answer. I couldn't. Ahead of us Smedley stopped, a blur in the darkness, then came back. "What did you say?" he asked. And still I stood there. Safaraz shook my arm—then fumbled in the side pocket of my sheepskin. The Major said, "What the hell's going on?" and there was a rising note of panic in his voice.

The torch flashed into my face. The light hurt my eyes but I couldn't close them against it. Smedley said, "My God— what have they done to his face?"

"He's out—out to the wide—on his bloody feet," said the Major. "Smedley—for God's sake *do* something." He started

197

to shake me and suddenly the rigidity passed and I buckled at the knees. I heard Safaraz say, "Put your hand on him again, low-born, and I'll slit your throat. Come, sahib." He got me to my feet—my arm across his shoulders and his round my waist, and then my feet were working mechanically keeping time draggingly with his.

Smedley said to the Major, "Tell Safaraz we're going up —up. It's our one chance, if only to hide and let Rees rest." And I heard the Major translate it into Urdu. Safaraz swung me left and scrabbled at the snow bank and then started to pull me up a step at a time. The inertia passed as quickly as it had struck me and I found myself climbing, but I still couldn't speak.

We were in a narrow gully. On that scarred hillside you had either to be in a gully or on the ridge that separated two of them, because there were no plane surfaces. This one was relatively easy because the torrent that coursed down it in summer had worn the stones into a series of irregular steps, and the wind, which was now behind us, had swept them clear of snow, so that even the Major was coping. We went up and up—climbing now like automatons—until Safaraz, who was leading, came to a huge smooth boulder which blocked the whole gully. He said, "Wait, sahib," and scrambled round the side of it and disappeared into the darkness. He was back in a matter of minutes and he took my arm and pulled me up the side of the boulder and over the top of it. It formed a ledge that sloped backwards, and the wind, striking the smooth outer face of it seemed, by some freak of aerodynamics, to be deflected upwards over our heads, leaving us in an area of comparative calm. Smedley said, "We're probably hidden from down below, and we're out of that bloody wind. Let's stay. What do you say, Rees?" I still couldn't answer.

"Leave him alone awhile," said the Major. "I've seen this happen to a bloke on the Frontier—two blokes. The Pathans got 'em and gave them the works. Some of this black bastard's brothers no doubt. They couldn't speak for a couple of days, and the poor devils would cry if you looked at them. Delayed shock, that's what it's called. Keep him warm and give him plenty of hot, sweet tea. Gawd! What a hope."

That is all I remember of that night.

It was broad daylight when I woke. The wind had dropped, it had stopped snowing and the sky was clear. I lay on my back looking up at it. My face felt stiff and sore and my eyes were hurting. I put my hand up to them, and as I moved, the Major said, "Lumme? Surfaced have you?" I turned over on my elbow. He was sitting hunched against the rock face, his knees drawn up under his chin.

I said, "Where are the others?"

"Moved round to the flank a bit. You can't see much from here. How're you feeling?"

"All right."

"You don't look it. What did them bastards do to your face?"

"Never mind that now. How long have we been here?"

"Not having a watch, can't say. It was dawn a few hours ago—five—six—how do I know? You've been out like a light. What's going to happen now, Mr. Rees?"

"You tell *me*."

"That's not right," he said accusingly. "You're commanding this show, aren't you? I didn't want to come— You others made me—now you say 'you tell *me*'. That's not right, Mr. Rees. All I asked was, what's going to happen now?"

He was still going on in this vein when Smedley and Safaraz dropped down over the edge of the gully above us. Smedley looked at me anxiously and said, "You all right now?" I said, "Yes."

"You passed clean out on your feet last night. We were having an argument about—"

"I remember what happened," I said shortly. "Never mind about that. What have you seen from up there?"

"Two patrols—going like the hammers of hell. One passed right beneath us, going back the way we came yesterday—the other cut straight out across the plain—going west. That was just after dawn."

"How many men?"

"Twelve in the one underneath us—fourteen in the other."

"They're reckoning on us heading back for the pass into Kashmir, obviously," I said, "and they're moving down to cut us off. Just as I thought. That puts an end to trying to get to the Indian fort."

"What do we do then?"

"I thought I'd made that clear last night. There's damned little we can do. I'm sorry—but it's no use blinking facts."

"Damn it all—we're not going to sit here and just freeze or starve to death, are we?"

I had no answer to that. For something to do I took my map out. Safaraz grinned at the Major. "There, ancient one," he said. "As I told you. My sahib reads the map and kam-puss. We march."

I fixed our present position as well as I could. Seven hours march north of the pass—say twenty miles at the speed they had driven us. The valley wasn't shown but I scaled off the distance along the range and marked it with a pebble. We had come perhaps two miles back along the same track—I moved the pebble. That put us almost due east of the fort thirty miles away—but between us and it a deep valley cut back into the plain—and the contour lines were almost touching. To circle round it would put another ten miles on. To climb down into it and up the other side looked impossible, even on paper. The only map route was the way we had come—down to the plateau again and along to the pass and then follow the track —but now we knew that two patrols were scouring that route. I tried to put myself in the place of the Chinese N.C.O.'s commanding them. There was nothing we could make for other than the fort, within a hundred miles—five days march at least, without food. Out of the question. It *had* to be the fort. It would *have* to be round the head of the valley or along to the pass and then down the track. All right then—I would picquet both these routes—moving out at top speed and leaving say three men under cover on each, and then I would fan out and comb the ground between the foot of the range and those picquets. Would I assume that the quarry would climb this enormous range behind us and move along the crest to the north and then come down in again, say twenty miles away in the opposite direction? And then essay a march straight across country, away from all tracks—making it all a distance of—I scaled it out—just over fifty miles? No—not unless the quarry was mad. No food—no sleeping bags or tents? As a Chinese N.C.O. I wouldn't have much faith in compasses either. No—the quarry wouldn't do that. I was pretty damned certain we *wouldn't* either. If we made ten miles a day we'd be lucky. Still—I stopped being a Chinese N.C.O. rather reluctantly, and became myself again.

"An eight thousand foot climb up to the top then another climb down," I told Smedley. "A fifty mile slog round in the opposite direction to the two routes I think the Chinese will assume we are likely to follow. Most of it at night—by compass. That's the best I can do. How does it strike you?"

"Bloody awful," he said. "When do we start?"

"We can start the climb now—this gully is fairly well screened from view down below. It will be late afternoon when we get to the top. An hour's rest only—then on through the dark. Did they feed you last night, by the way?"

"Nary a bite." My heart sunk lower. We just hadn't a chance. But I couldn't face the question in their eyes any longer. I got up. "Come on," I said, and started climbing.

We should have waited until dark of course. I hadn't thought of yet a third patrol. Thirty men was the most I'd have put the strength of that post at; twenty-six out looking for us, and about four left behind.

These fellows came round the foot of the cliff after we had been going about an hour. Safaraz spotted them first. He was bringing up the rear and he had stopped to let the Major make a bit of distance ahead of him, and had turned to look back. Smedley and I were on the only bit of snow on that whole climb—just where the gully opened out before driving into the slope again—and we were moving. We must have stuck out like sore thumbs. Safaraz called to us warningly but it was too late. We heard their yell thin and shrill through the clear air. That's the one thing the Chinese haven't learned—to keep quiet in pursuit.

They were a good two thousand feet below us—say an hour's hard climbing. I reckoned sundown was about an hour off also, and *we* were on easier going now. We might perhaps just make the crest when they reached the spot we were at now. We *might* just make it. We *might* get to the top as darkness fell. That was another thing they hadn't learned—to follow in the dark. They *might* think we would be turning south at the top—the obvious route. They *might*— They *might*—

Behind me I could hear the others gasping and panting as we climbed.

CHAPTER 23

We still might have made it. In fact there was one period when I was positive we would—when a plan so obvious, so startling in its simplicity occurred to me, that I stopped dead. These pursuers could yet be our deliverers. A narrow neck in the gully was all we required. A narrow neck where men could move only slowly in single file. Smooth-sided and steep, and with no cover for the pursuers once they had entered it, but with some at the top of it that *we* could get behind. Three pistols between us—two sevens and an eight—a total of twenty-two rounds. There were twelve of them, Safaraz said. They would all have burp-guns, and their fire-power would, on the face of it, overwhelm ours—but we would have the advantage of cover and surprise and superior height. Aimed shots from us which could, with luck and fire discipline, take the three leading men—perhaps a second three as the remainder turned and made for cover. Half their force gone. Two of us pinning them down while one of us crept back and got the weapons of the fallen men—odds almost even then, with us holding the advantage of height. Emergency rations on the casualties—and coming darkness our ally. Theoretically perfect. Theory always is.

It was the ground we wanted now. We had passed through two deep funnels that would have been ideal, but in my blind panic to get to the top no alternative plan had then occurred to me—and now we were on an open face, smooth unbroken scree that gave no cover. If we tried to make our stand here they would see us long before they got within pistol range and would be able either to rake us with their more powerful weapons before ours could reach them or, if they wanted us alive, send half their force round on a detour to outflank us and get between us and the top. No—we had to have a narrow defile. We had to have surprise.

We were bunched together now; Smedley and I just about coping, the Major an inert bundle being hauled over the scree by the superhuman efforts of Safaraz. Safaraz wouldn't be able to keep it up much longer. He had been doing three men's work ever since we left the camp, and even if his great heart didn't crack, his muscles and lungs would have to before long. I gasped the plan out to them—line by line alternately in English and Urdu. Ahead of us from our present position we could see nothing but the false crest that made a straight unbroken line against the sky. It moved ahead of us, mocking us like an oblique horizon. Once past that, and the broken outcroppings of rock might start again—and through them the funnel that would save us.

Try and imagine that slope. It went up from the plateau below us to the one above, a full eight thousand feet according to the contour lines on the map. The overall angle from bottom to top would have been about forty-five degrees, but it was not uniform. The whole slope was a series of saucers of varying diameters—from a few yards to three or four hundred. Some of the saucers were face up—some bottoms up—concave and convex slopes alternating irregularly. We were now in the lower portion of a convex slope—an upside down saucer—and it was the bulge of this that was making the false crest above us. What lay the other side of that bulge we could not see until we gained it. On the lower slopes of a convex saucer, we and our pursuers were intervisible. Once we had the bulge between us, cutting the line of sight, we could not see each other. Across a concave slope—a saucer the right way up—we were in full view of each other the whole time. It was far more complicated than that, of course, because sometimes a very big saucer—concave or convex—would contain many smaller ones. What we wanted, ideally, was either two big concave saucers adjoining each other but with their rims not touching by a couple of hundred yards or so, with a narrow gully connecting them across that intervening space, or, on the other hand, a similar sort of gully scor-

202

ing the lower bulge of a convex saucer. We had, as I have said, passed two perfect examples of this—one of each—lower down, and I make no excuse for passing them. They should have caught the eye of a recruit lance-corporal. Now I was praying for a third. There *had* to be a third, because the gap between us and the Chinese had narrowed to about six hundred yards and was closing rapidly, and we were intervisible. Had either side possessed rifles, and marksmen capable of using them, we could have picked each other off—but a pistol has no accuracy over fifty yards—a burp-gun perhaps twice that range. A .303 Service Lee Enfield in the hands of Safaraz, even perhaps of myself, and there would have been no problem, He was telling the Prophet that as he manhandled the Major up the sliding scree.

The Chinese did, in fact, open up once or twice with bursts of automatic fire, and the echoes reverberated from crag to crag, but where the shots themselves landed we could not tell. Certainly nowhere near enough to worry us—yet.

And then we were over the final bulge and out of sight.

We were in a concave saucer now—and it was the last. Across its four hundred yard diameter its further rim was the final crest itself. It was a sheer wall and at first sight it looked damned unpromising because the sun was dead at our backs and its dying rays shone straight onto it so, if there were any gullies in it we could not see them, because of the lack of telltale shadows. This gave the advantage to the Chinese because it was now shining onto us also, and when they emerged into the saucer they would be advancing onto us out of it.

There was not enough cover in the saucer for a partridge. Not a loose rock bigger than two fists together. If they caught us in here it would be the end. They could just circle us and close in, outranging us two yards to one. We had to reach the opposite wall and find a gully before they came up to the rim we were now crossing. There was snow in this saucer too. Lower down the wind had swept it clear.

We stopped and drew air into our tortured lungs. It was thin and lacking in oxygen. The Major sank down onto his knees. "We've bloody had it," he moaned and passed out finally. Safaraz bent down and hauled him up over his shoulder in a fireman's lift, but his blue lips and ghastly face told me that this would be his last effort. He still managed a grin though as he set off in a tottering run, the old man's head dangling like that of a dead scrub-turkey.

How we made that four hundred yards I don't know. We did though—and we reached the foot of the further rim just as the baying yells of the Chinese told us that they had breasted the edge and had seen us. We even found a gully—

made to order right where we needed it. Six feet wide and with sheer smooth walls—running straight into the hillside. Perfect.

We shot into it—Safaraz leading, then Smedley, then me. Yes—perfect—except that it had no cover—and it ended against yet another wall. No more than twenty feet high perhaps, and even with a few handholds in it. A fit man, commando-trained, shouldn't have boggled at it. It was the end of the line for us though. The perfect cul-de-sac. It was so complete and decisive that it left no room for despair, fear, anger or frustration. Just acceptance. Smedley even grinned and called it a certain specific creek and gave our estimated distance up it, without paddles. Safaraz dumped the Major on the ground and murmured, "There, ancient one. Some Japanis will die now. I am sorry you will not see it." Then we turned —literally backs to the wall—and waited with pistols cocked.

We couldn't see them because now the sun had dipped below the opposite hills, and the floor of the saucer was in deep shadow. But we could hear them—an N.C.O. barking staccato orders, and the others repeating them back as they used to in Korea. They probably couldn't see us either, but they quite obviously knew where we had gone because the scrunching of their feet through the thin snow onto the scree beneath it was getting louder and converging onto us.

Then they came into sight—blurred shadows against the greying snow. One of them yelled as he picked up our tracks, and the others bunched in on him. They were about a hundred and fifty yards off but they still couldn't see us. They probably wouldn't until the flashes of our pistols gave our position away—then would come the combined shattering volley. Anyhow, it would be quick.

Safaraz said, "I ask forgiveness for calling the sahib a boxwallah. The debt of my wages is cancelled."

I said, "Thank you, my son and brother. The road has been long but our friendship has lightened it. Allah bismillah— and may you never be tired."

"May you never be poor," he answered. It is the Pathan greeting and farewell, and translation cheapens it.

And now they were up to less than a hundred yards. We brought our pistols up together. "Wait for it," I said—and then the heavens opened and spat fire.

It was a solid wall of thunder and it nearly split our eardrums. It beat down on us from above and stupefied us. I remember thinking, "It doesn't hurt," and then wondering why we were still standing. But we didn't stand for long, because we were borne down under sheer weight of numbers and feet were pounding us into the scree—but they came from above, not the front.

And then, before the echoes had died, it had passed and there were leaping shapes between us and the Chinese, and yelling all round us. Hands grasped me and pulled me to my feet and bodies were pressing into me so that I couldn't get my pistol up. I couldn't see Smedley but I did catch a glimpse of Safaraz. He had got his knife out somehow but the press was too close on him also, and he was holding it stiffly above his head, trying frantically to slash downwards with it. And then a voice was yelling in broken Urdu, "Peace, fool! Friends." and I recognised the Tibetan caps.

There were nearly a hundred of them. Kampas. The savage tribesmen of Western Tibet. The only tribe they recruit into their largely irregular army. Bandits to a man when they aren't actually serving—but, in or out of the army, the most fanatically nationalistic of them all. The men who brought the Dalai Lama over the passes—and then went back to fight. The Jannissaries of the upper slopes.

All this came later, of course, when they had stripped the carcases of the Chinese of their arms, equipment and clothing. It came haltingly because only two of them spoke Urdu, and not well at that, so interpreting was a slow business. They had had us in view since mid-morning, I learned, using us as stalking horses for our pursuers—watching both parties from the heights, unseen by either—waiting, just one ridge ahead of us—for the perfect killing ground.

They were wildly jubilant at their booty. Twelve burp-guns with one hundred and fifty rounds apiece. Twenty-four grenades that made my flesh creep as they handled them exultantly and hamfistedly. Forty-eight compressed day-ration packs that stunk to high heaven of decaying fish, but which they were tearing apart with their teeth and chewing ecstatically. They shoved chunks of it into our mouths—poked out their tongues—grabbed us by the elbows and slowly gyrated with us in grotesque dances.

They hauled us up the last ledge like so many sacks of grain, onto the plateau above and into a dip where their ragged, hairy ponies stood picketed head to tail, with their muzzles bound to prevent their whinneying. They lit tiny fires with yak dung that they carried in bundles behind their saddles, and made up witches' brews of tsampa, buttered tea and the rotten compressed fish as a relish. It smelt like hell and it tasted worse, but we gorged like vultures on a carcass. They asked where we were going, and I told them Kashmir and explained the route we were intending to follow. They shook their heads firmly and assured us that the whole lower plateau was now crawling with Chinese and that there had been skirmishing between them and the Indian troops at the fort. That way was definitely out. There was only one route now—the track that their softer brethren from further east used, to avoid forced labor in the Chinese gangs. We asked if we could use it also—and they said yes; as men who would move Tibetan dead into the shadow of a prayer cairn we had acquired merit—and I realized that the jungle was not the only place where unseen eyes watched and news travelled over great distances without the aid of the inventions of the West. They even knew of the death of Uncle Stewart, and had a garbled version of our part in it. The post, guarded by only a few Chinese, had been over-run and comprehensively looted by them earlier in the day. We were bringers of goodluck, specifics against ague, bellyache, Chinese, and all the other ills that betided honest men. There was much toasting in greasy tea and much hanging out of tongues in salutation—and then, thank God, they rolled us in yak-hair rugs and let us sleep.

They had decamped when we woke, long after dawn next day, leaving only four of their number behind with eight ponies. These men sat regarding us solemnly, squatting cross-legged in the snow with their hideous two-inch-bore muzzle-loaders across their knees. Neither of them spoke Urdu but they evidently had their orders. They fed us again and then mounted us on the spare ponies and we set off along the ridge, but clear of the skyline, at a fast mile-eating trot which had the skin off our backsides within the hour but which was still preferable to walking.

We went steadily south, hour after hour. I marvel still at what those ponies can do on a capful of coarse parched barley a day. I tried to pinpoint our position on the map once or twice, but it was impossible on the move, and when we stopped I was far too tired even to care.

We camped that night on the ridge, and next day started to descend. I *did* make a stab at fixing ourselves by map and compass before we started, but I couldn't recognize any of the peaks now. We did about thirty miles that second day, and came at sundown to the top of a long pass running south-west. They camped with us again and fed us once more next morning and then hung out their tongues, grinned broadly and pointed down the pass. Then they had mounted and gone like the wind back north, bouncing in their saddles, yelling like fiends and driving the spare ponies before them.

"Funny buggers, them Kampas," said the Major. "Had to watch 'em in the old days. Pinch the eye out of a bloody needle, they would."

We set off down the pass—walking stiffly and wide-legged. We had a bad moment in the afternoon when, now over-confident, we came round a corner of the track and ran smack into a group of people drinking tea round a small fire

—but they were Tibetans—men, women and some small children—thirty in all. They were less surprised to see us than we were them, because they merely poked out tongues, made room for us and gave us tea in wooden bowls. When we had finished it, they gathered up their bits and pieces, beckoned to us to follow and set off down the track. We had been a little worried when our escort had left us without food—but this was evidently the arrangement. Don't ask me how they fixed it because I wouldn't even hazard a guess.

That day's march was a killer. We were below the timberline now and our clothes were bearing us down. We started to discard them, garment by garment, and to carry them over our shoulders—then they got too heavy and we threw them away, but the Tibetans merely picked them up and politely draped them over us again like Ancient Mariner's albatrosses.

We were still marching long after nightfall, the Major, out again, being supported by Safaraz and myself, and Smedley staggering in blind circles. And then we came to an open spur and we were pushing through camel thorn that tore through even our thick trousers, and finally we fetched up under an archway in a high wall and there were lights, and I was delirious because I could hear a woman's voice counting in English, "—nineteen, twenty—three children, Ethel—twenty-one—twenty-two—" I don't remember any more.

It was warm, and under and around me was a softness that felt and smelt clean. That much I knew before I even awoke. I opened my eyes but it was pitch dark. I sat up slowly and a hand in my chest pushed me back again gently. I lashed out and a man's voice said, "Easy, you sap."

I said, "Christ! I'm blind!" and moaned in self pity.

"Blind nothing," said the voice—then, "Claire! Round again—and cussing." I went to sleep again.

They took the bandages off some time later. I was sitting up propped against pillows. I saw Railton first. He was peering into my eyes through a small thing that had a light on the end of it and it hurt. He said, "No damage to the pupils—just severely blood-shot. Okay, you can leave the bandages off now. I'll have a look at the others." He got up from the edge of the bed and went out and I wondered what the hell an engineer was doing in a white coat and with a stethoscope round his neck. I must have wondered aloud because the girl said, "Because he wouldn't engage in illegal activities behind the screen of his profession, that's why. He's our chief undercover M.O."

I turned my head. She was beside me and behind me—and this time she was smiling. She was a different girl when she smiled. I told her so.

Claire took us all down three days later. We had to by-pass 'Pindi because things were hotting up and there were troop movements afoot. We had to be careful in Lahore too, and here she was nervous because she was out of her territory. I was glad, because I was able to take over now. We went to Yev's shop and once again he rigged us out—and once again it was on the house—and his blessing went with it—and another car, but unfortunately the same driver—but this time there were no blind hill turns. It was flat all the way to the Indian border—and beyond it to her father's farm.

I am writing this there now. Smedley has gone his way—by air from Delhi—to tell his syndicate, no doubt, that there's no percentage yet in drilling in Kashmir. The Major has gone his—his satisfaction over his acquisition of ten thousand rupees slightly marred by the loss of an odd twenty which he thinks that bloody Pathan must have picked his pocket for while carrying him. I have yet another meeting round that discreet table in New Delhi—and thank God there are now Indians *and* Pakistanis sitting there together for the first time since 1947. Safaraz is squatting outside on the verandah cleaning my shoes and singing "Zakhmi Dhil". I must remind him again that the Brigadier's memsahib understands Urdu.

Claire? She has gone back up the hills—and when they have finished with me in New Delhi I am going back too—if I have to disguise myself in ashes and cowdung, for there is much to be done up there.

And she's a different girl when she smiles.